I0763387

The Course of Fortune

A Novel of the Great Siege of Malta

Volume 2

Tony Rothman

iBooks
Habent Sua Fata Libelli

iBooks
Manhanset House
Shelter Island Hts., New York 11965-0342
Tel: 212-427-7139
bricktower@aol.com • www.ibooksinc.com

Library of Congress Cataloging-in-Publication Data

Rothman, Tony.
The Course of Fortune, A Novel of the Great Siege of Malta / Tony Rothman. — 1st. American ed.

p. cm.
1. Siege of Malta, 1565—Fiction. 2. Malta—History. 3. Religion—Christianity—History. 4. Fiction—Christian—Historical Fiction.
I. Title.
PS3569.A6887R8 2011
813' .54—dc20

Volume 1: 978-1-59687-427-5, Hardcover
Volume 2: 978-1-59687-428-2, Hardcover
Volume 3: 978-1-59687-429-9, Hardcover

April 2015

The Course of Fortune

A Novel of the Great Siege of Malta

Volume 2

Tony Rothman

CONTENTS

Map illustrations by Renee Zhan

Sardegna
Gozo
MARE ME
Com
Pantelarea
Lino
Lampedusa
Africa
Djerbé/Los Gelv
Zuara
BARBARIA

Sicilia

Cape Passero

Pozzallo

Malta

Birgu

Mgarr

Mdina/ Città Notabile

Zurrieq

ITERANEO

Tripoli

Book III

Beretta

The journey to Belgrade was long and arduous, the roads so rutted that Grand Vizier Sokullu, travelling a day ahead of the Sultan, was forced to repair them as best he could. Such measures did little to relieve His Majesty's gout, and each bump and jolt caused Soliman to grimace in pain. Each soldier's misery was worsened by the ceaseless, torrential rains, which swelled rivers and washed roads into oblivion. Natheless, the Sultan's army pressed on, halting for scarce a day at Sophia. Beyond, the floods only worsened and many camels drowned.

Throughout the journey, especially during the rains, when Soliman was unable to leave his carriage, I continued my tale. The Grand Turk seemed to find it of interest, the doings of these Knights whose beliefs were so foreign to his own. The telling only increased his wonder that such a disorderly band of cutthroats and brigands could have so humiliated the finest army in existence. Natheless, the Grand Vizier continued his threats against me and I knew my life was mine only so long as it pleased Muhibbi to listen, or until the present campaign was done.

One of the Sultan's few remarks was that he perceived I had become more capable of judgment as the history progressed, but natheless he felt I remained swayed by plain events, often failing to recognize their significance. I reminded him of the swordsman who stole a barber's razor, intending to pass himself off as a barber. With no knowledge of shaving, the swordsman died in misery when instead of beards he cut several throats.

As Soliman laughed, asking where I had come across such wisdom, I replied that if in my life I had found any, it was naught but the accumulation of experience, and he would forgive the young man in the first part of the tale for not being an old one. Moreover, as I had told him, I was no philosopher and never would be.

Listening to this speech, Soliman admonished me to mine events for wisdom and told me to get on with it.

Forty-Two

Seven years rolled by. Seven years in the Republic of Venice. It is not my intent to tell His Majesty of the wonders of that city, which everybody knows, for my city was another, another world, the world of the Arsenale.

It was a world. The place's very name, *arsenale,* had long ago been taken over by every other tongue to describe lesser establishments around the globe. Each morning as the Lion of San Marco looked down, two thousand and more workers flooded through those gates that flanked the Rio dell' Arsenale in order to labor at their assigned tasks. By the letter, apprentices or unskilled workers like Pietru and me were not arsenalotti, for that name was jealously guarded by the master carpenters, caulkers and oarsmakers who made up by far the greater part of the workers. It mattered naught; to the outer world, we were all sons, legitimate or ill. What mattered was the dazzling speed wherewith a galley could be built and fitted. After the debacle of Prevesa, the Venetian Council of Ten ordered that one hundred light galleys and twelve heavy should be kept at the Arsenale at all times ready for completion.

Ready for completion! Those masters turned out galleys so alike one another that a sober man could tell them apart only by the graffiti scratched on them and their berths. All the parts—the masts, the spars, the sails, the rudders—were fashioned to be used on one ship or the other. Once the carpenters completed the frame, "caulkers" fastened on the planking with nail and dowel. Then the cabins were built atop. Only now the boat was "ready for completion." The moment the Senate called a galley into service, the caulkers went at it again, filling the seams with tow and oakum and basting the hull with pitch and grease. How many times did I watch half the arsenal swarm aboard, fastening the deck fixings, providing the cables and posts, carrying on the oars. E'en as they finished the galley, it would be floating down the canal through the great wooden gates that opened before it and thereon to the sea.

Aye, anyone who had ever witnessed these final stages, from the lowliest peasant to the loftiest potentate, left calling the Arsenale the "eighth wonder of the world," for a galley could be assembled, launched and completely armed this side of an hour. With such discipline, and the Grand Turk next door, the Arsenale fashioned fifty or sixty ships a year.

As often as I marveled at the spectacle, I rarely took part. My job was another. I labored in the cannon foundries, one of the lesser Arsenale industries. Of course, all things are measured to another, and the Arsenale's very powder store was near the size of Fort St. Elmo. The sheds for cannon forging were hardly smaller. Natheless, next to the shipbuilding industry, cannon founding was named small.

My first task was insignificant. As the *marangona* fell silent on the first morning, Vannoccio said to me, "Can you use a hammer?"

"*Si certo*," I replied, "there's not much skill in that."

"*Allora, vieni*," he said and handed me the tool he grasped in his hand. I followed as he took an iron bar, thicker than my thumb, and thrust it into the coals of one of the many forges standing beneath this vast roof. When it was red hot, he carried it to an anvil and handed me the bar.

"Hammer!" he said.

I tapped, then under the foreman's disdainful commands of "Harder, simpleton!" whacked, until with difficulty I'd fashioned a small block on the end. At that, Vannoccio pointed to a little hollow in the anvil, shaped as a half-sphere, and handed me a punch of sorts, whose end was shaped in a like half-sphere. With more cries of "simpleton!" and "turn it!" ringing in my ears, I hammered the punch, shaping the little block in the hollow.

The foreman's stern words recalled Don Jerónimo's own long ago in Sevilla on the day I had first picked up a weapon and I knew the road to mastery would be long. I hammered and turned until Vannoccio ordered me to stop. He lifted the bar from the anvil and inspected my work, which remained attached to the bar by a stem that had passed through a hole in the punch. Satisfied, he chopped off the stem and handed me a tiny, smooth sphere.

"You have made your first arquebus ball," he said, dropping the hot object into my hand. As I let it fall to the anvil with a gasp, he said, "Now, fashion me a hundred."

It was like that, small things, then larger things. After I'd mastered arquebus balls, Vannoccio moved me to ones nearly the size of an egg. "What are these for?" I asked. Vannoccio pointed to the wall of the shed, where stood the largest arquebus I had ever seen. Nay, it was something more, identical in form, but almost too large for a man to carry. I walked over.

"A musket?" I said.

"Indeed," Vannoccio replied with a raised eyebrow, "you've never seen one?"

"No, only heard of them. How is one to fire such a thing and remain standing? It must have the kick of a horse."

Vanno picked up a tall wooden fork. "Mount it on one of these." Then he turned fully to me. "We must learn to make better muskets. They are the essence of an infantry."

Aye, some days later he walked up to my cluttered workbench and dropped amidst the metal shavings and droplets an armful of arquebus and musket barrels. "Why these?" I asked, looking up from my task, learning to join arquebus seams, just as Pietru, who was now one of the wine porters, came by with the regular ration.

"These barrels are from several masters. We need to learn which are the best. I want you to measure them ... " Taking his wine, Vanno continued: "The best are made by Signore Beretta of Brescia, whose family has held every Senate contract for the past thirty years. All the doges and the Emperor Carlos himself own specimens of Beretta's work. But his guns are as costly as they are excellent. With the Turks breathing down our necks and the Senate's requests up, we must learn to produce them more cheaply. Also, workers from his valley run away to Padova and Milano, stealing secrets. If we can make these at the arsenal, La Serenissima might maintain her advantage."

Thus it began. We forged barrels by wrapping iron sheet around steel rods. We attempted different lengths, thicknesses. Many argue that proper incantations and prayers must be said to fashion guns that fire excellently. At the Arsenale we pronounced no incantations. We sweated at the blazing furnaces, merely trying one thing after another and testing them in the fields, and each evening at the bell I passed by the doorkeeper and went home to Vanno's house, where I lived, and on Saturdays I collected my pay of two *soldi* a day.

Life in the Arsenale was governed almost as much as work on the Maltese forts had been. I learned quickly that a man not showing up by the time the *marangona* ceased ringing was struck from the rolls for the day. Guards prevented anyone *senza licenza* from entering, and every night we heard the watchmen on the fifteen towers calling out the hours; if a watchman didn't answer after the second call, he was sacked.

This was show. As first, the arsenalotti regarded Pietru and I with suspicion and avoided us. Thus free, we had little choice but to watch what went at this vast place and I began to wonder how anything at all was accomplished. The major industry was smuggling: Private shipyards paid better and masters used every device to spirit the Arsenale's supplies to their second workplaces. At day's end, the doorkeepers searched us all, but this only increased the thieves' ingenuity and everything from lumber to weapons managed to escape. As a last resort they forced us to carry our coats over our shoulders to reveal state property, but this accomplished nothing.

The other main industry at the Arsenale was drinking. Wine porters brought rations around five or six times a day, which was only just during summer when we toiled eleven hours. But each day I watched masters taking tubs down to the cellars where they stood around farting and then made off with any amount of wine they could. I don't know how the Senators thought they could forbid Saint Monday—when the masters were sleeping off throbbing heads from Sunday's drinking bouts—but they tried. When the ne'er-do-wells showed up on Tuesday, if they had their tools at all, they didn't know how to use them. By Malchus's Sanctified Ear, I weekly found them sleeping in the tool sheds, and once roused, they spent the rest of the day wandering uselessly around the yards merely to get paid. I began to thank the Turk for our industry.

One of these useless scoundrels was an apprentice named Jacopo, who was two or three years younger than me. From the first day, seeing that I was past the regular age for an apprentice, he began to make trouble. Before I'd learned to tell a forge from a bellows, his taunts began.

"What do you think you're doing! You think that seam will hold? *Zuccone!*" At first I thought he was merely drunk, and he may have been, for he persisted in that woodpecker way of drunkards. "This fool will blow himself up with a seam like that!"

Enough. I was on my feet, hand around his neck. Lucky for him, weapons were forbidden in the workplace. I fair lifted the *mezzacalzetta* off the floor. "You, little shit, should know I've killed as many men as toil in this room and I've strangled Turks with my bare hands. By God I won't think to snap your neck in two like a dried twig!" I threw the piglet to the ground. He got to his feet, oinking, and fled the work room like the terrified swine he was.

An instant later someone was boxing me about the ears. Vanno. "You'll take your fighting onto the street. I won't have it here!" Once he cooled down he asked me what this was all about and I explained. Then and there he said, "Very well, in six months we'll have a contest and see who can turn out the best arquebus."

Apart from increasing the other workers' regard for me, and my own zeal to learn the craft I had recklessly chosen, this incident also gave me an enemy who would cause a lot of misery. Right away arsenal officials were around asking Vanno what someone my age was doing here. He told them with a wink that I was his son returned from the wars and that I intended to make cannon. Were I still useless after six months, he'd turn me out.

Pietru had a harder time of it. He carried wine or wood or sailcloth, and sometimes they let him make arquebus balls, but he seemed lost. Tho' he could now make himself understood well enough in Italian, he found few friends and preferred to sleep in Vanno's stable.

"What is it, Xabaw?" I asked one day, seeing his sad expression.

My comrade seemed to have difficulty speaking his mind. "Francisco, you are good with things, I am not. You will become a cannon-maker; I cannot. I am older than you."

"Those few years matter little," I answered, thinking that this was not truly what gnawed at him. "You make farm tools. The difference is not great."

"Eh, I am happy to carry things if that is all they want, but I've never seen a place so big. Even the churches are big. There are people everywhere."

I perceived that Pietru longed for home but wouldn't admit it. "You have never seen a great city before, have you?" He shook his head. I was about to tell him another tale of Sevilla but halted, thinking—aye, Venice mayhap exceeded Sevilla, if not in size then in splendor. "Xabaw, we have sailed the seas and fought battles together. You have saved my life more than once and I have saved yours. I would not see you unhappy. Fortune has led us to the greatest city of the world. Does she so frighten you?"

The Gozitan nodded meekly.

Seeing a man of Pietru's bulk so overwhelmed forced me to chuckle. "Do you wish to depart so soon after we have arrived?"

Pietru rocked his head. Aye, he might have quit Venice forthwith had not the very next day we received a triple bolt of startling news: Turgut, coming to the aid of the French, had overrun Corsica. This alone was enough to put the entire Arsenale into a frenzy, but it was not all. Sulking because he hadn't been given Tripoli, Turgut convinced the Sultan that Morat Agha was unfit to rule the place. Soliman gave Morat the boot and appointed Turgut Tripoli's *Beylerbeyi*. As de Valette had foretold, Turgut had ensconced himself in the city and was already repairing it.

As for the third news: If I understood the vague account aright, Turgut had also carried off the entire population of Lampedusa isle into slavery. I knew at once that those poor fishing villages we had stumbled upon during the weeks of our shipwreck there no longer existed.

I slammed my fist onto the workbench and renewed my vow to someday kill this odious corsair, e'en as I realized I was in no position to do so. The news also caused Pietru to relent. "I decide later," he grunted somberly. The next day, Ix-Xabaw brought a caged bird with him into the workplace.

Six months to the day after he announced it, Vanno held his contest. In my anger against Turgut, aided by the nimbleness my fingers had possessed since childhood, I labored day and night to make a weapon that boasted a wheel-lock. Many say the wheel-lock was invented by Leonardo himself, but I say that man never invented anything. Leonardo drew pictures. Whoever first built that metal wheel with its spring inside and fastened it to the side of an arquebus, I name him the inventor. That man freed the hands of the horseman in battle, at least once he wound the spring. That wheel, triggered and creating sparks as it spun against the mineral held there, replaced the troublesome match. Of course, the wheel-lock often misfires and is so expensive that no one but noblemen buy it. As I hunched over the clockwork, copying Beretta's design, I could not help think that there must be a way of making the things dependable and cheap for the common soldier.

Well, with my wheel-lock, I handily won Vannoccio's contest. Jacopo offered his congratulations and I thought everything had ended amicably, but unbeknownst to me he began to nurse a secret hatred that went unrevealed for years.

To celebrate my victory Vannoccio took us all out drinking. While learning billiards at the tavern, we heard more startling news: The Genoese had booted Turgut off Corsica. Pietru and I sighed in relief, raising our cups to God, and those around us realized we had more than a feigned interest in such goings on. They told us something else too. Only days earlier a public festa had taken place in Roma to celebrate the election of Fra Claude de la Sengle to the Grand Mastership of the Knights of St. John.

Ix-Xabaw and I glanced at each other with open mouths. "Then d'Homedes is dead!" I cried. And: "May the World be swallowed by a quick Damnation, I'd have wagered my gun and my balls that Leone Strozzi would be chosen!"

Our reaction to the election excited everyone's curiosity and our drinking partners at once bombarded us. "The same Strozzi who was Captain General of the French Galleys?" Vanno asked incredulously.

"Aye, is there another?"

"You know him?"

"As a soldier knows his captain." We recounted our months at sea with Strozzi and the building of the forts, which only left the foreman more open-mouthed.

"And you left such adventure to come to the Arsenale! In the name of God, why?"

"Why did we come, Pietru?" I asked of my comrade, struck by the question.

Pietru shrugged. "Nothing grows on Malta."

It was a good answer. "*Si*," I said, "that island has lately reaped a bitter harvest, with the Religion in disarray, one military disaster after another and tribunals that ape the Inquisition while they destroy lives of the faithful."

"Then you did well," said Vanno, regarding my darker expression. "Venice has never had much truck with popes, as the Pope is the guardian of the faith and Venice is mistress of the seas—or was, until the Newfound World and the Turks changed everything. The Senate has all but pulled the fangs on the Venetian Inquisitor. You see, Francisco, here faith cannot compete with money, and tho' many heap abuse upon Venetians as friends of the enemy, you may have discerned that while the rest of Europe is in flames, La Serenissima these years is at war with no one."

Vanno was right; we had surely done well to leave Malta for this beautiful place, where one could curse properly without worrying about penalties for blaspheming. I was content and the past beginning to loosen its grip. As for the unexpected and exciting news about de Sengle, I told everyone what I could, but it took a long while to piece together the story.

Just half a year after d'Homedes' Pro-Inquisition had finished its work, You Majesty, Old One-Eye gave up his soul and was laid beside his predecessors in the Chapel of St. Anne. Once Strozzi dried his tears, he campaigned openly for the Grand Mastership and everyone at the Convent wagered their eggs he'd be elected. But at the last moment, one of the electors, a certain Gagnon, spoke out against him. Were the brethren charged with electing a great general, Gagnon said, the choice would naturally fall on Strozzi, but they were charged with electing a father to them all, and this Prior would only employ the Order's resources to prosecute his personal war against the Medici.

Gagnon's speech had an effect, and to everyone's astonishment Strozzi lost the election to Fra Claude de Sengle, the Grand Hospitaller, who was then abiding in Rome as the Order's Ambassador to the Vatican. Only months later did de Sengle return to Malta. Seeing that the new Fort St. Michel stood on an unfortified peninsula, he immediately ordered a wall built around l'Isola. I'm glad I wasn't there; backbreaking work began at once and within a year or two l'Isola was renamed Città Senglea in his honor. He also raised a mighty cavalier outside Fort St. Elmo.

Later I learned that de Sengle set the unfortunate Mareschal de Vallier at liberty, but refused to restore his habit. Mayhap he decided there was, after all, some justice in the charges brought against him.

We left the tavern, a rowdy bunch, singing to the new Grand Master, falling into the canal. Pietru was e'en quieter than usual. I could tell the news from Malta had increased his longing for home, which hadn't left him.

"*Iva*," he said, the gruffness of his voice at odds with his sentiments. "Francisco, I cannot live here. A man cannot smell the soil. I want to farm, catch birds. I want to smell the wind and the rain and the sea."

"The sea is all around us, Xabaw."

"*Iva*, but we do not sail it, Francisco. I go back to Malta. Maybe with the new Grand Master things will not be bad. Remember, I have not found my wife and children."

He smiled at that, as I did, and as I knew that nothing would now prevent his going, I did not try. "I will miss you terribly," was the only thing I said, "and will curse you to the Turks if we ne'er see each other again." We embraced. In the morning he was gone. I had lost one of the best friends of my life and was alone in Venice.

Forty-Three

The seven years rolled on. And with them seven years of that *guerre de course*, which had no beginning and no end. At the foundry I did not hear of, cannot tell of the countless engagements between Christian and Mahometan galleys, which resulted in naught but the next retribution and addition of fear. Large events of course reached us, and during my Venetian sojourn the government began publishing the *Notizie Scritte*, for which one paid a *gazetta*.

It wasn't until late 1554, when Georgius the miner came with a shipment of copper, that I learned more of the strange fate of Leone Strozzi, Prior of Capua. By the Body of St. Alfonso, Your Majesty, there was a man who wrote his destiny with his own hand!

E'en while d'Homedes lived, the situation in the town of Africa where Vergã and I had begun our adventures had turned grim. The two thousand Spaniards Emperor Carlos had sent thither mutinied for lack of pay. Carlos, desperate to be rid of the town, offered it to the Religion and d'Homedes—mayhap de Sengle—promptly dispatched Strozzi to reconnoitre. But the Prior realized that the place was impossible to hold and the Knights refused to accept it.

The Vice Roy of Sicily, Don Juan de Vega, viewed the refusal as treason and halted all corn shipments to Malta. The Council sent Strozzi to Palermo to make amends. Well, as Pietru later told me, Strozzi escaped Malta because his chief servant had poisoned the same Gagnon who'd foiled his election as Grand Master. What's true is that Gagnon was dead and Strozzi left in a hurry.

No sooner had he arrived in Palermo than the Prior received word that Henri of France desired him again to become Captain General of his Galleys. Thinking he might thusly wreak his long-sought revenge on Cosimo dé Medici, Strozzi accepted. Carlos, tho', had already ordered the Vice Roy to keep a close eye upon Strozzi and, so, at Don Juan's palace the Prior became the sort of guest d'Aramont had been of Sinan at Tripoli. While they were lunching, Strozzi's lieutenant rushed in to say he'd sighted five enemy galiots, likely Dragut himself. Strozzi asked leave of Don Juan to do battle, promising to return before lunch was over.

Strozzi never finished lunch. He fled to Malta, where he resigned as Captain General. Immediately Jean de Valette became his successor. Strozzi made for Toscana, in French hands, to attack Cosimo. Pietru joined the undertaking and saw everything with his own eyes. While waiting for French reinforcements, Strozzi decided to amuse his men and laid siege to a small town, Scarlino, no doubt only a stone's throw from where we'd met up with Georgius himself on our way to Venice. But a peasant, lying in the rushes, spied Strozzi advancing at the head of his men and shot him in the side. Mortally wounded, the Prior of Capua died a few days later. That would have been summer, *anno* 1554.

By this time Carlos had ordered Africa razed. The great towers, walls and bastions that had been the envy of every town on the continent were at last undermined and blown to rubble, and the place was all but erased from the face of the earth, as Balthazar had advocated on the very day I first met him.

Throughout such great goings-on I merely worked at a furnace or at a bench. As was my wont, I'd done my best to put Malta behind me, and for a time succeeded in burying the past. But the past is not unlike Lazarus, and whenever word reached me of an exciting engagement, I cursed myself for my absence. Thoughts of Isabella returned e'er more frequently, yet we could not surmount the gentle Appennino or the suspicions separating us and we never wrote. All the same I kept her kerchief even as I visited the Venetian whores, whose part of the population rivaled Malta's. I maintained my skill at arms with constant practice at one of the many fencing schools in the city.

During those forays I watched the shadow of the campanile fall across the clock tower, regarded the new library across from it, which was said to be the world's greatest, and wondered at the opulent visage of the basilica. I traversed the booths on Piazza San Marco offering pilgrimages to the Holy Land and stood among the crowds on Ascension Day, when the Doge cast a golden ring into the waters and married Venice to the Sea. Often I was visited by angels of the ear, which are everywhere in Venice.

When you walk across the Piazza, you hear the sound of trumpets, and you hear them when trumpets are not present. I came to believe that Venice was music. She reveled in pageantry and spectacle. Only once did I see men burning books on the piazza—Jewish scriptures shortly after Joseph Nasi made his daring escape. This was not usual. La Serenissima is no place to weep.

What confounded me above all was the very idea of Venice. On Sundays, Vanno led me through her great labyrinth. He averred that La Serenissima's days of glory were over and often pointed out a decrepit palazzo where a more magnificent one had stood three centuries ago. My eyes saw none of the shabbiness that so offended him. I saw palazzi whose ornaments belonged to the East no less than the West, and that more than a few Moors walked among the brilliant robes of the nobility without rings on their ankles. Turkish and Persian merchants wearing huge turbans argued with customs officers as they unloaded their *caramusali* at the docks. I saw even Jews with yellow *O*'s sewn on their backs or wearing yellow hats and turbans.

It disturbed me.

"On Malta," I said to Vanno as we crossed the Rialto Bridge one day, "the only Jews and Moors are slaves."

"What is that to us?" he replied sharply. "I told you, Venice will trade with anybody."

"Even with the Turk, against whom you prepare for war?"

My master laughed. "Especially with the Turk."

"The Knights would ne'er consider trading with a sworn enemy. Do you Venetians lack faith?" Surely Strozzi had been right: The Venetians were harlots who slept with the enemy.

"Faith?" Vanno scoffed as he bought a loaf of bread from a baker. "You mean the faith of your insignificant Knights of St. John? Bah! They could carry on their Crusade against the Infidel from now until Judgment Day, but as far as the Turkish elephant goes, they're doing nothing but drilling holes in the eyes of fleas. La Serenissima is clever: She makes her foe soft with trade and to back it up we have—the Arsenale."

I considered this as we sat down on the side of a canal and ate the bread. "Tell me, Vanno," I asked, "what is a republic?"

Vanno spit up everything into the canal. "Boy, you've been living in one for a year now!"

"Yes," I nodded, "but what is it? No king or prince sits on a throne here. Who then rules? Men speak of this council or that council and of senates and doges, but I can't make anything of it. Is the Doge a king?"

"I would say," Vanno answered, tearing off a new piece of bread and putting it into his mouth, "he is more like a canary in a gilded cage. Once a year he throws a ring into the sea." I asked how the Doge was chosen, to which Vanno replied, "The Great Council chooses him. Only the Devil knows how."

Without the slightest understanding, I nodded. Venice was truly rife with councils, all of which seemed to do nothing but fight. I fancied the Doge to be a Grand Master, surrounded by his ten advisors, the *Signoria*. "But if the Great Council chooses the Doge, does this mean the Great Council or the *Signoria* rules?"

Vanno stared at me. "Money rules. Three hundred years ago you bribed the right person and became a noble, and for all I know you pay to become a doge. For us, the small people, the main thing is to pay taxes. You can pray where you want."

"The former seems to be the same everywhere," I sighed. "Wouldn't a king be simpler?"

"Simpler, aye," answered Vanno. "But no Venetian would put up with it. And boy, consider: La Serenissima has stood in this lagoon now for over one thousand years."

Such conversations were rare; our job was to build armaments. For a time I continued making arquebuses and muskets. One indisputable thing was that longer arquebuses and cannon could fire a ball further and truer than shorter ones, although the reason for this provoked never-ending arguments. One day Vannoccio declared:

"Those who claim that shooting far lies in the secret of the width of the bore are arming themselves with lies taller than a deer can jump."

"Vanno, you are surely right," I replied. "The Turks fire arquebuses a good nine palms long. Mayhap we should copy them."

We built some and, indeed, they proved to shoot further and with greater accuracy. But they also proved unpopular with the men because of their weight and because they took longer to load.

I rose to cannon. I will not describe, Your Majesty, all the details of the cannon-founding art, for they are myriad. As my hands grew ever more calloused, I learned to make gun patterns from fir logs, to fashion them to the final shape of the cannon and to provide them with ornaments in order to make them beautiful. I learned how one covers this pattern with pork fat, then loam and how one then makes a clay mould around it, strengthening the whole with iron bands. I learned how to bake the mould and to remove the pattern from the rear by melting the wax and ramming the pattern against a wall with many men. I learned how to make moulds for the breech and I learned how to position the iron gun-core in the center of the mould so that it would be true, for otherwise the ball would not fire straight—or worse, the gun would explode. I learned how to finish a gun by drilling out the core with a bit driven by a wheel.

Most of all I learned the secret of bronze. I learned to build furnaces of brick and construct wheels driven by water or horse to work the bellows. I learned what wood to choose for the fire, be it elder, or hornbeam, or black poplar. I learned how to bake the furnaces and plaster them with ash. Then I learned the right portions of tin and copper that make excellent cannon metal. Amid the fluxes of heat and sweat I learned to stir the melt with a stick of chestnut and I learned, as we lit the fire beneath the metal, to pray to God.

My first mould broke during the baking and the second during the pouring of the bronze. Vanno only laughed, after he had beat me about the shoulders, saying therein lay the art. When I had finally produced a small gun that fired, it blew up. The core, assuredly, wasn't straight, making the metal thinner on one side of the mould. Slowly, encrusted in a constant armor of soot and grime, I progressed from demi-cannons to full cannons and then to the longer and heavier culverins.

In all this, I learned, lay much art indeed. Masters around the Middle Sea all followed the same philosophy, but their methods varied as much as French and Spaniards. Why was Venetian ordnance the finest? I say we could fashion a gun that was shorter and lighter than one turned out by Spanish or Ottoman masters—no mean thing on a galley where you count your weight. No one will buy a Genoese gun these days—they will explode in your face.

No less an art than casting a gun is using it. One must know the amount of powder and its composition, and how much hay to pack between the powder and the ball. Most of all one must be able to aim. This is a highly paid skill.

"Heed me," Vanno said one day when we were on the mainland testing cannon. "Good guns, ancient and modern, always fire straight. If they do not, it is your mistake."

Yet many trials showed that when we fired, sometimes the ball dropped before hitting the target, especially at a distance. This puzzled us. Aye, things fall to the ground when released, but a cannonball traveling so fast ought not to be subject to the earth's influence.

"Still it drops," I said to Vanno, observing the target.

He shrugged stubbornly. "I tell you that the ball travels in a straight line, but when the distance is great, the flight finishes in an arc. If this happens you must raise the gun."

That we did.

Guns are useless without gunpowder. "With this invention," the foreman declared, touching off a crucible one day, "the inventor surpassed all men of every age from the creation of the world up to the day when he announced it." Man, like angels, had penetrated e'en unto God with his divine intellect, but nothing compared to the invention of gunpowder, for with this he could harm his fellows more than with all the poisons in all the herbs and animals of Nature, even with earthquakes and the very thunderbolts of the sky. For all these things, Vanno said, afforded some hope of escape, but with gunpowder there was no such hope, not the slightest.

Natheless, he taught me how to compound charcoal, saltpetre and sulphur into gunpowder, how to grind the ingredients to the proper fineness and how to recognize good powder from its color and by its action on a piece of paper. He averred that the best saltpetre is made from animal manure transformed into earth in stables, or in human cess pits that have not been used for a long time. And he declared that people who claim that powder makes no noise when fired in guns are liars.

With each cannon, Malta receded further. It became part of a former life, and Spain a life before that. From time to time we received word of the Knights, but from Venice, Balthazar's words that the Knights were a relic of a past age, like the Baptist's hand, seemed truer than he likely intended.

A visiting merchant told how de Valette and Dragut had lately encountered each other off Sicily. A second related how Dragut had offered Parisot five thousand ducats to become his lieutenant, and a third swore that de Valette countered by offering Dragut Malta for Rhodes, but that the corsair laughed and said not to be troubled—he would take Malta soon enough.

What was true was that Turgut and Parisot were at loggerheads. Jean de Valette, now Captain General of the Galleys, took to the seas with a righteous vengeance. He wielded his implacable hatred against the infidels in Barbary, Sicily and the Levant. He seized galleys and *caramusali* with their cargos of soap, spices, linen, hides and slaves. de Valette—I could hear the vow— had sworn that if every Christian were defeated, so be it: He alone would drill holes in the eyes of the fleas that sat on the ass of the Turkish elephant.

Yet for every time we heard the name de Valette, we heard the name Turgut ten times. Neither age nor foe diminished his strength, and the very mention of his beard was enough to excite disbelief and awe. Truly, while the latest merchant put down his tankard to give us his news, a strolling musician who'd been sawing with a sort of stick at a stringed box he held under his chin put down his instrument to listen. We asked him what instrument it was that made such a pleasing sound. He claimed it as his own invention, a *violino*, but was more interested in hearing about the corsair who ravished Italy and Spain with abandon.

As the merchants usually told it, Turgut's foe was Romegas, who now commanded Parisot's private galleys. He never lost an engagement; he took on six ships to his one. Many swore he didn't sail but flew across the sea, and others that he'd made a pact with the Devil. Mahometans silenced their babies with his name, while Christian slaves prayed to him for deliverance. Much on his account, I learned, His Majesty's wife Roxelana never ceased urging her husband to be done with the Knights. For the repose of her soul, she left upon her death a large sum of money to finance an expedition to destroy Malta. To what extent this is true, His Majesty knows better than I.

But Romegas could not escape the wrath of nature unscathed. E'en the *Notizie Scritte* reported that extraordinary day in September, *anno* 1555, when the fiercest winds—a Dragonara—roared through the Great Port.

A huge wave swept into the harbor, washing over everything, and with it came something hardly ever seen—a giant waterspout. Knights, townspeople—those who weren't drowned immediately—watched with terror as that funnel ripped the Order's banner from its moorings atop St. Angelo and threw it all the way to Gallows' Point. They watched it pick up galleys in the Port like children's toys, toss them about and cast them back into the water. No one could describe the shriek of the winds and many were certain God had loosed the end of the world. After a full watch, the spout vanished as suddenly as it had appeared, leaving behind it a strange, deathly calm.

Every person in Birgu ran down to the docks to find the harbor full of overturned boats and corpses. The Religion's galleys had been manned, ready to depart at dawn next, and all the galley slaves chained to their benches had drowned. Grand Master de Sengle instantly ordered the Knights and workmen to rescue those still alive and right the capsized boats. As the day, then night wore on, the workers counted six hundred dead. Early next morning these workmen put ropes to one of the Order's galleys and were preparing to right it when they heard a tapping from beneath the keel. Quickly they brought drills and saws and cut a hole into the keel. Out popped Romegas' terrified pet monkey and then, fully waterlogged, out crawled Romegas himself. He had spent the entire night clinging to a board below the keel, up to his neck in water, breathing in an air pocket. Other Knights found this way were rushed to the Hospital. Those more alive than dead limped to the Church of San Lorenzo to give thanks to God for their miraculous deliverance. But Romegas himself had not been fully delivered. From that day on his hands trembled so much that he could not drink a glass without fear of spilling half its contents. No one, tho', ever noticed this tremor in the thick of battle.

That, Your Majesty, was the appearance of those seven years from my workplace. I never heard anything of Vergã or Balthazar. It was as if they—or I—had dropped off the edge of the world. Ah, a few other morsels of news did reach the Arsenale. By 1556 the same de Sesse, who opened the gates of the Gozo citadel to Turgut and Sinan, had bought his freedom through wealthy relatives. He presented himself before the Council on Malta, was arrested, tried and reinstated as a commander.

His Majesty may also recall that in the same year Emperor Carlos retired to a monastery. He made his son Philip of Austria King Philip II and bequeathed the Holy Roman Empire to his younger brother Ferdinand. *Anno* 1559 Carlos, Soliman the Lawgiver's great foeman, died.

One further event, Your Majesty, which was certainly brought to your attention at the time. *Anno* 1557, Grand Master de Sengle died after a short illness. Jean de Valette, his way having been cleared and having then risen through all the high posts of the Order, was elected Grand Master of the Knights of St. John.

Forty-Four

My apprenticeship was ending. For Vannoccio's approval I intended to cast a great culverin, adorned with legendary animals to make it more terrible, but that year famine struck Venice. The supply of grain withered and the price of bread became exorbitant. No more as you walked across Piazza San Marco did you hear the sounds of trumpets and witness the Dogaressa leading a resplendent procession of nobles, guildsmen and two hundred thirty-five ladies-in-waiting adorned in damasks, satins, pearls and precious stones. As you stepped across the square, you heard echoes and felt the presence of ghosts. Beggars knelt on the street corners before they too entered the other world, and the docks were lined with people attempting to flee this one.

One evening, before sunset, I approached San Girolamo, having been scouring the city for food, when a voice called out, "Signore, are you called Francisco?"

I looked up to see a Jew. I knew him as such because of his yellow turban and the square cut of his cloak, but otherwise he appeared a stranger.

"You do not recognize me, do you?" the gaunt figure asked without expecting a reply. "I am the doctor who treated you on a boat, ah, six or seven years ago. You were fleeing Malta, as I was."

"Forgive me," I said regarding him with full perplexity. "I have no memory of that voyage, as I was senseless and near death. I was told that a Jewish physician indeed saved me. If you are that man, then I owe you my life." I bowed at the waist before him.

"I did naught but what my oath required." The elderly physician appeared to be in a hurry. Aye, he said: "I must go now before they close the gates."

"What is your name?" I called after him as he limped off.

"Miguel Rodrigo," he said as he disappeared into the *getto*.

"At least he is not a Marrano," I said to myself, "a pig."

Because I had sold guns to the nobles of Venice, I had enough money to buy bread, when it could be found. The next day I bought a loaf for a week's wage and took it to the getto. The Venetians called it that, "casting," because an old foundry once stood there, but now Jews were locked up at night there for their own safety. No law forbade me from going in, yet of course I had ne'er before set foot inside the crowded island, with apartment piled atop apartment, and now I felt shivers go down my spine at being surrounded by so many of this kind. I sought out Rodrigo, finding him at the top of one of these buildings, and gave him the bread, which he and his wife accepted with gratitude. Then I merely left by one of the gates, passing the two guards, and stepped onto the little bridge.

Standing on the other side with three of his mates was Jacopo. At first they gaped, then took a step onto the bridge toward me. I unsheathed my sword and they backed off. Laughing, they disappeared into the alleyways

The next morning, as always, I went to the Arsenale with the ringing of the *marangona*. The works were quiet. Each day since the hunger began, fewer and fewer masters had been showing up, tho' the guilds were opening their strongboxes to buy bread. The truth is, people were dying. At length Vanno arrived. His cheeks were sunken for lack of food, his beard almost entirely grey and he looked one hundred years older than on the day I'd first met him. As he asked how work on the culverin went, Jacopo appeared.

"Jew pig," he spat, straight to my face.

On Malta I would have killed him. Here, after nearly seven years, I stared sharply, then broke into derisive laughter. "I was run out of Spain because of base accusations that I was a Moor. Now you call me a Jew. Will you next accuse me of being a Turk?"

Jacopo told Vanno where he had come across me and I explained how it had happened. The foreman dismissed Jacopo, but a moment later he erupted as if I had sold Venice for thirty shekels. "How dare you buy bread for a Jew!" he shouted. "Joseph Nasi and his Mendes work for the Turk to destroy this city! It is because of them God has sent this famine upon us! He is punishing Venice for sheltering Jews. Get out of my sight!"

Tho' I had worked for Vanno seven years, I saw that I did not fully know him, or Venice. I put a loaf of bread I had bought onto his bench and walked out of the Arsenale.

I then killed Jacopo, mayhap. One of the *battagliole sui ponti* was brewing, those regular street brawls that sometimes drew in thousands of men and which had become riots with the famine's onset. Armed with shield and cane, I sought out Jacopo in the narrow alleys and crush of combatants. When I finally found him on the second day of fighting, I broke his arm and cracked his head. The women leaning out the windows above cheered me. Whether he lived I don't know.

But Vanno was right: God was punishing Venice. The famine was beginning. The mainland became inundated, and the Rialto, forcing one to take boats through the squares. Then came the pox. Some said it was the great leprosy, others only the *morbillo*. Whatever this scourge's exact nature, it raced through the city, leaving so many people ill and dying—children especially—that the Lazzaretto, the island that had long been the quarantine place for the sick, overflowed with water and people. During the famine roving bands of the hungry followed you with ravenous eyes and if they so much suspected you had a crumb to your person, you were a dead man. Now, if they saw the red of the corruption in your eyes, they fled in the other direction. Venice had become shrouded with mists, and beneath this mantle roamed only phantoms.

One day a fever seized me. Had I become a victim of this pox? My health had been good and I'd been near few people of late. After Vanno dismissed me I could no longer appear safely at the Arsenale and I begged for work at private shops. I cast guns for one of these foremen who had taken a liking to me until he found out why Vanno had let me go. I worked for another for a few days until he ran out of money buying food and then for a third until he died. Then there was nothing, no work, no food.

I found myself wandering the streets without three coins in my purse and knew that if the fever did not kill me, starvation would. More than once I defended myself against those roving wraiths, uncertain I was not already one of them. Nearly delirious with hunger and not knowing whither my feet carried me, I looked up to see the door of the *Ospedale S. Giovanni dé Cavalieri di Malta*. Tho' it was hardly two paces from where I stayed, in all these years I had never thought to go there. This day angels had guided me. I saw them departing and I did not hesitate to enter the courtyard.

The place overflowed. A physician greeted me with the customary hospitality, but he pointed to all the sick, occupying every bed and every archway, and said that tho' he might keep me quarantined with the others, as I saw ... The thought of being locked up with so many ill and dying only convinced me that I would fall to the contagion, had I not already. While I stood there pondering the best action, another physician wearing the traditional black robe entered the cloister. He too greeted me, I him, and for some moments I dumbly faced this red beard, not perceiving that before me stood an old acquaintance.

"Dr. Jean!" I suddenly cried, forgetting myself and embracing him.

"Francisco," he replied, equally astonished, "we had given you up for ... dead."

I turned as another figure strode into the courtyard, the unmistakable cross emblazoned on his mantle. For a moment we regarded each other as if through time, attempting to bridge the old faces we knew with the new ones we saw. In truth, this monk had not changed much. His hair was yet raven black, his beard finely shaved to follow the rugged contour of his jaw. His physique was as lean and muscular as of old. Tears sprang to my eyes; at the same moment, ignoring probity and safety, Lord Balthazar embraced me.

"It is a bittersweet joy to see you after seven long years," I said, hardly able to speak, "on the very day I may have been struck down by this plague."

Immediately Vigo examined my eyes and nose and asked if I showed any rash. I told him no. "I suspect your fever is of hunger, not of ... sickness. But sickness preys on the weak. When have you eaten last?"

"Two days ago," I answered. "Meseems."

He immediately brought bread and fruit. I put some to my mouth and nearly fainted. Grabbing me by the arms, Dr. Jean and Balthazar led me onto the street.

"Where are we going?" I asked. "The streets are not safe. They're infested with people who will kill you as soon as look at you."

"Do you have a room?"

"Yes."

"Thither."

I awoke sometime later to find myself surrounded by bread, fruit and wine, and both my guests staring down at their patient.

"You call this a room?" Balthazar said, examining my finest arquebus as he sat at the tiny table. "How is it you can live in such a place and yet own such an excellent wheel-lock? You might have sold it for food."

"Not while I live," I answered, sitting erect, rubbing my eyes. "I fashioned it as a gift for a fine nobleman I once knew. To my chagrin, he who I intended it for refuses to use ought but a sword."

"You made this?" Balthazar said and cast an admiring glance at me.

"Aye," I nodded. "I considered forging a two-hander, but swords are not my craft and other masters make better ones."

A sly smile crossed Balthazar's face. We attempted to speak of other things. It transpired that years ago Pietru had told them I was working at the Arsenale, and upon their arrival a few long weeks ago they had searched for me there, but by mischance I had not labored at that place for two months. "Pietru?" I inquired.

"He is alive, fighting, searching."

"Always ... " All of us were searching for the words capable of spanning the chasm of years that separated us. *"Por las Revelationes de San Juan!"* I exclaimed suddenly, grabbing a cup of wine, "what are you doing in this accursed city?"

"Ah," said Balthazar, leaning forward on the table as he drank, "few, I say, would call Venice accursed, but under present circumstances, I take your meaning ... Dr. Jean and I are traveling."

"To Constantinople," offered Vigo.

"To Constantinople!" I shouted at the top of my voice. My ears deceived me.

"To search for rhubarb," the doctor said.

Throwing aside the cover, I fair jumped from the bed, but Dr. Jean bade me take care. Once more I leaned back. "How do you plan to get there in the midst of this ... calamity? All arriving ships are quarantined and few can be leaving. If they are, the Turks will certainly quarantine them at their own ports—should anyone aboard be left alive."

"Truly," sighed Balthazar, "we have not arrived at a propitious moment."

I suggested the overland route via Belgrade, but we could not agree that it was a whit safer than the sea route. Vigo said he intended to visit the Republic's botanical gardens in Padova. Someone there might know of a merchant intending to travel to Constantinople. "No, I should first speak to Lorenzo Priuli here, for his garden is ... renowned."

"The Doge himself!" I blurted out.

"Well, yes, I suspect so," reflected Vigo.

"I fear you are too late," I said. "He has recently died."

Balthazar now cut us off with a wave of his hand, saying that in any case the problem remained: What was the best way out of Venice?

For a moment Vigo stroked his beard, then shrugged again. "I propose we ... *wait*. The ... fact is, if you have observed the price of food since our arrival, the famine is ... abating. That can only mean one thing: sufficient people have died from this pox that food is becoming more plentiful. The infection shall soon run its course as well. Each day we see fewer patients at the hospital. God's wrath is spent."

"I assume you are coming," said Balthazar, arching his eyebrow, "once you regain your strength."

"When I regain my strength," I smiled, "you, old man, had best take care."

To end a famine by a contagion was a horrible design to contemplate and La Serenissima's sins must have been great indeed. But in the end Vigo proved correct. Hunger and sickness were abating. The doctor's investigations revealed a wealthy merchant, a Persian called Chaggi Mehmet, who was planning to sail for Constantinople as soon as possible. With no questions asked and for a suitable fee, which Balthazar paid without murmur, this Mehmet took us on as partners to open rhubarb routes through Turkey. While the affairs were being settled, we secluded ourselves in a monastery on one of the outer islands of the lagoon, where my strength returned.

Tho' there was an infinity I wanted to hear about from Balthazar and the good doctor, they had made themselves surprisingly scarce. Moreover, the Knight had become perceptibly more taciturn, as if that great weight he had of yore sometimes borne on his shoulders had grown until it now oppressed him. But a few days before departure, he motioned me into the monastery's courtyard. "Let us see how you've held up," he said and we had at it with rapiers.

I was amazed that the Knight's strength had not diminished by a hair's breadth, and in no way could I get the better of him. Natheless, after a full glass I too was holding my own and neither had he made any progress. With a laugh Balthazar finally called a halt and gave me his hand. "I see," he said, "you've not only learned to talk like a Venetian but fence like an Italian. Good. Whither we're going you may need all your skill. Rhubarb is a formidable opponent."

"Balthazar," I answered, "Something burdens you. I have hardly gotten a joke or story from your lips these weeks, and I'm anxious to know of your doings over the past years."

"Of course," he conceded readily enough and went on to say that he had mostly been in France. "After Tripoli and that business with Cubelles I felt, like you, that my presence at the Convent was unnecessary, and I returned to my estate." I suspected that was far from all, and sure enough, after cajoling enow, I got an admission that for several seasons Balthazar had maintained a liaison—platonic of course—with a poetess whose marriage did little to deter her from her amours.

"There was a woman!" recollected Balthazar, warming to the theme in spite of himself. "Louise Labé, she was called. I met her during the battle of Calais. *Moy foy*, I fully mistook her for a man—dressed in armor as she was. At a certain moment a foe had unhorsed her and had dismounted for the kill. But I took care of him and when she removed her helmet to thank me—those tresses tumbled to her shoulders and—I beheld Athena herself. She proved a good archer and not a bad swordsman. Many of her poems are secretly dedicated to me ... "

I laughed. It was good to know the Abbé had not entirely changed. I asked about Malta.

"You would recognize it," Balthazar nodded reluctantly. "With trade, Birgu grows ever more crowded. The number of souls there is mayhap twice what it was in your day, and l'Isola—now Senglea—is fortified on three sides, but all is not as I would have foreseen." He paused, accurately reading the expression on my face.

"You'll recall that in former days I averred that the Knights must remake themselves. Parisot has perceived the Knights' disarray and taken it to heart. But he has not looked to the future; rather he has taken his design from the past. Within days of his election he issued a *prammatica* on dress. Having considered how vain and dishonest is the fashion in clothes on the island, in order to avoid the utter ruin of man, you understand, de Valette was forced to—ban stockings of mismatched colors. He has also restricted the wearing of embroidery and silk and divers manner of clothing ... "

Balthazar sighed. To say the least, I hardly knew what to make of this intelligence. "I would have thought he'd have more weighty matters on his mind."

"Oh, he does," the Abbé said, and fell completely silent.

At last the morning of departure arrived. My two companions, adorned in the cloaks of well-to-do merchants, had piled a fair amount of gear on the dock, including a heavy strongbox, locked and chained. Vigo went over the papers of one Dr. Claude de Thézan-Venasque while a pair of spectacles perched on his nose. "Age," he conceded, "but Murano does make the finest spectacles in the world." Earlier I had stopped at the Arsenale to give Vannoccio a loaf of bread, but the foreman was not there and I left it at his bench.

Forty-Five

We set forth on a round ship of Venetian design. I had never before sailed on a two-masted merchantman, with a lateen sail aft but elsewise square canvas, although these galleons, as people called them, had become common enough in recent times. She may have been built at the Arsenale itself. As we cast off, I prayed that the strange boat was up to the voyage, which would be long and dangerous.

For an hour I stood on the castle watching Venice, the city that had been my home and not for so many years, sink beneath the waters of the lagoon, and long after she was gone I continued to watch. Only when we were well out in the wintry sea did I turn to find Comte Niccolò Contremaret at my shoulder, regarding me.

Before he could utter a word I said in a way that brooked no retreat, "Now, tell me of rhubarb."

He smiled mysteriously, glanced over his own shoulder. "Dr. Thézan-Venasque can better expound on its medicinal properties, which are miraculous, but I am certain, Vincenzo, you are aware that this past spring a treaty was signed at Cateau-Cambrésis."

"I heard about it," I nodded, grasping the rail, "but with Venice dying, I paid scant attention."

"I understand," replied the Comte gravely, "tho' the treaty is assuredly the most important event of the past decade. With it, France and Spain have at last recognized that their interminable wars have bankrupted them. Italy is at peace—"

"—as she is in ruins."

Niccolò nodded with a perceptible sadness. "Aye, but no more splendid ruin could be wished...With this treaty, the Ottomans are denied French assistance and their ships are barred from French ports. The Grand Signor is hardly pleased, but he has all but made the Mediterranean his private lake and our friend Turgut continues to terrorize this lake—"

dé Pesci, is whether in seven years you ever quit the grime and cinders of that arsenal to step foot inside San Marco's."

"You surely know," I answered, glancing between him and the waters of the Adriatic, "that the common people are permitted inside but once a year on the saint's day, or perhaps on some other special days. But yes, once I got in."

"And … ?" The Comte's voice and eyes revealed infinite patience.

"I wept. I did not think such a marvel could be wrought by the hand of man. More than at any other moment of my life, I felt the presence and glory of God and finally, mayhap, I understood what you had felt that day in the Sistine Chapel."

Niccolò nodded. "We see the Venetians do have faith ... Since then," he went on unexpectedly, "I have had a yet more profound experience. It was on another of our useless endeavors to squeeze money out of the Pope, and indeed Paul invited us to the same Sistine Chapel to hear a Mass written by one Giovanni Palestrina, dedicated to the memory of Pope Marcellus. They said it was the first time this Mass had been sung. I tell you, in my life I had ne'er heard such a glorious sound, and I was certain that angels had descended to earth and were carrying us to heaven. This Palestrina had touched God with his music, or perhaps better said, God had touched him, and through him, all of us."

We fell into silence then, each mantled in his own thoughts. My companion's voice had deepened across seven years, or had become more resonant, sterner. I grasped for words.

Our voyage continued down the Adriatic. The Uskoks miraculously spared us but the elements did not. We endured one storm after another and more than once I thought this boat so heavy at the top would capsize. But each time we somehow came through, waterlogged, alive, and after near a month put into Candia on the Venetian Isle of Crete. Chaggi Mehmet needed to take aboard more goods, but that evidently was not the full story. Niccolò disappeared without a word for nearly a full day. In his absence, I wandered about the fortifications, striking up a conversation with a young painter of icons. This Domenikos presented me with one of his images, but my eyes found it foreign and I passed it on to someone else. When Niccolò returned, as silently as he had departed, we resumed our journey, northward toward Constantinople.

Storms slowly lessened and on a calm day Dr. Claude abruptly began explaining that half the world was after rhubarb and that the Hospitallers could not be left behind. According to Dioscorides, the plant, with its large, hairy leaves and thick black roots, alleviated all manner of ailments of the spleen and liver, relieved cramps and convulsions and helped heal wounds. It was a principal ingredient of mithridatium, like theriac a known antidote to many poisons. "And of course it serves as a purgative."

"Where is this plant found?" I asked.

"Ah ... this is the ... *mystery*. Marco Polo tells us that the finest rhubarb comes from somewhere in China."

"China!" I exclaimed, cutting him off with a hint of severity. "Do not jest with me, Dr. Claude. China! We'd be gone for years, if we were lucky to come back at all."

The doctor nodded, pursing his lips. "Some say it grows near the Volga. All agree rhubarb comes through Turkish lands. With Chaggi Mehmet we need to determine the best source and variety."

Hereat, Niccolò joined us. "Have you ever wondered during your sojourn in Venice, Vincenzo, why with the Knights on their knees Soliman has not finished them off?"

I suspected, somehow, it was not due to the medicinal properties of rhubarb.

"Soliman now has well over sixty years to him. If the reports we receive are true, his empire has been cast into war because his surviving sons are locked into a battle for the throne. He killed off the most talented, Mustafa he was called; of the two remaining, he has apparently cast his lot with a drunkard, while the other has fled to Persia."

It seemed to me that that would have settled the matter.

"If the matter is settled," Niccolò replied severely, "then Philip's plans, Malta, and the whole of Christendom, are in the gravest peril."

Tho' we played cards and draughts in the cabins, Niccolò was always wary of speaking openly. Near Chios he mentioned that the Grand Master had restored the habit of the Mareschal de Vallier. "For this act Parisot is to be honored," the Comte said.

Recollection of the most despicable episode in the Order's history inevitably brought to mind another Knight. "Meseems Nicolas Villegaignon would be pleased to hear this news," I said, sliding my draught. "I have often wondered what became of our inscrutable Chevalier."

Now, as Niccolò captured two of my pieces, his countenance brightened. "You haven't heard?" he said with an air of astonishment.

I shook my head, astonished at his astonishment. "Not a word."

"By God," he went on in a new tone, bordering on the rapturous, "Durand has become one of the most notorious men of Europe! Only a few years after we last set eyes on him he set sail for the Newfound World! To Brésil I say, where he and his comrades founded the first Huguenot colony and lived among the cannibals—"

"Cannibals!" I exclaimed, taking up Niccolò's tone of wonder—before I abruptly halted at something even more incomprehensible. "*Huguenot* colony?"

"*Mort de Dieu*, truly you don't know!" cried Niccolò, turning full on me. "Villegaignon apostatized."

My eyes practically burst from my head. "Old One-Eye and Cubelles were right all along!" I erupted, incredulously, angrily, God knows what, slamming my fist on the table and capsizing the board. "*O Reniego aquel Puto de ruyn Ladron, que motejava Nuestro Senor en la Crux!* the great Knight reveals himself to be a foul heretic after all!"

Strangely, at this juncture Niccolò sighed. "They set sail with both Catholics and Huguenots," he said, stroking his beard as if lost in thought, "and founded a colony at the mouth of the River of January. *Apparentemente*, the savages remained peaceful, but near warfare erupted amongst the colonists. Villegaignon himself returned only this past year, the Catholics calling him a heretic and the Huguenots calling him a traitor. Earlier he sent his comrade André Thévet back to France, bearing many things they'd discovered, including an herb used by the savages for relaxation and which is now sweeping Europe."

"What is that?" I asked.

"They call it tobacco."

"Yes, I've had news of it, but the Order cannot be pleased with Villegaignon."

"Truly. de Valette ascended to new pinnacles of dudgeon on learning of this betrayal by his old friend. Durand will be defrocked, if he hasn't been already ... And yet," the Comte went on, soberly, "Villegaignon and Venice have much in common; they belong to no faith. Perhaps those of his cast and not us, not Parisot, are the men of this new age."

Comte Contremaret's incredible tale had relaxed him enough so that I finally put to him the question that had been on my mind since we'd set eyes on each other in Venice: Had he news of Isabella?

The Comte had. While in Firenze en route to Venice, Balthazar de Marans des Homes-Saint-Martin had discovered Isabella Guasconi's mansion, an easy walk from the fortresses of the Strozzi and the Medici. When a servant admitted Balthazar the Signora was out, but the girl ran to fetch her as the Knight waited in the colonnaded atrium amidst the statuary and played with the dogs.

Not long after, the Abbé rose at the fountain, astounded to see a veiled woman adorned in a dress of the finest Sicilian lace, and whose arms were graced with gold bracelets and pearls. "Balthazar, *che piacere rivederla,*" Isabella said with joy, pulling aside her veil and extending her hand. As he bent to kiss it, he noticed that the *imprese* she wore on her necklace carried an image of a triangular candleholder in which two of the candles had gone out.

"You have done splendidly for yourself in Florence, Isabella," Balthazar said as she took his hands and bade him sit with her by the gurgling water.

The regal lady blushed but nodded all the same. "Trade has flourished, mostly silk and olive oil. I've published a book of poems, which has brought me some renown." Pulling a small volume from her *borsetta*, she held it out. "Allow me ... "

"I shall read it with the greatest pleasure," the Knight replied, accepting it with a bow. "But you who are as fair as Botticelli's *Primavera*, if not Venus, disguise you beauty with a veil, Milady."

Again Isabella blushed, touching her banded hair, which Balthazar saw she had fully dyed the prized blond. "It is my own conceit. I am privileged to serve some hours each week at the hospital. It would be unseemly were the sick to recognize me ... Of late the physicians here have been recommending toad broth as a cure for heart ailments. Have the Knights heard about this?" Balthazar protested that he was hardly the one to ask but would pass on the information to the physician with whom he was traveling. "Enough of me," Isabella went on, calling for wine. "You must speak of yourself and tell me all the news from Malta."

Balthazar did not speak of himself. As for Malta, Isabella well knew that the year before last Parisot had issued a *Citazione*, recalling all members of the Order to Malta under pain of being defrocked. "All of us rushed thither, expecting a Turkish descent, but Parisot had been misinformed and, I believe because of the war between the Sultan's sons, the invasion has not come. Your Godfather has levied ever higher taxes to pay for the new fortifications and the *università* complain ever more bitterly, but ... " the Knight faltered.

Hereat, Isabella abruptly rose to her feet and turned away. "Yes, I know, Balthazar, you don't need to tell me that Parisot hangs anyone who crosses him. Let us not forget the Jewish slaves he discovered secretly advising the Turks to invade … "

"Aye … " As Balthazar accepted a goblet from the service presented him, it seemed to him that Isabella's eyes glistened with tears. "But I can truly say that under him the Convent has become a more of a convent. Perhaps the Order can be proud of that. I say also that he and your mother miss you dearly."

"As I miss them," she said, clasping her goblet to her breast, "but my life is ... here." Isabella glanced distractedly around her.

Seeing her discomfort, Balthazar took her arm and they began strolling about the atrium. "Tell me, Isabella, how is it that the great lady you have become is not married? I should think half the city's men would be at your feet."

"Oh, they are," Isabella laughed lightly, "but ... " She shook her head. "I cannot express it. Growing up on that barren island ... I think I have simply grown accustomed to my own company. I yet hope ... Balthazar, you have not said a word of yourself. What brings you to Firenze?"

The Knight revealed only that he was travelling to Venice to open rhubarb trade with the East and that, as she was en route, he thought it most proper to see her.

"I am grateful," she said and at once commanded that he stay for several days so that she might organize a feast in his honor.

The banquet was grand. The young widow had surrounded herself with courtiers, ladies of more than one sort and artists. She improvised verses with the poets at the table. To a statesman by her, she offered harsh views of Cosimo, who ruled Firenze as a dictator, and the Turks equally. She commissioned one of the painters to make her portrait "in the style of Raphael."

When between courses she broke off the lascivious dance to which she had at length acceded, e'en grabbing Balthazar's arm so that he might join her, he chided: "Parisot would never stand for such debauchery, Milady."

"My friend," she laughed, "there are more reasons than one to escape the Convent." But when Balthazar remarked she had apparently become a patron of the arts, Isabella demurred. "In a small way. I do willingly pay for anything that might endure our mortal defilement, particularly as my own ashes shall be naught but verses and whispers into the ears of potentates." She caught her own sharpness. "Forgive me, Balthazar, I have no right to take such a tone with you."

Balthazar smiled as he might, but through the entire evening, e'en as she brazenly revealed her leg like a peasant or played the lute not at all unpleasantly, it seemed to him that Isabella remained alone, as if she belonged on a *fregata* between a barren island and glorious Firenze.

It was only the next afternoon, as the Knight prepared to resume his journey, that she faced him at the door and said, "Tell me, Balthazar, what news have you of Francisco?"

"None, Milady. His friend Pietru told us, *uertu de Dieu*, six years ago, that he found work at the Venetian Arsenale. Since then we have heard nothing." The Abbé kissed Isabella's hand and departed.

"That is all?" I asked, somewhat surprised.

The Comte nodded. He could or would not offer me anything more.

"She claimed I betrayed her before Cubelles' tribunal," I recollected painfully as we climbed to deck. "I sought to protect her. Rather, it was she who gave me up. I've not understood."

Niccolò regarded me with the same paternal gaze as of old and put his arm on my shoulder as we gazed over the sea. "There is buried much in her soul ... Vincenzo, in this life there are questions you will never have answered; if you have not understood that by now, you had better in all haste. Recall the words of your countryman:

"—from Tripoli, his new home."

Niccolò glanced at the running clouds above and watched the wind fill the sails. "Philip wants him booted out."

I nearly pissed in my pants. Then: "Hah! My testicles will hang from Turgut's galley! You and I know better than anyone what that dream cost the Order in the year of the *razzia*—"

"Truly," nodded the Comte, "but with the treaty signed, the King of Spain's hand is free. He sees the *kairos* is upon us and preparations for an expedition against Turgut are well underway." A crewman ambled by then. "In the meantime," Niccolò went on, "we are to search for the origin of true rhubarb ... Tell me, what did you take from Venice?"

I had expected this question from the Comte and yet had no good reply. "I now have a craft, as my father would have wished, tho' I ne'er decided whether the faith of the Knights or the industry of the Arsenale is the foundation and bulwark of Christendom."

"Surely casting could not be all you learned in such a place," the Comte said, smiling.

How this new man differed from the old, I could still not fully voice, but with each passing day I heard ever more of my old friend within the new and took comfort. "After Spain and Malta, Venice ... perplexed me."

"I am pleased to hear it," the Comte said.

"They believe themselves Catholic but ... Do you know, a few years ago the Pope attempted to bring the Index. The booksellers' guilds knew that every book burnt meant less money for them. So the Venetian Inquisition, fearing a true uprising of printers and booksellers, promptly withdrew it. By the Incarnation of Christ, they laughed the Pope out of Venice!" I could only shake my head. "They call La Serenissima a republic—and with so many rulers she seems in a perpetual confusion. For that reason perhaps the air there is freer to breathe. I see why Strozzi so despised the Venetians. In his eyes they might have been heathens. It took me seasons to grow accustomed ... "

As I made this speech, I was struck that Niccolò listened without interruption. "Yes, I believe you are right," he said, and only when I had finished. "The Venetians have put their faith in second place. Such is strange to contemplate." Hereat he grasped the boom anchoring the lateen sail and turned directly on me. "What I want to hear from you, Vincenzo

Talk to me not of the frowns of fate,
or adverse fortune; nor offend my ears
with tales of slavery's suffering in Argier,
nor galley's chains, heavy, disconsolate.
Speak not to me of fetter'd madmen's woes,
nor the proud one from his glory tumbled down:
dimm'd honour, friend abandoned, broken crown:
These be heavy sorrows; but who knows
to bend his head beneath the storms of life
with holy patience, he the shock will bear,
and see the thundering clouds disperse away.
But give to mortal man a jealous wife—
then misery, galleys, fetters, frowns, despair,
loss, shame, dishonour, folly—What are they?"

Forty-Six

His Majesty will appreciate that anticipation and dread consumed us as we approached the Bosporus and Constantinople. Three devout Christians, two having taken up arms against the Mahometans, were sailing into the clutch and breath of the Antichrist himself. Tho' the day was chilled, I lifted my hand from the rail to see sweat dripping from my palm. We glanced nervously amongst ourselves, watching the Antichrist's unmistakable shadow loom above this kingdom, beckoning us into his cold embrace, and certain that his Evil Eye had descried us on the deck of this boat. Our breathing slowed, became as one, ceased.

Yet, I acknowledge that if a spell had been cast upon us, it was not entirely one of fear. As the galleon passed through the straits, a city likely without peer on the entire earth rose larboard. Far exceeding Venice in size, from within the walls girding this profusion of roofs, gardens and domes, rose five mosques grand beyond imagining, their towers stretching toward heaven. San Marco might have sat comfortably within any one of them. As the city teemed with dwellings, the straits teemed with ships. Galleys with lateen sails and blue wreaths draped from their prows, merchantmen, caravels and an infinity of smaller boats glided past the Sarai, which sat hard by the water surrounded by a forest of green. This palace was as enormous as it was nearly shorn of ornament. As it floated by, we knew that the Sultan himself sat on a throne there, and with each passing moment we felt the heart of the Antichrist pulse louder under the great vault of blue.

Chaggi Mehmet joined us at the gunwale. "Welcome to Constantinople, Gentlemen, or as the Turks here say, *Eis teen Polin*, 'Into the City.'"

We did not dock at Constantinople proper. Rounding the tip of the cape we put into a road, the Golden Horn Mehmet named it, no doubt as fair any in the world and longer even than the Great Port of Malta. There, at the base of a hillside opposite Constantinople, we docked at a place called Galata, or Pera. I was at once perplexed and astounded. Judging from the aspect of this town and the churches therein, we'd hardly left Italy.

The crew prepared to disembark. "Messeri," said Mehmet. "I remind you that weapons are not permitted on the streets here. I suggest you stow yours in your trunks."

We did as advised.

"This must be the largest city in the world," I whispered to Niccolò, watching a steady stream of caiques ferry passengers across the Golden Horn to the colossus sitting on the opposite shore.

"Indeed," said Mehmet, overhearing, "they say here reside half a million souls."

I swallowed hard. That was three times the number of Venice or Sevilla. But there was something more, much more. "Will we not be taken as slaves?" I asked, my heart already pounding.

Mehmet only laughed; no, he guffawed. "Everyone here is a slave to the Sultan. We will make your presence known to the Venetian Bailo and you shall become *mustemin* for a year. Have no fear. You are guests."

At that juncture, several armed janissaries boarded the ship to secure the cargo until duties were paid. Chaggi Mehmet, a Mahometan, would receive the lowest tariffs. After he dealt with the customs officials and put the strongbox under guard, he led us to the ornate palace of the Bailo. There, four or five more janissaries standing at the gate eyed us suspiciously, even cursed us, but allowed us to pass. Walking through an Italian loggia, we spoke to Venetian officials who would inform the Turks of our presence. For the moment that seemed to be the end of the matter. Maugre the foul looks of the janissaries, it struck me that no Persian merchant could remain in Malta —or Venice—so easily. We next hired a house for lodging and once more I became convinced we had by some magic traveled around the Mediterranean and returned to Italy.

"You have," said Mehmet, gathering his fur cloak about him. "Galata was founded by the Genoese. If you wish, you may go to church today." Thereupon, Chaggi retired to his own lodging in the vine-covered hill above and, while I pondered his strange remark, Niccolò paid some men to carry our baggage to the house he'd procured.

The Comte lost no time in getting down to it. As Thézan-Venasque sat on a low bed piled with cushions, I on a chair and Niccolò on a stool near the crackling fire, he said in voice muted and full of urgency, "Gentlemen, the time has come for me to divulge the full purpose of our journey hither to Constantinople. I have told you the Christian forces have been preparing an expedition to Tripoli. What I have not told you is the scale of this undertaking or its present state. Planning has been going on for a full six months and involves Spain, the Papal States, the Genoese, the Neapolitans and the Knights. Should these plans go ahead, a fleet of one hundred sail will set forth from Malta in approximately six weeks—"

"One hundred sail!" I blurted out unintentionally.

Niccolò quickly hushed me, glancing toward the window. "Yes," he answered, *sotto voce*, "joining this enterprise will be upon fifteen thousand men—"

"This is a true ... *invasion*," observed the doctor in like tones, stroking his beard. "I had not entirely imagined ... "

"Yes, for the Glory of God, King Philip, the Pope, Andrea Doria and Jean de Valette are determined to rid the world of the great scourge Turgut, once and for all."

"Doria?" I whispered thereat. "He must have ninety years to him."

Niccolò crossed his legs at his place. "Ninety-three, to be precise. His grand-nephew Gian Andrea has assumed command." At this the Comte allowed himself to warm his hands as well as a brief sigh. "I do not know that we have received a bargain—for that one has but twenty."

"Six weeks ... " I muttered. "They will set sail in February—yet winter?" Tho' my voice remained low, my incredulity mounted with each answer.

"That is my guess," the Comte nodded. "There have already been numerous delays, but they will sail—in winter. Surprise is the essence of this attack, and that explains our presence here. We must know what the Turks know about the undertaking."

"Sooner or later," said Thézan-Venasque, testing the plush of the divan with his hands, "they must discover it. One cannot keep an enterprise of such magnitude ... secret ... *in perpetuum*."

"Nay, one cannot ... *in perpetuum*. But with God's grace it can be kept secret until the last moment. If the Turks now prepare a fleet, then they know and the plans must be changed—or struck. We must discover immediately what the Turks have learned."

I stood, leaned against the door, pulled my cloak tight. "How, my dear Comte, do you plan to do that?"

Niccolò glanced up at me. "Firstly, we must find Franculi Nicolo Rhodiot, the Order's chief agent in Constantinople. We have had nothing from him of late and know not what has become of him. We must also make contact with one Giovan Barelli, a Greek living here, who may be able to help us."

"This problem seems equal to the first," I scoffed. "How are we to find them? And six weeks! By God, if you are right we will have to discover them in three or four if there is any chance of getting word to Malta with the fastest *fusta* on the seas. With a full galley—we have one or two weeks ... at most."

The Comte nodded soberly, his eyes saying, aye, God has not dealt us a favorable hand. "It is unfortunate that pox and weather so delayed us. On the morrow I will make inquiries with the Bailo. In the meantime, Dr. Claude, you are to work with Chaggi on opening the rhubarb routes. We have not revealed to him our true purpose and he has not inquired. So shall it remain. You are to speak with him only of rhubarb, but use your eyes and ears to find a way into the Porte. Vincenzo, in the morning I want you to go to the Arsenal. If necessary, ask for work."

Truly, I had heard much about the Turkish Arsenal, the only serious rival to the Venetian. "Where is it?" I asked.

Niccolò shook his head. "I believe it is hard by Galata. It should not be difficult to find. Getting in I leave to you. Gentlemen, these matters are of the utmost urgency to all Christendom. You are to use only our assumed names. You are not to speak a word in public of our true purpose. If anyone asks why you are here, lecture them on the benefits of rhubarb. Dr. Claude, this should be easy enow for you." For the first time, Niccolò gave out e'en the hint of a smile.

Thézan-Venasque got up and made to bid us good-night. But before he could open the door I said, turning to Spanish, "Niccolò, *soy inquieto*."

"What ails you, Vincenzo?" he smiled.

"You are a man of arms and I also. The weight of this endeavor on our shoulders is great, and I fear other arts are needed for its successful completion."

Claude nodded. "I also have misgivings about this ... *venture*," he said. "I am a physician."

"My friends," Niccolò replied, laying his hand on my shoulder. "The Religion's intelligence has been sorely lacking in recent years. Parisot has not only banned hose of mismatched colors, but has resolved to put an end to this sorry state of affairs. He personally ordered me to undertake this *venture*, and my vow of obedience has left me no choice. Truly, wars are not won solely on the field of battle. This circumstance requires us to use not our arms but our heads." He tapped his temple with his finger.

In listening to Niccolò's speech, I could not but be reminded of the rogue Vergã's more succinct words on this account years back: the Order's intelligence was shit.

"You, Comte, not we," the doctor said, taking the words from my mouth, "have sworn an oath of obedience. I have sworn to aid the sick, of all faiths. I agreed to come to search for rhubarb. I apologize for my ... *naivety*, but this other business does not ... suit me."

"Aye," I nodded. "Arriving in Malta lo those many seasons past, I ne'er imagined I would end up a spy in Constantinople. That art belongs to another. I say it again." For a moment all words ceased, until I put it another way: "You are a Chevalier of the Order of St. John. Would you call this valor, Niccolò?"

The Comte remained silent for a long time. At length he emptied his lungs and answered, "Once in Tripoli you bowed before Turgut and I observed that by such small concessions we erode our faith. We would all prefer to vanquish our foeman on the open lists, but I remind you, Vincenzo, the golden days of chivalry are no longer with us. I have sworn my obedience and I will fight with whatever weapons are at my disposal."

"You begin to sound like a Venetian," I answered.

He who I called Niccolò said, "Amen," but e'en so, he was right. I had made my bed by accepting this undertaking and would lie in it.

Forty-Seven

The next morning Niccolò did not go to the Bailo's palace. Rather, as singers near and far called the infidels to prayer, he threw a cloak over his shoulders and hurried down the hill past a tall circular tower with a pointed roof that dominated the entire town. At the bustling dockside he easily found a ferryman who rowed him for a few coins across the Golden Horn to Constantinople itself. On the far shore he climbed the hill, quickly becoming lost in the dense warren of streets. Everything in this quarter was dominated by a fresh mosque of astonishing size. Niccolò paused for a moment, breath visible in the cold air, craning his neck at the great domes and towering minarets. He swallowed slowly. If the intent of this mosque, which surely must be the most splendid in the world, was to impress everyone who beheld it with the infinite power of the Allah's Deputy on Earth, it succeeded.

With a church or mosque standing in every direction, Niccolò needed to ask several times in several languages where he might find the one he sought, the Church of St. Theodosia. The ancient, white, domed church was not at any great distance, and gaining it, the Comte entered without hesitation. Inside, he told the priest he was searching for one of his parishioners, a Giovan Barelli. The grey-bearded man in his white and gold chasuble bade him wait and sent off a young boy. An hour passed while Niccolò repaired in his mind's eye the damaged iconostasis and the burnt image of Christ on the throne.

At last a voice said from behind him in perfect Italian, "The Eastern Savior is decidedly more severe than the Western, would you not agree?"

Niccolò turned to see an elegantly-dressed, wiry merchant with sparkling eyes and a curly beard. "Yes," the Comte replied, in less perfect Italian, "more severe and sadder. But the Catholic Church has of course fallen into gluttony and sloth."

"So the Greeks believe."

That was enough to let Niccolò know he was speaking with whom he sought. "You are Giovan Barelli?"

"Some call me that. Do you know when the Ottomans conquered this city a century ago, they butchered every one of the worshippers in this church? Come, let us walk." Barelli said a few words to the priest in perfect Greek, crossed himself from the right and ushered the Comte outside. "How did you find me?" he asked and began to stride briskly through along the quiet streets as veiled women passed.

Niccolò was impressed by the city's greenery. "Friends on Crete told me to ask at this church. Parisot speaks of you with high esteem."

"I have not seen him since one of his forays to Crete several years ago, when he did me a great service. I have heard he has become Grand Master. I am certain he will restore to the Order its former glory—if he does not expel all the Knights first."

The Greek paused, glancing up at the same mosque Niccolò had passed earlier. "These bloody dogs of Hagar seek to convert everyone to their cursed religion," he said, gathering his furs close. "That is the only reason we are allowed to live here in peace. But the Greeks will someday rise against the Infidel, and Byzantium will be restored to its people." They walked on in silence for a few minutes before Barelli broke it. "What brings you to Constantinople?" he asked.

Niccolò, yet unsure how much to trust this lively stranger, would not divulge everything. "I must find one Franculi Nicolo Rhodiot, a friend of Parisot's. He seems to have vanished. The matter is urgent."

"I do not know him," Barelli responded. "He sounds Greek, but in Stambul one never knows. He could be Italian, Cretan, Turkish—or all of them. Come, we will try to find out."

The merchant led the Comte under these cloud-pocked skies to a great covered bazaar. Inside, as dusty light streamed through the domes, the Greek stopped at several shops, speaking to the owners in flawless Turkish or Greek as the matter required. While Barelli talked with these loose-robed merchants, Niccolò watched men and women scurry on their daily chores through the noisy, cluttered arcades within which he found himself. The place appeared endless, stall upon stall unto thousands, each decorated with flowers or calligraphy.

"Buy these fine porcelains! this excellent cloth!" Niccolò imagined the shopkeepers to be shouting. Skins of all sorts hung about him: martirs, zebelins, wolves, fox, sable, bucks ... Precious stones, jewelry; arms—swords, bows, bucklers; silks, carpets. Many slaves. There in a big open space at the juncture of the arcades, hundreds of Christians, stripped naked as at Tripoli, running back and forth under the bastinados of the slave-drivers, the buyers examining all their parts for defects. The lamentable sight strengthened the Comte's resolve to succeed in his mission.

Barelli turned back to him. "This may take some time," he said.

"Time is precisely what we do not have," answered Niccolò gravely.

"Give me until tomorrow evening," Barelli said. "Where can I find you?"

The Comte told him and the Greek said he would come to Galata at the appointed hour. Just then a dispute broke out between a buyer and a seller at one of the grain stalls. A janissary came running and Niccolò watched as he beat the merchant with a stick for his sharp practices while a man on horseback holding a bird on his finger looked on. The Comte took leave of Barelli and walked out of the bazaar, sensing apart from the skins and slaves, a sharp, piquant odor he had never before experienced.

At the morning hour when the muezzins were calling the faithful to prayer and Niccolò was setting off under a dreary sky across the channel, Dr. Claude was saying his Paternosters. Having performed that duty, he blew into his hands to warm them and repaired to Chaggi Mehmet's office down at the dockside. The doctor, too, could not rid himself of the sense that his party had journeyed to an Italian city with its red-tiled rooftops and Roman-style churches. Paying little attention to all the people about, he scurried down the hill past the fish market, where in the rising sun turbaned mongers heaped their catch in great square bins. Before the smell of the fish overwhelmed everything, Thézan-Venasque also thought he sensed a pungent and totally unfamiliar odor.

Mehmet's office sat right on the Horn, beside a warehouse. Most of the day the doctor reclined in his furs on voluptuously pillowed divans thinking it sinful. He watched Mehmet and the other traders perform washings then pray on rugs several times, and he listened to them discuss the possibility of receiving a concession to bring rhubarb from Rus, Persia and beyond through the Empire. All agreed that naught would come without time and perseverance.

"Esteemed Chaggi," said the first of them, "Most of your trade has heretofore come through Saracen lands, but I am certain you know new routes through Turkey are absolutely ruled out. The best you can hope for is permission to trade along old caravan paths."

Another threw doubt on even that much, pointing out that the Lawgiver—may Allah grant him glory and long life!—had recently granted certain privileges to the English. The Armenians had also been attempting to dominate these routes. A third raised a finger, saying the question was really about taxes and protection. To gain such a concession, every official along the route would have to decide whether Chaggi's merchandise could be protected and at what cost.

"And of course," said the first, "all this is only after the Imperial Divan has approved it. Or unless you find a friend in high places. Have you considered instead trading with Frank lands?"

Chaggi nodded and sighed. With the recent war between Turkey and Persia, he had indeed brought most of his goods via southern routes. Such havoc! "Yes," he sighed, perceiving the magnitude of the task set before him, "there are many hurdles to be overcome. But perhaps Allah in his wisdom perceives the benefits of rhubarb."

The same damp morning a distant gun awoke me at sunrise, and after saying my prayers I had also set off, for the Arsenal. I made my way without difficulty; many on the streets spoke Venetian or French and my destination was known to all. But not for a moment did I lower my guard. With each step I feared arrest, or being taken into slavery, and the fact that no one so much as cast an eye on me did nothing to lessen my apprehension.

The number of peoples I saw here disquieted me. Jews walked freely among the crowds, without wearing the least sort of mark. Venetians, French, Greeks, Turks, Moriscos, all crowded the piazzetta and gathered about the fountains. Not a woman on this winter day dressed in ought less than a cloak of velvet, crimson, satin or damask, with clasps of gold or silver and arms covered with bracelets and precious stones. One might have taken them for nymphs or brides, rather than ordinary women on their way to the baths. E'en having lived in Venice for long years, a deep unease, a sensation of uncleanliness gripped me, that infidels should mingle so readily with believers. Overpowered by a desire to wash, I pushed my way through this crowd, and as I did so a foreign odor made itself felt, so sharp that I turned my head each time it attacked my nostrils.

At nearly a trot, with glances over my shoulder, I passed through the gates. Before me, at a distance down the waterfront, lay the Arsenal. From where I stood, I perceived only that it was long and narrow. Dozens upon dozens of sheds stretched out along the bank of the channel and the works were surrounded on three sides by high walls. I swallowed hard and made down the path, attempting to lighten my spirits with a song, without success.

Just before I gained the works I came upon another walled place hard by it. My only thought was how to get around, until I saw hundreds of Christian slaves being herded out of the gate there. Seeing these poor wretches shoved and cudgeled, I realized at once that I had stumbled across the bagno, the prison for galley slaves. Suddenly one of them bolted in my direction. With pitiful cries he threw himself on me, naming me his deliverer. I stood frozen, like a hero of antiquity turned into rock, with my arms spread helplessly. Thus I remained until one of the slavedrivers leapt onto him, cursing and beating him. I let this *agozzino* drag him away, my heart pounding in my breast, and walked on to the Arsenal, at once ashamed that I had done nothing to help a fellow Christian, all the while thinking, *uscança dy guerra*.

As soon as I reached the Arsenal, the slave was forgotten. Squatting around a fire before the gates, five janissaries devoured a breakfast of garlic, cucumbers and onions. Eight years had passed since I had first beheld these warriors outside the walls of Mdina, but on this morning they remained no less formidable in costume and more in bearing. I sucked in my breath, refusing to be cowed, at the same time uncertain how to gain my object. One of them got to his feet and swaggered over in his kaftan, addressing me in what I took to be Turkish, but I understood nothing. I replied in Venetian, at which this dark fellow cast at me an annoyed look and waved me violently off, crying "*Drizza!*"

Recognizing the command, I answered in the lingua franca, "*Mi far cannone. Mi voler lavorar in arsenal.*" Whether he understood my words or my pointed finger, I don't know, but he stood aside and with a brusque wave of his hand let me pass. Through the gate, I breathed.

The Turkish Arsenal was narrow and laid out along the water's edge, but I thought if it did not exceed the Venetian in measure, that made it large enough. I counted more than one hundred sheds sheltering galleys, either finished or being built. Yet as enormous as the place was, it appeared strangely empty. Nothing like the beehive of Venice greeted my eyes and I doubted that more than a few hundred people labored here. Puzzled, I at length asked a carpenter where the casting sheds might be and he said the Imperial Foundry was at a place called Tophane, which tho' not distant, was on the other side of Galata, on the banks of the Bosporus.

I retraced my steps, going through the town again, and soon thereafter passed through a gate into the Gun Foundry. I stepped onto a field of Mars. From every side cannon muzzles pointed at my head. Pieces large and small, from Rhodes, from Hungary, from every other place the Ottomans had conquered, cannon, a culverin twenty-two palms in length, a Turkish mortar with a mouth so wide that I climbed into it ... I suddenly realized I had never seen a collection of captured Ottoman arms—anywhere. The Foundry itself was of great size, with scrap heaps everywhere, barracks, casting sheds and a building of high walls and a dome at the center. As I strode nervously about, inspecting the weapons and blowing into my hands for warmth, a fellow of middle years covered in soot approached me from one of the sheds and asked what I wanted.

He was Venetian.

Once I regained my tongue, I responded that I was a master of gun casting and asked whether any work was to be had for the day or week. Lorenzo, this foreman, said not much, but they were making some new pieces and I might lend a hand.

I followed him into the casting shed and found it not unlike those of the Venetian Arsenale. Great wooden posts supported the roofs and birds roosted on the beams. The chief difference was that along one wall sat the largest weapon I had ever set eyes on. So gigantic was this basilisk that it lay in two pieces that screwed together and I failed to encompass its girth with my arms. A pyramid of stone balls sat by it; each ball must have weighed hundreds of *libbre*. This was, in all likelihood, the largest gun in the entire world, and it was not alone. Near to it other monsters rested on stands, not so enormous, but longer than any cannon we would forge in Venice. Now I swallowed hard indeed. "How is it that the Ottomans yet use *pedreri?*" I asked, putting on a brave face. "No one else but the Portuguese still throws stone. In Venice we couldn't afford to make the balls."

"In Venice there are not enough slaves to cut them," the foreman said.

There was no arguing with the reply and I asked Lorenzo why so few men were about the Arsenal and the Foundry.

"'Tis true," he answered, waving me to a gun mould hanging by ropes from one of the formidable beams above. "Far fewer masters work here than in Venice. Only thirty or forty unless there is a call, then craftsmen from all over the land flock here."

I helped him grasp the mould with several novices. "And how is it that a Venetian master comes to work at the Turkish Gun Foundry?"

Lorenzo did not answer directly. He motioned the gang to rock the mould into the wall. We did and knocked the wooden pattern out of it. Eventually Lorenzo replied. "They pay well," he said, and I spent the day working for the enemy.

That evening the three of us gathered again in Niccolò's room to discuss what we had gleaned. Taking much the same position I had the previous night, I spoke first. "I got into both the Arsenal and Foundry with little trouble. They do not employ so many people constantly as in Venice and it was explained to me that little work is going on now. Were they aware of the invasion plans, surely I would have seen a more fevered activity."

"This is good news, I would say," agreed the Comte, smiling. "Did you learn anything else?"

"Only that their guns are the largest I've ever seen, the heaviest, and judging from their length, probably the most accurate." Shaking my head, I described the basilisk in the foundry shed. "The master also spoke of the new *Kapudan*, Admiral of the fleet, Piyale Pasha, who replaced our foe Sinan a few years ago upon that one's death. Piyale is from Croatia or Hungary, a Christian somehow. His talent is such that he was allowed to marry Soliman's granddaughter. The cannon master said Piyale has but thirty years and is far more resolute than Sinan. He never hesitates and can launch a fleet in a day. Indeed, meseems we have come to a country geared for warfare."

"They *have* all but taken over the Mediterranean," observed Dr. Claude, who thereat said he had learned little except that to set up trade routes in the Empire was an intricate business. The Ottomans seemed to be a people in love with laws and regulations. How one was to see through them he could not perceive.

The Comte sighed. "Yes, but we must see through them to get into the Porte. I fear that is the only way to learn of the invasion."

"Into the Sublime Porte?" I asked, this aspect of the plan only now being revealed. "The Sarai? *How?*"

Niccolò shook his head. "*Moy foy*, I don't know. Our Rhodiot has vanished from his former abode. I did find Barelli. He will come hither tomorrow eve and tell us whether he has located the other. He hates the Turks—or appears to—and speaks every language perfectly. I think we must trust him."

The evening next, Giovan Barelli appeared at the house, saying he believed he knew where we might find Rhodiot. "He is not unknown in Galata. Come."

"How is it," I asked Barelli, "that this empire opens it arms to so many and can be intent to destroy them all?"

"Ah," replied the Greek.

He led us to a tavern down near the dockside. E'en as we entered, that odor we had all experienced overwhelmed us. "What is that smell?" we three exclaimed as one.

Barelli merely smiled. "There, I believe that is the person you seek." Our eyes followed the arc of his finger—past men seated everywhere on cushions or rug-covered benches, playing bones or cards, almost every one of them with a cup in hand—and at last landed at the extremity of the room. There, a Christian of my age but wearing the robes of a rich Turk reclined on a colorful carpet against a mountain of pillows as three dancing girls, clad in scarves and silks, moved before him with such lascivious motions as would melt marble.

We sat down at his side.

"Are you Rhodiot?" asked Niccolò severely.

The fellow, with astonishment written all over his face, nodded.

"We need to talk to you."

In the meanwhile, Barelli had said a few words to one of the tavern boys, who quickly brought us a tray bearing four cups, which he set down before us. From these very cups wafted upward that most strange, bitter odor that had disturbed us all so keenly. Each of us peered down his nose into a thick, brown liquid, and, following the Greek, we cautiously put those hot cups to our lips and had our first taste of coffee.

Forty-Eight

Niccolò dragged Franculi Rhodiot to his feet, robes and all, leaving us almost no time to speak of coffee—the doctor admitted he had already refused the drink at Mehmet's office and swore now never to touch the potion again; I remained uncertain. Before we could collect our senses, Niccolò had hauled the sinful Knight back to the house and had thrown him onto the cushions of the sitting room.

"It is plain to all why you have vanished!" roared the Comte. "Why were you not at your former abode?"

"I—I left it," stuttered Rhodiot, as he got clumsily to his feet.

"Yes, we see, for taverns and whorehouses, where you drink *c—coffee* all day and abandon the Order to which you have sworn obedience to dire peril!"

"Sir!" replied Rhodiot, gaining some composure, even as his aspect remained comical in his eastern robes, "Were weapons permitted in Galata, I would challenge you for those words. Apologize!"

"Tell me what the Turks know about Tripoli!"

Rhodiot gaped and shook his head. "I have no idea, Sir, of what you speak."

"Precisely. You know nothing, which means we know nothing. Can you get us into the Sarai?"

"How, Sir, do you expect me to do that?" Rhodiot answered haughtily.

"With your brains," Niccolò scoffed and once again shoved the useless spy to the cushions. Then he turned to the rest of us. "We must enter the Porte, but thanks to this rogue's weakness for Turkish delights, the Order is bereft of means."

At this juncture Barelli stepped forward. "I have perceived much from our conversations, Signore. It is certain that you are here on an undertaking for Parisot, but if I am to help him, you must take me fully into your confidence."

"You trust this stranger?" cried Rhodiot.

"More than I do you." Hereon he addressed the Greek. "Parisot believes in your qualities, Sir, and that will have to suffice." He told Barelli everything.

The Greek listened attentively and answered, "Any fool can walk through the Imperial Gate into the palace's first courtyard, for it is open to all. To walk through the Gate of Salutation into the second courtyard, however, requires an official purpose. To walk through the High Gate, the Sublime Porte, into the Imperial Harem is inconceivable, and to walk into the Imperial Divan is merely impossible. Yet, you must indeed step into the Divan or, better, the Harem. You should think in terms of years." Niccolò was about to object. "Yes, I know. You have weeks ... days." Barelli fell silent for a moment. "The fastest path through a gate is often not the most direct. By imperial *ahdname* the Venetian Bailo is the legal administrator of all Franks in Galata. You may be certain he has friends and ears in the highest places. I understand he is shortly to give a banquet. We must do our best to get invited."

The next morning Barelli and the Comte exerted every means at the palace to be presented to the Bailo and were successful. Antonio Barbarigo, the Bailo, received them the same afternoon.

"How is it," Barbarigo asked with marked curiosity, offering Niccolò a seat in his grand Italian sitting room covered with eastern rugs, "that a French Comte with an Italian name becomes a trading partner to a Persian in Venice?" To which the Comte merely replied that the world was growing rapidly in this age and asked the Bailo in turn how it was that the Ottomans so readily accommodated foreigners.

"Do not be so deceived by your easy presence here," replied his host with a small hint of gravity as they sat down. "Upon landing you paid a *cizye*, a head tax, and after a year you will leave my protection to become a *zimmi* subject to the Sultan's laws. Eventually you will become an infidel slave to the Grand Signor." At that Barbarigo laughed. "But perhaps you will not stay so long, Comte Contremaret, if rhubarb proves unattainable."

The guests made no request of the Bailo to hasten negotiations with the Porte and the Bailo made no offer, but upon learning that the Comte had recently been on Malta, Barbarigo inquired with yet greater curiosity whether Niccolò had met the Grand Master. Niccolò unhesitatingly replied yes, hoping the connection would prove advantageous, but the Bailo frowned, declaring the Knights to be a veritable nuisance.

"With every infidel vessel they capture, the Sultan's anger grows. If it had not been for the chaos here in the past few years, I am certain he would have already put an end to them."

The Comte reminded him that with the great powers at war amongst themselves, the Knights had of late been the only Christian force protecting the Mediterranean. "Of course, Eccellenza, with Cateau-Cambrésis signed, our potentates might at last rally their defenses and strike back."

"Comte," answered Barbarigo skeptically, "Europe is exhausted; she hardly has sufficient strength. The Knights themselves ... " He shrugged, offered his guests some coffee and figs. "How are Malta's fortifications?"

"I would say—"

"The Knights are, unsurpassed in military arts," Barelli interrupted, accepting the fruit. "While still Captain General, the present Grand Master saved several of my ships from capture by the Turks, at the same time taking a pair of theirs. A remarkable display of seamanship and valor." At that moment, some of the mist surrounding Barelli's association with de Valette lifted in Niccolò's mind.

"What sort of man is the new Grand Master?" asked Barbarigo.

"He belongs to an age when the world was simpler," replied Niccolò before Barelli could speak. "In that, *Fide et fortitudine* might be his motto."

"Not *fide non armis?*"

"No, Parisot believes God strengthens his arm. He may be correct."

"Well, Comte," smiled their host, "I see you are a *homo factus ad unguem*."

"No, merely *homo sum; humani nihil a me alienum puto*."

"Delightful, really," Barbarigo said. "The two of you simply must come to the banquet in two days' time. Cancel any other plans you might have. I can guarantee an event." The Bailo graciously saw his guests to the door.

"Well," sighed Niccolò on the street, "we seem to have succeeded in one mission, at least."

Barelli nodded, putting his hand on the Comte's shoulder. "Truly, but you must not appear overly anxious to win the Bailo's confidence. As they say, *festina lente*. Also, remember, you are here to gather information, not to give it away."

Two evenings later, Niccolò and Barelli set off from the house: The Comte, in a new robe brocaded with silk and gold and edged by ermine, would have outshone the Doge himself in resplendence; Barelli, wearing a shimmering kaftan clasped with gold and a tasseled hat that towered above his head, did not cede place. Despite their magnificence, I felt a sharp unease as Dr. Claude and I watched them walk toward the palace.

Antonio Barbarigo had invited three hundred guests of all nations. It seemed to Niccolò that each spouse or maiden intended to outdo her rivals, and the banquet hall blinded one's vision with gold and silver, carquants, tablets, silks and crimson caps wound with golden bands, all adorning women who walked so far above the ground that they appeared to float. These women aspired to be not merely nymphs but goddesses. Regretfully, the Comte was unable to pursue their company as he waited to be presented to the host.

"How are the negotiations for rhubarb proceeding, Comte?" the Bailo inquired.

"Very well, Eccellenza. *Sans doute, l'affaire s'achimyne.*"

At that the Bailo turned to the next guest. Niccolò made a point to be presented to several Turkish officials, who dressed more plainly in their heavy kaftans, but with wound hats towering no less than a *braccio* above their heads. These officials, a few of whom appeared to be Viziers, spoke no western tongue, but Barelli was able to serve as *dragoman*. His efforts proved to be of no sensible value, for the Viziers knew little about the House of War and exhibited less curiosity.

"How is the health of the *bey* of the Franks?" one inquired, Barelli explaining that by *bey* his interlocutor meant not governor but king, but that he could not ascertain to which king this Vizier referred or whether he meant the Emperor himself.

Niccolò and Barelli threaded the crowd with ears vainly sharpened for word of Tripoli. A few Jewish doctors—including the personal physician to the Sultan—and merchants mingled among the crowd. One of these told Barelli that Joseph Nasi himself had been invited, but Nasi so detested the Venetians—and Christians—for their treatment of him, that he vowed to finance a war against them before he entered the Bailo's house.

"Could he do that?" Niccolò asked Barelli, taking him aside by the arm.

"Yes, he could," Barelli answered. "And he will."

A gong sounded.

Servants brought venison, partridge and peacock. The Westerners alone partook of the wine, imported by the Jews present. The Comte's increasing thirst for intelligence was hardly slaked by the drink and at each moment his desperation mounted. Fortune changed slightly when he found himself seated next to the Austrian Ambassador Busbecq, who—jumping casually among six tongues as he imbibed ceaselessly—failed to mention a word about Tripoli. Surely, Niccolò thought, this Ambassador would know anything that was to be known. Indeed, when Busbecq's tongue had loosened sufficiently, the Comte delicately mentioned rumors about large events unfolding in the western Mediterranean, but Busbecq shrugged, saying he had heard nothing whatsoever.

Leaning to the Comte, he did narrate *teste- à-teste* an extraordinary tale that confirmed what Niccolò had himself told us on the voyage to Constantinople: The kingdom had been embroiled in civil war for the past two years. Of Soliman's four living sons, three were born to his wife, Roxelana, but the eldest, Mustafa, was of a Crimean concubine. All agreed that only Mustafa had been capable of succeeding his father, but Roxelana, determined that one of her own sons should become Sultan, used witchcraft to convince her husband that Mustafa intended to usurp the throne.

"*Uouz comprenez*," elaborated Busbecq, "that this put Mustafa in an extremely dangerous position for, according to the barbaric custom of the Turcz, once one son is selected to ascend the throne, the others must be murdered. Truly, under her spells, Soliman summoned Mustafa to Constantinople, where as he watched from behind a curtain in a tent, the eunuchs ambushed and garroted him. Mustafa's young son was soon dispatched in like manner."

Of Roxelana's three, the youngest, a humpback, incontinently died in terror and the path to the throne was opened to the two elder sons, Selim or Bayezid. But immediately upon Mustafa's death a pretender appeared, claiming to be Mustafa himself, having miraculously escaped his father's ambush. Thousands of rebels flocked to his standard and success followed success, until the day Bayezid himself captured and hanged the imposter and his followers. *Toutefois*, intelligence convinced the Sultan that Bayezid himself had suborned the false Mustafa.

"Were it not for the intercession of his mother, who pleaded for mercy, Soliman would have without fail executed his own son. But two years ago

Roxelana died. *L'affaire fut dans l'eau* and Bayezid declared open warfare on Selim."

The armies met at a place called Konya, twenty thousand men on each side. Tho' Bayezid was the worthier, Selim was aided by supernatural forces when a great blast of wind from a saint's tomb blew sand into the faces of his brother's soldiers, blinding them. Fleeing, Bayezid reached Persia, where Shah Tahmasp showered him with fabulous gifts. *Dans les coulyssez*, the Shah was in fact bargaining with the Sultan for Bayezid's release. Would Soliman grant Baghdad to Tahmasp in return for the rebellious son?

"The Sultan, *certainment,*" Busbecq concluded, "has no desire to relinquish Baghdad to the Persians. That is where affairs now stand."

Niccolò understood that what he just heard was the best possible news for Christendom. The war between the sons had not only saved Malta from an invasion, but the Sultan had chosen the worst possible successor. Selim, Busbecq assured him, was pompous, corpulent and the least talented. Soldiers nicknamed him "stalled ox" and *sarhosh*—"the sot." Mustafa would have invaded Europe, and Europe would have trembled. Selim would stay home drunk.

"Christendom needs only, I believe," concluded Busbecq, "to hold out until the Magnificent dies—if it is able. Tell me, Comte, do you think it is able?"

As Soliman listened to my own relation of this story, I thought I beheld a tear falling from the eye of God's Shadow on earth, but convinced myself I was mistaken.

Niccolò's answer to the Ambassador was forestalled by the entry of three dozen Galatan dancing girls, who made those we saw in the tavern appear plain and unschooled. Afterwards the guests were treated to a comedy, *Cupid and Psyche*, followed by a tableau depicting Colombo's discovery of the Newfound World. One of the Viziers leaned over to Barelli and asked him if he knew where this Newfound World was. When Barelli told him, the Vizier expressed amazement, as he maintained the earth was flat.

Niccolò departed the banquet feeling naught had been gained—to the contrary, that precious days had been wasted in pursuit of this road.

"The fact that we yet heard nothing of invasion plans is a good sign," objected Barelli on the street.

"Does no one speak directly in this kingdom?" Niccolò said in despair.

"No, but at least you are making yourself known to the Bailo."

"Ach," muttered the Comte and went home to bed.

Niccolò slept uneasily, and for good reason. Late afternoon next, while Thézan-Venasque drank coffee in Chaggi Mehmet's office, one of the servants announced a well-dressed Armenian merchant. Bowing deeply with his hands on his breast and speaking a respectable Venetian, the stranger, having ascertained that he truly faced the Persian Chaggi Mehmet, glanced around with such agitation that Mehmet needed to assure him that it was permissible to speak in the physician's presence.

"I come from Bayezid, son of Soliman," the Armenian said.

Another silence engulfed the room as Mehmet arched an eyebrow and shot an amused frown at Thézan-Venasque. At length he replied that Bayezid was presently guest of the Shah in Persia.

"That is true, esteemed Chaggi," the visitor answered, "and he will pay handsomely to one who will aid him escape the Shah's hospitality."

Thereat Mehmet put his hands on his hips and laughed heartily. "You expect me to believe Bayezid sent you? Hah! What proof can you offer?"

Taken aback, the Armenian answered that he could bring proof in a day's time, at which Chaggi said, "Very well, bring it," and dismissed him. Once the merchant had departed, Mehmet wheeled on Thézan-Venasque and laughed again, soberly. "Dr. Claude, we have just received unsettling news. We are traders. Why would such a fellow come to us? I tell you agents of every sort swarm about this city. One must be on one's guard always. And now ... Can you explain this to me?" He peered at the doctor severely.

"No," replied the physician. "I cannot. You are more experienced in such matters than I."

"Well," said Mehmet, "let us see whether our visitor returns."

At the house, Thézan-Venasque recounted what had taken place. "The good-natured Chaggi's suspicions are raised, and he may ... umm, no longer trust us. Perhaps we must divulge everything."

"Would you put your trust an infidel?" Rhodiot asked. Barelli had thought it was less dangerous to keep this slothful agent by us than set him at his own devices. The question Rhodiot posed was not simple to answer and I breathed deeply, as did Niccolò and Thézan-Venasque.

Barelli himself had been listening attentively. "Chaggi's suspicions are not the most urgent problem," he said. "Today you are in considerable danger. The question is, from whom? If your visitor appears tomorrow, he will bring proofs, probably letters. Whatever they may say, your heads are forfeit if you allow yourself to be drawn into this subterfuge. Rather, Mehmet must tell this courier only that he would speak to a scribe at the palace—about rhubarb trade into Persia. Any person has the right to present a petition to a clerk at the Sarai. Chaggi must know this, but do not hope that you will gain access to the Porte by such naive means. Natheless, it is now of the utmost importance to keep up appearances. Only Mehmet and the doctor should go."

"It is a good plan," said Niccolò.

"It is not a plan," answered Barelli, "merely a move."

The next day the Armenian appeared at Chaggi's office with a letter bearing a royal *tugra*. That should have been sufficient to ensure its authenticity; Mehmet natheless found it incredible that he should hold in his hand a letter from Bayezid offering to pay a ransom worth several kings, were his escape from the Shah to Frankish lands effected.

Dr. Claude had already spoken to Mehmet about an answer to such an overture and Mehmet promptly handed the letter back to the Armenian. "Tell your master I am a simple trader. I will go to the palace tomorrow to petition for the right to bring rhubarb through Turkey, that is all."

The Armenian bowed and backed out of the room.

That evening Barelli said to those gathered about, "Dr. Thézan-Venasque, you and Mehmet must not fail to appear at the Sarai tomorrow. In the meantime, Vincenzo, continue to listen for anything at the Foundry. Niccolò, you and I need to get closer to the Bailo to find out who is behind this. Messeri, we must exert all possible means. It is possible in this that the mountain has come to Mahomet, but that would be a miracle, and miracles are rare devices indeed."

Barelli departed and I said to Niccolò, "Comte, we have been in the infidel capital for a week. In a few days it will be too late for a galley to get through to Malta in time to warn them about anything."

"I am well aware of that," nodded Niccolò wearily, laying a hand on my shoulder. I had rarely seen him so at a loss for ideas. "Now let us get some sleep."

Forty-Nine

The next morning Mehmet and Thézan-Venasque made their way across the Horn to Istanbul and the Sarai with a petition Mehmet had had drawn up by his best scribe. They passed through the massive Imperial Gate without difficulty. Indeed, Mehmet had been in this courtyard more than once before. Thézan-Venasque cast about uneasily, at the stables, the wooden walls, at the janissaries milling around an ancient Byzantine church they seemed to have changed into an armory. Every sort of person was to be found here amidst the cypresses, from the lowest to the highest; yet with almost everyone dressed in the simplest kaftans, Thézan-Venasque could hardly distinguish the common people from imperial officials. The quiet of the place unnerved him; even the horses made no sound but for the tread of their hoofs on the ground, and the low, unornamented buildings caused the doctor to feel he had entered a nomad's lodge rather than a palace.

As they waited to be received by an imperial scribe, Mehmet bought some sherbet from a seller who walked about with a tank of the drink strapped to his back and who drew it off through a tube. Others near the Gate of Salutation gazed curiously at the stuffed heads of executed officials sitting atop marble pillars. Dr. Claude bought a peach from a fruit seller and bit into it. After some hours, an official emerged from an office, asking who they were, and after a few more hours a clerk sitting on a rug admitted them to the same office. He accepted the petition and told them to return in five days' time. Thézan-Venasque and Mehmet bowed and left.

At the same moment that the merchant and the physician were entering the Sarai, the Comte and Barelli were presenting themselves at the Bailo's palace, but the Bailo was himself en route to the Sarai on official matters and unable to receive them. I returned to the Foundry. The situation had changed not a wit from previous days. While we toiled at the furnaces, I again asked Lorenzo the cannon master how it was that so many foreigners labored at this place, as the Turks themselves regarded all foreigners with a vague suspicion.

"It is true that these people are backwards by nature," Lorenzo replied, "and believe their Prophet said that those who imitate a people become one of them. But their priests tell them it is permissible to copy Christian weapons for their jihad against the Infidel. Fight like with like, they say." Lorenzo further averred—as indeed the damned *chavush* had many years ago—that they banned printed books, for God's word must come direct through the hand of the Prophet. What's more, they frowned on timepieces; hardly a one of them knew what time of day it was beyond morning, afternoon or evening, and they even prized bows above arquebuses. Such suspicions were made clear to me that day when they cast a gun. I was told to leave the casting shed, along with everyone excepting some priests and nobles, for fear of the Evil Eye.

Later, before I departed the foundry, I asked Lorenzo why he did not work at the Venetian Arsenale. He again said that the pay here was better, but when I asked whether that was the lone reason, he shrugged.

At the house that evening, Barelli's first question was whether Mehmet and the doctor had been received by a scribe. Dr. Claude nodded, drawing himself up to the crackling fire as he recounted their four-hour wait and their instructions to return in five days. The Greek was puzzled. "Four hours? Five days? This seems too swift," he said.

"Ah," interjected Niccolò, rising in frustration. "Every door is closed and opened to us, who knows which? We are blind men in a maze."

Barelli advised him to take heart and I reported only that these people feared the Evil Eye to such a degree that they did not allow infidels to be present when they cast their great guns.

Five days later, Mehmet and the doctor returned to the palace to be told that their petition was in the hands of the Head Clerk and that they should come back in a week. The Foundry showed no unusual activity. Mayhap the Christian forces had truly achieved surprise and the Turks had no knowledge that Tripoli was soon to be invaded. So much was good news. What unsettled me was what we would do if suddenly the news should turn.

"It is now too late for any galley to get through in time," I said to Niccolò at the house as I built a fire, "and in a few weeks more a galiot. I have a bad feeling about this. We must arrange for a *fusta*, should matters come down hard."

"I have begun to do so," he replied, "as I have also sent a messenger to Crete, telling them how matters stand and requesting that Romegas be waiting for us at all times, from now on."

"Romegas?" For some years I had given no thought to that Knight. I had not for an instant forgotten his apprentice, Blaij Vergã.

The Comte nodded, rubbing his hands above the flames. "Yes, he has been reconnoitering the eastern seas this season and we made plans to rendezvous when this business was complete. However, as we know, plans change ... "

Those words held truth. As we spoke, Thézan-Venasque was walking home from a coffee house. Suddenly, he thought he spied Chaggi Mehmet ducking into a small mosque with the very same Armenian merchant. The doctor waited out of sight until at length the two emerged. Now there was no question and he quickly returned to the house.

"You're late," Barelli said. Dr. Claude nodded and immediately told us what he had seen.

"We are being played by Chaggi," said Niccolò angrily. "He must know our game—"

"—or is trying to find out," observed Barelli.

Rhodiot paced angrily back and forth in the room. "I say we off both of them."

"Idiot!" hissed Barelli without pause. "One could do nothing worse. Whoever has suborned those two would know immediately what we are about. We must continue to play Chaggi as he is playing us. I know the danger in this, but the alternative is fatal. Remember, the advantage is ours; he may have suspicions but he knows nothing. Doctor, I fear you must do everything to uphold appearances, at whatever risk. From now on, we will not meet unless necessary and then only in Christian churches. I shall send you word by my chief servant each time. We may hope the enemy yet has no knowledge of me. I ask you to find separate lodgings."

Despite his reassuring words, Barelli left us quaking in our boots, certain we were watched, lacking evident means to further matters at the Porte.

In this desperation Niccolò resolved to pay a visit to the Austrian Ambassador, Ogier Busbecq. The day was near freezing and the Comte thought he noticed a few flakes of snow. He stopped to buy a pair of gloves. Crossing the Horn to a crowded quarter of Stambul, he ducked into several taverns and churches to be certain he was not being followed. The Ambassador's residence sat high on a hill, at some distance from the water. Niccolò found Busbecq playing tennis at the court he had recently built for himself. The loquacious fellow bounded over to him and offered his hand.

"Good-morning to you, Comte," he said in Latin.

"Good-morning, Ambassador. Is it not a cold day for sport?"

"No better way to keep warm," Busbecq replied, passing to French and wiping his short, greying hair and beard with a cloth. "This is the life, wouldn't you say, in the Refuge of the World? What more splendid existence could be imagined? Come, join me for coffee—or do you prefer wine?"

With his arm around Niccolò's shoulder, Busbecq led his guest past a large cage of screeching monkeys and through the courtyard, where he brushed aside a sable with his foot and petted a wolf. An astonishing number of animals roamed about—horned stags, gazelles, deer, lynxes, cranes, wolves and even a bear, the last being chained.

"As you see," the Ambassador remarked, "I am a great lover of animals ... By the way, you are in luck, today is Friday, and we may watch the Sultan en route to his devotions." He ordered a servant to bring coffee to one of the upstairs rooms.

Busbecq threw open the windows and bade his visitor step onto the veranda. Both the palace and the great mosque rose before them in the near distance. Niccolò decided to take the stag by the horns. "Sir," he said, "as the Hapsburg Ambassador in Constantinople, you certainly have a better idea than I of affairs at court. As I said to you at the Bailo's dinner, we hope to receive a rhubarb concession from the Sultan and at this moment have a petition circulating at the Sarai—"

"—where it will undoubtedly circulate until Judgment Day."

"Precisely. I am hoping you might advise me."

"Where is this petition now?"

"I am told with the Head Clerk."

"Not high enough, I fear. But to become Head Clerk, one requires a patron, usually a Vizier. One should determine who the patron is. Ahh, coffee."

Niccolò accepted the cup presented to him by the servant. "Is it possible that the Sultan might be induced to show interest in this matter, or is such a question naive?"

Busbecq chuckled. "I am afraid that is a distant hope. The Sultan has become a veritable recluse in the Harem. I myself have had only two audiences with him. The closest you are likely to get to the Sultan is today. Behold."

As they drank coffee and watched, a procession slowly moved by: A groom leading a white charger caparisoned in gold and jewels—the stallion had hung from straps in the stables during the night to ensure it walked with a halting gait. Atop this horse, none other than the Lawgiver, simply dressed in white; following him, sheiks, armed janissaries, mounted silahdars in red, all surrounded by crowds who returned the salutations of the Padishah with flowers and good wishes. For a moment Niccolò shut his eyes and was unnerved; apart from the soft murmurs of the people, the procession might have been enfolded in sleep and the world in midnight.

"You know," remarked Busbecq, "whatever you think of these Turks, around the Sultan no man owes his dignity to anything but his personal merit and bravery. This is why the janissaries are so formidable in war. They are all the Sultan's slaves. No distinction is attached to birth in this empire and each man carries in his own hand his position in life, which he can make or mar at will. How superior to our own ideas—with us there is no opening for merit; the prestige of birth is the sole key to advancement in Europe."

Niccolò was taken aback by the Ambassador's words. "You would abolish the nobility?" he asked, intrigued in spite of urgency.

"We could do worse," Busbecq said, jovially. "We could do worse. Now, Comte, if you have not already experienced it, let me introduce you to sherbet, a delightful drink of fermented raisins, ice and water ... "

That evening in an empty church on other side of the channel, under the severe and compassionate gaze of the Eastern Christ, Niccolò reported his experience with the Ambassador. I again felt possessed by the uneasy sensation that Abdallah-al-Waryagli in his long-ago conversations had not entirely dissembled about this kingdom.

"Did Busbecq agree to help?" was the only question Barelli asked.

The Comte shrugged with a perplexed expression. "He advised that we identify the patron of the Head Clerk, but Busbecq is too much of a diplomat to speak directly, and I am not enough of one to decipher his nuances." There was another matter. "Signore Barelli, you show both an enthusiasm and an aptitude for this our enterprise. From the day we take our leave of this accursed city, one way or the other, I invite you to assume charge of the Order's mission here. Parisot has left the decision to me. I can assure you that the rewards for success will be great and no expense spared. You have my word." For one of the few times in my life, I saw the Abbé-Comte cross himself.

"I would be honored," replied Barelli, "to serve de Valette and the Knights against the Infidel, and I pledge my life to do so." He walked up to a wooden image of the Savior that stood before the altar, crossed himself in the way of his faith and kissed it. Then he returned and took the Comte's hand.

"To this end," Niccolò said, "Dr. Thézan-Venasque must begin schooling you at once in the use of the Order's ciphers, which will be of critical importance." The Greek nodded readily. "I would also turn over to you our strongbox, which shall go a long way to easing the difficulty of this venture. We should do this immediately—just in case."

"It is not a simple matter," I interrupted. "How will we get the strongbox out of Chaggi's office without raising his suspicions further?"

"You shall have to steal it," said Barelli.

Within several days Thézan-Venasque had located the extra keys in Mehmet's office and removed them unnoticed. The greater danger was the night patrols of janissaries with their shrouded lanterns, the midnight fishermen with their nets at all places along the Horn and the watch at the warehouse itself. Late one night, Thézan-Venasque made as if he had just come out of a tavern and approached the watchman. The guard, by now familiar with him, readily accepted the doctor's offer of the new tobacco from the West, which was in fact *afione*, available everywhere here; before long the fellow was fast asleep at his post. Dr. Claude waved the three of us out of the shadows and moments later the box was on a caique headed to the opposite shore, the keys back in their proper place.

The next day the Comte appeared at Mehmet's office to discuss the state of the rhubarb negotiations, only to find his trading partner in a frenzy over the stolen box.

"Do you realize, Sir, " roared the Comte, "this puts our entire enterprise in peril? That box held enough gold and jewels to ransom the Sultan himself!"

Mehmet apologized profusely. "A thousand pardons. All this is of course of the gravest concern, Comte. I shall alert the authorities and the Guild of Thieves immediately and make every attempt to recover the money. I cannot understand ... Watchmen guard these buildings all night."

With deep bows he begged the Comte to sit and join him for coffee. At length the Comte relented, disclosing that he had a separate cache of jewels that would see them through the nearest weeks, but now it was imperative that the negotiations be brought to a successful conclusion as swiftly as possible.

We breathed a little easier when Chaggi evinced no suspicion of the true warp of events, and a few days later decided we had turned this matter entirely to our advantage when the merchant and the doctor returned again to the Sarai to be told a Vizier now considered their petition.

"Must this mean," I asked Barelli at our next meeting, "that Chaggi has a more direct route to the Porte than he has let on?"

"It may be. We have no way of knowing and must play this out. *Corragio*."

But the game took a sharp turn against us. A week later we met in another empty church, this time on the hill behind Galata, where many of the ambassadors made their residence. Rhodiot was absent. We waited and waited until the city slept fast. All of us paced, certain in our bones something had badly miscarried. Suddenly the errant spy burst in, pushing and dragging that Armenian merchant, who struggled to break free.

"This one has been following me," he said, hurling the knave violently to the stone floor. The Armenian immediately scrambled to his feet and bolted for the door. At once Rhodiot and I were on him and brought him down hard.

"We have known about you for some time," said Barelli. "What do you know about us?"

The Armenian refused to speak.

Barelli struck him across the face. "Did Chaggi Mehmet send you?"

Still the Armenian remained silent and Niccolò grabbed his arm, twisting it so tightly behind his back that he fairly wrenched it from its socket.

"Yes, he sent me," the man finally admitted, clenching his teeth but refusing to scream. "And he knows everything."

"You're lying," the Greek replied, striking him again.

Rhodiot, leaning against one of the church's columns, interrupted the questioning. "It makes no difference. If we let him go now, we may not see the sun rise."

In spite of the distaste the rest of us held for Rhodiot, we were forced to agree. The Comte nodded to Barelli. We gagged the Armenian with a kerchief, marched him down the deserted streets to the other side of the hill and drowned him in the Bosporus. Commandeering a caique, we weighted the body with stones and dumped it into the middle of the cold straits.

"Soon enough now we shall discover whether the enemy knows of our association," said Barelli once we had returned to shore. "We must have no further direct contact, Comte. Our predicament has become far too dangerous. Leave messages for me at the church where we first met. The priest there can be trusted. If your head remains attached over the next weeks, inform me when your mission is concluded. I shall lie fallow for the time being and resurrect myself as soon as it appears safe." The two men embraced and the Greek disappeared into the night.

The rest of us walked back to Galata shaking. "We must of course pretend nothing has happened," said Niccolò. "Let the next move be Mehmet's, and let us hope it is not to the neck."

"Comte," the doctor said, steadying his nerves, "our necks are but a ... *minor* affair. However, while we have run in circles from merchant to ambassador to Foundry to Porte only to put ourselves in ... *some* peril, it has become evident that time is draining away."

My agitation was too great to allow the physician to proceed in such calm tones. "What the doctor wishes to say, Comte, is that time has run out. While we have laid our necks on the block, it has become too late to warn anyone about anything by any means. Only God knows when the invasion will begin, but He will ordain it without our intelligence."

"Do you think I am not aware of that?" answered Niccolò with sensible annoyance.

"Then what is our further purpose here? Why do we not escape while our heads remain attached, rather than wait for the scimitar to fall?"

The Comte hummed softly to himself. "My friends, Turkish scimitars are sharp and I do not fear them. I rather fear failing in this our mission. Word of the invasion will come hither. We shall wait until we have the Porte's reply in hand."

"As I deny and defy the Evil Spirit with both my Hands!" I erupted. "You are mad. Natheless, I shall not abandon you to this madness."

Words were easy. From that day on we glanced over our shoulders even in churches. I began to drink coffee and Dr. Claude, contrary to his vow, seemed entirely unable to stop; what's more, this mysterious elixir left us all more on edge than we already were. I prayed at one of the Galata churches. Each night I went to sleep in a room I had hired some weeks before, expecting never to see the sun again.

None of us could say why our heads remained fastened. From the morning after we had disposed of the Armenian, Mehmet appeared unnerved. He suspected us, and each glance he threw in our direction was more distrustful than the last, but he knew only that the Armenian had simply vanished without a trace. He made no overt move. Each day he informed us that our petition continued to make its slow way up the unfathomable spiral of the Ottoman court. Each day Niccolò courted diplomats and ambassadors, became a frequent guest of the Bailo and befriended Ogier Busbecq. Yet, while we retained our heads, we remained blind to the inner workings of the Sarai.

I could bear it no longer. "Do you remember, Comte," I said one night in a church, "how in the old days you so often spoke of Folly, of the Order's blind march to disaster? I name our presence here Folly. We have no eyes or ears in place at the Sarai. These diplomats have been dealing us their own hands and, as we remain alive, it seems almost certain that someone in the Porte is using us for his own designs."

"I agree, Vincenzo, but as Barelli said, we required years. I regret that our enterprise has been stalemated, but I have no further thoughts."

"I do."

The Comte cocked his head in surprise.

"Some years ago, in the dungeons of St. Angelo, you spoke of how you had wronged your beloved, a Jewess in Venice, and that as a result, her family had fled to Constantinople, where they prospered. I ne'er knew what to make of that story, but if it held any truth, seek her aid."

"Surely, you cannot believe ... "

"Throw yourself at her feet and beg forgiveness, Comte. Perhaps it will be forthcoming."

A deep sadness encompassed his features. Without another word, Niccolò got to his feet, crossed himself in front of the altar, and walked from the church.

Three weeks before the Feast of the Annunciation and the New Year, Mehmet informed us that he and the doctor would be received at the Divan. He warned us not to expect a favorable or e'en firm decision. "It is too much too hope for, as we have not found a suitable patron. But we shall dutifully appear at dawn tomorrow."

"I fear it is now that the design of our foe shall become evident," said Niccolò later, "and that the sword shall fall."

The doctor sighed. "Comte, if I return from the Divan with my ... *beard*, you can be certain that I will confine my practices to medicine from this day forward."

"And every member of the Order shall be indebted to you for it, as they are indebted to you for this undertaking." Thereupon Niccolò embraced the physician. "Now, I myself have an appointment with Destiny," he said and vanished.

At sunrise next I was awoken by the gun followed by a knock on my door. Cautiously, I rose and opened it a crack. Niccolò.

"We have been thoroughly duped," he growled, stepping firmly into the room. "We are nothing more than pawns in an elaborate game being played out in the palace."

Clearing my head with a swig of wine, I asked what he was about.

"A few weeks ago, I sought out the one you spoke of. Some wounds, I fear, are too deep to be forgiven at any price, but one may always purchase knowledge, if not wisdom. I have learned this: A certain Equerry at the palace, one Lala Mustafa, has been attempting to obtain advancement at the expense of a bitter enemy, a Vizier who is patron of the Head Clerk and thus Chaggi Mehmet. It was Lala Mustafa who forged the letters from Bayezid, e'en as he convinced Soliman that the letters originated with the Vizier—an act of high treason."

Puzzlement had overcome me. "I do not see what this has to do with us," I said, taking another swig.

"Directly, nothing—we *have* been pawns in this game. We did well not to take the bait of those letters, or our heads would already sit at the palace gate. But the Equerry intends to create the impression that the Vizier has suborned us into freeing Bayezid and thus has hurried along our petition to the Vizier. It is quite believable, as our announced intention is to travel to Persia."

"W—whose side is Chaggi on?"

The Comte shrugged. "I suspect he is trying to have both rhubarb and gold. We know only that the Armenian spoke to him, not what passed between them. Were I Lala Mustafa, I would have had the Armenian convince Chaggi that it lay in his interests to be certain we received a rhubarb concession as quickly as possible and set off for Persia."

I stood aghast at the plot's risk and intricacy, but Niccolò scoffed. "I am told this is a commonplace. We are, after all, in Byzantium. One thing is certain: The Equerry, through Soliman, will see his hand played at the Divan today, and if Mehmet and the doctor appear, their heads will roll."

"But they have already departed!" I exclaimed. "Audiences begin at dawn."

"*Mort de Dieu!*" exclaimed the Comte. "I must ensure that they do not set foot into that pavilion. I am off." Niccolò's cloak swirled and he vanished.

By the time the Comte had crossed the Horn, Mehmet and the doctor had passed through the first courtyard of the palace and had been stopped by a *bostanci* outside the Gate of Salutation. Only after they showed him the summons they had received from the palace were they permitted to pass into the second courtyard. Thézan-Venasque was again struck by the silence. He failed to convince himself that a single person coughed or spit, and the janissaries stood so still at their places that they seemed painted rather than alive. A gazelle leapt before him and he stepped back, aware now of a persistent sound—the pounding of his own heart. He breathed deeply, attempting to still himself, and managed to take in his surroundings. No statuary greeted his eyes and only haphazardly placed gardens and fountains lent the place ornament. The tallest structures to be seen were the chimneys on his right, atop the royal kitchens, from which wafted the smell of onions and game. Before him stood the forbidden Sublime Porte itself and to his left a square pavilion where the Imperial Divan was just beginning its morning deliberations. A crowd had already gathered under the ornamented wooden roof. Mehmet told him that it would be a long wait before their petition was heard. This was not a relief.

They stood in silence with the others for some hours. The physician, aware only of his thumping heart, could not perceive by what means he remained upright. Suddenly, tho', a *chavush* of fifty years or so passed through the Gate of Salutation, rushed by them and whispered to one of the guards that he had urgent news for the Divan. Within moments, all was a silent commotion. Mehmet and Thézan-Venasque pressed closer to the pavilion in order to ascertain what had taken place. The doctor found himself entirely helpless, not understanding a word of Turkish. Eventually Chaggi was able to get close enough to hear something before the high officials retreated into the chamber itself.

"This emissary, Abdallah, has come directly from Turgut. That is all I could make out."

As little as it was, Thézan-Venasque instantly understood that their continued presence at the palace had been rendered useless. "Our petition will not be heard *today*," he said. "Let us be off."

"But why, doctor?" Mehmet replied, grasping Thézan-Venasque by the arm. "Let us be patient. They may yet hear us."

The doctor looked at Mehmet aghast. Wrenching himself free, he fairly bolted from the courtyard, leaving the merchant behind. He passed through the Gate of Salutation, and crashed into Niccolò, who stood on the other side, vainly attempting to convince the guard to let him by.

"Come," said the doctor, grabbing Niccolò by the arm. "*L'affaire fut dans l'eau*. We must get out of this city as quickly as possible." He told Niccolò what had just taken place.

"We are lucky—that *chavush*'s news has surely saved your head." He went on to give the doctor all his own intelligence. "But we cannot leave just yet. We must learn more exactly what word the *chavush* brought and what the Turkish answer will be."

The physician peered closely at the Comte. "Vincenzo was right. You *are* mad."

"Perhaps. But a *fusta* bound for Crete is waiting at the docks. As soon as we get to the other side, have your belongings brought aboard. Without delay."

One had neither to be a spy nor know exactly what the *chavush* had told the Divan to perceive what the Turkish answer would be. Within hours, foreman Lorenzo had orders to take some pieces to the Arsenal. We loaded the cannon on a barge and towed it the short distance around Galata to the sheds. Workers were already pouring into the Arsenal to finish up new galleys and launch them. Under the gaze of janissaries and *bostancis*, all carrying arquebuses or cracking bastinados, I found myself caught up in this activity, hauling new pieces and old onto the galleys. I could not leave the yard without peril of being beaten or shot. Worse, the galley slaves were already being herded out of the nearby bagno and being chained to the benches. If I attempted to flee, I could easily find myself among them. By mid-afternoon we could watch the fleet assembling on the far shore, below the Sultan's palace. Evening came and I somehow knew that if I did not get away soon, I would be stranded in the heathen capital for the rest of my life. My chance came when *Kapudan* Piyale Pasha himself appeared at the yard to inspect the progress of the work. Such was the commotion and the numbers of soldiers accompanying his entrance that I managed to walk out the back of one of the sheds unnoticed. Hurrying to Galata, I counted more than forty ships at the ready. Others appeared every hour.

The moment the Comte and the physician parted company on the Galata side of the Horn, the Comte ran to the house, had his own belongings stowed on the *fusta*, then without hesitation made his way to the Bailo's palace, asking to be received. The Bailo was gone. The Comte paced for some hours, gave up and left. As he hurried down the street, Barbarigo himself appeared, beside himself with agitation.

"The most extraordinary news, Comte," he said, unable to contain himself. "Four of Dragut's galleys arrived this morning. The Spaniards have seized Los Gelves—"

"*Los Gelves!*" exclaimed the Comte. "In the name of God, what are they doing on Los Gelves?"

"I have no idea," replied the Bailo, raising his hands. "For certain Dragut is in desperate straits at Tripoli, with only fifteen hundred men under his command. All the corsairs wintering with him fled as soon as they heard the Spanish fleet was approaching."

"Extraordinary news indeed, Sir," said Niccolò. "But if you will excuse me, I have some urgent business of my own to attend to. *Mille grazie.*" He bowed, leaving the Bailo in his agitation and puzzlement.

I found Niccolò and Thézan-Venasque at the dockside, waiting for me next to a fifteen-bank *fusta*. "Are you satisfied?" I asked him. The Captain had already got permission of the harbormaster for departure of this small vessel carrying a trade delegation to discuss coffee with the authorities on Crete. "Let us be off before we find ourselves rowing a galley ourselves."

"There is one thing yet to be done," Niccolò answered. "We have already stowed your bags. If I have not returned in two hours, sail without me." With that he jumped into a nearby caique, almost capsizing it, and pointed to the opposite shore.

What followed was easily one of the longest two hours I have ever spent, sitting on that boat, expecting at each moment Mehmet with a corps of janissaries and a Vizier to appear at the dockside and seize us. I did not breathe.

At Constantinople, Niccolò made his way to the Church of Theodosia and asked to see Barelli. The priest sent off the same boy and once again Niccolò heard the perfect Italian behind him.

"The eastern Savior is more severe than the western, is it not so?"

"And sadder."

"I am surprised to see you here, Comte—and not altogether pleased."

"I have not a moment," replied Niccolò, glancing at the pale frescoes around him. "We are vanishing with the westerly wind as I speak. Everything now rests in your hands. Do better, my friend, do better. Take years." Once more they embraced.

Niccolò had one foot out the door when Barelli's voice accosted him. "One thing, Comte. Take Rhodiot with you—or kill him."

Stepping off the caique at Galata, Niccolò dashed into the same tavern where we had first discovered Rhodiot and without a word yanked that one to his feet, pulling him from the embrace of the girls he was entwined in, spilling his cup. When the cause of all our misfortune protested, Niccolò made the tip of his dagger felt in the small of his back and marched him out. "Yes, I know, no weapons in Galata."

As the last sands fell, Niccolò shoved his unwilling passenger aboard the *fusta*.

"*Ribalza!*" shouted the Captain and, as the oars dipped into the water and the sails filled with wind, the boat slid into the Bosporus.

"How did you know we could make it?" I asked at that moment.

The Comte smiled. "Look at this confusion," he said, passing his arm over the great picture of gathering ships about us. "I also suspect that the heads of Mehmet and a certain Vizier are by now adorning the palace courtyard, and no one knew where we were to be found."

Still, we did not breathe until we were well out of the straits. Only then did I say, "Balthazar, I trust you do not intend to make a habit of this occupation."

"Francisco, my friend, you have my word on it."

Dr. Vigo nodded, averring that from this day on, maugre the custom of our age, he would devote himself solely to medicine. "I also think I shall never develop a taste for ... coffee."

Fifty

"Give a hand."

Pietru brushed away the fly crawling about his ear, took the bisket he had been eating out of his mouth and glanced up from the rock he had perched himself on. Nearby, some men of one of the *asentistas* were loading armfuls of hides and sheep's wool and as many jugs of oil as they could carry onto a boat.

"*Mur inharaq*," Pietru replied and went back to his meal. These *asentistas*, who King Philip had contracted for the undertaking, had caused only trouble and Ix-Xabaw wanted to have nothing to do with them. But the fellow walked across the dirt, yanking Pietru to his feet.

"Lend a hand, I say."

Pietru quickly sized up the Spaniard and kicked him in the balls, then as he was reeling, punched him in the mouth. At once three of the others were on him, but four Knights sped over and put an end to the brawl. "*Mur ahxi 'l-ommhok*," Pietru growled, picking up a stone from the piles all around and returning to work.

He climbed to the ramparts with the brown stone on his shoulder, went down to fetch another. At this moment Ix-Xabaw thought he had spent his entire life hauling rocks—on farms, on forts. The only difference between Malta and this place was that here the stone was darker. He was bending to grab a stone when a Knight told him to help drag up a cannon. Pietru stopped, wiped his hands on his soaked shirt and glanced about. It was May—bright, hot. Thousands of soldiers toiled everywhere to the soft crash of the surf and the rustle of palms. Camels and horses wandered aimlessly about; they had all but ceased to bring stone as the hammers and chisels slowly fell silent. E'en while the men got this thirty-six *libbre* in place, atop one of the bastions, someone was hoisting a Spanish flag, someone else a Genoese, a third the red and white banner of the Knights.

The fort was complete. Pietru crossed himself and kissed his crucifix. By the Blessed Mother he had witnessed a miracle. He'd have wagered a pig it would never happen in his life. It wasn't just the shortage of wood, stone and lime on this accursed island. They'd been raising the huge castle nearly two months. The Knights built one wall and bastion, the Sicilians another, Gian Andrea's men a third and Gonzaga's men the forth. Work often came almost to a complete stop because ... well, because the island people gave little but camels and because the *asentistas* spent most of their days buying up oil, horses, camels, wool and barracans, and loading their boats. The Knights' wall went up fastest—as for the rest ... *X'jitnejku?*

The past three months were a turbulent fog for Pietru. From the start everything about this undertaking went wrong. The chiefs had been planning it for nearly a year, almost since the day the big treaty was signed between France and Spain. At last the Christian forces would prevail against Dragut! The Grand Master and the new Vice Roy of Sicily, Don Juan de la Cerda, Duke of Medina Coeli, had railed the loudest, but then word came that Dragut intended to confront them. The Duke began to shake like a lamb, saying they should attack Gelves instead, which had hardly any defenses.

de Valette would have none of it: "The King has ordered us to wrest Tripoli from Dragut, for the Glory of God and Christendom!" he thundered in reply. de Valette only wanted to take Tripoli because King Philip would give it back to the Knights, most swore. Nay, the Grand Master told the truth: Philip had ordered them to seize Tripoli.

But delay after delay beset the Christians. Troops needed to be levied from Spain, Italy, Germany, the fleet assembled. By the time the ships had gathered in Sicily, it was late in the season and weeks of storms prevented the fleet from leaving. Finally in December the weather broke. Every matelot knew it was madness to depart, but the Duke ordered the fleet to set sail. Forty-nine warships and thirty vessels of burden left Zaragoza—twelve thousand men, they said, but the weather knew better than the Duke and forced the fleet to put in at Malta. For two full months storms ravaged the island. The Great Port stayed thick with ships and Birgu's whores had better business than they'd ever known.

All this time the leaders feared that word of the preparations would reach the Grand Turk in Constantinople and they resolved to set sail as soon as the sea allowed. The Religion put in five galleys, a galiot, two galleons and some smaller boats. Four hundred Knights volunteered, fifteen hundred soldiers and more common laborers, all under the great commander, Captain General Fra Carlo Urre de Tessieres. Ix-Xabaw signed on at once, hoping to rid himself of the nightmares that had not let him sleep in nine years.

More signs came from Heaven. A fever swept Malta, killing two thousand men before a boat had left. Pietru was already convinced that God had cursed the expedition. Natheless, on the tenth of February the fleet at last set sail towards Tripoli. On the Birgu docks, Pietru stood among fourteen thousand men who crowded aboard more than one hundred vessels. It was the largest armada Spain had assembled in forty years, since the Emperor Carlos's doomed invasion of Algiers, *anno* 1519.

The ill omens continued without cease. A few days out, the fleet touched down at Los Gelves, Djerbé, for watering, then continued on to Tripoli. But Dragut himself was prowling about. At the same instant he espied the fleet moving past him, the Christians likewise descried his red and white banners sliced by the blue crescent. Quickly, Dragut's two galleys made for that same channel of La Cantara where he had been so desperately trapped during the year of the *razzia*.

"After him!" cried Gian Andrea Doria, seeing that Destiny had put the corsair into his hands, as it had put him into the hands of his great-uncle nine years ago. He signaled that a squadron of five boats should at once after Dragut.

In the confusion at Djerbé, Pietru had been loading water onto the *asentistas's* galleys and found himself aboard one of the five. The Captain lofted the red pennon and the chase was on. League after league, the *comito* cursed the oarsmen, he and the *sotto-comiti* lashing their backs. Glass by glass they gained on Dragut and it looked as if they would have the corsair trapped again—in the exact place he had made his fabulous escape, the stuff of tales across the Mediterranean. Pietru loaded his gun and waited. Now some round ships appeared on the other horizon. Their flags showed they were out of Alexandria and the squadron's Commodore signaled his Captains to wheel about.

Puzzled, the Gozitan steadied himself on the *ballestriere* as the galley shuddered and groaned. "Where are we going?" he asked the fellow at his side.

"Can't you see, fool, those are merchantmen crossing our paths! Booty for the taking!"

So they went after the round ships. Within a few hours the men were boarding and they spent most of the day engaged in plunder. Seizing his chance, Dragut stole out of La Cantara and made for Tripoli, while his lieutenant Uluj Ali, commanding the second galley, sped straight away to Constantinople. Pietru never had much of a say in anything, but after that he resolved not to stray from the Maltese companies.

"*Allahares qatt nispicca wahdi*," he muttered.

His vow did little to prevent the omens from becoming darker. After Dragut had fled, the fleet touched down several times on Los Gelves for fresh water and in each place were met by some small resistance from the people there. Two hundred men were lost and Alvaro de Sande, one of the leaders, was wounded. At length the fleet departed Djerbé and landed on the North African coast. When Pietru learned that they had put down at some flats near Zuara, he shivered at the memories of that disaster. Try as he might, he could not understand what they were doing on these sand banks.

At once they dug wells among the palm groves and soon hit a stream. Pietru lifted some of the water in a pot and sniffed it. "No," he said, shaking his head.

But other men averred the water was fresh and clear, and drank greedily.

That night, his squadron was cooking some game around the fire. "Why did we land here and not attack Tripoli?" Pietru asked the Knight, Vallés, who commanded them.

Vallés laughed. "Now that we failed to capture Dragut at Djerbé, he is back at Tripoli and Gian Andrea and the other Commanders are no doubt arguing about whether to go after him. We'll sit here until they decide."

Before they finished eating, men began falling ill, and within a few days, dying, as they shitted out their innards. Even as Pietru helped bury Vallés, the weather turned, becoming bad again. Not bad—furious. The sky opened with thunder and lightning, and the wind churned itself into a tempest, ripping the palm leaves from the trees. Standing on the beach with his fellows, Pietru watched helplessly as the *capitana* of the Sicilian fleet smashed against one of the Order's galleons, shattering both to pieces and sinking them. The Gozitan crossed himself. In the lingua franca, he knew, *fortuna* was the word for storm. He did not reflect on this.

Aloud he said only, "God has put the Evil Eye on us."

Still the men sat sweating and swatting flies on the beach, waiting for a decision. Word came down that, truly, the chiefs were bickering about whether to move against Dragut in Tripoli or go back to Los Gelves. At length, scouts reported that the numbers in Dragut's stronghold weren't great, and that many of the other corsairs, upon seeing the Christian fleet, had fled. Natheless, the war council decided to retire to Los Gelves.

This time they took Djerbé without much difficulty. The people there were poisoning the wells with aloe, and one day two thousand peasants attacked the Christians with shouts and swords, but they had no horses or guns. A single volley from the Maltese arquebusiers killed a large number of them and sent the rest running. After, Duke la Cerda made a treaty with the local sheik and prevented the troops from molesting his people.

Pietru watched la Cerda in some sort of rapture strut before his troops, boasting to one and all, "I am the first general to enlarge Philip's dominions since he ascended to the throne of Spain. To commemorate this great victory and to demonstrate the possession of Los Gelves by the Spanish Crown, we will build a fortress here."

Work began at the beginning of March on the north shore of the island, at the site of an old castle a cannon shot from a tiny town of a few white dwellings and a market. With peace made with the local people, the *asentistas* spent all their time trading and buying and loading their ships until their bellies were crammed. Pietru cursed those hired sailors under his breath even as he asked himself why he was building this fortress. Did they plan to stay? Nobody would tell them anything.

Flies, insects were everywhere, over everything. Pietru, suspicious of the food on this island, ate little but the bread that had been brought on the galleys and birds he trapped. Many of the men, catching sight of the long-tailed mutton all around, could not resist. Before long, so many were falling ill that Captain General Tessieres decided he must inform the Grand Master.

When word reached de Valette in Birgu, he ordered a fast *fregata* back to Djerbé with notice to the Vice Roy and the Captain General. Pietru heard it, as always, when rumors swept the building place. Even after so many lips, Pietru discerned the wrath in the Grand Master's voice: Djerbé cannot be held. Abandon work on the fortress. If the Vice Roy foolishly persists, the Captain General must return to Malta at once.

de Valette's message came too late. By now an extraordinary number of men were desperately ill. One night whispers swept through the camp that Gian Andrea aboard his galley was himself on the verge of death.

"He's already died," one Roya declared; most agreed.

But the Vice Roy wouldn't leave off the great monument to his valor. Seeing nothing was to be done, Tessieres loaded the Religion's galleys with the sick, most of the Knights and sailed back to Malta. The Captain General, Pietru later heard, himself died a few days after his return.

"Now what are we going to do?" Roya grumbled at the camp.

"Looks like we're going to keep building this damned fort."

"What for?"

"Because we're paid to."

Pietru had been singing a song to himself, or growling it:

"*Min jitma fit-tama,*
It-tama tqarraq bih,
Jaghmel ir-rieh fil-bomblu,
Jahseb li jsiefer bih."

"What's that about?" Roya asked.

The Gozitan shrugged. "It says if you hope too much you are like a sailor trying to bottle wind. The chiefs have hoped too much. Eh, they are trying to bottle wind. It is stupid. The omens have spoken."

They kept working. de Valette sent three galleys with fresh troops under old Fra Bernardo de Guimeran. They arrived at the end of April. Two days later the Spanish troops from Naples departed when they heard rumors of a Turkish fleet near Sicily. After another week, the thousands remaining on the island had been burned almost to the color of the rock, but they managed to finish the fort. It was big, bigger than Fort St. Elmo.

"Now what do we do?" Pietru asked with Roya, arms on their hips as they surveyed the barely finished castle with its four round bastions and square buttresses betwixt them.

Another great argument, they heard, was going on amongst the leaders as to whether the garrison would be supplied by sea or not. Fed up, some of the *asentistas* began to leave; most of the troops milled about, everyone wondering the same thing: "What do we do now?"

Days later, their question was answered. The watch atop the bastions spied the *fregata* from Malta well out, hoving in furiously. As it reached the beach, the *ciurma* raised its oars and the boat ran itself onto the sand. Without a moment's delay, the crew jumped ashore, running toward the castle gates. Soldiers quickly gathered 'round, making way for Colonel Alvaro de Sande, who came out to greet them. Pietru managed to get close enough to hear.

"Sir," a Knight from the *fregata* said, "the entire Turkish fleet was sighted off Gozo four days ago. Eighty-six sail. They are headed this way."

Pietru pushed his way fully through to the men standing before the castle gates.

"Pietru," I said.

Fifty-One

We had raced to Crete ahead of the Turkish fleet, driving the *ciurma* to exhaustion and beyond. As the rowing gang raised the oars and the *fusta* slid to the dockside at Candia, Balthazar said, "I pray Romegas is about. He should be expecting us," and the Knight jumped over the side.

I threw my bag onto the embankment after him. "I must warn you, Balthazar: If Blaij Vergã is here, I will kill him." Seven years had passed since that day on the docks, but I remembered it as yesterday. He was a mortal enemy, nothing more, nothing less.

"Stop talking like a Spaniard and set it aside," replied the Knight as we walked in the shadow of the fortifications. "Vergã has proven himself again and again these past seasons and is Romegas' trusted man."

"He is a base rogue who stole my future and when that was not enough, attempted to steal my life," I said as we entered the town. "If I do not kill him, he will certainly kill me."

Balthazar did not hesitate. "Let him try."

Luck was with us. Balthazar again disappeared for the day, but the next morning, an urchin he'd paid to let us know the moment any ship flying the Knights' colors arrived, ran to our inn and told us the Romegas himself had put into port. At once we were on our feet and sped down to the dockside to meet him. Crowds had already gathered, so great was his fame, and we pushed aside the people there to get near him. The galiot was the Religion's own, its brilliant vermillion wales, the red and white lateen sails, the eight-pointed cross, all glistening. There, shouting orders from the poop with a monkey perched on his shoulder, stood the Chevalier Romegas. I had not set eyes on him for at least seven years. No longer the youth I had first met on Djerbé, above me stood a man in the bloom of life, his swarthy face broader and his beard no less ragged than of yore, his voice as loud and manner no less imperious. He showed no recognition of me as he greeted Balthazar and Rhodiot, joking we were only a few weeks late.

"And we must be off to Malta without delay," Balthazar said at once.

"Yes," interrupted Rhodiot. "We have learned that the Turkish fleet is sailing to relieve Dragut."

Balthazar shot a glance at the former spy, but nodded. "I fear the *Kapudan-i Derya* Cara Mustafa and *Kapudan* Piyale Pasha himself are hot on our heels. Above forty sail, mayhap sixty."

"So soon? Are you certain?" Romegas asked with full disbelief. It was then that I first noticed the pronounced tremor in his arms. As if the import of Balthazar's news had been too grave for e'en this fabled Knight, his hands began to shake with such severity that his monkey took to caterwauling, and only with some difficulty did he steady both himself and the animal.

Romegas begged forgiveness with a terse, forlorn nod—strange for him—and Balthazar continued. "They were assembling the fleet faster than the Devil himself. We could hardly credit our eyes. They cannot fly with their heavy galleys as we have, but, *uertu de Dieu*, I say we have not a moment to lose."

"Come then," answered Romegas, "we'll be off tonight." At once the Commander ordered his crew to provision the galiot and be ready to sail that same evening.

Neither did Blaij Vergã, who had stood behind Romegas during the entire conversation, at first recognize me. I recognized him. He was e'en more powerfully built than memory sanctioned, his shoulders having broadened, his muscles granite. A scar not present seven years ago ran down his cheek and on his tunic he wore the half-cross of a confrater, its upper shaft lacking. Balthazar hadn't told me he'd become a confrater, and my disbelief and resentment were limitless. After Romegas had given the order to provision the boat, those of us from Constantinople turned to disembark, but Vergã stepped up to me. And laughed.

"I thought you were dead," he said. Blaij could hardly contain his amusement.

"I am harder to kill than a stupid ox can suspect," drawing my sword.

At once Balthazar interposed himself between us. "*Calla*. Our mission is too urgent for duels. Vergã, were I Francisco, I should kill you myself. But as a Knight of Justice, I am ordering you to put this quarrel aside, or

I will see that half-cross stripped from your chest. Francisco, as your friend, I tell you there comes a time in any fight when the vanquished must extend his hand."

Balthazar said not a word more; with perceptible reluctance, Blaij Vergã and I took each other's hands and, once again, became friends. At that moment I truthfully felt a great weight lift from my soul.

We set sail. The galiot flew westward with the wind, as if Lucifer and all his black angels were breathing on our tail, as we knew they were. During meals in Romegas's cabin, I learned of Blaij's exploits, which were considerable. At Romegas's side, he had taken ship after enemy ship and had displayed such bravery that many proposed the bastard should become a Knight, should it require a dispensation from the Pope himself. Vergã boasted that in some ports there was a price on his head, tho' not as great as the reward the Turks offered everywhere for Romegas himself. When we'd met up with them, Romegas was after a Calabrian renegado, Cocia-Cocia, who was so evil men called him the Executioner.

"He got away from me this time, but someday, I'll eat his balls for breakfast," Romegas swore. Vergã added that they'd come within a sow's teat of getting him, but to their annoyance had to make for Candia.

I listened to the braggart with more amusement than envy. After all, a lifetime had passed. Balthazar, tho', as if peering into my soul, recounted: "Not long ago, one Knight of Malta, de Guzman—an acquaintance of mine by the way— quarreled with another Spaniard. Fearing the Inquisition would spoil the settlement of their dispute, they arranged to meet on Avlona, a territory of the Grand Signor. To be sure, they had the Turkish Sanjak-bey judge them, a Spanish renegado who lords over the place. Hah! Is it not too much of a muchness, *ce n'est pas ius uerd mais uerd ius*, two Christians fearing death by the Inquisition, attempting to kill each other on Turkish soil with an infidel as arbiter?"

We raced on.

We put into the Great Port of Malta in early May, by now *anno* 1560, and the sight of that harbor brought back every awe and bitterness. Starboard, the new cavalier towered above St. Elmo, and to port three corpses swung from the gallows. Castle St. Angelo had not perceptibly changed, but when we rounded the apron into Galley Creek, I was filled with the sense that I had arrived at a place at once familiar and unknown.

The creek bustled with more ships than in former days. Across it, the wall we'd heard talk of in Venice ringed every side of l'Isola but the one facing us and, as the exhausted *ciurma* raised its oars, the distant silhouettes of slaves and soldiers raised themselves at the landward end of Birgu.

I could scarce recognize the town. More houses crowded the Borgo, inns, forges, more women. At the same time it displayed an air sensibly more somber than formerly. I can hardly say why. Aye, none of the Knights wore mismatched hose, and many within eyeshot scurried about in nothing more than their black habits. Balthazar and Vigo themselves had donned their own proper vestments before we stepped ashore.

"Should we not go directly to the castle?" I asked, as our small company passed through the gates and the physician bid us farewell.

"Nay. de Valette has moved from the Grand Master's Palace to a new mansion he has built in Birgu. He says he finds the wind up there disagreeable."

As we walked in the direction of the Monsignore's house, an elderly monk approached us, not far above the auberges. At first I paid scant attention to him whose mantle and wide-brimmed hat in no way distinguished themselves from any other Knight's, for my eyes were fixed to the side, where by him walked a full-grown lioness. Only when Balthazar and Romegas bent to kiss his ring, did I realize that after these many seasons I faced Jean de Valette. I kissed his ring in turn, feeling that tho' he must now have above sixty years, and tho' his beard was grey and his hair receding, Parisot could yet pass for an altogether younger man. For a moment de Valette looked on me without expression, then his countenance subtly changed and I knew he well recollected me.

"Eminenza, we have news," Rhodiot put in immediately. "The Turkish fleet approaches."

de Valette frowned. "I would not have expected them for another month," he said, absently stroking his animal's head.

"I should expect them far sooner than that," answered Balthazar.

"Are you certain?" Inscribed on the Grand Master's face was the same disbelief that had been written on Romegas's own when he heard the news. "How is it possible? More than three hundred leagues and with heavy galleys."

"We cannot be certain, Eminenza," said Balthazar. "But the Turks assembled that fleet with the speed of Hermes and the wind has since been at our backs. I would wager my soul that we have no more than a week ... two."

de Valette scarce hesitated before giving his answer: "Fra Balthazar, you must warn the forces on Gelves. In your absence, the entire enterprise has miscarried because Gian Andrea, a shadow of his great-uncle, possessed not the heart to attack our sworn enemy Dragut, and because the Vice Roy of Sicily, losing sight of our right and proper goal, has squandered two months building a fort to no purpose on an untenable island. Depart tomorrow morning; convince them in our name to abandon Gelves. Romegas, sail eastward again to reconnoitre the enemy. Thank you, Messeri, for your efforts. Come to me with a detailed report this evening, Balthazar. Rhodiot, you shall be rewarded. I go now to serve dinner to the poor."

He extended his ring, and when I kissed it I thought I discerned the hint of a smile. Then he gathered up the leash of his lioness and moved along the street.

I accompanied Balthazar the few steps to the Auberge de France. He lay his hand on my shoulder. "You are not obliged to sail with me tomorrow to Djerbé. God willing, we shall see an orderly retreat from that island. I do not yet perceive the full import of the Monsignore's words, but I fear this mighty coalition so painstakingly assembled has torn itself apart. If so, the danger will be great, mayhap greater than we have ever faced."

"Does not Niccolò have thoughts on such a circumstance?"

Balthazar sighed. "Alas, I do not recollect any. Perhaps e'en his vision does not extend into this new arena we are entering."

"Balthazar," I said, seeing my friend's disquiet, "I once swore to kill Turgut. I have never forgotten that vow. For reasons I do not discern, the Almighty has seen fit to twine your path and mine again. I can tell you only one thing: After years of testing guns, my aim is better." I took the Knight's arm. "We have been through much together, Balthazar. I cannot imagine we shall fail to survive this."

We embraced. "Sleep on't," he said, stepping into the auberge, "and if you are willing, be at the dockside at dawn."

There were more bells now. As they rang the Ave Maria, I walked into the Church of San Lorenzo to offer prayer and to ask for guidance. Despite my assurances to Fra Balthazar, I had e'en less a stake in these affairs than when I first set foot on Malta nine years ago. I asked for a sign. That evening, as I gazed on the angels above the church altar, no visions came, but I left the church knowing full well that on the morn I would accompany Balthazar to Africa.

I wandered the streets asking if anyone knew a *quiraca* called Flaminia. *Quiracas* there remained aplenty in Birgu—a coin in the hand would bring them like flies—and for sure de Valette had been unable to exert his authority over them. Before long I was directed up the hill to a fair-sized house on the landward end of town, surprisingly near the Guasconi household, which I avoided. I put my fist to the door. A young girl of five or six years let me in. I stopped at the sitting room to see Flaminia herself in a *teste-a-teste* with a customer.

She glanced up at me and after an expression of utter disbelief flashed across her face she jumped to her feet, exclaiming, "O Madonna!" Then she slapped me.

I bowed. "You have done well for yourself, Mistress Flaminia," I said, glancing around the well-appointed rooms. "You now have a house."

"Little thanks to you," she said archly, but not unkindly. The whore was only in her middle twenties now, no less voluptuous and more sensuous than before.

"I came only to beg forgiveness for vanishing abruptly those years ago. Circumstances did not permit me to say *à Dios* ... Is this your daughter?" I tussled the hair of the little one.

"Yes, this is Francesca. Say hello to Francisco."

The girl curtsied and ran into another room.

"I am glad to discover you survived that Inquisition and have prospered. It is well you no longer need my money, for at this moment I have not a *taro* more than when I first set foot on Malta. If a Knight is keeping you, tho', I'd advise not to let him know of your other activities. It might be dangerous."

"He is on Djerbé," she replied with a knowing smile. "Will you stay, *mio cuore,* after I bed this other fellow?"

"No, I too will be off to Djerbé in the morning and must rise before the sun."

Flaminia kissed me on the cheek and I departed. On the street I walked up to the Guasconi house and stood before it for a long time, but in the end I saw little virtue in presenting myself there and went to find a room.

I did not sleep a wink for the anticipation that consumed me. By the time Balthazar appeared in his battle dress, whistling, I was already pacing the docks.

"Don't," I said. "It's the sign of the Devil."

"You're right," he answered and ceased. An hour passed while we waited for Hugh de Copones, the other Knight Parisot had dispatched, who had instructions for a ten-bank *fregata*. We wasted another hour pounding on every door on the embankment, trying to rouse a captain who would find us some oarsmen. At last we were ready. A big wave would put an end to us in this tiny craft, but it would be swift. Just as we were making to embark, a *luzzu* pulled up to the docks and some fishermen jumped ashore in the greatest agitation.

"The Turks!" they cried as if they'd lost their heads. "Off Gozo!"

Balthazar and de Copones lost no further moments. "To Gozo!" they both shouted to the oarsmen. The Knight turned to me. "It must be some scouts. The fleet cannot have arrived so quickly."

Balthazar was wrong. As we neared the Gozo channel, we saw the enemy ships come into view, then loom before us. We counted, again.

"*Mort de Dieu*," Balthazar breathed, crossing himself. "Eighty-six sail. Piyale Pasha has crossed the Mediterranean faster than anyone before him."

"Will they attack Malta?"

"No. They will attack the armada."

In that instant it seemed the enemy ships grew larger. Without waiting a heartbeat de Copones cried, "*Eia!*" The oars dipped and the *ciurma* hauled for dear life south, to the Isle of the Lotus Eaters.

Fifty-Two

"The entire Turkish fleet was sighted off Gozo four days ago," said de Copones to Alvaro de Sande before the castle gates on Los Gelves. "Eighty-six sail are headed straight towards us. You must abandon this place at once."

E'en as the Knight pronounced those words, Pietru, me, Balthazar, de Sande could sense the panic sweeping the men gathered around. Within moments, the *asentistas* were running for their boats. While men scattered this way and that, no less than roosters lacking heads, Balthazar put it to the stout, bald-headed Colonel: "Where is Doria?"

de Sande tilted his beard toward the water. "Sick, on his galley. How much time do you think we have, brothers?"

"Not enough," replied Balthazar. "All of us overjudged the time it would take Piyale to sail from Constantinople, even I when I gave him every benefit of wind and skill. The danger is as immediate as it is grave."

At that instant a captain of the German mercenaries rushed up to them in his half-suit and gartered hose. "Señor," he said to de Sande with a heavy accent, "our contract does of us not reqvire garrison duty. Ve must be embarked first."

"*¡Cierre ese hocico!*" shouted the heavy Colonel, at once furious. "You will await orders or I'll be certain you're hanged, treacherous dog!"

Balthazar and I glanced at each other. Memories of Tripoli were flooding back, to him more than to me, but the stakes were no longer a small garrison of six hundred men. The stakes—I abruptly paused, better comprehending today how crucial that small episode nine years ago had been for the whole Mediterranean. Aye, the stakes from the loss of that tiny outpost had now risen to fourteen thousand men and the entire Spanish armada.

"You shall await orders," de Sande repeated to the *landsknecht*, thrusting his finger into that one's face, then turned to us who had just arrived.

"Come, you monks, we must inform Doria at once." He ordered some men into the very *fregata* we'd just run aground. As we pushed the boat into the surf, I watched men fighting for a place in the caiques in order to be first on the galleys.

We found Gian Andrea in his cabin aboard his *capitana*, voiding his bowels into the pot. At first sight I could hardly credit that this pale, snot-nosed boy in a nightshirt commanded the largest fleet Christendom had assembled in half a century. When begging forgiveness for his sickness he stretched himself out on his bunk, looking for all the world as if his hours on earth were fast expiring, I thought he must rather be a down-on-his-luck Knight in a Maltese tavern. When Balthazar gave him the news that the Turks would soon be upon us, his eyes widened and he ran quaking back to the pot. Watching him, my nostrils filled with the stench from his ass, I still could not credit that any sane man had made this whelp Admiral. I understood that God had placed Christendom in the gravest peril.

For a second time Gian Andrea made excuses for his bowels, but his shivering frame and the wild glances he cast in all directions belied the simplicity of those pleadings. "What do you expect me to do?" he said as panic besieged him. "Fight?"

"That is one road, Admiral," answered de Sande severely.

The Captain General now turned to Balthazar and de Copones. "If your report, Messeri, is correct," he said, grasping the post by his bunk in an attempt to steady himself and his nerves, "we are greatly outnumbered."

"The odds are not so unfavorable," de Sande made the reply, "as when your great-uncle faced Dragut off Genoa eight years ago. We have fifty-four heavy galleys and the island at our backsides for protection. The Turks know the prowess of well-manned Spanish galleys."

"They are not well-manned!" Gian Andrea spat, losing the attempt to contain himself. "How many have we lost to this sickness?"

"Spaniards can always make a fight."

The sick one shook his head, violently, curled around that post, and looked up again at the Knights. "What number of the Turkish fleet are warships?"

Balthazar and de Copones glanced at each other. Then from Balthazar: "Almost all of them, Signore, so far as we could tell."

"You see, it is out of the question."

There was no convincing the terrified boy as now he sat disheveled on his bed, now half-stood, half-leaned on the post. de Sande grasped one of the cabin posts as well, evidently impeded by his own weight. "What do the other Commanders say, Admiral?"

"How would I know?" Doria half screamed, laughed, waving his hand wildly. "Do you see any about?"

"Then allow me," said de Sande, bowing as he was able, "to gather a council of war, Señor."

With a curt nod, Gian Andrea waved us all out of his cabin.

"*Si, O reniego la Ley de quel Puto Mahomet,*" erupted de Sande when we had climbed to deck, "we are in a terrible fix. Let us find the Don Juan de la Cerda, Don Sanche de Levye of the Neapolitans and the other Commanders without delay. I fear the best we can hope for is an orderly retreat."

By now it was well past dark. de Sande glanced at the near full moon shining on the placid sea with silhouettes of galleys everywhere and lost no time in ordering Doria's Captain to send skiffs out for the commanders of the Sicilian, Neapolitan, Papal and Maltese contingents. He himself waved us into the *fregata* to go after the Vice Roy, de la Cerda, who was at the fort.

We found la Cerda and de Guimeran, who had taken command of the Maltese infantry, inside the castle surrounded by Italian and German officers who were insisting that their infantry be let aboard the galleys—immediately.

"All in good time, Gentlemen," la Cerda answered, placidly. "You will not be abandoned, I pledge my solemn word on it."

The German was not to be placated. "*Die Zeit draengt!*" he shouted, planting the tip of his huge sword in the dirt. "*Wir verlangen, augenblicklich an Bord der Galeeren gehen zu düerfen!*"

"Your fears are unwarranted," la Cerda said to the *landsknecht*'s babble. "Admiral Doria will sail to Tripoli to parlay with Dragut for the corsair's surrender. During that time we will have ample opportunity to embark the troops before the Turks arrive."

"You are a madman!" the German screamed so violently that his feathered hat nearly toppled from his crown. "You have to no purpose built zis fort and now you intend zat every man among us here die!" He pushed his way past la Cerda and strode toward the beach.

"Señor," said de Sande to the Vice Roy, interrupting. "Doria requests your presence in his cabin at once for a council of war."

The Vice Roy swiveled to de Sande. "Colonel, I leave it to you to keep these troops in order while we decide what is to be done." He indicated the German Captain. "Put that man in irons if need be." Don Juan de la Cerda immediately walked out of the gates and embarked for Doria's *capitana*, leaving de Sande to deal with the garrison.

The sight around us was not to be believed. Thousands of men in the castle hurriedly gathered their weapons and kits and ran to the shallow cove, which sat hard by the fort, struggling to get on one of the few galleys that crowded that small place. Others waited on the beach, feet awash in water, hoping to find a caique to ferry them to the galleys, but there were too many men, thousands.

In the midst of this, I spied Pietru Galea, sitting immobile near the castle gates as others dashed frantically past him. "Pietru," I said, as I had earlier, turning to him. He stood and we held each other at arm's length, regarding each other with an inexpressible joy infused with an incomprehension about all that was taking place. My stocky friend now had above thirty years to him. The round head, burnt almost black, had grown near bald and boasted more scars than I could count; he had lost more teeth and the rest were rotten, but the muscles of his arms by now had been tempered in Vulcan's forge. We did not say anything for a long time, unable to speak of former times in the midst of this ...

"How many men are here?" I finally asked, finding no other words.

He shrugged in that old way of his. "I think more than five thousand on land, the same on the boats, the others trying to get to the boats."

"Did you ever find your wife?" I said.

"No," he said. "Someday ... "

We went to the beach, where de Sande and his officers were attempting to put order into the troops, holding them back with halberds and threats, shouting that they must await the Admiral's command before embarking. We joined him as he ran back and forth at the edge of the surf, attempting to organize the men into a semblance of their companies: Spaniards here, Sicilians there, Neapolitans, Maltese...the Germans, who still insisted they be let go at once. He might have chosen to restrain a herd of cattle.

It went on like this until the break of dawn, when finally the Vice Roy returned from Doria's galley. "The Admiral orders that everyone be embarked," he told de Sande.

"The armada will not put up a fight?" the Colonel asked.

la Cerda shook his head. "No one advised it. Every one of us voted ... "

" ... to flee?"

"Yes."

The stampede began. Pietru vanished in the crush of men, all of them pushing, stumbling, falling. As de Sande's halberdiers held others back, Balthazar and I managed to climb onto one of the boats ferrying men to the galleys and both of us grabbed oars. de Sande himself remained on the beach, vainly trying to put calm into the evacuation. The sun rose, flooding the scene with its harsh, blinding light, and those sands before the castle appeared to come alive. A sea of insects swarming into the water, swarming onto larger insects in the hopes of being carried to safety. The confusion was such that Balthazar and I had ended up with some Sicilians who insisted we row to one of their galleys, which lay not far out. Gaining it, we climbed aboard. From the *ballestriere*, we watched the sea of boats about us making their way out to the dozens of galleys lying in every direction on the water, returning to the beach thick with men.

Then it happened. In quick succession, sails and pennants began to pop up above the northern horizon. One here, another there, a third, a fourth ... Within the space of moments, near ninety ships faced us. The Turkish fleet had arrived but a day behind us and the Spanish armada was trapped. The panic now became complete. Every captain held only one thought in his mind—to escape. I glanced over to one of the *asentistas's* galleys, nearby. The crew was frantically unloading from the holds everything they had so greedily bought or stolen in the past months, hauling it on deck and hurling it overboard. Bales of wool, jars of oil, anything to lighten the load. Our own crew, stricken with the same dread, followed suit. Of a sudden the waters around us became thick with every manner of debris.

"Not the food!" shouted the Captain of the vessel on which we found ourselves.

Nobody listened. Before my eyes crewmembers hauled a horse and two camels to deck and, as the creatures struggled, dragged each one to the edge of the boat and pushed them overboard. The animals crashed into the water, bellowing and neighing, and thrashed about wildly for their lives.

At first the enemy, closing, appeared to be stowing their sails for engagement. But Piyale Pasha discerned the complete disorder among the Spanish fleet. For a moment I regarded Balthazar, who stood transfixed by the approaching enemy. "*Mon Dieu!*" he exclaimed suddenly, "they're hoisting sail."

"*¿Como?*" I cried. "For battle? That is mad."

Without hesitation, Balthazar ran to the Captain. "The enemy is hoisting sail. They won't be able to hold formation and they're giving us targets. We can bring down those masts and sink them all."

The Captain laughed. "There's only one thing to do now—be fucked or get the Devil out of here." He gave the order to the *comito*.

"*Remate cani!*" the *comito* roared the ancient cry. The lashes fell onto bare, scarred backs and the *ciurma* heaved for their lives.

It was for naught. Piyale's fleet, under sail, bore down on us faster than I would have thought possible. In less than a glass, one of the lead galleys was heading directly to our starboard. Before the Captain could give a single order, the deck under us shuddered under the impact of the Turkish armaments and an instant afterwards we heard the roar of the guns. A moment later the ship lurched again, another boom, and with an immense groan the stern lifted. Balthazar slid on the *ballestriere*, grasping at a cable to keep from going overboard. I tumbled to my knees, struggled to right myself. As I got to my feet, the boat let out another roar and titled further. Now Balthazar lost his grip and went over. In his half-suit I knew he would sink quickly and I half dove, half fell after him.

The water was clear. I saw the Knight struggling at a distance below me, bubbles all around, and I went for him, grasping him under the shoulders and, with every strength I possessed, tugged his weight to the surface.

"Save yourself if you can," he said, gasping for breath. "Or both of us will be lost."

"Quiet, it cannot be half a league to shore."

We hauled for land, my arm ever around him, but neither of us were men of the water and the sixty or seventy *libbre* of armor on him proved too much. "We must get this steel off you."

Desperately, I attempted to loose his pauldrons and cuirass, now letting him drop while I worked the laces, now grasping him. At the same time, Balthazar was doing his own to cut the straps for his tasses. Finally, the breast and back plates fell away, sinking to the bottom with the metal skirt. That was the worst; the brassards proved easier. At last the two of us turned landward again. But our strength was exhausted and that half league would see our doom. All about us men were in the same dreaded predicament, struggling against the weight of their armor, drowning.

Spying a floating spar, I threw one arm over it, the other under Balthazar's shoulder. This piece of wood proved our deliverance. Clutching it for life, we made past those bales of wool and jugs of oil, past horses and camels, dead or lowing their death moans. A dead rider sprawled across a dead horse; a barking dog on a plank, a seagull perched on a sheep. All the while the battle continued to rage. Nay, God would not have called this a battle. Turkish cannon boomed near and far. Smoke wafted over us as distant shouts and screams reached our ears. Heads barely above water, we watched one Christian galley after another blown to splinters and disappear into the sea without putting up the least fight. All around ships burned; men everywhere dove for their lives. Half lying across our raft, we saw Piyale take the Pope's *capitana*, sink the Sicilian, capture the *capitane* of Monaco and Terranova. Here and there a Christian galley resisted only to be sunk or taken by the foe, and a few galleys with vermillion wales appeared to be making good an escape. We could not discern, gasping for breath and spitting water, much of what was taking place in the sea off Djerbé, but by the time Balthazar and I struggled to the shore and collapsed on the hot sand, it was evident that the Spanish armada had been destroyed.

Soldiers helped us to our feet. All along the beach men were pulling their fellows, dead and alive, from the surf. Thousands stood here, those who had not been embarked before the Turk appeared, watching the debacle unfold before their eyes. Within an hour or two, it was over. Far more than half the galleys had vanished. No one was quite certain how many got away. Piyale was already towing near twenty to a point along the coast, well beyond the town, from which all the Djerbens had fled. We knew the Christians still alive would e'en now be being chained to their own benches. Everyone watching this horrific spectacle remained speechless as the sky filled with the thunder of the Turkish victory salute.

At length I discovered Pietru, who had not managed to embark, and then de Sande approached, trying to judge the strength of the remaining forces.

"Do you know what has happened to Doria?" Balthazar asked him, stripped to a wet, quilted underjerkin.

"No, not yet," replied de Sande. "His *capitana* is there." He pointed down the coast.

"What about the Vice Roy?"

"Ashore, here in the castle. Help me get the men inside. The Turks will doubtlessly attack soon."

The soldiers did not need to be reminded of their peril and willingly took refuge inside the fort they had completed scant days before. As de Sande was gathering the senior men about, including the Vice Roy, four or five of Doria's officers ran through the gates, helping, carrying the Captain General himself, who was too sick to walk. They said the contrary winds had prevented them from making good an escape, but luckily they were able to gain the shore in one of the galley's boats. Later some men said they saw the *capitana* run aground on a shoal. de Sande's council took place at the Admiral's bedside inside the stone commander's quarters. By now the day was hot, the air moist and thick.

"How many men are here?" the Vice Roy asked from his place on a barrel.

de Sande's aspect was of a man who had not slept all night. "I believe five thousand," he breathed.

"Do you mean to say we have lost nine thousand men in this enterprise?"

"Thus far," the Colonel replied dryly, taking a cup of wine from one of the men. "But the fort is well provisioned."

"How well provisioned?"

"Summer is upon us; look at the sweat on you. We had enough food for the better part of a year—for half this number of men. Wine will run out and water will become the chief concern. We should have built the fort at Rocchetta, where there is a deep harbor and wells. As it stands, we shall have to use the wells in the marketplace of this deserted town."

Now Doria propped himself up on the bed. "Gentlemen, you are straying from the important matter. The Turks will soon attack. How can we hold out?"

"By God, we have no choice, *Sir*," spat de Sande. "The greater number of galleys have been sunk or captured in this ... this ... " He threw up his arms. "Not enough heavy vessels remain by us to confront the foe; for the most part there are only some *fregate* of scarce use to anyone, which matters not because half the soldiers are too ill to man them. Piyale is today occupied with securing his prisoners and making his prizes fast. But, yes, you are correct, tomorrow there will be an attack."

"How many men does he have?" Doria asked.

"Who can say, *Sir*? With a fleet that size, ten or twenty thousand, as you well know. If we are lucky he has not brought sufficient siege guns for this endeavor." The Vice Roy and Doria glanced at each other. de Sande continued. "We have guns and powder. We had best ready them."

Doria nodded abruptly and waved de Sande out of the room.

We spent the remainder of the day positioning guns, counting rations, measuring powder, distributing arms. My prized wheel-lock lay somewhere at the bottom of the sea, as well as my rapier, and I took up a plain arquebus. Only late that night did anyone get to sleep.

At dawn, one of the serving men rushed up to de Sande. "Señor, the Admiral and the Vice Roy are not in their quarters."

The Colonel nodded. "Yes, I know. During the night they and their entourage took nine of the *fregate*. They will send a relief. Do not despair, we have provisions for many months." Not long after, de Sande approached a few of the Knights with somewhat different words and a less brave mien. "Brothers, the Admiral and the Vice Roy fled during the night. I could not prevent it. The scoundrels vow to send a relief ... There is nothing for it but to make the best defense we can."

Soon after hearing this news, Balthazar sought me out atop the garrison. By now the staggering import of what had taken place yesterday had begun to make itself felt and Balthazar showed no cheer. "You see," he said, vainly attempting to find a jest, "you would have done well to heed my warning and stay behind."

"I made the decision," I answered, not entirely convincing myself.

"I thank you for it. You saved my life. Francisco, I cannot make light of this circumstance. I say we have just witnessed the worst disaster to Christendom in half a century. Why? It is more than that beardless Admiral or these undisciplined mercenaries. These men have fought so long, they have forgotten what they are fighting for. They have lost faith; if not faith, purpose." For only a moment did Balthazar then pause. "You see the outcome," he chuckled somberly, regarding the enemy begin their disembarkation. "For ten years now, we the Knights have watched as our great foe has spread his shadow wider and wider, until on this very day he completely surrounds the Mediterranean; no one remains to oppose him. While Soliman lives, the next step is Europe itself. Mark my words."

As we stood on the ramparts of the fort, we continued to watch Piyale's forces take up position beyond the small, empty town. The hot, moist wind swept over that fort, carrying with it a greater loneliness than any man trapped within had ever felt.

Fifty-Three

de Sande's first act was to have the chaplain lead a prayer in the bailey of the fortress. Every man among us knelt, his hands on his sword, and asked the Almighty for deliverance. The Colonel then ordered a thousand arquebusiers into the deserted town to protect the wells and another thousand to the south of the fort to prevent the Turks from emplacing artillery there. Of no less urgency he sent out a third company to cut wood for a palisade to be built around the remaining boats moored at the castle's side. Most of the others who were not sick remained on the walls, I among them.

The danger confronting us was everywhere visible. No fewer than ten thousand men were setting up camp beyond the town and in the palm woods to the south, with more disembarking from the ships every hour. Not since Mdina nine years ago had I witnessed such a host and its import needed no explaining. The enemy showed itself to be in little hurry. Piyale sent out the irregulars, the *azabs*, to fashion gabions from the palm trees to provide protection for trench digging. At the same time, the *Kapudan* began to disembark his cannon, some of which I myself had loaded in Constantinople. All this was done to the accompaniment of musicians who marched around gaily crashing cymbals and playing on horns. It would have been comical had it not been so threatening. As the hours passed, tho', it seemed that Piyale had not foreseen this siege and so had carried few big guns hither, for which I thanked God. I felt a hand on my arm and turned to see Pietru behind me.

The sight of that weatherbeaten face and crooked nose cheered me to no end. "There has not been a moment for me to discover where you have been these past years since we parted in Venice," I said, slapping him on the shoulder. "Tell me. I have missed you, Xabaw."

He shrugged and spoke in Italian. "Eh, I went back to Gozo, to my farm, but there is no one on the island, a few hundred men, no more. I heard only the wind. After a year I went to the Port and built walls for Grand Master de Sengle. I went on some caravans as an oarsman, then with my gun. That is all."

"Then you have taken no new woman?"

He shook his head. "I would farm again. I am tired of fighting, but the Turk—I fuck him—he leaves me no peace."

Nodding, I slapped him on the back once more and, a thought coming into my mind, I scampered down the steps to the powder stores. As I opened the caskets one by one and inspected the powder, Balthazar happened to enter, searching for armor.

"What are you about?" he asked, surprised to find me here.

I rubbed the powder between my fingers as I examined it. "I wanted to see the amount and quality of the stocks, and to think."

"You know of powder now?'

As I recounted to Balthazar Vannoccio's words in the Arsenale, that from this invention there was no hope of escape, not the slightest, we both knew we were soon to test the truth of them. "Yes, I know of powder. This cask will do better for middle cannon than arquebus, but I was hoping to find here the ingredients wherewith to make ... fire. Greek fire."

Balthazar cocked his head in admiration. "You are a master of that art as well? Truly, we should have talked more these past months. You did learn something during your stay in Venice."

I laughed. I learned that people who claimed powder makes no noise when fired in guns are liars. "Fire is an art any fool can master. Many say the ancient Byzantines held some great secret wherewith they set aflame enemy ships, but Vanno always held that the only secret is that modern masters have misunderstood the old ones." I sighed. "I ... I see here no means, no tar or pitch or liquid resin. Perhaps in the boats ... " My words stopped then.

"You cannot be pleased to be trapped in this fort," Balthazar said, regarding my somber countenance.

"What sane man would be pleased?" I exclaimed, turning to him. "You have seen the faces of these soldiers. They are terrified—and for good reason. Certain death awaits us."

"I meant to say you cannot be pleased with me. To be here for no discernible reason but that I am."

I could not deny the contrary emotions coursing through me. "Aye," I said. "I had not intended this, but now that my life begins to have a trail, I see that I have not intended most of what has transpired. I have struggled to stay my proper course, but find myself too weak. Do you remember that day at Tripoli when we stood on the hill with Sinan as his guests?" Balthazar nodded. "I thought then that I was caught up in a sweep of events so great that no man could resist. I feel the same now, this moment."

"Marcus Aurelius said, did he not, 'Life is a struggle and a sojourning in a strange land.'"

A mournful sound escaped my lips. "Men have learned nothing further since, have they? Had I not met Blaij Vergã, surely everything would have turned out much different."

"Perhaps you should thank him."

"He has said as much. Eh, we have put that aside ... But I vowed to kill Turgut and worked seven years in the Venetian Arsenale for an unspoken end. Here I find myself, and Turgut is nowhere to be seen ... Am I still a youth who cannot shirk adventure ... ? It seems I shall always be *esforzado*." I glanced up from the casks. "What of you, Balthazar? I have said it before, but since Venice you have not seemed entirely yourself. Sterner than the man I knew, fewer jokes and tales ... I can hardly express it."

He nodded. "*Moy foy*, the role of comte did not sit well. I am a soldier, not a spy. And when I beheld the great mosque Soliman has built to himself, I think I at long last perceived the stature of our foe." Balthazar paused for a moment, glancing at the powder casks. "The Turk may be invincible."

His words alarmed me. "You of all people, a Knight of St. John, cannot be losing heart."

"Nay," he smiled ruefully. "Francisco, if I am sterner, it is because I harden myself to fight a sterner foe. I am also now a man of middle years—"

"You yet have the strength of any man I know."

The Knight shrugged, nodded. "My arms yet serve. But I have campaigned now on and off for twenty seasons. To what end? Since our arrival, I have attempted at every moment to divine why this great undertaking, carefully planned by our potentates for a full year, has fallen into complete disaster. Doria, the council, refused to attack Turgut in Tripoli. la Cerda built this fort on an untenable island, despite the Grand

Master's warnings. These men have no vision beyond themselves; I said as much yesterday. They no longer understand why they fight. Our princes must form standing armies, as the Romans did, or we must discover a new ideal, which I do not perceive. Faith alone no longer suffices against the Grand Signor." Fra Balthazar paused, finally, and reflected. "Niccolò accords the Ottomans a place among the empires marked by excellence, a union of energy and talent that makes them—not us—the inheritors of the Assyrians, the Medeans, the Persians ... the Romans." He paused again. "After our sojourn in Constantinople, I believe Niccolò may be correct."

"Balthazar!" I cried, fully overwhelmed by alarm, "to hear a Knight of Justice speak so! From your lips—heresy!"

He sighed, chuckling. "You did not take to coffee. Francisco, I have ne'er been so singleminded as Parisot or Romegas and I shall never be Grand Master. If we survive this ordeal, I should like someday to retire to my estate and write down my thoughts, if I can ever gather them together properly. I doubt I should find any readers, alas ... "

"Balthazar," I said, suddenly finding myself close on tears, "if we should not survive this—"

He raised his hand. "Let us vow, my friend, never to overly mourn our fate and never to say farewell. Our task today is to survive the test that God has placed before us. If this day be our last, we have no regrets of each other." He turned away. "Now, if I can find some proper armor ... "

At that moment the sound of scattered arquebus fire reached us from the ramparts. I glanced once more at the Knight and ran up to my station.

The Turks had sent in their azabs to prevent our men from cutting down trees for the palisade and now some skirmishing was going on under the palm leaves. The arquebusiers along the walls and those de Sande had sent to the south were lending their fire, which was almost useless, as no one could see anything. The sun was by now high in the sky, the day hot and our sweat running. Some of the Knights had been setting up a makeshift hospital along the walls, for many of the men remained grievously ill, but there were few surgeons about and almost no physicians.

When the cause of the shooting became known, other Knights, Balthazar amongst them, took broadswords in hand and made a sortie to the woods to confront the azabs. At the same time de Sande ordered a Knight, le Chausaille, to drag some of the remaining boats ashore and anchor them with dirt, e'en before the palisade was built. I joined Chausaille and his men. With hands clasped to the ropes, a hundred of us dragged seven galleys and galiots to the shore between the castle and the town. Then we began to fill their holds with sand and dirt. Engaged in this activity I searched for pitch and resin, still hoping that I might do something by way of fire weapons. As the sun caked the dirt onto us, I found pitch and tow for the repair of ships. The tow would serve for matches, but the pitch was of insufficient quantity and of the wrong consistency for my aim.

While we labored on the beach, the Knights were taking care of the azabs in the woods. In any engagement with the Turks, I learned, those poor bastards, hardly schooled in arms, are sent ahead like pigs and they die in great numbers. They did that day, as the Knights and our infantry chased them through the trees, cutting them to pieces as the rest of our men cut wood. The moment the axes were through those trunks, men hacked off the leaves, ran the trees to the beach, sharpened the ends into points and began to dig in the palisade around the vessels we were securing.

Sometime around midday, when our feet were burning and skin peeling, arquebus fire began on the far side of the town. We craned our necks to see what was going on at that place, whose single square and few lime-covered dwellings scarcely made a town at all. Natheless, the foe would have a hard time digging trenches and getting siege guns close to the fort as long as our men were arrayed about that little marketplace. Sure enough, the janissaries had begun their first assault and the gunfire continued for hours. Throughout, men, including some Djerbens who had foolishly remained with the Spaniards, were running back and forth with carts and barrels to the wells. de Sande never ceased trying to increase the stores of water within the fort, but if the wells were taken, we would certainly die of thirst.

For those of us working on the boats, by sundown our throats were parched and our stomachs crying out for food. But bread came from the fort and water from the marketplace and we knew that our men had held.

The night was quiet and most of us who had been engaged on the boats or building the palisade returned to the castle. Eighty or one hundred men had been lost that day, to the Turks or to sickness, but e'en as we threw the bodies into a ditch outside the walls, those who remained alive were grateful to de Sande for the leadership he had shown and to the arquebusiers, who had not allowed the janissaries overwhelm them.

Some men were sitting around a fire, making a meal of fish, speaking of what we would do if we ever got out of this mess alive, when Balthazar sat down and entered into conversation with a fellow who had been next to me for some time. Only then did I recognize him as none other than Ramon Caravajal, who I had not set eyes on since we dragged a gun to Mdina, nine years ago. He said he had been in the Indies and that he had wrenched off an elephant's leg from its body. "By God, if I had put forth a little more strength, I would have run my arm down to the beast's heart and entrails and forced him to disgorge them through his mouth."

I laughed as another Knight boasted that he had tossed the heads of all the Moors he had killed so high into the air that, before they came to the ground again, they were half-devoured by flies. Forced to wave a mass of flies off our food before each bite, I thought it likely true. Now one of the Germans left among us began to grumble how he hadn't been paid, or disembarked, only to face certain death at the hand of the Turks.

Caravajal sneered. "Go where you please. Go to the Turks, if you want. *Los Soldados Espanoles no van à la guerra come obreros, segùn el uso de los Soldados Mercenarios, si no à ganar Gloria, Triumphos, Victorias, y Reputation.*"

"*Was saget er?*" the German wanted to know.

Someone translated and with an enraged cry the German jumped onto Caravajal. Those rest of us leapt on them but only with difficulty broke up the fight. By morning the German was gone.

The men continued building the palisade. As for the galleys we had anchored on shore, de Sande intended to use the vessels as a sort of gunnery platform, and so we dragged pieces small and large to those boats and emplaced them with the others already aboard. The janissaries made another assault on the town, but once more our arquebusiers held them off. We had the feeling that Piyale was merely testing, searching for our weaknesses while he established his camp. To be sure, the preparations went on for several days without a full-scale assault. The constant activity kept our spirits from sinking as they might have otherwise. They did sink, five or six days after the sea battle, when another twenty galleys flying the dreaded blue crescent rounded the coast. Turgut had arrived.

"Mayhap," said Balthazar as we watched the corsairs erect their leader's white marquee on the far beach, "the reason you are here has become manifest."

"Mayhap." The omen shone brightly.

Almost immediately Turgut's forces began to disembark the siege guns.

"They are too distant to do much damage," I said needlessly. "They will have to bring in trenches." Thus far our arquebusiers in town had prevented much trench-digging. The Turks would have to clear the arquebusiers out before they got very far.

Turgut had other plans. Later that day he sent out azab sappers to open trenches to the south, farther than the arquebusiers could shoot and nearer to the palm woods. But de Sande wasn't going to let him get away with it. Our cannoneers on the fort chased the dogs away with salvos, tho' at a distance of three hundred fifty paces, they were putting more fright into the enemy than damage. Finally, the azabs and slaves regained their wits and began digging under protection of their gabions. At that point de Sande sent out our troops to confront the foe. The fighting was fierce and the enemy retreated from the spot he had chosen.

Piyale and Turgut then decided to assault the palisade. It came. Azabs ran screaming and yelling at us through the space between the town and the fort, exposed to fire from our men on the ramparts. They fell by the dozens, but there were hundreds of them, carrying sword and spear. Those of us aboard the galleys fired at them everything we had, over the fence, from the muskets mounted on the wales, to the falcons, the sacres and the full cannon. The noise never ceased and truly my whiskers became forged in cannon fire. At one moment the enemy reached the palisade and we were overwhelmed with numbers. I cast about, finding a small barrel of gunpowder, thrust a match into it, lit it and hurled it over the fence. The explosion knocked us all nearly senseless, but it put enough fear into the enemy that they retreated for a few moments. Luckily several hundred of our men then sallied forth from the castle and drove them off.

Piyale and Turgut could see that our gun battery was going to cause them trouble and the next day they sent some ships against us from the seaward side. When our sentinels gave the alarm, we were hard put to turn the guns we had brought aboard around to face them. Luckily we'd dismantled the parapets from the boats and managed it. The first shots our men unleashed fell short or went wide and I told them my aim was better. They gave me the match and my first ball struck one of the galleys headed for us, putting a hole in its hull. By this time the gunners in the fort had trained the heavy cannon up there on the enemy boats and together we beat them off.

It went on like this for a week, assaults every day on the palisade, on the marketplace, skirmishes near the trenchworks. The trenches crept closer, but all this time we did a good job of holding the foe at bay. Finally, toward the end of May, Piyale ordered his janissaries to assault the town once more. After a fierce struggle, in which hundreds on both sides were killed, our men retreated from the marketplace and the wells fell into the hands of the enemy.

Fifty-Four

Hour by hour—nay, moment by moment—the enemy trenches now closed in on the fortress walls. I knew the sappers would try to get as close as thirty or forty paces for battering, hardly farther than one can spit, but mayhap with the heavy Ottoman guns they could do with fifty. Sure enough they tried, while those of us on the boats constantly bombarded the infidels from the flanks, giving them a great deal of trouble. Natheless, when de Sande saw that they were finally emplacing a dozen large pieces and a dozen middle ones in the trenches, he gathered together a council. Balthazar remembered most of all the closeness of the air and the buzzing of the flies.

"We must get word to Malta," an exhausted de Sande said as they sat in that chamber on barrels and stones. "In this heat, the water in the cistern and barrels cannot last more than a few months, even if the walls do. I intend to send a boat, but the risk is great. Who will volunteer?"

None of the Knights stepped forward, for not a man of them wished to appear eager to desert the fortress at such a grave hour. de Sande then chose Barthelemy d'Alba, a man of my age, and told him to find a crew and take one of the remaining *fregate* that very night. There were few left to us.

The battering started then, the rumble of the guns beyond the walls, a few bits of stone and dust falling from the ceiling of this place. No one paid much attention.

One of the Spaniards present said he'd reconnoitred the Turks and that the Christians were missing a chance to act. Piyale had all his men ashore, including the *ciurme*. He had taken all the armaments from the galleys, including the Christian ones, and had dismounted their rudders for fear that the slaves would seize them and escape.

"What are you saying?" asked de Sande as he wiped his bald head.

"The infidel galleys now have less than fifty men aboard each of them. We have yet three thousand men who can fight. Let us take the chance and seize the galleys. The prisoners there will join us."

Most of those present, de Sande as well, scoffed at the suggestion. "What you say may be true. But between us and those galleys lies the entire infidel army. By God, to get there we should have to capture the town again, and the wells, beyond which Dragut now sits enthroned in his marquee."

"Perhaps we should do that," offered Balthazar, as another faint shudder made itself felt and more dust fell from the walls. Unfortunately, the castle was of an old design, four walls square; at least the Vice Roy had made certain they were thick. "To reach the galleys is certainly impossible. Yet, our foe has begun his demolition of these walls. We can sit here until he breaches them or until we starve, or we can attack, and try to dismount his guns. We have yet a substantial force of men."

de Sande asked to think on't and pushed his heavy frame to his feet. That evening in the dead of night, Barthelemy d'Alba and a small crew stole away in one of the last *fregate* to advise Malta of the situation. From the ramparts we watched the oars dip into the water and we prayed for them and for us.

The same evening I chanced on Pietru, who I found helping guard the big cistern near the south wall of the fort. He was playing with a small lizard as it crawled over his arm. "I am glad to see you are alive, Xabaw," I said. He nodded. "How long will the water last?"

Pietru did not know. de Sande had rationed it from the start. Between the big cistern and the smaller jugs and barrels, he thought another month.

"We must find more water, somehow," I suggested.

At that, Pietru handed me the halberd by him and walked outside the fort, coming back with a forked twig. As on that day in Italy seven years ago, he took it in his hands and wandered around the walls of the fort, by the wounded, by the shit pit, everywhere. Soon men were following him around the yard, not a little curious as to what he was up to. At the corner of the southwest bastion he paused. Then he found a pick and started digging. The other men joined in. After a glass of digging, some dark water began to bubble up from under the walls. All the soldiers around cheered and called the Gozitan a hero. Others fell on their knees to the brown dirt, thanking God for His intervention. Ix-Xabaw showed himself to be uncertain, saying it had seemed to him that the ground there looked dark. The stream proved to be meager, not nearly enough for our needs, but everyone regarded it as a favorable omen. de Sande decided we would risk a sortie.

We poured out of the fortress at dawn, two thousand men. The Turks were not expecting an assault and we caught them with their pants down. As they scattered for their weapons and horses, we streamed into the town, arquebusiers first, firing a salvo, having one chance to reload and firing a second before the janissaries got their wits together. Even as the Sultan's infantry retreated behind the wells and buildings, they began to return fire with deadly effect. Men began to fall in every direction, but our force had with it the Hand of God and the enemy continued to fall back.

The Knights had come up behind us, wielding their broadswords. I felt somehow Balthazar's presence and turned. Sure enough, armored in a cuirass and helmet he had found, he followed at my shoulder, and together we pressed forward through this marketplace. So much dust had now been thrown up into the air that we were as if lost in a morning fog; I perceived nothing but the shouts, the ripple of the gunfire and the flashes from the arquebuses. A large janissary stepped from behind a wall directly before me and at once we were grappling with each other. He knocked me to the ground, and stepped on my rapier, snapping it, but his loose clothing did nothing to protect him and Balthazar ran him through. I cast about for another weapon, spying a halberd lying on the ground next to one of our fallen men. At a loss, I snatched it up and we rushed forward. Amidst the sounds of gunfire and the flash of powder, our men were everywhere killing a great number of the enemy, who fled in all directions as we pursued them.

Suddenly, we found ourselves on the far side of the town. Those about me pointed to three large cannon, that which we had come for. Without hesitation we grabbed rocks and with them drove spikes into the touchholes, rendering the guns useless. The task done, I glanced up. The corsair encampment spread eastward from our feet. Five paces from us rose Turgut's tent. Surrounded by guards, the dreaded corsair himself stood at its entrance, that incarnation of Evil who had eluded Christendom time and time again. In that instant time halted its advance. My eyes perceived every detail of the beard, the surcoat, the pointed boots, the creases on his brow, the turban not fully wound, the expression of disbelief frozen on his face. The old man of seventy and five years could not credit that the foe they had so securely trapped had turned upon them. I held no doubt that God had set Turgut in my path. I took ten strides across the space with the halberd outstretched.

"Gozo!" I screamed, aiming straight at the corsair's neck.

Time took up its advance and what happened next has never been fully clear. One of the guards in that tableau now coming alive deflected my blade downward and the halberd tip entered Turgut's thigh. Eyes wide, he stared at me as he let out a strangled cry. A second guard lifted his scimitar to slice me in half, but Balthazar took that one's head from this throat with a swing of his sword. Two others of Turgut's men struck Balthazar in the side and he fell. By this time more Knights were with us. I don't know how it happened, but I managed to lift Balthazar onto my back and, with the help of a nameless Knight, carry our senseless comrade back to the town. We put him down near the wells and I stripped off my shirt to bind his wound, but so much blood was flowing that at first sight I was certain he would not last the sands of a glass.

"You will not die on my account!" I shouted, emptying my lungs at him over and over again, but he did not respond.

While we knelt in the marketplace, I saw that the battle was turning—against us. Our men had diverted their attention from the foe to rounding up food and supplies. Now they ran in all directions, to the buildings and from them, carrying with them anything they could find. Seeing this, the janissaries had regrouped and with the horsemen who now appeared were calmly, steadily driving our men back with arquebus fire and deadly arrows. The Knight with me, who named himself Mas, helped me carry Balthazar back to the fort; not long after, the army itself began flooding in, having tossed away its advantage.

Inside the castle, I gave Balthazar over to the physicians by the hospital wall, but I knelt by him the next day and night. For that time he never came to his senses and I thought, surely, he who had saved my life twice in a single engagement was sending his soul to Heaven. The heat added its wrath. In the African sunlight armor and blades became too hot to touch, and the number of flies only increased with the number of dead and the amount of shit piling up in the pits. Yet, the Order's physicians stitched up the Knight and applied their salves. Whether it was rhubarb or a more miraculous herb, or my ceaseless prayers, I know not, but after the second day, Balthazar opened his eyes.

The bombardment had recommenced shortly after the battle and the first thing he said was, "At least the walls have held." We were yet unsure whether he would survive.

The walls had held, but the enemy was now battering us with eighteen large cannon and smaller ones. The *boom-boom-boom* was continuous, accompanied all the time by distant cymbal crashes. We did our best to give them trouble with our own pieces, and we did. More than once a good shot from the walls or from our beached boats dismounted one of their guns, but they always brought up another. The foe was now entrenched. We made no further sorties.

Naturally, word that I had wounded Turgut swept through the castle and many men sang my praises. E'en Ix-Xabaw nodded in admiration. For years after, I thought of that moment before the corsair's pavilion, which from the first had seemed a dream. The halberd, Balthazar's presence there, and Turgut's himself. I did not feel I myself had been present, acting.

Balthazar, struggling against his delirium, said, "The *kairos* was upon you and you seized time by the forelock."

The Knight had mentioned that word before. I did not know exactly of what he spoke, but from then on I was convinced Destiny had been in it.

Toward the middle of June, late at night, the watch spied four galleys approaching the fort from the side opposite the enemy. Soon, they had launched their boats and our men cheered as through the gates walked a company of Knights from Malta. de Sande was roused and greeted them. Within moments everyone who could walk had gathered around with the keenest ears.

In the firelight they told us that Gian Andrea and the Vice Roy had gained Naples. We also learned that due to the skill of one of the Knights' pilots, the Order's four galleys had escaped Piyale, and this pilot had also guided thirteen others safely to Malta. Twenty were in Piyale's hands, which meant ten lay at the bottom of the sea.

"You cannot imagine," said one of the Knights, "how the reports of the armada's destruction have spread, like fire from capital to capital. Old Doria himself has been taken ill by the news and they say he will not survive it. People weep in public as if Armageddon has taken place on these shores. Across the continent princes are calling it the worst disaster of our century, and every Christian prays daily for your salvation, and their own, for they know that nothing now will stop the Grand Signor from making a descent on Europe."

"Damn Europe!" de Sande erupted. "Will my men be relieved?"

The Knight hesitated. "I may speak honestly with you, Señor: We are not the relief. de Valette has sent these four galleys to carry the wounded from the fortress. Philip is making feverish efforts to organize an expedition and succours, but you understand, now that the fleet has been destroyed, the task is not simple ... "

"May we expect a relief or not?" shouted de Sande again.

The inconstant light disguised much, but the Knight shook his head. "I do not know, and by God that is the truth," he said, crossing himself. "Our duty now is to get the wounded and sick off this cursed island. Let us make the attempt before dawn."

We spent the night putting as many of the wounded and sick aboard the galleys as possible. As I helped lay Balthazar in one of the boats we both looked at each other and said, "I expect you to stay alive." Then he added, "You have not yet entirely fulfilled your vow."

He was correct; I had not. I watched the oarsmen push the caique from shore and stood there for a long time. When the Turks recommenced the bombardment, I returned to the fort.

Little changed over the next weeks. The enemy continued its bombardment. We fought back as we were able. No relief appeared. As July advanced the heat became unbearable, so oppressive that one could not stand in the sun for more than a few moments at a time. Had we sufficient water, we might have made do, but the cistern was near dry and the stream Pietru had discovered was small and hardly fit to drink. Our lips and throats became ever more parched. Some food remained but wood for cooking grew scarce. Those who ate raw meat fell ill, and so as our stomachs cried out we walked about the fortress more like skeletons than living beings. With each passing day ever more became sick and died, and each night a handful of men eluded the sentries and deserted to the enemy, deciding that it was better to risk slavery than face the sure death creeping toward us.

We had grown indifferent to the crash of the balls into the curtain, e'en as we knew that sooner or later those walls must come down. We could not grow accustomed to the heat, which grew without limit until we could scarce move. We shat rarely and our piss, when it came, was clear. The whole fortress smelled of piss. Toward the middle of July, de Sande sent out another *fregata*, requesting immediate relief, but received no reply.

"Europe has forgotten us, Xabaw," I said to Pietru one day on the beach as we watched four of the galleys collapse into cinders. de Sande had ordered them burnt to prevent their capture. We were saving three, God alone knew why. At the moment flames consumed the largest of them, I thought I heard those damned barbarian trumpets and we returned to the fort.

The wood ran out and then the water ran out. A Sicilian who practiced alchemy distilled two dozens of barrels of fresh water each day from seawater and de Sande offered him half his estate if he could only increase the supply, but he had not sufficient means. After this attempt failed, you could see men everywhere stretched upon the ground with their parched lips gaping, saying over and over again the one word "water." If a doctor happened to give them a cup, they would struggle to sit up, drink it, then fall to the ground again, exhausted. It was at this time, when the water ran out, that our hopes ran out too, and we passed the point of despair and became reconciled to a quick end.

It was close on the last day of July when de Sande called together those who could still stand. Perhaps there were a thousand of us. The Colonel himself had lost so much weight that his clothes flopped around him as were he a filthy doll. "Men," he said, "we can no longer hope for a relief. If we sit in this fortress we are certain to die of thirst. I for one would prefer to make a brave end and die with my sword in hand."

The rest of us cheered him and we spent the day making preparations for a final sortie. Plenty of weapons were about, so many of our comrades had died, and I found myself a good sword and an arquebus. "Xabaw," I said, but words failed me. I was too exhausted to feel bitterness. We embraced and got such sleep as we were able.

Morning came and the Turk took the decision from our hands. The Infidel resumed his bombardment and soon the east walls fell with a terrific roar. When the dust cleared, we faced a large breach and beyond it, Turkish cavalry.

de Sande wasted no time. He raised his sword, shouting, "For Christ and Philip!" and we followed him out through the gates and the breach, cheering and yelling.

We did not stand a chance. Within moments our force was surrounded by the enemy, who fairly laughed in our faces. de Sande cast down his sword and everyone else followed. One of the Knights on the gunnery platform kept up firing, but he was soon wounded and taken. As the Turks rounded us up, they dashed cheering into the fortress and cut the heads off all the sick and wounded. They carried these heads and hundreds of others they'd already taken to a spot some paces to the west, where they began piling them up. Laughing, they mortared those grim heads as they stacked them higher and higher, saying this pyramid of skulls would remain for ages to come as a monument to Allah of their great victory. We watched them with horror build this tower of staring eyes until it was at least five times the height of a man. Then they marched us to the galleys where the other Christian prisoners had been kept since the defeat of the armada. For a moment our column halted, directly before Turgut himself. I stared at the old man, as he stared at me. I expected my head to roll the next instant, but as on that previous time in Tripoli he betrayed no recognition.

At the camp, they said, were five thousand prisoners. Piyale Pasha took some days to prepare for departure, after which the iron rings were fastened around our ankles and every one of us was chained to a bench.

Fifty-Five

Piyale Pasha's return to Constantinople after the ides of September was the most triumphant the Turks had ever witnessed. The fleet arrived in the dead of night but Piyale, seeking to make the greatest impression, waited for morning before entering the Golden Horn. With the dawn call to prayer, thousands streamed down to the harbor and no one who watched the procession ever forgot it. The Turkish galleys, painted red with banners flying, majestically towed three and twenty captured vessels behind them. The victors had stripped the Christian galleys of their parapets, spars and rudders, and reduced them to mere hulks, making them appear mean and contemptible next to their own. A Spanish standard proudly emblazoned with Our Savior on the Cross had been captured by Piyale's troops and the *Kapudan* ordered it dragged in the water behind Doria's galley. In that way the prizes were pulled slowly along, as dolphins played alongside them, and the great crowds on the banks of the Horn cheered the victorious Admiral.

Soliman himself had come down to the colonnade in his garden at the base of the Sarai to watch the spectacle. Every Turk greeting the Admiral, from the lowest to the highest, boasted, "Who can resist us, now that the Spaniard is vanquished?" Yet, later many said of His Majesty that so schooled was he to meet each change of Fortune that all the cheers and triumph of that day failed to wring from him the slightest smile or sign of elation.

Alvaro de Sande, Don Sancho de Levya and the other prisoners of rank had been treated as befitted their station, and they watched the cheering crowds from the poop of Piyale's *capitana*. Be assured, the men rowing the Turkish galleys were little aware of any triumph. In their state of utter deprivation after months in that accursed fort, many lacked the strength to survive the long journey to Constantinople and they died in great numbers, only to be tossed overboard without ceremony. Those who remained alive ate ravenously the biskets thrown at them, the beans, the few olives and water. Pietru, having spent years as an oarsman, did better than most, rising and falling to the drumbeat in a silent resignation. My muscles ached without limit, the oars chaffed the skin off my hands, e'en as I wrapped them with strips torn from my own shirt; assuredly my bones alone would remain if my arms did not fall from my shoulders first. Like every other prisoner, I was unable to comprehend the fate that had befallen me e'en as I was mortally terrified of it. I prayed to God and asked why he had forsaken His children. So broken were we in spirit as well as in flesh that the words *uscança dy guerra* ne'er entered my mind.

After parading us through the streets to the taunts and jeers of the common people, our captors marched us to that same bagno next to the Arsenal I had stumbled upon only months before. My heart froze. Did the Almighty truly intend this? I had no time to reflect; the numbers of prisoners were so great that we could not all be fit in the bath house and our captors pushed hundreds on to an old mosque in Pera.

For days Pietru and I sat locked up in this place. We slept on the stone without straw or blankets and our jailors fed us only dry black bread and water, which we shared with vermin of every description. Many of the men's stomachs could scarce endure perpetual water drinking. "*Porta vino!*" they cried, thinking anyone would understand, but no amount of pleading convinced the janissaries to bring wine or ought else. They treated everyone alike, young, old, strong, weak. The sick they regarded as good as dead. Sometimes when confronted with our pleas, the janissaries beat us with their sticks for their own pleasure, but for far longer hours we only sat on in this dank, crowded kingdom of rats whose air soon became too thick with our own filth to breathe.

After a week—I don't know—some men and women brought pots filled with broth and little chunks of meat, which we devoured with the bearing of famished wolves. Our visitors told us that the Austrian Ambassador himself, Busbecq, was organizing the citizens of Galata into supplying the captives with food and other necessities. These merciful souls also tossed us what little news they had: Don Sancho de Levye, Pierre de Massues-Vercoiran—that same Knight who helped me deliver Balthazar—and some other noblemen were being kept in the Tower of Galata, only a stone's throw from us, and a few days after our arrival some of the highest prisoners had been taken to the Sarai. The Turks paraded them through the streets, taunting them at every step, and forced them to wear their armor back turned to front. Some of the officers collapsed in the Divan from exhaustion and one or two were actually dying. In all these matters, Soliman had been so impressed by Alvaro de Sande's brave resistance that he offered the Colonel a command of an entire army should he abjure his faith and profess to the Prophet Mahomet. de Sande replied that he would sooner live in chains, and the Sultan granted his request.

While de Sande sat in the tower, we in the mosque-prison looked with evil eyes onto the clever ones who'd secretly tarred a few coins or jewels to their scalps wherewith to fee the jailors, or onto the high-born ones who managed to see Busbecq, declaring they could repay a loan. They gave him every imaginable story about their valor, wealth and connections, and often convinced the soft-hearted Ambassador to put up a surety for their ransom.

The rest of us had no means. Shivering at night in our chains on the mosque's hard floor, tearing at our worm-ridden bread, we knew naught of what would become of us. Our visitors told us the Turks might sell us to a rich family or send us to Hungary for labor. They might keep us in Constantinople for the same purpose or chain us again to a galley's bench. No one needed to tell us that in all these prospects the likely outcome was our own death. We prayed night and day for our speedy deliverance, convinced in the depths of our souls we would soon awake from a horrible dream. The weeks wore on and when enough in the bagno had been sold or died, most of us were moved to that lightless, walled place.

The truth thus slowly dawned: With tomorrow's rising of the sun, the dew would melt away, but this living nightmare would go on. We were forevermore Soliman's slaves. When at last we yielded to this truth, our spirits plummeted to the deepest abysses of despair. One moment I cursed the Almighty for abandoning me to the wrath of the Antichrist, the next moment I readied to give myself up to His Will.

"Wherefore," I cried, "didst Thou grant me to survive the Infidel bombardment on Gelves, assault after assault and months of hunger and thirst besides, only to cast me into this Hell from which there is no escape? How have I offended Thee, O Lord?" Ne'er, not at Mdina, not on Djerbé itself had my faith been so sorely tested. I cursed myself for ever having left Venice, and Spain so long ago. I cursed the Turks, but received no answer from God.

Wrath overcame us. The prisoners fought ceaselessly over the few coins in our possession and forced newcomers thrust into our midst to pay a tax on pain of horrible punishments. More than a man died, pummeled or tossed high and dropped to the stones. Had we the strength, the rest of us surely would have killed each other, and there would have been mercy in it. Each time I caught sight of a rope, I regarded it hard as a gallows for myself. Two things alone saw me through this time of darkness. The first was Pietru. He too prayed daily at one of the altars they allowed in the bagno and, like every Maltese, he cursed the Turks without cease. Yet his spirits seemed not to have sunk to the depths of my own, and he often sang to himself in his gruff voice so unsuited to song.

One morning, after we had been kept under lock and key forty days, our guards marched us out of the bagno. An Agha came along to examine us, like horses. He turned our hands, felt our muscles and peered at our grinders, dividing us into one group or another. The weaker ones were sent off, whither we knew not. The janissaries chained and ferried the rest across the Horn and everyone was certain we would be taken to the bazaar, stripped and sold, but it proved otherwise. The weaker slaves had been sent to the bazaar for auction, while the stronger were being kept for the Porte. This was the worst possible news, for, being slaves of the Porte itself, we'd have no master who might ransom us. As my spirits plummeted yet deeper into blackness, the guards cudgeled us toward the far wall of the city, where we were to build a new mosque and hospital ordered by Soliman's daughter, Mihrimah. On this march I begged Pietru to say whither came his strength. I do not think he understood me.

"How do you talk so, Francisco?" he boomed. "The Turks took my wife and children. Now they have taken me. I will die here. I put the Evil Eye on these Turks."

"You sing songs." One might call it singing.

Pietru cocked his scarred head as had I confused him. "I have always sung songs, Francisco. I sang songs when I ploughed my farm, when I carried rocks for the forts on Malta and on Gelves. Eh, I have always sung."

"But we are slaves now," I replied with a sensible anger. "How can you sing?"

Now my companion with the crooked nose reflected, mayhap more than he had in his entire life. "You have lost much, Cikku. You have built great guns in Venice. You have spoken with Grand Masters. All that is gone. I have never had anything more than the wind and the birds."

"You have lost your wife and still hope to find her," I said, yet vexed.

"You must hope, Cikku, but not too much. Hoping too much is like trying to bottle wind." He began to grunt his song about the wind, then broke off. "Since the *razzia*, I have hauled rocks and fought the Turk. No one cares how many rocks I have hauled or how many Turks I have killed." He did not seem to know what he wanted to say. "No one will remember."

"I will remember," I said. "God will remember."

The same day, as we labored on the new mosque, I overheard two other prisoners talking. While in conversation, one of them, none other than Ramon Caravajal, muttered, "*Uscança dy guerra.*" The words, which I now heard for the first time since Djerbé, struck me with renewed meaning. It was simple to shrug off another man's captivity as "usage of war." When oneself is enslaved, the world assumes a different color. To our captors, we weren't worth a pig's bristle, and I could expect no more help than that faceless prisoner who, on the day I first walked to the Arsenal, so desperately launched himself at me. By the same coin, tho', I should expect nothing worse. Aye, de Valette had survived *uscança dy guerra*, as had countless others. So could we.

This small understanding, and Pietru's warning not to hope too much restored to me a measure of spirit. We must not hope too much but we must put what little strength we had to regaining our freedom. "Xabaw," I said as we put our backs into the work, "Balthazar on Djerbé charged me to survive. I now make that charge to you. Let us pledge to each other that we will not die in chains." We took each other's hands and made the vow.

Fifty-Six

Survive, then, but how? Pietru began to gather animals to him, birds mostly, but also little furred animals like weasels, and shared with them his food. For my part I packed despair into my purse and cast a hard eye on the ordeal God had set before us. I at once thought of Giovan Barelli and had I the meagerest idea of how to find the Greek in this vast city, I would have sought his intercession. But I did not, being unsure even of his true name.

Swiftly my hopes turned to Lorenzo at the Gun Foundry. Somehow I must get word to him that I was held in the bagno. This bagno, I regarded our prison, had unlike the slave quarters in Birgu at one time been a true bath house. Not a window allowed steam to exit or light to enter, and its courtyard was surrounded by a high wall. The Turks cared little about what went on inside and ages ago prisoners had made Catholic and Greek altars in some of the steam rooms. Much gambling and card-playing and smoking of *afione* took place at night, when we were locked up with the rats, but the only way out was through the single door. The good citizens of Pera continued to bring us food, tho' amount diminished as they forgot us.

I resolved to speak to one of the janissary guards. My chance came on a cool morning when we were being marched to the mosque. They had this day removed the chains and so I approached the nearest of them with a bow. The fellow held a stick, for in the city janissaries are permitted no weapons beyond this or a staff, and under the heavy kaftan I perceived the body of an athlete, no rarity among these feared troops. My hope of a quick release faded rapidly, tho', when I addressed him in the lingua franca and the blockhead failed to understand a single word. With an angry wave he passed me on to another, but with this one I had no better result. I cursed aloud, understanding then that these janissaries were schooled more in their bodies than in their noggins and that needs be I would learn Turkish.

Some days after, a Genoese woman came with food to the bagno. Pushing aside everyone in my path, I grabbed her by the shoulders and implored her to seek out Lorenzo at the Foundry. Only weeks later did she return with the news that Lorenzo was nowhere to be found. Some said he was traveling, others averred that his year as a *mustemin* had gone by and as he had no wish to be subject to infidel law he had returned to Venice. I went on cursing and laboring at the mosque.

Winter came and with it the wind and rain. Our toil ceased not for a day, tho' by then they had mostly stopped beating us. The dark season was cold and we had nothing to wear but cotton tunics, and many captives lost the will to live. The rest gathered around the fires in the bagno and slept hard against each other for warmth. Through the janissaries we picked up our first words of Turkish, and through our visitors we learned what we could of the outside world. We heard that Busbecq had begun bargaining for Colonel de Sande's release. We heard that old Andrea Doria, having fallen so bitterly ill at the news of Gelves, had died without recovering and that every Ottoman forthwith offered thanks to Allah. Of greatest import, we discovered that someone had accused Soliman of neglecting Mahomet's prohibition on wine and the Sultan proclaimed that henceforth none would be brought into Constantinople, e'en for Jews and Christians. The news caused the sharpest alarm, for wine was necessary for our diet, and many of the men doubted they could survive without it.

"The Grand Signor has lost his mind completely," Caravajal spat as we shivered in a circle under the flickering light of the oil lamps. His Majesty will forgive me for repeating such a slander, but this is exactly what I heard.

"He's an old man who becomes more superstitious each day," added another, as he threw a four of swords into the center. "He surrounds himself with women and astrologers. He's dismissed his boy-singers and burned their instruments because a witch promised him heavy punishment in the hereafter should he not give up suchlike amusements."

"How do you know this?"

"One of the janissaries told me."

We called in a guard and put the question to him in our feeble Turkish. He nodded, yes, Soliman *Kanuni* was old and no one paid attention to him anymore. Picking a wriggling louse out of my hair, I asked who then ruled their empire. The guard shrugged, grinned toothily. "The Grand Vizier, and the *yenicheriler.*" The janissary's answer was my first inkling that this the Greatest Empire of East and West was not cut from a single stone.

"These people do have the most peculiar customs," said Caravajal, farting. "They will not go to stool in the presence of others and always walk off to a distance."

"Have you seen that the men make water in the same posture as the women?" put in the fellow beside me, brushing away a rat with one hand and sweeping up the coins in front of him with the other.

Anyone would admit it was strange how often Mahometans washed, five times a day before prayer.

"The oddest thing is how they go around picking up the smallest bits of paper and stuff them into the nearest nook or cranny for fear the name of God may be written on them." It was true; every wall you looked at had little pieces of paper stuck into the chinks.

"Yet none of them can read."

"Can you? Knave of roses." One called Argensola tossed the card. But there was something to it; in this vast city there were no books but for the Quran.

"What do you say about their veneration for the babbling idiots who walk the streets?"

"Mahomet was an idiot."

We all laughed. It was the laughter that kept us alive. At that juncture, tho', Argensola gathered a tattered blanket he had managed to buy around his shoulders and asked what the words were to become a Mahometan. Suddenly a great silence descended upon the circle.

"*O reniego los Infideles del Hijo de Dios!*" erupted Caravajal angrily as we all turned on the fellow. "You dare contemplate it?"

Argensola shrank from our gaze, fairly vanished into the cracks between the stones. "Nay, of course not," he stuttered after an infinity of time, "but I have heard if you say those words, the infidels set you free."

No one raised his voice then, for after months of captivity who among us would lay his hand on the Holy Book and swear that the thought hadn't entered his mind? Our temptation was sharpened by the rumor we had lately received, explaining why no relief force had come to Djerbé: Philip had been frantically organizing one, but upon learning that his friend the Vice Roy of Sicily had escaped alive, he abruptly reversed his orders and abandoned the island. Knowing now that the King of Spain himself had cast us into the jaws of the Antichrist turned each and every one of us into a bitter man. I could not but wonder what Nicolas de Villegaignon would decide under present circumstance. I began to pray for my soul.

Throughout this conversation, Pietru had been silent, feeding a little bird perched on his outstretched finger. Now he spoke. "The Sultan may be an old man," he said, "but who opposes him?"

"If I ever get out of here alive," Caravajal spat vehemently, "I'll kill Philip for his treachery, and then I'll kill a Turk for every scar on my back and every stroke of the oar I've suffered!"

Each man around Caravajal muttered his angry assent, but the boast was empty. Day by day I better understood Balthazar's words at Djerbé that the Turks had all but grown invincible. Visitors to the bagno, confusion and fear writ on their countenances, told us the Grand Signor planned an invasion in the coming year. It would be to take la Goletta at Tunis, the greatest and last Christian fortress on the Barbary Coast. Or the descent would be on Europe itself through Italy. If so, it would bring the end of Christendom.

Spring came and we suddenly found ourselves part of that invasion. One day in June, *Kapudan* Piyale Pasha walked out of his lodging on the Arsenal grounds and a great commotion ensued. Before we knew it, Pietru and I were chained naked to a galley bench of Piyale' s own *kadirga* with enough Turkish *buenas boyas* and conscripts about us to prevent a revolt.

"*Ala! Ala!*" the *comito* cried and we heaved, praying that we would survive the expedition, which was now said to be la Goletta. We rowed for weeks, through the Marmara, down the Aegean, toward the Morea. No words can convey the hell a galley slave endures, yet I concede, Your Majesty, that if there be circles of Hell, the screams of the slaves, the scars on my back and festering sores on my ass told me that Turkish galleys sat on a circle a *dito* more exalted than our own. The *gumiler* whipped us less often than the *comiti* and *aggozini* flogged Mahometan slaves, they cleaned the *kadirgalar* more often of our stool and the slaves even received a small part of the spoils, as much as the soldiers. Nor did the soldiers distain from speaking to us; it seemed to make little difference to them that we were slaves or not.

Piyale was a wonder to behold. Pietru and I often watched him closely from our bench near the poop. With only thirty years to him he was lithe, resplendent in robes and jewels. To my eyes he hardly appeared a Turk. People said Piyale was born a Christian and had been found orphaned near a ploughshare during His Majesty's siege of Belgrade. Seeing that he was suitable for the Seraglio, the troops presented him as a gift to Soliman and the boy soon rose to great heights, marrying one of the Sultan's granddaughters. The Admiral's reputation was formidable. Three years ago with Turgut he had laid waste much of the Italian coast, and on the day when he unexpectedly hoisted sail against us at Djerbé, I myself had witnessed his daring and resolve. I'd already begun to wonder at the number of Christians in the service of the Grand Signor. I could not yet grasp it.

We rowed on, not knowing our goal. The strange thing about this expedition was that only fifty ships had set sail, not enough for the feared invasion of Europe, mayhap not e'en for descent against la Goletta. To be sure, one day off Zante, a *fregata* overtook the fleet and Piyale abruptly ordered the armada to return to Constantinople. With a puzzled glance at me Ix-Xabaw shrugged. "Eh, it's better than rowing to Tunis."

I decided to learn to what was transpiring. During our next rest, after I had gulped down my ration of water and *peksimet*, I called out to the janissary who was shoving his way by us on the *corsia*. "*Hey! Nichun biz dolasip turuyoruz?*"

At first he only glared at me. Dark, tall as I, he wore his battle dress and smoothed his dark, heathen moustaches, thicker than I had ever seen on a face, and which fair trailed off the end of his chin. As he cast his hideous visage at me, I had the strange sense I had seen this janissary before, long ago.

"What is it to you, cur?" he said without stopping. "You'll row as you're told."

"Say," I ventured. "Were you on Sinan's galley at Tripoli nine years ago?"

That one halted his advance and peered at me with curiosity. "*Evet*, I was. Were you there?"

"Aye, on the Ambassador's *fregata*. You walked past me."

"And now you are a slave."

"*Mundança de Fortuna*," I answered.

The janissary laughed. "No change. Always the same. We sent you Spanish dogs yelping back to your kennel. No one opposes us now. We'll make the entire world our dominion and you Christians will all be our slaves!"

The arrogance of the janissaries never ceased to astound me. They shave their beards down to these barbaric moustaches in order to appear more fearsome to the enemy. They shave everything away on their crowns, too, but for a lock, declaring that should the enemy overcome them, they wanted something wherewith their heads could be carried. Yet I wondered whence this boasting. "You haven't told me why we are turning."

His eyes could hardly conceal his real surprise. "*Isminiz nedir, it?*" he said.

"Francisco. What is yours?"

"Yakhshi ," he replied, amused.

At the start of the drum he moved on, but the next day when he passed I said to him again, "You have still not told me why we've turned about."

"Do you think I know everything, dog? Bayezid, the Lawgiver's son, is held by the Shah of Persia and Soliman can't convince this baby Shah to release him. It looks like war. The old man can't trust his own son, that *sharosh* Selim, and so troops are now called back. You may be marching into Persia behind my ass."

So, I reflected, that affair with Bayezid, into which we had been so dangerously drawn not a year ago, dragged on and, it seemed, had saved Europe. Christendom would kneel with thanks for the barbaric custom of brother killing brother among the Turks.

By the time we put into Constantinople a few weeks later, talk of war with Persia had died away. Negotiations with the Shah over Bayezid went on. The galley slaves faced work on the mosque again. Two mornings after our return, as we were being marched out of the bagno, one of the janissaries waved me over to help him with three drunkards they'd just found lying outside the gate. Foreigners. They'd been going at it too hard in the nearby Galata taverns, doubtlessly fearing the disappearance of wine.

"Who are they?" the janissary asked.

"*Shu iki adam Ingiliz galiba*," I said. Then I looked at the third one in the dim light of sunrise. He was a Moor with about fifty years. As the janissaries roused him, I reached back in time. There was no doubt in my mind. Here before me lay Abdallah al-Waryagli. God had finally placed him in my hands. "*Dikkat!*" I cautioned the janissaries. "He is a *chavush*."

We got the emissary to his feet, but some time passed before he came to his wits. With dull eyes he peered at me.

"*¿Usted no tiene ni idea de quién soy yo, verdad?*" I said to him. He continued to stare at me as through a haze. "When I last had eyes on you, you were on a boat trying to escape Malta and I was doing my best to put an arquebus ball into your chest. And I would have, had not the Lord sent a miracle to save you."

Suddenly recognizing me, Abdallah bolted on wobbly legs in the direction of the town gates. I laughed. "You have nothing to fear. As you see—" I held up my arms.

Abdallah-al-Waryagli walked back and regarded me from head to toe. "You are Francisco, yes. Of course. I am, to say the least, surprised to find you in Pera."

"As I am surprised to find a devout Mahometan drunk beside the bagno."

"It was a ... misunderstanding," said the Moor with more than slight embarrassment. "These Englishmen ... Why are you ... ?"

"As you see, our positions have been somewhat reversed."

"Somewhat." He peered at me again, the fog slowly lifting from him, as I explained that I had been among those captured at Djerbé. "You once saved my life," said Abdallah, "if not twice, and I swore that mine was yours."

"I tried to kill you once."

"For good reason. Now you save me again from a certain ... inconvenience. This has been written in the Book of Destiny." Then and there Abdallah turned to the janissaries. "I will buy this slave from the Porte. Whom do I see?" Again he addressed me. "You will buy yourself from me by securing a ransom or working it off. What can you do?"

"I can cast guns."

He cocked his head curiously. Later that day al-Waryagli, thro' means I did not comprehend, spoke to the proper *zindanchi* and the transaction was completed. I moved from the bagno to the emissary's house on the hill behind Galata. The next morning I would begin work again at the Imperial Gun Foundry.

Fifty-Seven

Dawn next the morning gun sounded from Tophane and one of al-Waryagli's servants escorted me the short distance thither from the *chavush*'s house. Near here, on a dark night a year ago, our company had drowned the Armenian. Passing through the field of captured pieces the Turk and I entered the Imperial Gun Foundry. Lorenzo's surprise at seeing me was no less than mine at seeing him.

"By God, what are you doing here!" the grime-covered foreman exclaimed in Venetian.

I pointed to my ankles. "You mayhap have heard of what last year transpired on Djerbé ... My master will permit me to work here if you will."

Lorenzo readily agreed. To my question where he had been all these months he made no answer. At that moment a procession of Pashas entered the casting shed, followed by soldiers shepherding along twenty or thirty sheep. With this noisy flock baaing about our legs, the foreman motioned for me to bow. I followed his example, crossing my hands on my chest and bending toward the Viziers and the Sheik, who stood before us in their robes of high office. "We are casting a great gun this day," Lorenzo said.

He meant I would not be allowed to the casting pit for fear of the Evil Eye. But Lorenzo himself followed the sheep into the next shed. Amidst this crowd was also Yakhshi from Piyale's *kadirga*. I spent the day showing the novices how to bake a new furnace. Tho' I couldn't be present for the gun casting, I knew well enough what was taking place around the pit. The furnaces would have been going since yesterday to produce sufficient heat. The workers would be stripped to sandals, thick leather sleeves to protect their arms and a cap pulled over their face with only holes for the eyes.

As Lorenzo and his men threw quintals of copper and tin into the furnace bowls, the Sheik and Viziers were chanting over and over again, "There is no power and strength save in Allah." In the name of the True Faith, they tossed some coins into the molten sea, while some of the men stirred the melt to be certain nothing solid remained. Now the time keeper gave the signal to open the gates and the glowing bronze began coursing from the furnaces down the channels into the mouth of the gun below. At the same moment the priests slit the throats of all the sheep and cupped the blood in their hands, adding it to the rivers of molten bronze. For a full glass the pouring continued with a more exacting care than needed for a bell. Everyone watched with stilled breaths, but the great mould held and the Sheik lifted his arms and offered prayers of thanksgiving to Allah.

Late in the day Lorenzo appeared from the casting shed carrying proudly a rich new robe of honor. "How is it," I put it to him as he approached, "that you, a Venetian, are allowed to participate in the casting?"

Lorenzo gazed at me with a smoldering eye.

"You've turned Turk!" I exclaimed with sudden understanding.

"As you will," he growled darkly, put on a turban now that he was away from the pit, and departed with the others for a celebratory feast.

Yakhshi the janissary also passed by then in full dress, instantly recognizing me. "Francisco the cur," he laughed in that swaggering way of his, "what are you doing here?"

I answered, as he addressed me, in Turkish, as I wiped the sweat from my brow: "Making guns for the Infidel."

Full of haughtiness but amused natheless, he regarded me as we stood under those beams against the cooing of roosting birds. "So you do more than row. Can you shoot guns?"

"Cannon or arquebus, yes. Better than a janissary, I'd wager."

Arms bowbent, Yakhshi laughed again. "What would you wager, pork-eater?"

I needed only a heartbeat: "An arquebus against my ransom."

"*Bitti*. I must go into the country. Find me at the Arsenal the morning after the full moon."

That evening the servant brought me back to Abdallah-al-Waryagli's home. His *konak*, his town house, stood on the hill behind Galata, surrounded by a garden and a wall, with its own cistern for water. The house, stone on the bottom and wood on the top, with windows woven of wood and decorated with colored glass, was spacious enough that the *chavush* had given me a room with another slave downstairs. Upstairs, carved wooden screens closed off the women's quarters, where his wife and youngest daughter stayed.

The Moor required nothing, other than I repay the large sum he had spent to buy me, either by putting my name to a *mukatab* to work it off or by securing a ransom. When I returned from the Foundry he bade me sit with him on the floor at a round copper table, ordered his wife to bring coffee and said, "You will want to begin writing letters for your ransom. Believe me when I say these things are not carried by a swift wind. Do you know someone who might pay for you?" I hesitated long, pondered, nodded. "Good, we will see."

"Should I attempt to escape?"

"You may judge the risk. You yet wear the *kadina* on your leg and are easily identified as a slave. With Allah as my witness, if I catch you in the attempt, I will have you beheaded ... The janissaries certainly will. To reduce any ambitions I have pointed you out to them and for the present you will be escorted to the Foundry. Have you been treated well after Djerbé?"

I stared at him with a ferocious incredulity. "God knows there is no such thing as a fine prison. You have been able to judge that for yourself. We were deprived of food to the edge of starvation. Were it not for the good Christians of Galata, I'd be dead. Many of my comrades are. We slept in chains and the guards beat us at their pleasure for the first months." I paused, tasting the coffee Abdallah's wife Fatma had brought. "The galley is hard, but we are harder."

"You can make your life much easier here, Francisco," he said.

"How is that?"

"Profess to the True Faith."

In younger years, I would have spit up the coffee in my mouth. Now I answered with a sterner countenance, "I am professed to the True Faith."

At this the dark *chavush* laughed merrily. "You say so! Was God ever married to beget a son?"

"What do you mean? Do you deny Christ is the Son of God?"

"Any man whose head is filled with sense denies it. Christ was a great prophet, yes, but to call him the son of God is the most errant blasphemy and you Christians will burn in everlasting hell for believing it." He paused. "I shall not dispute with you, Francisco. You are blessed to have been taken captive to the greatest city in the world. Now you see with your own eyes that when I spoke of its splendors years ago I spoke the truth. Wonders stand everywhere about you. Refugees from the cruelties of Christendom stream here and make their fortunes. All you must do is profess—"

"—and?"

"You will be free. Pronounce the *shahada*, 'There is but one God and Mohammed is his Prophet'."

"Nothing more?"

The emissary took another sip of coffee. "You must believe it. Then your salvation is at hand. Otherwise there is no hope for you, *kafir*, in this world or the next."

I did not entirely grasp Abdallah's meaning; mayhap did not wish to.

"Open your eyes, Francisco," he went on with a wave of his arm, taking on a new tone. "Soliman, Prince of the Faithful, rules the vastest empire on earth. The greatest *gazi*, he will take the Holy War to the West, and Christendom shall topple before him like the rotten house that it is."

Abdallah-al-Waryagli's eyes fairly glowed as he made this speech. I could not recall from times of old having seen him so fired. Surely the triumph at Djerbé and the recent wars between Christian princes had made our enemy bold and insufferable. Perceiving this, I resolved that I should ne'er submit, never turn. Yet in the moment of this my resolve, I saw that much of what the *chavush* said was true. I had fled Spain with base lies at my back, that I was eighth-part Morisco. This city, this empire, would embrace such a man with open arms. The fingers of temptation beckoned. I could not but recollect Balthazar's remark about Villegaignon and Venice, that perhaps their ambiguous faith was that of the future.

Natheless, a great shudder passed through me as my soul recoiled in horror at the Moor's proposition. I gave no answer and instead asked about a matter that had been unanswered for nearly a decade. "Tell me, was it indeed you who sent ciphered messages to warn the Turks about the expedition to Zuara those years ago?"

"Of course," Abdallah replied easily, "tho' I never determined exactly whether my messages reached Aga Morat in good time. I believe they did and decided the battle."

"And the letters we found in the cave. Yours as well?"

"I am uncertain," he said with twinkling eyes. "Several slaves put their captivity to good use and spied on the knights." My owner thought that to speak further of it served no purpose. "I give you now paper and ink. Do not, however, attempt to write in ciphers."

That night, by the light of a small oil lamp, I penned my first ransom letters, to Balthazar, knowing not whether he was alive. Swallowing what morsels of pride remained to me, I wrote also to Isabella, not knowing whether she would remember me or care. I made two copies of that pitiful note, sending one to no more exact address than Firenze and the other via her mother Lady Emilia on Malta. I prayed for my deliverance and went to sleep on a mat.

After a week I got paid at the Foundry and, slipping out of Abdallah's house at night, went over to the bagno. There was a risk in this, for the guards might easily seize me again by mistake. Luck was with me. Around the entrance stood some janissaries listening to a wandering beggar who had pleaded alms for a story. Laughing at the tale being told, the jailer paid little attention when I gave him half an *akche*, and he let me in. I found Pietru sitting against a wall feeding his animals. "Take these," I said, handing him all the coins in my bag. "It will be easier for you—but do not spend it on *afione* or infidel talismans."

Smiling, he accepted the money. His countenance, tho', quickly betrayed a deep despair. Pietru had no one to turn to for a ransom and saw nothing in the future but oars, lashes and stones.

"Listen to me, Xabaw," I said, "I have begun working in the Foundry. I will bring you money each week and, with time, I will find you work there."

He put little stake in it. "The only hope for me, Francisco," he said, "is to escape or become a renegado." He hesitated and glanced away. "Would it be so terrible to turn Turk? On Malta we call God Alla. It should be easy for me."

"Xabaw, do not think of it, on peril of your immortal soul. I am writing letters for our ransom. I will never abandon you and you must never abandon hope. Someday this nightmare will end, I swear to you." Crossing myself, I added, "Do not forget you wife who endures no less. Never forget our vow."

We clasped each other's arms, renewing our pledge, and I departed.

Fifty-Eight

"God alone knows the new moon," they say here, believing it the utmost blasphemy to ask into matters of the heavens, and most don't believe in the next moon until they see it with their own eyes. I suppose they have an easier time believing the full moon.

On the morning after the full moon, I walked without escort to the Arsenal, where I found Yakhshi the janissary and his comrades standing around a brass pot near the Admiral's quarters with little to occupy them. Catching sight of me, he grinned ferociously beneath those big, drooping moustaches, at once fetched two arquebuses from a store room and waved me after him. With long strides we walked inland, past a great field where bowmen were practicing, and toward a nearby woods. His mates, curious as to what was about, followed. I had yet to put to rights the comical effect of the spoons the janissaries wore attached to their headdresses with their reputation. They called their colonels "soup makers" and the army of janissaries the "hearth," but it would never have entered my head to name these surly, tattooed ruffians "cooks."

Yakhshi halted at the edge of the wood with this unruly band around us and I smelled trouble. "So, pork-eater," he said, pointing to a tree thirty paces off, "you think you can shoot." Yakhshi handed me one of the guns. Two or three palms longer than any arquebus I'd fought with, the gun was clumsy to load and he finished first; we lit the matches. The other soldiers began placing bets.

Yakhshi 's first shot hit the target, mine missed. "I am not accustomed to such long guns," I protested. The kick was fearsome.

We loaded and shot again, both hitting the target. On the third shot, I missed; he hit. We shot twice more. I hit once, missed once, as did he. One of the janissaries, alarmed that he was losing his wager, struck me in the shoulder with his stick, and I quickly perceived that the business had turned serious.

"Do you yield, Francisco dog snout?" Yakhshi said as the smoke cleared.

"*Hayir.*"

We traded weapons and continued. With each *thhhppp* of the guns, the men around heaped on me more and more abuse. I attempted to cool my blood and think only of the task, but after ten shots, I yielded. At once all the janissaries began shouting, attempting to shame the unbeliever into becoming a Mahometan. This was too much and when the same fellow raised his stick again, I grabbed his arm and kicked him in the stomach. An all-out brawl erupted, fists and curses flying in every direction. The mêlée ended badly for me, with my arms pinned to the ground and that same whore lashing me on the stomach with his stick. I refused to cry out. Had he kept at it, the swine would have burst my innards and I would have died in my silence, but Yakhshi, desiring of obtaining his prize, soon put an end to it. As the others stomped off, their headdresses in disarray, the janissary looked down at me and said, "You owe me a gun, *kafir.*"

"It will be finer than this one," I answered, getting to my feet and attempting to recover a small esteem as we walked back to the Arsenal.

If I was bruised and disgruntled, Yakhshi revealed himself in high spirits. "I have defeated you and the Sultan will whip the breeches off your Philip. We already have! Hah! What a filthy mess you infidels made at Djerbé! By my forelock, the House of War cannot stand against us."

By now, a blind man could see that after Gelves the blustering arrogance flaunted by Abdallah and these janissaries held the entire empire in thrall. "Where did you learn to shoot so well?" I asked, attempting to put the brawl behind me.

The big man only continued his mockery. "How stupid can you be, *kafir*? I am a slave of the Sultan, a *yenicheri*."

He spoke those words, "slave to the Sultan," with a pride that escaped me, tho' by now I had heard the declaration often enough. "You were of the ... *dev* ... ?"

"The *devshirme*, of course! All janissaries are collected."

As I stood beside him, Yakhshi relived that day when he was a boy of fourteen, when an officer of the janissaries leading some royal horsemen swept into his village in Natolia and took him from his parents. His mother was running around like a lost hen, desperately trying to hide him—anywhere. She let him down a well, but the soldiers, laughing, well knew this ruse and pulled him up soaking wet. "I see the tears in her eyes. She implored them to leave me. My father tried to calm her."

"They snatched you from your mother's very arms!"

"*Evet*," Yakhshi laughed, "it is the way."

Never in my wildest dreams would I have thought to hear of the Collection from a janissary himself. Neither could I imagine a more barbaric means of recruiting soldiers; the reason for it escaped me. "Why you?"

"Because I was suitable, fool."

Yakhshi did not, it seemed, regard his impressment into the janissaries as in any way unusual and I needed to ask again: why him, why not others?

"It is *chilik*," he replied, finally understanding what I was at, "one from forty families. Now I am a *Boluk-bashi* and I have collected boys myself. The laws do not allow the Sultan to take sons of important men or priests or of good descent. We do not to take only sons because their fathers would lose them for farm work. Orphans are undisciplined and become thieves. Boys who squint are stubborn and perverse. Boys that are too short are trouble makers and boys that are too tall are stupid. The Sultan does not take fresh-faced and beardless youths, for the enemy laughs at them."

"Who does that leave?" I asked, puzzled.

"The *yenicheriler*."

I shook my head, seeing we did not comprehend each other. "Do you long for your family?" I asked, rather than pursue it. "Do you ever visit your mother and father?"

Hereat Yakhshi, arms bowbent, stared at me in outright disbelief and to my complete astonishment burst into a rage. "How dare you, *kopek!*" he shouted. "They are infidels my enemies! My father is the Sultan. I have no mother. For every *yenicheri* it is the same."

Still something eluded me in this soldier's speech. Thinking my Turkish was too poor, I decided to ask no more about his parents. "They circumcised you?" I did ask, "at fourteen years?"

"Of course," he answered with pride, "you, *kafir*, would not be able to bear it." Humor restored, he went on to say that after the circumcision, the best-looking boys were schooled in the palace and often became high officials. The strongest worked in the gardens and become *bostanciler*, which also led to great privilege.

"I was sold for one gold piece to a Turkish farmer. This is the usual. I worked for him for seven years, while I learned to shoot and to fight with a sword. Then I returned to Istanbul to work at the Arsenal and joined the *yenicheriler*." Others worked in the dockyards, or in the Foundry as apprentices or patrolled the streets. "Always we strengthen and practice."

He halted at the field where the archers were shooting, called one of them over and handed me the bow. It was not fashioned from a single piece of wood, but of the sinews and horns of oxen held together with glue and tow. I am by no means a weak man, and after rowing a galley for months would have challenged a bull, but may I renounce my mother if it is not true, that string was nigh impossible to draw, so much stronger than our own bows was it.

"By the gashes in my face!" I let out the oath.

"Hah!" the janissary laughed. "Pork-eating *kafir*."

"Of what use is a bow in our day and age?" I rejoined, once more trying to salvage my pride. I'd all but forgotten the argument on this account that had taken place nine years ago on my voyage to Africa.

The bowman walked to about ten paces from a wooden target in the form of a door, and within the time it would take me to get off a single shot with an arquebus, he put six arrows into that target, arrayed in a neat circle around the center white, which was no larger than a coin.

Other archers engaged themselves in a distance contest. They sat crosslegged in absolute silence, awaiting their turn. When an contestant's turn came, he bowed to the ground, as if praying, took a shorter bow than the first archer had used and launched his shaft. They marked the furthest shot with a rock, and I say it was three hundred paces—farther than any arquebus or crossbow could fire. The victor received a white handkerchief. We walked on, I pondering of what use an arquebus was in this day and age.

"These archers have practiced their art their entire lives," the janissary said, answering the question I hadn't voiced. "Targets are everywhere around the city." It was true, on each street and piazza you saw them. "But it is easier to teach a stupid man to use a gun. With bow or gun we will conquer you. Then we will conquer the Newfound World."

"You know of the Newfound World?"

"I have heard of it, but I do not know where it is."

"Sail toward the setting sun," I said, by now having had my fill of this insufferable Yakhshi, "until you drop off the edge of the earth."

"If we drop of the edge of the earth, how will we reach it?"

Thank God further conversation was spared me, for at that moment the same pig who had beaten me ran up to us from the direction of the Arsenal. He raised his stick at me again, but Yakhshi grabbed his arm. "He bore the strokes in silence, like one of us." Then, in the greatest agitation, the other spoke directly to his chief, who responded in like disquiet. Within moments many men had gathered around in a circle, all waving and shouting with such animation that I could not follow the words.

"What has happened?" I finally asked Yakhshi.

He answered with a grave face. "Bayezid, Soliman's son, has been executed in Persia, strangled. The Sultan's will has prevailed."

"Was not Bayezid the superior son?"

"*Evet*, he was."

One of the other *yenicheriler* broke in shouting, "We must tip the pot against the Sultan for this act." Others nodded their assent and the shouting increased.

The reason in this escaped me. Not many moments ago Yakhshi had told me the Sultan was their father.

"A father does not rule his sons," the *Boluk-bashi* replied to his men. "But the time for revolt has passed. When Mustapha was strangled, we had our chance and lost it. Now we are stuck with the Sot." Almost as if the thought entered his head too late, he shrugged: "Remember, we are getting paid these days."

This time I did take my leave of the turbulent group and speedily hied to the casting sheds where I found Lorenzo. Taking one glance at my bruises he said, "What the Devil happened to you?" and I replied by asking whether he had heard the news.

"Yes," he said, "it is spreading like wildfire. Soliman sent the Shah Tahmasp gifts enough that he allowed Bayezid to be executed." But the foreman was not disturbed that the janissaries spoke of overturning the pot. He only took up a breech mould he was making and nodded without looking at me. "It has happened before. These brutes stand outside the law. They think nothing of demanding tooth rent for the wear their damned grinders get while chewing, and they have more than once decided which son would succeed his father." He glanced at me quickly, which was all he ever did since admitting he had become a renegado. "They have nothing to gain by a rebellion now. Every son but Selim is dead and the dynasty must continue."

I told him that one of the dogs had cursed his own mother, but Lorenzo only shook his head derisively and went back to his work. "He named her an infidel," I pressed.

Now he did stare frankly at me as if I were myself a wandering idiot. "Blockhead, don't you understand—every janissary is taken from a Christian family."

At this thrust to my ignorance I must have stood there gaping. The Turks' most ferocious warriors—Christian slaves! Not only the janissaries, Lorenzo said, again averting his eyes, but every government official, from the Grand Vizier to the lowest agha of the janissaries. Only priests and judges were Turks. The thought was so enormous that I could scarce absorb the import.

"Must it be spelled out for you?" he mocked, glancing at me for a final time. "The janissaries are raised without kin. They have no loyalties, save one—to the Sultan."

That night Abdallah confirmed everything. "You see how wise the policy is. Unlike your undisciplined rabble, these men do not fight for money, for booty; they fight only for the Prince of the Faithful, the Padishah of the World. More, the cavalry, the *spahiler*, hold their *timarlar* at the pleasure of the Sultan. They fight, he awards them land. Each soldier may say with pride he is a slave of Soliman. This, Francisco, is the first true army since the time of the ancients. The first that has something to fight for. Death? What can death mean to our warriors, when each man knows that when he dies in battle he will enter the Gardens of Paradise, where under the shade of date leaves he will lie in the arms of the divine *houriler*, where he will partake of the forbidden juice of the grape and where the climax of love will last a full ten thousand years? That is why we will conquer you, *kafir*."

I tried to imagine what Balthazar would have to say to all this, and failed. Yet after this roiling day I understood better why the Infidel had defeated us the Christians time and again. The Turk had created a great mechanism whose sole purpose was to make war. That night the streets were noisy with shouts that the janissaries had gone on a rampage, killing Jews and burning synagogues. I blew out my oil lamp, praying that the entire city would be reduced to cinders. It would not. I lay awake, certain now that Bayezid had been killed, Soliman would once more turn his eyes westward with his great machine, and I was convinced more than ever that I had fallen captive to a barbarian people.

Fifty-Nine

Fra Balthazar de Marans des Homes-Saint-Martin could hardly contain his surprise, not to say his incomprehension, when Grand Master de Valette asked him to greet Nicholas Durand *dict* Villegaignon at the docks and conduct him hither to de Valette's own house in the Borgo. Surprise yielded to outright disbelief when the Chevalier Villegaignon and no other stepped off a vessel at Galley Creek. Villegaignon remained handsome beyond compare, Balthazar discerned at once, tho' his blond hair had turned equally grey and his gait befitted an older man rather than a younger one. The Knight's sojourn in the Newfound World had apparently not diminished his taste for extravagant dress, and the gold-threaded doublet he wore shone like the sun in the evening light. Balthazar had foreseen a doublet; natheless it alarmed him. After bowing to the Grand Prior—if Durand remained Grand Prior—Balthazar handed him a mantle of the Religion he had carried down to the docks, draped over his arm.

"Fra Balthazar?" Villegaignon asked, recognizing the other and at the same time disclosing his perplexity.

"*Mettez-le, s'il uous plait, Frère,*" Balthazar replied. "Parisot has of late tightened his strictures in the Convent. Forgive me, but exaggerated habiliments are banned absolutely. Should you wish to avoid eternal damnation—in addition to six month's confinement in prison—I suggest you take it."

Villegaignon scoffed but acceded, having his servants mantle him directly on the embankment. The entourage began to move toward the gate. Ten years had passed since the two monks had laid eyes on one another and their acquaintanceship had never been close, making it all the more difficult for Balthazar to find a suitable porte into conversation. de Valette had worsened matters by failing to forewarn Balthazar of his invitation to Villegaignon. Overwhelmed by curiosity, Navarre considered whether to inquire into the reasons, but his thoughts were cut short after only five paces when several Knights emerged from the gates, marched briskly past them and boarded the galley.

"Halt!" Villegaignon shouted. Finding his command ignored, he strode up to the nearest of those Knights and spun him about. "By God, I ordered you to halt. I'll have you strung up, I swear. By whose authority do you board this vessel?"

"By the authority of His Holiness the Pope, the Grand Master and the Inquisitor, Bishop Cubelles."

The Chevalier Villegaignon stood frozen as rage and incredulity warred for his countenance. "I trust you have no Calvinist literature aboard," whispered Balthazar to the other urgently. "You perhaps have not heard, Monsieur, that this year past His Holiness has officially established the Inquisition on Malta. Domenico Cubelles has become Inquisitor of the Apostolic Church of Rome. Parisot himself orders all incoming vessels searched for the works of Luther and to burn them. Tell me quickly, or I fear the matter could turn grave."

"No, they will find no literature of Calvin aboard." Villegaignon turned with an expression of utmost severity to his companion. "Do you suspect me, Monsieur?"

The sun had all but set now, giving the limestone fortifications a brilliant golden sheen, much like the threads of Villegaignon's outlawed doublet. "Forgive me, the Monsignore has provided no details, but I had ... with the scandal throughout France—"

"Yes, I know." Villegaignon's expression remained hard. "You understood I had apostatized. My enemies intend everyone to believe it ... But as you see, Brother, Parisot has called me to the Convent."

That was no less a miracle than a girl emerging a virgin from the Court of France, reflected Balthazar. How could it have transpired?

As if peering into his companion's mind, Villegaignon offered, "The Grand Master has read my *Response aux Libelles d'Iniures* and is satisfied with my profession of faith."

Balthazar felt as after an insubstantial meal, unsatisfied, but Villegaignon had no better idea than he of the reason for the summons. "Parisot said only that the matter is of the highest importance. I trust we shall discover more presently. I do confess to some surprise at this Inquisition. de Valette can be no friend of Cubelles."

Balthazar sighed without cheer and recounted how Parisot had fought long against the imposition of the Holy Office in Malta, believing it inconceivable that the very Convent could be infected by the Lutheran plague. "Natheless, Parisot knows he has lost this battle, and the Inquisition is here to stay."

As soon as the small group passed through the gate, Villegaignon perceived that much had changed in the Borgo. Balthazar pointed out the new Auberge of Italy, which accommodated a fair hospital. Recent taverns and houses made their presence felt, but the greater change was less sensible. Yes, every brother in sight walked the streets wearing nothing more than his black habit and carrying only a rosary in his hand. Strange to see! This was not what disturbed Durand.

"Navarre, do my eyes deceive me, or are there few women and merchants on the streets?"

Balthazar chuckled. This sort of thing had happened before. "*Ouy*, Parisot has of late established a *Collachio*, where all the Knights must reside, as on Rhodes. He intends to cut them off from the ... *remainder* of the citizenry. I foresee that this measure will last a few more weeks."

"You always were a seer, Fra Balthazar."

Both Knights laughed.

Balthazar escorted Fra Nicolas to the Auberge de France, where his servants deposited his trunks, and thence to the Grand Master's new house, which stood not far from the Post of Castille on the landward end of Birgu. de Valette personally greeted his guest at the door and ushered the two Knights into the sitting room.

"It is a pleasure to see you after so many years, Nicolas," said de Valette, taking the other's hand. "I trust your journey proved not too arduous."

"Since Brésil I find I am no longer the youth I once was," Villegaignon replied with more truth than humor, "but my sovereign lord has summoned me and ... " he paused slightly, smiling, "it is good to see an old friend."

At the mention of Brésil a shadow passed furtively across both Knights' faces, vanishing as de Valette's servant brought drink. Parisot motioned for his guests to sit. The new house was larger, tho' hardly less austere than the old one, Balthazar noted, with the same image of the Virgin and rusted shackles above the dining room doorway. Parisot's lioness padded in, curled up at her master's feet and was soon purring quietly, but the parrot in the dining room squawked from time to time.

"You undoubtedly wish to learn the reason I called you here," the Grand Master said, taking up his goblet.

Villegaignon answered with a barely perceptible nod.

"As you know, the Council of Trento has this year begun its third session. The Order intends to send a delegation and I would like you, Nicolas, to lead it."

Balthazar nearly dropped his glass.

Villegaignon himself seemed stricken as by a bolt, and the skepticism writ on his countenance hadn't diminished when he finally replied: "You entrust me with such a mission, Parisot?"

"Do you not feel you are qualified, Nicolas?" A certain point on the Grand Master's words made itself felt as they hung in the air, but Durand did not answer directly, asking instead for clarification.

Parisot stood now, careful not to disturb his animal, and began his old habit of pacing. "I require a man with a golden tongue, one whose unquestioned nobility shall gain him access to the many cardinals and ambassadors gathered at Trento. You shall remind them, Nicolas, of our ancient Religion, its cult of divinity, hospitality and military service, which it has exercised now for five hundred years at great cost and anguish. At every occasion you shall narrate how our income has been prejudiced in Hungary, Bohemia and England by the Lutheran peste, which perverts men's souls to evil. You shall explain that the Religion is defending all Christianity against the power of the Turks and the Barbary corsairs, and that the cost of building the fortifications on this island has been *grandissima*."

Hereon, the Grand Master paused in his words, even as he continued to pace. "Messeri, the Grand Turk is preparing a final descent upon Christendom, and after God saw fit to destroy the armada we had sent against him at Djerbé, the Religion now stands alone in protecting all Christians. Our reports from Constantinople—accursed origin of all plagues—become more frequent and we believe the invasion will fall on this island, the Convent. We have always had at heart our sworn duty to protect Christendom, but we must raise more money for the defense. You, Nicolas, shall impress upon the delegates at Trento that, with the confiscation of our commanderies in England by the apostate Henry, income has fallen, and tho' Queen Mary through the good recollections of our Order restored our rightful belongings, they have of late been confiscated once more by the abominable woman who now holds the reins of government in that country. If those slothful ambassadors persist in not understanding our need for ready money to confront the enemy, you must tell them that the cost of all the things necessary for living on this island has of late doubled."

Abruptly the Grand Master halted his march before the fireplace and fell silent, as if to his surprise he had run out of things to say. He sat down, stroking the head of his pet and said, "Nicolas, are you prepared to undertake this task?"

"*Remis velisque*," replied Villegaignon quietly.

"Excellent!" exclaimed de Valette, rubbing his hands together. "Gentlemen, you will remain for dinner."

Here Balthazar rose and excused himself. "Eminenza, you and Fra Nicolas have many seasons to discuss. Allow me to accept the invitation on another occasion." With that he bowed and turned to the door.

"Fra Balthazar," said Villegaignon, "please join me for falconing tomorrow at nones."

"With pleasure," replied Balthazar and took his leave.

The following morning at the appointed hour, Balthazar and Villegaignon left the auberge for de Valette's stables just outside the town walls. The Grand Master had offered the use of horses and one of his own prized falcons for their sport. As Balthazar threw a saddle over his mount, Villegaignon discerned a momentary grimace shoot across the other's face. "You are in pain, Monsieur?"

Balthazar dismissed it with a wave. "I came close to giving it up on Djerbé two summers ago, but God willed a miraculous recovery. On occasion I do feel a constriction in my side, that is all." He smiled. "*Vulneratus non victus*."

"*Vincit qui patitur*," Villegaignon answered with some appreciation, saddling his own horse, "but what a catastrophe Djerbé has turned out to be, Brother! Christendom's best men killed or captured. Scum alone remains to us. We were fortunate the Turk did not invade last year or this for, *rebus sic stantibus*, we would have seen the end of civilization. Why has there been no descent?"

Balthazar had no opportunity to reply, for as Villegaignon took the hooded falcon onto his glove from one of de Valette's servants and they prepared to ride off, Bishop Cubelles himself appeared at the stable door surrounded by four halberdiers. Cubelles had hardly changed in the decade since Balthazar had sat before the Tribunal. The dark face, all but hidden by the great and now grey beard, as of old seemed naught but to peer outward from the depths of Hell.

In the name of His Holiness the Pope, Cubelles ordered Villegaignon to follow him to the Bishop's Palace.

The falcon fluttered its wings and screeched; Glancing at Navarre, Villegaignon erupted in laughter, even as he stroked the head of the bird to calm it. "You jest, Eccellenza. I am here at the request of the Grand Master himself."

"Satan bows to neither rank nor office; nor does his implacable foe, the Holy Inquisition." Cubelles motioned for his men to prevent the exit of the two Knights and the bird screeched again.

"Stay as you are," counseled Balthazar, dismounting, "I shall summon the Monsignore at once." The halberdiers crossed their weapons. "Do you intend to question me again as well?" he said to Cubelles. When that one failed to reply, he pushed his way past the blades. A short while later he returned, running, with de Valette and his lioness by him.

"You dare!" roared the Grand Master to the Bishop and his guards. "Stand aside at once and allow our honored guest to pass."

The halberdiers hesitated, not perceiving the best course of action. Cubelles, tho', refused to yield. With a finger leveled at Villegaignon, he replied coldly, "Every cardinal and prince in Europe knows of this man's terrible apostasy, which will leave him burning in Hell for eternity. John Calvin himself has publicly—publicly, I say to you—declared the Chevalier Villegaignon to be an unspeakable atheist. No one shall stand in the way of the Holy Inquisition's intent to question him, be it the Monsignore himself."

Drawing himself up, Parisot answered with complete and utter scorn, "We see the Inquisitor now brings the words of the heretic Calvin as evidence against his subjects. Stand aside, creature of perversion! The entire world embraces the Religion's service to Christianity, and that its honor should be sullied with base suspicions and accusations is an affront to our protector the Lord Christ."

But the Grand Master's anger hardly eclipsed the Inquisitor's. "Lest Eminenza forget," Cubelles' rejoined, "His Holiness himself has declared to his everlasting sorrow that Luther's putrid corruption has insinuated itself into the blood of the very Order of St. John. No better example is this man standing before us." Again the Bishop lifted his finger. "That he is allowed to set foot in the sacred Convent is the unspeakable disgrace. Let him burn at the stake."

At that Durand paled sensibly, even as wrath shrouded his creased face, but Parisot abruptly changed his tone. "Fra Nicolas has been selected by us to travel to Trento and remind Cardinal Boromeo and His Holiness of the affection in which they hold the Religion. He shall speak to Pius of the great service you are performing in our name of ridding Malta of the Lutheran plague, and I am certain the Pontiff will look with favor upon you."

At that juncture Parisot's lioness growled significantly and the Bishop graciously stepped aside. Villegaignon, however, had lost all appetite for falconing, and whilst the Grand Master apologized for this small inconvenience, the Chevalier begged Balthazar to postpone their meeting until dinner.

After vespers had rung, Balthazar and Villegaignon met under the grimy stone arches of a tavern in the lay half of town. Without delay, Durand quaffed down a flagon. Balthazar chuckled. "Let me add my apologies for this morning's disturbance. Eminenza is in a difficult position. The truth he cannot face is that Lutheranism has indeed descended upon the island, particularly among the German and English Brethren. On the other hand, as he foresaw long ago, Knights and soldiers have used the Inquisition here to their own ends, ceaselessly denouncing each other to the Bishop just to be rid of enemies and gain wealth." Balthazar now also drained his cup. "But," he smiled, "let us speak no more of such troubles. You were asking me something this morning before the ... interruption."

Durand sullenly placed on the table before him several leaves of paper he had carried rolled up under his arm. Picking meat off the fowl the tavern keeper had set down, he only at length said, "I was asking why there has been no Turkish descent this year."

Balthazar shrugged, pouring two more glasses of wine and throwing a bone under the table for the dogs. "Three years ago I helped emplace a good man in Constantinople. We now receive more trustworthy reports than of yore. Last year the Grand Signor was distracted by the affair of Bayezid, who is since dispatched. What happened this season is hardly clear. The Turk was occupied with his wars in Hungary, but thro' the Hapsburg Ambassador Busbecq, Emperor Ferdinand and Soliman have just concluded a peace. The Grand Signor now receives tribute and, I fear, a free hand.

"Worse, Sicilia saw a terrible harvest and grain is in short supply here, everywhere. Parisot has rationed bread at the auberges, and he spoke truthfully when he said the cost of almost all things on the island has doubled. Turgut has also been prowling about for wheat. *Mort de Dieu!*" Balthazar suddenly exclaimed, "that damned corsair has the kingdom in a noose! The raids on the Spanish coast increase by the day and the terror is now so constant they say, 'The Eastern shores of Spain are the West Indies of the sea-wolves.'"

Hereon the Knight sighed and raised his cup in a salute. "We were pleased to receive one instance of good news. As part of the peace, Busbecq managed to secure Alvaro de Sande and Don Sancho de Levye's release and escorted them home. It took a mere two years." Villegaignon had not heard this report, a small mercy. "But," concluded Balthazar, regarding the other straight in the eye, "this is not at all why you desired to see me, Fra Nicolas."

Villegaignon nodded at his interlocutor, whose intelligence was far keener than he had of yore desired to admit. "What did you make of Parisot's performance yesterday?"

Some pigs wandering into the eatery distracted Balthazar for a long moment. "You and he, Sir, falconed together on this island thirty years ago," the Knight replied, ending his silence.

"Much has changed since. Speak freely, Monsieur."

Balthazar leaned back and ran his tongue slowly over his lips. "Very well. I believe you were as surprised as I was."

"He is deadly serious," nodded Villegaignon as he unrolled the papers before him; the Grand Master had put his instructions into writing: "'Fra Nicolas is to give advice *et procurar il bene et utile tanto della republica Christiana como per la nostra Religione ... Item: Accorendo idonea occasione narrarete la opportunità del sito di queste nostre Isole et quando è necessaria alla conservatione et difese di tutta la christiantà ... Item: narrarete che gran somma di denari spende ogni anno ...* '" Slowly the Chevalier raised his eyes. "The Council at Trento is discussing reforms that will change the face of the Catholic Church forever. You know this, I know this, Parisot knows this. In these instructions ... " Durand tossed the papers aside, " ... is not a single mention of the Church or of the Faith ... or of God."

"Perhaps this is why he asked you to go," said Balthazar levelly. "For there is no mention of God."

"Sir?" Villegaignon replied, half rising from his place.

"Pâce." Balthazar waved him down, perceiving a deep satisfaction that after all these years Fortune had at last availed him of an opportunity to match wits with the celebrated Villegaignon. "What do I make of the Monsignore's performance? I say that as you may have changed, Parisot has as well, to the extent a man changes. He no longer will bash a fool's head in out of mindless anger, but in certain respects his ruthlessness has deepened."

Villegaignon gazed at the reclining Knight severely. "Your tone *is* offensive, Monsieur," he said, "and your insinuations. I name Parisot the most devout Christian on earth."

"Let us then agree to call him devoutedly ruthless," Balthazar continued to smile. "We see it plainly in these papers. The Order requires great sums of money to fight the Turk. He stops at nothing to get it. We need spies in Constantinople; he puts them there. If the Maltese cause trouble, he hangs them. No, Parisot is ruthless, but hardly a fool. Should it further his aims, he is willing to compromise his faith by sending a compromised ambassador to Trento."

Listening to this speech, the creases on Villegaignon's aging face deepened, and without a word he rose once more, this time to depart.

"Monsieur," Balthazar said, seeing he had gone too far. "Accept my apologies. I do not intend to insult you, merely to understand you. In spite of your vanity, your mind is too keen not to realize that you are a compromised man."

Abruptly, Villegaignon sat down again and tore off a piece of meat from a bone. "I do not perceive whither this discourse, Fra Balthazar," he answered with somewhat lessened heat, "but I tell you plainly I never apostatized. We traveled to the Newfound World with Catholics and

Huguenots. As you might imagine—Can you picture the fiercest religious disputes in the Brésilian forest surrounded by crocodiles? That is the situation I found myself in. *In fine*, I was forced to forbid the Calvinist rite—"

"They say you executed insurgents."

"They say!" Villegaignon suddenly erupted with full malice. "Those children of the Devil whose throats are open sepulchres and whose tongues are laden with asp venom! What do such snakes know? After ten months of every sacrifice, those three renegade monks incited my men against me for no reason other than to harm our religion! For my troubles the Huguenots name me the Cain of America. The Catholics long ago decided I was a heretic, merely for sailing with the Huguenots."

Durand took a long drink while drumming his fingers loudly on the tabletop. When he'd calmed, Balthazar, having also taken a long drink, observed dispassionately, "With this you prove my point, Brother. You are a compromised man. If the Monsignore proposes to send you to Trento—"

"—it is as he said. He requires the highest nobility, my connections to the Queen Mother of France, such as they remain, my languages ... " Villegaignon was attempting to force composure, convince himself.. "Perhaps most of all he requires my friendship at a crucial moment."

"Very well. By your own words he does not require your faith. *Virtus post nummos.* That is all. As Parisot compromised himself this morning with the Bishop, he is ready to compromise himself with you. "

Villegaignon sat back now and regarded his strange interlocutor. "You do not entirely approve of Parisot, Fra Balthazar. Will you follow him?"

"Monsieur, let us be frank. Neither of us are children. Whatever you may think of Parisot, no man sees farther in the art of war. Unlike d'Homedes and other rabble, he learns from past mistakes. If he says a descent will fall on Malta, it will. He is my superior and I have taken a vow of obedience. Of course I shall follow him."

"You are a sly fox, Fra Balthazar," answered Villegaignon. "Let me pose my question so you cannot escape: Will you follow *his faith* willingly, against the Turk?"

Balthazar now laughed merrily. "You have at heart remained a lawyer all these years, Fra Nicolas. Let us walk." The two men left the tavern and soon mounted the ramparts overlooking Galley Creek. The night was clear and the stars were coming out, reflecting in the water. "For we the Knights what could be simpler than to stand firm, without doubt, against the Infidel? Yet, I tell you, in Constantinople I saw the greatest adversary. Soliman welcomes all who flee Christendom. There are no Inquisitions among the infidels—"

"Calvin, you may know," Villegaignon interrupted, "contends that the Grand Turk has been sent against Christians as a scourge for papal pride—"

"Luther said the spirit of the Antichrist was the Pope, and his flesh the Turk."

As the two men gazed below, watching inspectors rummage through the newly arrived ships, Durand turned abruptly to his companion. "Do you truly believe, Fra Balthazar, that God intends the Turk to convert the entire world?" Here, Villegaignon quickly cut off the other's speech. "Beware of compromising yourself, Brother," he said, half in jest.

Balthazar, tho', leaning against the wall, faced Durand anew. "You have not permitted me, Fra Nicolas, to answer your first question. In Constantinople I saw also an empire where printed books are outlawed, that lacks but all painting or statuary or music, where no one knows anything of the world beyond its borders. If nothing else, I would fight for those things."

"Not for faith?" Villegaignon pressed, returning to his first point.

"You and I are alike in many ways, Durand," Balthazar sighed as they walked on, "cursed by sailing to new worlds. I will say this. Whatever the outcome of the present struggle, whether or not these great fortifications hold, in the stream of things, Parisot, the Knights have already lost. The Grand Master does not comprehend that Luther has changed everything once and for all time."

"You, Fra Balthazar, hold with Luther?" Villegaignon asked with yet heightened intrigue at the second mention of the heretic's name.

Balthazar smiled. "Nay. But I discern with Luther the shackles of past ages have begun to loosen. For all I know without Luther there would have been no ... no—what is his name? that Polish monk with his outlandish ideas. Parisot fails to perceive that the Crusades are over and that he merely stands in the great wash of history, which does not course to his feet, but flows past all of us."

"You are a complicated man, Fra Balthazar."

"These are complicated times, Fra Nicolas."

Several days after their conversation, Villegaignon fell seriously ill and announced he would return to France without attending the Council of Trento. The Grand Master appointed another to replace his friend and asked Balthazar to accompany the delegates. Balthazar, for his part, requested that he instead be allowed to escort them as far as Firenze and travel on to Constantinople. The Grand Master, regarding Balthazar, said only he would consider it.

Sixty

For the second time in three years Balthazar entered the courtyard of Isabella Guasconi's mansion in Firenze. On this occasion he found her in the gardens playing croquet with friends and servants. As on that previous visit, joy lit up her face when she caught sight of the Knight and she ran to him with her hands outstretched, but today Balthazar wasted little breath in getting to the salt of the matter.

"Signora," he said, taking her aside, "a few months ago I received by some miracle a letter from Francisco de Barai. He says he has also written to you. Have you received word from him?"

Even before learning the contents of the letter a shadow crossed Isabella's face. "No, I have had nothing, Fra Balthazar."

"Two summers ago," the Knight explained, "we both fought at Gelves." The very name of that island was enough to cause Isabella to instantly regard him with horror. "As mayhap you know, I was wounded and carried safely to Malta by the galleys your guardian sent thither. Francisco stayed behind, trapped with the others." He thence handed her one of the pitiful missives I had written from Constantinople describing all that had happened since.

Isabella had not finished the letter before it fell from her hand and, clutching at the cross I had given her, she fairly collapsed into Balthazar's arms. The Knight called for aqua vita at once. When Isabella came to herself, she paced before Balthazar with hands clasped at her silver girdle and her long dress flowing behind her.

"What a great wrong I did him, those years ago, and now this is the bitter fruit of it. I had not the strength to resist that horrible Inquisitor, who threatened me with such dire consequences ... I thought to ... Par—" Her breath ceased; she cast at Balthazar a gaze of pure terror; of a sudden tears coursed to her eyes and she grasped for her handkerchief.

"Isabella," Balthazar said, taking her arm, "who can say which events, which decisions have led Francisco into the lap of the Infidel? Perhaps you did him a wrong, I know not, but I think it not this wrong that has led him to slavery in Constantinople. Rather blame King Philip, who abandoned our forces while they were in the most dire straits conceivable. In any case, Francisco seems to have passed from immediate danger, tho' his missive was written on a year ago—"

"A year!" Isabella cried. "So long to reach you?"

"The miracle is that it did not miscarry and found me when I last returned to Malta. Be of stout heart, Isabella, if he is working at the Foundry there, he will be well treated—"

"Well treated!" she exclaimed in disbelief and anger. "O Balthazar, every man I have known who has returned from slavery is hardened for life. Is it any wonder that they begin here to call cruel men *captivi*? I do not except my own Godfather, Parisot. *Oimè*, I pray thee, Balthazar, I would not see that of Francisco. When I last had eyes on him, he had already become all too hard."

With the croquet game going on behind them, the Knight lowered his head. "What is hard for a woman, I fear, is of little consequence to a man. Isabella, there is hope. Meseems of the three voyagers, Francisco is not the careless Palinurus, but more like Ulysses, who learns from his travels—"

"Not Plato," said Isabella, looking up at him with a returning equanimity, "who travels to learn?"

"I would not go so far," replied Balthazar and smiled ruefully.

Isabella picked up a stray ball that had rolled to her feet and tossed it back to the others. "Have you ever given him these thoughts?"

"I regret to say, no. Someday I shall. What will you tell him, Isabella?"

Hereat Isabella hesitated, her face darkening. "Ten years ago," she laughed somberly, "Francisco and I believed our destinies to be intertwined. We were children, Balthazar. Despite Parisot's will, I have contrived not to take vows of poverty, chastity and obedience." For an instant she paused, her old haughtiness returning as she glanced at the colonnaded atrium and the merry guests about her. "I make my way in Firenze with my pen and the right word to the right ear. I do not scorn my life ... Yet I see that to escape Malta is not so easy. My destiny and Francisco's were perhaps intertwined after all, tho' not in any way I would have foreseen."

"Isabella," said Balthazar, sensing again that same apartness he had perceived on his last visit, "I shall travel to Constantinople to negotiate a ransom—"

"I am coming with you," the young woman said. There was no hesitation this time.

But the Knight merely shook his head. "It is impossible, Signora. In the first place, I am presently en route to Trento to accompany the Order's delegates, and will not be at leave to depart until they are safely deposited. In the second place, the journey is dangerous—"

It was Isabella's turn to shake her head. "Fra Balthazar, your pleas fall on deaf ears. Dead husbands have their value and I will go with you or without you, and that is the end of the matter."

The arquebus I forfeited to the janissary proved to be of gold. I fashioned a trustworthy wheel-lock for him and adorned its stock with brass and ivory, ornamenting it with elaborate designs. So pleased was Yakhshi with his prize, which shot as far and as true as the best Turkish guns, that he bragged to all his comrades of it and within days I was besieged with orders for like weapons. Before long I had made enough money that I was able to move from Abdallah's house to rent a small room of my own.

There is wisdom in losing certain contests. From the day I had taken up work at the casting sheds I knew a fateful choice faced me. I might sign the paper Abdallah had offered, the *mukatab*, but at the pay of the Foundry I guessed I should spend ten years buying myself from him. In despair I continued to write Balthazar and Isabella, never receiving a reply. I did not know whether Balthazar was alive, whether the letters had miscarried, or whether those in whom I placed my hopes had abandoned me. The Knights, all knew, never ransomed their own; every slave fended for himself. The unknowing on every side was the worst prison of all, and from my ever-hardening deliberations one issue and one alone emerged: Pietru and I must escape.

Early on I decided we must secure safe passage on a boat out of Constantinople, but this design quickly revealed formidable obstacles. The tariff was far higher than the money I had thus earned, and Pietru still spent his nights chained in the bagno. I discerned no way to free him. Natheless, I resolved to devote all my labors and prayers to traveling along the road I had chosen.

Without great sums of money the rest was unimaginable and so I worked feverously at the casting sheds. I showed the Turkish masters how to make fire pots, clay vessels filled with unctuous liquors disposed to ignite easily. For some time I tried various combinations of powder, pig fat, aqua vita and the like to learn how to make the mixture stick to armor once it exploded. Finally I stumbled upon the ingredients that caused the resin to fasten onto steel like glue, and the barbarians were very happy when I imparted this secret to them. We demonstrated these *granadas*, these pomegranates as I thought to call them, for Piyale Pasha himself in a field near the casting sheds. So impressed was he by their quality that he awarded me a crimson silk robe.

It entered my head to cast a basilisk. I told the chiefs at the Foundry that I could make a gun no smaller than the monster that lay for all to see in the shed, and like it in two pieces, but I could make it lighter by a better use of brass and tin, and a more economical thickness. Lorenzo opposed my plan, saying that the gun would explode and that many smaller pieces could be cast for the same cost and labor. I was not to be deterred and descended on the Foundry chiefs daily, even begging Abdallah for his intercession. After many deliberations, which went as high as the Grand Vizier himself, Lorenzo told me with displeasure that I was to be allowed the attempt. Suddenly, confronted with the prospect, I gulped. Never had I cast a gun of such size; few men had and none, ever, of the Venetian Arsenale.

We spent from one full moon to the next and half of another making the moulds alone. Work on the demon was impeded by the fast of Ramazan, when the infidels are forbidden to eat from dawn to the time the stars come out again at night. As a result, no one has any strength for heavy work and little gets done. Natheless, in six weeks we managed to complete the moulds and the only thing left was the casting. I demanded of Lorenzo that I be present.

"You cannot," he said as we lowered the mould for the breech into one of the two huge pits we had dug, "for you are an infidel, and you have designed one of the greatest guns."

"And should not the designer of the greatest gun in the Empire be allowed to cast it himself?" I persisted.

Lorenzo refused to aid me, even as we built towers around the moulds and strengthened them with stone, rope and iron to make certain they would not crack under the force of the metal. Seeing my way blocked by this renegado, I sent a request to the Sarai through Abdallah. At length, because I had provided good service to the Foundry for well o'er a year, the new Grand Vizier, Ali Pasha, consulted with the astrologers and *ulemalar* and granted a dispensation that I should be allowed to direct the casting of my own piece. The furnaces were lit and the bellows worked ceaselessly for three days and nights until the bronze was as liquid as water—the fateful moment had arrived. Forty Sheiks and Viziers, not to say the Sheik-ul-Islam and Ali himself, arrived for the ceremony. Prayers went on all morning and seventy sheep were sacrificed during the pouring, which took a full hour and consumed well over three hundred quintals of ore, including four old cannon. Several more days passed before the metal had cooled enough for the forms to be cracked open, but when the breech and barrel of the basilisk finally emerged from their wombs and we cleaned them, everyone said this would be the finest gun they had ever set eyes on.

After we reamed the halves and screwed them together with capstan-spokes fitted into the sockets we'd moulded for this purpose, we tested the beast by loading it with a quintal and a half of gunpowder and hurling great stones of seven hundred *libbre* full across the Bosporus. When I touched a match to the breech, lightning flashed as from the heavens itself, followed instantly by a roar such as no man had ever heard, and the very earth quaked as were it rending itself asunder. The heat every explosion produced made the gun so hot that it needed cool for an hour; natheless the monster held and the Sheik christened it "destroyer of cities." At seeing my success, Lorenzo stomped off in red envy, but Yakhshi, who was also present with Abdallah, slapped me on the shoulder, saying the pork-eating cur could do tricks. Abdallah told me that the Grand Vizier wished to speak to me and we three walked over to the water's edge, where the Pasha awaited.

"You have done well," Ali Pasha said, ordering his slaves to bring me armfuls of silks and furs. "In days of old, many great basilisks were cast, but we have not seen such a large gun made here in my lifetime." I crossed my arms and bowed before him. "Were you not an infidel you could become chief of the Foundry."

"I am honored that you say so, *Hazretleriniz*."

"Why do you not embrace the True Faith? The heights to which you may rise will prove limitless. Who knows? One day you might be presented to the Sultan himself."

"I am content with my present position, *Hazretleriniz*," I answered, bowing again, deeply.

"I advise you to consider it," he said, mounting his horse. Then he added from the saddle, by way of afterthought, "You are aware the Porte has recently concluded a peace with the Bey Ferdinand?"

Somewhat puzzled by Ali Pasha's remark, I nodded.

"We made a good bargain. Fighting will cease and we shall receive tribute for the part of Hungary we allow the Bey to retain. It does mean your weapon will not travel to Hungary. It is very heavy, in any case." The Grand Vizier rode off.

When the galleys returned to Constantinople at the end of the season, I found Pietru at the bagno, alive. I regarded the man before me. He stood. He was filthy, lice crawled on what little hair he had left. His mouth lacked a few more teeth, further scars crossed his arms, another his face and sores festered everywhere on his skin. But he stood. We embraced. He stared at me, as if he could not recognize this stranger in his baggy trousers and loose jacket, looking as much like a Turk as a Christian. I led him by the arm to one of the chapels, far from prying ears.

"Xabaw," I whispered, "if we are ever to get home again, we must escape this city. I shall soon, I think, have earned the money to purchase passage for us on a boat, but it is all for naught unless we get you released from this bagno."

He regarded again my fine dress. "Can you buy me?" he asked without artifice.

"Nay," I shook my head, "only a Mahometan may purchase a slave."

We gazed for a long moment at each other. I said it then: "I will turn Turk and buy you. It is the only path out of here."

Strangely, at hearing my plan, Ix-Xabaw laughed with his rough voice. "Eh! Where is the sense in that, Cikku?" he said. "I told you: I'll become a renegado. Then they will release me. It will also save you money."

"Who will release you? You are a slave of the Porte." Pietru didn't know. "Let me think on't," I said, gave Ix-Xabaw a purse and left the bagno.

I sought out Abdallah-al-Waryagli and as night fell I found him at sup with his wife and children, who were examining on their lessons from the Quran. He invited me to join them and I sat down on the carpet beside the copper tray while the servant brought rice and Abdallah's beloved yoghoort. Fatma was full of the match between their daughter and the Chief of Hounds at the Sarai, but she quickly perceived I had weightier business on my mind and discreetly left us, saying she would attend the puppet theatre.

"So," Abdallah said, observing that I had become a renowned master at the Foundry. "What more could you wish for, Francisco?"

"My liberty," I answered.

"Ah," he said, scooping up the remaining rice with his hand, "after you have taken up the Faith, why don't you marry my daughter or perhaps the Chief Confectioner's daughter? She is very beautiful and the match would be quite advantageous to you." I regarded him with horror filling my eyes. "You should have signed the *mukatab* I offered," he went on pleasantly. "Because you have become so valuable, I must increase its amount and that of your ransom. You should fetch a high price, truly."

Hereon I discerned the game the devil was playing. "I will sign your bond," I said, sitting upright, thinking to fast correct my mistake and retain such protection as it might afford. Abdallah nodded, agreeing to draw up a *mukatab*. "And tell me," I now asked, "should I take up your faith, would you release me as you promised?"

"You," the Moor said, raising his right forefinger, "are like the student who stole the Talisman of Illumination from the Sheik, forgetting that possessing it would avail him nothing until his mind was opened to it." Abdallah gestured for his servant to bring coffee. "I have said that you must not only take up the Faith, but believe. Your task is thus to convince me that you believe. Who knows? Perhaps it will take years. Revelations, after all, are given only to the Prophet, and you are not the Prophet, *kul*."

We gazed at each other and brought the cups to our lips.

Sixty-One

The cardinals and bishops at the Council of Trento declared it improper that an ambassador representing a society of lay brethren should sit among them, and so the Order's delegation was refused admission. Wrangling went on for months. Finally Balthazar, despairing of any resolution, took his leave of Villegaignon's replacement Martino Royas, and returned to Firenze shortly before the New Year, 1563.

"Forgive me for the interminable delays, Signora," he said, kissing Isabella's hand as she greeted him at her door. "It is hardly a surprise that this Council has dragged on for years. Sisyphus had an easy time of it by comparison."

Isabella Guasconi wanted to know one thing only as she led him into the atrium, where a shaft of sunlight illuminated the well: Had he any further news from Francisco?

He had not, while in Trento. "Mayhap some word awaits at Malta."

"I did receive, *in fine*, a letter from him, written many months ago," she told Balthazar, fetching the dirty and worn missive from her bedroom. "His padrone there makes the conditions for his release ever more difficult and he despairs of getting free, but he is alive and in good health."

None of this surprised the Chevalier and he hardly glanced at the note. "Such negotiations depend entirely on the whim of the padrone and always involve much haggling. I will need to return to Malta for money—and a ship."

This suggestion far from pleased the padrona of the house. "Malta, Fra Balthazar? If Parisot should discover—"

Balthazar raised his hand. "Isabella, for you to undertake this voyage can serve no purpose and I advise against it, but you are a grown woman now."

Signora Guasconi regarded him with curiosity. "Do you think that makes a difference to Parisot?"

The seas were strangely quiet this season, and the journey to Malta without incident. Immediately upon arriving at the Convent, Balthazar sought out de Valette, whom he found as the Council adjourned for the day at the Grand Master's Palace atop Fort St. Angelo. In recent years an outside staircase and a balcony had been added to the old Castellan's quarters, as well as a nymphaeum with a garden about it, and so everyone now called the house a "palace," tho' it was not a *dito* more palatial than before. Parisot was sitting quietly on a stone bench beside his lioness, regarding with evident displeasure the nymph facing him. Kissing Eminenza's ring, Fra Balthazar reported how things stood at Trento—the Grand Master should not expect any money out of His Holiness soon—and he remarked on the puzzling lack of corsairs on the seas.

"It is puzzling," replied de Valette, getting to his feet. Balthazar regarded the habited monk, realizing with force that Parisot was far from a young man. His sixty-fifth year must be upon him now, his hair gone on his forehead and white elsewhere. But he yet moved with grace and strength, and his mind showed few signs of having dimmed.

"We have received word from Barelli," Parisot went on, turning from the nymph to Balthazar, "that there will again be no armada this year. Why? The Turks have Europe on its knees. Dragut's dogs have seized four thousand Christians from the Granadan coast. With the succour of those pirates, the Moriscos there will soon be in open revolt. Yet Soliman makes no descent. Each year he delays, Philip rebuilds more of his fleet."

"Truly, the Grand Signor has not seized the *kairos*," observed Balthazar.

"This great silence troubles me," de Valette went on as they moved toward the steps leading down to the fortress' main gate. "So soon after Djerbé, Europe is again lulled into carelessness ... and whosoever is deceived is unwise. Fra Balthazar, the danger is as real as it is immense. Our foe's appetite is insatiable and, as you know, he must now intend a descent upon Europe."

Balthazar nodded. Aye, he had said as much himself. "Such a design, tho', seems mad."

"*Ouy*," Parisot chuckled, "but as with all tyrants, he shall at length choke on a morsel he cannot digest. Natheless, I would know what Soliman's eunuchs and concubines are advising him today."

As they crossed the moat into Birgu, Balthazar, without a word of Isabella, reminded Parisot of his desire to travel to the Levant. He could meet with Barelli and determine more exactly the state of affairs.

"I was about to suggest it," answered Parisot. "Sail with Romegas when he returns."

Balthazar had not foreseen this eventuality and fully understood that it would prevent Isabella from accompanying him, which was after all not for the worse.

Moving away to prepare for his daily office of feeding the poor, de Valette added, "I intend for him from this time onward to be in charge of reconnoitering the Levant."

The very next morning, the guns atop St. Angelo sounded in salute, and Balthazar and Isabella found themselves among the curious crowds running down to the docks as de Valette's two personal galleys slid into Galley Creek.

Before long Commander Romegas himself stepped off the *S. Gabriele* in full battle garb with his monkey on his shoulder, leading two turbaned prisoners of noble rank. Following them, his men pushed several hundred Moors, Turks and negri off the two boats. As the people began to perceive the numbers, they filled the air with great cheers. The disembarking crew told eager ears that after a ferocious fight Romegas had seized a heavily armed galleon belonging to none other than Rais Sidi Mahomet Ugli. It had been laden with merchandise, but so damaged during the battle that after a glass it sank and Romegas had his hands full to save the men aboard, who were bound for Constantinople and Mecca. One of the two high-ranking prisoners was Rais Ugli and the other was the Governor of Cairo.

Leaving Isabella, Balthazar approached Romegas. Before he could get out a word, Romegas chortled, "Hah! We'll ransom that one for eighteen thousand *zecchini*. Not a bad haul! I only regret that Cocia-Cocia got away again. I was so close to him I could smell his ass. I kiss the cross before you, Balthazar—someday I'll have his heart on a plate." He put his crucifix to his lips.

Only then was Balthazar able to raise the matter of the Levant. Once Romegas understood, Balthazar returned darkly to Isabella. "You may be certain the Grand Signor will not be pleased when he hears of this capture," he said, then added: "But what to do about you, Milady, I confess not to know. Once, tho', I was on intimate terms with the poetess, Louise Labé, who would not have hesitated to don armor—"

"*Oimè*, Fra Balthazar," Isabella rejoined with equal annoyance and amusement, "you have spoken of her more than once. But if I have never made it clear to you, it is neither my habit nor desire to imitate that which I so little admire."

"Well then, Isabella," Balthazar looked on her as the crowd dispersed, "I remain at a loss. Romegas declares that Hell will freeze over before he allows you on his galley. *Moy foy,* 'twould be easier were you a captured slave."

Too true, Isabella conceded. "Tis unfortunate that the Order's sisters no longer maintain convents in the Levant," she said. "I might then join one of the hospices as a nun or a nursing sister. Natheless, Balthazar, I insist you get me to Constantinople, by any means."

As the sun fell, Isabella dined with her mother, Lady Emilia, in her old house. Tho' it had not been a year since they had last seen each other, Emilia seemed to have grown sensibly older; the crow's feet creasing her eyes had markedly deepened, if not from the passage of seasons, then with concern. She, like every Christian, worried over the Turkish threat, Dragut's continued depredations, over the harvest. She worried over the reasons behind her daughter's unexpected visit. Mostly she worried over Isabella's continued widowhood.

"Isabella," she said at the table, "it is high time you remarried. You are yet tolerably young and with your fortune, suitors are not wanting. I have letters from half of Italy asking for your hand."

In some concession Isabella lowered her eyes. "I know it," she answered. "Do not think me opposed to marriage, Mother. I long for children of my own, and yet ... Our poets sing of love, but in my heart a fear of it beats no less loudly than a yearning. Oh, words fail me in this."

"How strangely you talk," her mother responded. "You are past the age for love, in any case. We must pick a suitable husband. I suggest—"

"Mother, I beg you, cease! At this moment I cannot bear to listen." Isabella fully stopped her ears with her hands, pushed her plate from her and rose to her feet. "My fate is to be content to leave my poems behind me, as a man leaves his work." Abruptly she burst into tears.

Lady Emilia could in no way fathom her daughter's emotion, was indeed angered by it, and neither could she discern what to do about it. A helpless annoyance was about to erupt into a full-blown argument when one of the servants announced the Grand Master.

Seeing Parisot at the door, Isabella rushed to him, fairly burying herself in his chest and, tho' surprised at his goddaughter's tears no less than her presence, he warmly enfolded her in her arms, asking the reason for both. Isabella answered only that Balthazar had visited her in Florence and she availed herself of the opportunity to accompany him on to Malta. As for her tears, "Mother insists on marrying me off again. I find myself unable to accommodate her wishes at this time. Please understand."

de Valette added his voice to Emilia's. "Understand? What is there to understand? I also insist."

"Insist, insist!" Isabella erupted angrily, stamping her feet like a child. "What do you intend to do about it, Parisot? Hang me if I refuse?" Abruptly she halted, stepping back to arm's length and gazing straight into his face. "Forgive me, I had no cause to speak so rudely. I find few men worthy of consideration next to those I have long known."

With that, as Parisot stared impotently after her, Isabella returned to her old room and began to scribble furiously her confusion of love and armor:

Di là 'l disio, e di qua la paüra
Tanto m'affligon, che sceglier non posso
se verso il prode gir, o dargli'l dosso.
Folle! Perché cerco amor e calura
fra'l duro usbergo, e l'aspra freddura?

With his instructions to scout the Levant and to ferry Fra Balthazar at least as far as Crete, Romegas ordered his crew to hoist the galleys from the creek. They repaired the damage from the recent engagement, scraped and tallowed the hulls, provisioned the vessels. Parisot's four hundred galley slaves were marched out of the bagno and chained. When all was ready for the Commander's departure, the treasury prepared a strongbox for Barelli and it too was carried aboard—but now, as Balthazar had foreseen, transporting that heavy cargo proved infinitely easier than shipping another burden.

"With apologies, Signora," Balthazar said on the Birgu embankment as his servant took his armor aboard, "I am obliged to advise you to return to Firenze. Otherwise, that Greek round ship yonder shall sail for Crete in the next few days. If you should unwisely be aboard, we shall rendezvous in Candia at the Venetian church."

It seemed to Isabella that Balthazar pronounced these words with the casual air of someone who had lived by the sea and the sword, and with that halo of fatality she sometimes discerned about him. The Knight's proposal went further to anger than to please her, but she sensed he was no longer to be pressed on this matter. Discerning no other road, she acquiesced as he kissed her hand and boarded the *S. Gabriele.*

Sixty-Two

With trembling hands, Isabella bought passage on the round ship *Santa Sophia*, which, guarded by sixty arquebusiers and crossbowmen, set sail two days after Romegas had departed. Despite the sun and blue sky, Isabella knew in her bones that Balthazar had spoken truth: This journey served no purpose and everything that had taken place at the Convent portended only evil.

A week out of Malta she stood on the stern castle of this oddly built ship, bedecked with both square and lateen sails. The wind was light and the sea calm when five specks swiftly emerged out of the southern blue. As the specks turned into galleys, and as their canvases slowly unveiled the red crescents on them, the blood drained from the face of the crew member standing nearest Isabella and she knew at once that her premonitions had come true.

"It's Cocia-Cocia," the sailor breathed, slowly crossing himself.

"W ... who is that?" she managed to ask and grasped the crewman's arm before he fled.

The glance he shot at her was of one who had seen his own end. "Signora, this renegado has said that if he is to spend eternity in Hell, he wants to give Christians a taste of it while he lives on earth. Cocia-Cocia is the Executioner." The ghost shook away her arm and ran below.

Isabella watched helplessly while those corsairs under full sail and oar gained on the lumbering round ship. She'd been told countless times that to be taken by a mad corsair was a different fate altogether than to be captured by the Turks. She crossed herself, paralyzed by a dread she had not experienced since the *razzia*. The passage of time, she discerned, had not increased her bravery; to the contrary, it only made her more vividly aware that life hangs by a thread. At this moment she sensed an angelic presence, the passing of a dark wing across her face.

The ship turned under her as the *Sophia*'s Captain, Morelli, attempted to flee. But this only increased the ardor of the attackers and within moments the infidel galleys had closed on the round ship, the nearest intending to ram her. At that moment Morelli showed he was more than a simple merchant. With a deft stroke of the helm he turned the ship sharply starboard, evading the enemy's spur. The corsairs shaved so closely against the merchantman's broadside that all their oars went to splinters with a tremendous din of snapping timber and infidel curses all twined together.

"Irons!" Morelli shouted, and his men threw hooks onto the galley and pulled it close, even as he sent his arquebusiers and crossbowmen into the rigging. To the Captain's cries of "*Fogo!*" his men began giving it to the barbarians with bolt and ball, even as the corsairs desperately hurled themselves onto the deadly anchors that had shackled them.

No one was paying the slightest attention to the passengers. Isabella, for all her skill with language and horse, had never fired a gun, and could do naught but close her ears and pray as the *Sophia*'s batteries lit into Cocia-Cocia's remaining galleys, then rushing to aid the crippled vessel. For an hour Morelli put up a stout defense, himself hurling a keg of gunpowder onto the trapped galley's deck. With a terrific roar and flames it blew a hole into the center of the hull and the vessel quickly went down, carrying all those chained with it.

For a time all was quiet, until the four surviving Turkish galleys took up positions off the round ship's bow and stern. An instant later the *Sta. Sophia* took hits fore and aft. The ship shuddered, sending splinters high into the air. Isabella lost her footing and fell to the deck, hitting her head against a spar as she did, and nearly losing her senses. Another silence surrounded everything as she struggled to her feet. The corsairs were giving Morelli time to realize that further resistance was hopeless; then they signaled for his surrender.

The infidels boarded the ship, throwing the few dead overboard, tossing the wounded into the hold, and forcing the crew and male passengers to the galleys, where they were beaten and chained. Finding the holds filled mostly with Sicilian cloth and wheat, the barbarians groaned and cursed loudly, but the ship itself hadn't been too badly damaged and would fetch a price. In the midst of the commotion, Isabella thought to attend the wounded below, but one of the Turks blocked her from going down, and so she stood fixed on the poop deck, shoved every way and that.

At length the largest galley pulled alongside and its Commander boarded, one whose arms were scarred and tattooed such that not a fingernail of pure flesh was to be seen, one who wore a red scarf round his bald head rather than a turban, and who sported heavy moustaches instead of a beard. He approached Morelli and, speaking perfect Italian, complimented him on his defense. When he caught sight of Isabella, and stepped in the noblewoman's direction, Morelli interposed himself between her and the renegado. Cocia-Cocia's scimitar was out and the next instant the Captain's head was on the deck. The blood splattered over Isabella's face, she turned, held her stomach and retched. Cocia-Cocia laughed, forcefully turning her head toward him. She'd never seen such emptiness in a man's eyes. She managed to slap him, but such was her shock at this moment that she could only dimly comprehend the unspeakable evils to which these sodomites were about to subject her, and she was hardly aware when two galleys of the Knights of St. John appeared on the horizon with the sun behind them.

Balthazar stood by Romegas on the poop of the *S. Gabriele*, watching the enemy galleys take up position four abreast, starboard of the *Sta. Sophia*. "It is Cocia-Cocia," said Romegas, feeding his monkey a nut and fairly rubbing his hands together. "O ye spawn of Satan, this time ye shall not elude me. Have I not sworn, Balthazar, that someday I'd eat his balls for supper? Tonight will be the feast, my mouth is watering."

The numbers arrayed against him—four galleys and a seized merchantman—made not the slightest impression on the Commander. Natheless, Balthazar observed keenly, he did consider the situation—briefly. Romegas sensed at once that the wind had fallen; the *Sophia* was becalmed and could flee nowhere. Before a moment had passed his eyes lit up, and within another breath he was everywhere, ordering the sails struck, giving instructions to his *comito*, signaling to Gaspar la Motte, commander of the *Philippe Corona*, receiving a buckler from the hands of his servant. As the Abbé donned his own helmet for the engagement and took a simple broadsword from his man, the two galleys split off and proceeded until they were each near three hundred paces from the two outer galleys of the enemy. Balthazar stepped onto the *corsia* amid the hundred and fifty *gente di capo* aboard, steadying himself against another for the dash and ramming, but strangely, Romegas nodded to the *comito*, who in turn ordered the *ciurma* to begin rowing in a large circle.

Before Balthazar could discern what was taking place, Romegas had brought the forward pieces to bear on their target and an instant later the centerline gun roared, followed in quick succession by the *demi*-culverins and *sacres*. E'en as the *S. Gabriele* lurched under the recoil and smoked wafted over slaves and *gente* alike, the animals below began screeching and Romegas's monkey scampered into the Captain's cabin. But the gunners reloaded and on the next pass fired again, again striking their targets. Balthazar could hardly credit the distance; it was beyond the range of all but the best gunners with the best ordnance. The enemy attempted to return fire, but under this bombardment were having a time of it. When they finally got into position, their gunners were defeated by the range and almost all the balls fell harmlessly into the water.

"They should buy Venetian ordnance," Romegas laughed within earshot of Balthazar. "And hire Venetian gunners."

Cocia-Cocia aboard the *Sta. Sophia* had abandoned Isabella the moment he'd spied the galleys of the Knights and was bringing the merchantman's guns to bear. But his men didn't know the location of the powder stores and ran about like chickens. Worse, they didn't have the feel of the boat and could do nothing to maneuver it. Seeing that the galley being bombarded by the accursed Romegas was on the verge of sinking, and the one under attack by la Motte was seriously crippled, Cocia-Cocia spat an oath, boarded his *capitana* and made to engage the foe.

la Motte realized he faced the Executioner and prepared for ramming. At the same moment, Romegas ordered his crew to do likewise against the last infidel galley. "*Fora!*" His voice was as a sounding trumpet.

The *fischietto* quickened the drumbeat as the *comiti* took their sticks to the slaves beneath them, all the while shouting, "*Ala! Ala! Remate cani!*" The *ciurma* cursed and shat on its benches as both galleys lurched forward. Sliding along the sea, they took on the aspect of two stallions, gathering strength and speed until, trotting with head lowered and fiery eyes, they hurtled themselves across the blue lists at one another.

"*Via!*" shouted the *capomastro* to the arquebusiers and musketeers crammed on the prow. "*Via ! ... Alesta! ... Fogo!*"

The fusillades engulfed the prows of both vessels in smoke and noise and men crumbled against their mates or fell headfirst into the water. Still the galleys sped towards each other to the drum and splash. Corsair arrows flew everywhere and Romegas's galley quickly became a hedgehog, quills jutting everywhere from its snout. The infidel arquebusiers were reloading, intending to get off a second salvo, but Romegas had not for nothing greased the hull of the *S. Gabriele*; nor had de Valette in vain purchased light Venetian armament. The corsairs had no time.

"*Via!*" shouted the *capomastro* to his gunners, waiting to the last possible moment, yea 'til he could descry the eyes of his foe. "*Fogo!*" The guns spat their charges directly into the hull of the enemy ship. At this moment, half the Christian *ciurma* aboard the corsair vessel saw what was to take place and, as if conspiring, dropped its oars. The corsair veered starboard and its shots went wide. Its gunners had no second chance, for in that instant the *S. Gabriele's* ramming spur crashed through the corsair's hull.

Romegas's men let out a cheer and cast irons to the other ship. The boarding began. Blaij Vergã was among the first to cross that short space, where one misstep would send you to Neptune forever. He had done this often enough, received wounds enough, but each time wondered how it was that Romegas never failed. Was it Lescaut's hand-picked crew? Luck? Daring? Nay, by now Blaij viewed the Commander as invincible and the enemy did too. That aura was his true shield and it would protect him this time as it did the others.

There was hardly a place to swing a sword, and for every man Vergã struck down, another instantly appeared in his stead. But as he and his fellows moved slowly, deliberately forward, slaves had loosened the nails of the chains that bound them and were rising against their captors, grappling with them with their bare hands. Before long the infidels realized they could not prevail and began to cast down their weapons.

From the *Corona*, things looked differently. When la Motte's galley collided with Cocio-Cocio's *capitana*, the corsair's spur had put a hole into the *Corona*'s hull. la Motte prepared for the worst. But to his amazement, Cocia pulled away and dashed off into the sea. The Executioner had sensed the battle was lost. The *Corona*'s crew let up a cheer.

"O, you Calabrian dog's prick!" Romegas called out, seeing his opponent flee. "You have escaped the faith, but you shall not escape Romegas!"

There remained the *Sophia*. Vergã himself decided to end the nuisance the corsairs were causing with musket and arrow fire and ordered the *ciurma* of the captured galley to bring her alongside the round ship. When the Christian slaves proved wary of further danger, Blaij called out, "We take that ship, your chains come off and we share the booty." Hearing the charmed word, many of the *gente* who'd boarded themselves shoved dead and wounded slaves aside and took their places at the oars. At the prow, protected only by raised shields, Balthazar found himself pressed to Vergã.

"That ship must not be sunk. There are Christians aboard, including the Grand Master's goddaughter, do you understand me?"

Blaij nodded and passed on the word to the gunner. Quickly they pulled alongside the *Sophia*, arrows, arquebus shot and musket fire raining everywhere. Heedless of the danger, Blaij hurled an iron over the round ship's gunwale and climbed, calling his fellows after him. For a moment Balthazar stood back, impressed by this rogue in spite of himself, then grasped a rope and was after him.

The corsairs' skeleton crew on the *Sophia* realized soon enough that its Commander had fled, that it was outnumbered and quickly being surrounded. Within a moment all action stopped, Balthazar and Vergã not having received the slightest wounds. In a panic, tho', a few infidels on the quarterdeck had seized the remaining passengers, among them Isabella.

The fellow with the knife at her throat glanced about frantically, having lost his wits altogether. In order not to inflame him, Isabella for her part made no struggle.

"You have no hope of escape," Blaij called out in Spanish, then in Italian. "Release her and you'll live." The fellow's eyes only darted more rapidly and he tightened the grip on his captive. Vergã turned his gaze to a second infidel and bore his eyes into him. That one, seeing there was no hope, threw himself onto the first and with a thrust of his kris into the side, slew him as Isabella tore herself free. The others cast down their arms, just as Romegas climbed aboard. The Commander had witnessed the entire outrage. He strode over to those few holdouts, decapitated the one holding the kris and cracked another's head with the flat of his blade. Those remaining instantly dropped to their knees, begging for their lives, which were spared.

Romegas at once ordered his carpenters to begin repairs and readied to escort the *Sta. Sophia* to Crete. At the same time he placed skeleton crews on the two prizes, preparing to tow them behind de Valette's galleys.

"It seems we are ordained to travel together in any case," said Isabella archly to Balthazar on the deck of the *Sophia*.

"It does indeed," the Knight replied with a slight bow and a small smile. "Again my apologies for the inconvenience, Signora. These things happen, alas."

Isabella shot a hard glance at Balthazar and turned to Vergã, who stood by them. "And it seems I am indebted to you for my life," she said to him, extending her blood-spattered hand. "I thank you for it, Señor."

Vergã bowed and kissed it, saying, "It was my honor," to which Isabella made no response.

That evening they all dined on lasagna in the Captain's cabin of the *Sta. Sophia*. Romegas naturally wished to know what Isabella Guasconi had been doing aboard, and she replied openly that she was en route to Crete to establish a trade in Cretan wine, which the Venetians did their best to dominate. The explanation satisfied Romegas well enough, who was in a boisterous mood, having taken some hundreds of slaves in the battle.

"Eh, have no fear, we'll get you to Crete soon enough," he said, pouring drink for everyone. "God was with you. Better, God was with you for having sent me."

Isabella caught herself staring at Romegas's hands, which trembled so much that he needed to steady one with the other as he tilted the decanter, and she wondered wherefore God had given this small Achilles heel to His avenging angel. If the Commander noticed her distraction, he ignored it.

"I declare we have shown Soliman a lesson this day, ah?" he said with a tone of expectation.

Balthazar nodded. "Of that there can be no doubt," he answered, voice perfectly balanced between affirmation and irony.

As he frowned at the Knight, Romegas's hands shivered anew, whereat Isabella interrupted. "How many prizes have you taken this season, Commander?"

"The Governor of Cairo should count thrice," Romegas answered too seriously, going on to complain that as Commander of the Grand Master's personal galleys, he should have rank equal to the Captain General of the fleet. "Balthazar, who has taken more prizes? I have offers from every king in Europe to lead their navies. His Holiness ... "

Before Balthazar might respond, there was a knock on the cabin door. One of the boys opened it and a small group of Christians who had been freed earlier entered, requesting leave to thank the Commander. More than one dropped to his knees in gratitude. A woman held out her newborn and said she would name him Mathurin, in honor of their deliverer. With good humor, Romegas took the babe in his arms, sprinkled some wine on its forehead and blessed it.

When the passengers had departed, Isabella asked Lescaut directly, "Commander, throughout the Mediterranean they say you have never lost a battle—"

"That is true," he said, smiling.

"To what do you credit such astonishing success?"

The seaman leaned back, his face sensibly flushed with drink. "To the Almighty," he answered simply, "who has made Romegas invincible. You see these hands that tremble so. After the Dragonara and the night I spent under that overturned galley, God sent me these tremors as a sign that nothing worse could happen."

"Have you never been wounded?" Isabella asked, incredulously.

"Of course, but what are such cuts? Arquebus balls, arrows ... If you do not fear death, they cannot harm you."

"It is true," added Blaij Vergã, "he cannot be harmed."

"And you, Señor?" Balthazar cocked his head toward Vergã. "Can you be harmed?"

Vergã seemed indisposed to answer the Knight, but as the steward brought sweets, Isabella also turned toward this dark confrater whom she knew only as Francisco's old companion, who had murdered his own mistress and attempted to kill Francisco himself. "Señor?" she said, acknowledging to herself that Vergã had the most piercing eyes and a natural, easy command about him. How was it he who had saved her?

"Only cowards fall, Señora. Be bold, refuse to retreat—" he cast a glance at Romegas—"and the fight is yours."

"If a man believes he cannot be harmed," Balthazar said idly, raising his cup, "I should think the excitement would be gone."

This time Vergã did deign to reply. "The excitement, Señor, always lies in besting one's enemies."

Romegas was nodding, whereas Isabella had lowered her eyes, unable to entirely grasp either the famous Knight or his lieutenant. Throughout her life she had been schooled to believe that excellence of mind and body were inseparable. What had she failed to comprehend?

"Vergada does all right," said Romegas. "I've decided to lend him a galley so he can prove himself on his own—for a share, of course. Then he can marry one of those Greeks he's taken a fancy to—or several of them." Romegas guffawed, as did Vergã.

"It's true," Vergã admitted. "Every woman in the Greek islands has been offered to me."

"But for those who've been offered to me," corrected Romegas. "Remind me some time, Vergada, about that dispensation from the Pope. Maybe we can make you a Serving Brother, at least."

Accustomed as she was to the speech of sailors, when it did not amuse Isabella, it wearied her. Rather than excuse herself she gathered all the daring she possessed and turned her eyes directly on the Commander. "I have heard, Sir," she ventured, "you treat your captives with extreme cruelty, and from what I saw today, I might agree with such sentiments."

It was as if Romegas had parried the remark a thousand times. "Signora," he said scornfully, "my treatment of barbarians serves as a warning to those ass-fuckers who behead Christian captains, leaving the dresses of noble lades splattered with blood. Now, Signora, you have put to us enough questions. What of you? Half of Christendom wants to know why you remain unmarried."

Isabella made no answer, cocked her head bemusedly at the question that had become so popular of late, and brought her glass to her lips.

"What is this?" chuckled Romegas. "Doesn't she know the proverb, 'In an old barn is fine threshing, but an old flail is good for naught.'" Also raising his cup, Romegas guffawed loudly at his own jest.

"Of course I know it," Isabella answered with sudden mirth, "but *si hallo un marido bueno, no quiero tener el temor de perderlo; y si malo, que necessida he del?*"

"If I find a good husband," Blaij translated for the Commander, "I do not wish to be exposed to the fear of losing him; but if a bad, what need to have one at all?"

After a pause, everyone around the table broke into laughter and the conversation passed on to other matters.

The small fleet proceeded eastward. A few days out from Crete, Romegas was standing again with Balthazar on the poop of the *S. Gabriele* when the watch reported the sighting of two Turkish *caramousali*.

"Let's take 'em," Romegas said.

Sixty-Three

All a man needs to do to turn Turk is raise the forefinger of his right hand and pronounce the fateful words, "*La he, la he, ill allah Mahomet, rasaul allah*," there is but one God and Mahomet is his prophet. Some, wishing to have their oath sealed, go to a religious judge, a *qadi*, then participate in a more elaborate ceremony: The apostate is wrapped with a turban and given an arrow to hold in his right hand. He mounts a stately, caparisoned steed and to the beating of drums and the playing of horns he is paraded about the city in order that all may recognize him.

More than once I witnessed the ceremony and, staring fixedly at my right forefinger, I thought surely the hard, inconceivable fate would fall to me. At table Abdallah-al-Waryagli never insisted on my conversion, for by custom the offer is made but once, but hardly an evening passed when he did not extol to me the superiority of the Quran or speak of the rituals of the Mahometans. He never failed to ask what my sentiments were and always I answered in the same words: I had yet to find my way. Inwardly, I wept. I consoled myself alone with the thought that, regardless of what I might do, in my heart I would always remain true to my faith and that God would see fit to forgive me. We had been slaves for well over two years, and I knew I must decide quickly if I were to free Pietru while both of us remained alive. One night at supper, tho', not long after the basilisk had been cast, Abdallah let slip, "Of course, when you have become a Mohammedan, you may no longer be ransomed."

I instantly perceived that the stakes had risen again, sharply; should I become a renegado, I would sacrifice my chances to be delivered by Christian friends. At the same time the steady diminishment of those hopes was pressing me to turn. A fever seized me, as I were standing on a precipice between two abysses, peering one way into slavery for the remainder of my mortal life and the other way into eternal damnation. But when al-Waryagli told me of the pilgrimage to Mecca, required of all

Mahometans, I at last perceived that this is where the foreman Lorenzo was when I vainly sought his aid from the bagno. With the realization came a chance to both free Pietru and save my soul.

"Lorenzo," I said to the foreman as he passed my place in the Foundry with a mallet in his grasp, "the Grand Vizier, Ali Pasha himself, has told me that I could become chief of these works should I profess to the true faith."

As so often, the foreman answered with naught but a sullen, burning gaze. "I know you harbor scant love for me," I went on, carving an ornament for a new culverin. "You did everything to stand in the way of the casting of the basilisk, but if I profess, within a short time I will surely be standing in your way." Still he made no answer. "I well see your lust for position, but I say again, if I turn, your way is blocked. Were I to swear not to turn Turk, would you do me a service?"

"Go on," Lorenzo said, finally, tossing the mallet in his hand and looking up at me.

"You are a renegado and so may buy slaves. I will give you the price and a commission if you buy a friend of mine out of the bagno."

After some thought the Venetian stilled his hammer. "It cannot be done. He is a slave of the Porte. His owner is the Sultan himself."

"My owner Abdallah bought me from the bagno. It can be done. It has been done."

"Then ask Abdallah to dirty his hands with this intrigue!"

The foreman spat when he said it, but his boneless snarl met with only a decisive refusal from me. "That I cannot risk. You have my offer. What do you say?"

Lorenzo's hunger for place defeated his weakness; he breathed deeply and agreed. My fear, tho', that Abdallah would get wind of the plan was great and I made Lorenzo swear not to utter a word to a living soul. For his part he made me vow never to take up the Mahometan faith in my mortal life. So grave were we that he raised his forefinger in the way the infidels do when taking oaths, and I held two sticks crossed and kissed them before letting them drop. Thus was the deal struck.

We could not act as yet. Pietru was chained to a galley through much of the season *anno* 1563, and the morning and evening guns at Tophane sounded many times over while I baked and cast, awaiting his return. As my anticipation grew during those endless months, a subtle change took place at the Arsenal and Foundry. More craftsmen asked for work each day, more galleys went under construction and the masters received more orders for the casting of guns.

"Whence have these new novices who don't know a hammer from a chisel appeared among us?" I asked Lorenzo, but he had no answer, other than that the Porte had requested new arms. Abdallah professed ignorance as well. Those of us who labored in the Arsenal and Foundry had our own thoughts: Slowly, imperceptibly, preparations for the long-awaited invasion of Europe had begun.

I became certain of it in June or July, when thirty janissaries appeared at the Gun Foundry, including Yakhshi , escorting an old man of nearly eighty years. At once I found myself quivering in my shoes. Turgut and no other. His escort pointed to my great basilisk and some of the lesser pieces lying by it. Seeing this, I quickly I threw down the work in my hands and made to go out to another shed, but Yakhshi caught sight of me and waved me over to the *Kapudan*. Slowly, now quaking from head to toe, I walked across the space, thinking I should fulfill my vow with the heartbeats remaining to me and take Turgut to Hell. No swords were about, except those the janissaries carried today. The hilt of the *Boluk-bashi*'s scimitar beckoned but in the instant I made to grab it, Yakhshi took me by the arm and presented me to the most dreaded man on earth.

As I had once at Tripoli, I bowed, certain again my life had run its road. I'd well forgotten that on Djerbé itself Turgut had had no recollection of me. He'd looked death in the eye so often that to him the image of that faceless attacker rushing at him with a gleaming halberd was merely another incident of war. The Admiral spoke pleasantly in Turkish, asking me about the basilisk, its weight and where I had learned my art. During our conversation I was able to gaze comfortably on him. Like the others standing about, he was dressed in loose pants and a jacket, fitting for the hot months, and he was distinguished from his men only by his age and the enormous white turban he wore. For an instant I thought that I was looking onto de Valette. Maugre his fully white beard and his deeply creased face, his eyes retained a sparkle and he spoke with alacrity. He spoke with the ease of a man who had known high power all his life.

"How will you feel when your basilisk rains its destruction on Christians?" he asked me.

I shrugged. "Philip might have considered that when he abandoned his troops at Djerbé. Such are the winds of Fortune, and I have nothing to repent of."

E'en as I uttered these words I realized the mention of Djerbé might rekindle Turgut's memory. It did not. He nodded thoughtfully, then with arms bowbent burst into outright laughter. The others joined in and soon everyone was laughing raucously. The birds above began to chatter. "It is well you failed to kill me on Djerbé," Turgut said, slapped me on the shoulder and moved on, ordering one of his escorts to award me a silk.

Turgut's visit convinced me of the necessity to escape Constantinople as quickly as possible. Who knew what chaos would reign once invasion preparations had taken hold, who would be chained to a galley and who would be sent to cast guns in the field? I cursed to myself; these hands were bound until Pietru returned. At last, late in the summer, the galley he rowed appeared and once more I thanked the Almighty when I found Ix-Xabaw alive in the bagno. His appearance had not much changed over half a year. His muscles bulged but his eyes appeared empty. He muttered in a low, almost incomprehensible voice that the fleet had spent all season searching for grain and hadn't engaged the enemy.

"I have not forgotten our vow," I said to him sternly, pressing into his hand a purse, "and neither shall you. Be prepared—the time is nigh."

At once I returned to the Foundry, taking Lorenzo outside to the field of guns. There I put in his hands a sackful of *akcheler*. "If you betray me in this," I said, "I shall not rest until I see your head on a pike. Now see to what we agreed without delay."

The steel in my voice—more, I'd say, his own ambition—served to temper Lorenzo and he set about to fulfill his part of the bargain. With the money in hand, he dressed himself in his finest robe, went over to the bagno and found the *zindanchi* at the gate chewing the fat with the janissaries. Tho' Lorenzo was far from delicate, his task was; Pietru Galea was of the fifth share of the spoils belonging to the sovereign, and to buy him was surely a violation of the Mahometans' law.

Overcoming his own weakness, the foreman stepped up to the *zindanchi* and said, "Eh, dungeon-man, I want to talk to you." The big, grubby slave-keeper could see that his visitor was from the Foundry and had seen high favor from the Porte. He shrugged and followed that one to a distance, near the big field where the archers practiced. Today the elite horse, the *silahdarlar*, rode with blinding speed past the targets, putting shafts into them. Lorenzo went on: "I need to buy a slave in there. He worked in the Venetian Arsenale and'd be helpful at the Foundry."

The *zindanchi* now examined this cannon-maker from head to toe, from the sandals, to the baggy pants, to the silk robe and turban. "Who's sent you?" Receb, as this one was named, asked Lorenzo. "I can't sell these slaves. Anyway, your turban may be wrapped, but you look like a Christian *kopek* to me."

"I'm no Christian," answered Lorenzo with heat.

Receb frowned. "Prove it."

The foreman said that anyone at the Foundry could tell him, but this didn't satisfy the dungeon-man. Lorenzo said he'd been to Mecca and Receb asked what was there. Lorenzo told him. Receb asked him to recite prayers and Lorenzo did, saying also that he performed his ritual cleansings and attended mosque on Fridays. The dungeon-man paused, stroking his unshaven chin, still little convinced and thinking he should take this fellow to a *qadi* to be certain.

Now Lorenzo, at last, displayed real strength. "Wait a moment," he said and dropped his breeches.

Receb stared. "You have indeed become a true believer!" the dungeon-man laughed, but then shrugged. "It makes no difference. I cannot sell you the slave."

"You can. For what purpose have been questioning me if you cannot?"

Despite all this, the *zindanchi* would not relent and for a long time silently watched the *silahdarlar* ride and shoot. "On the other hand," he at last remarked, "if this slave is stolen property, perhaps he might be returned to you." So saying, he turned around and Lorenzo walked back alone to the Foundry.

From the angry expression on the foreman's face, I at once discerned that the affair had miscarried. "What has happened?" I asked with undisguised urgency.

"He refused to sell me the slave," Lorenzo replied. "But he said something might be done if the slave is stolen property ... What could the bastard have meant?" Suddenly, the Venetian's countenance brightened. "That's it! He wants me to come to him through the Guild of Thieves."

"Why?"

"To protect his ass, of course."

The next day Lorenzo set off for the Sheik of the Guild of Thieves, finding him in his office next to a mosque in Constantinople. Lorenzo complained to the old man that a slave of his had been stolen and ended up in the bagno. The Sheik, inviting the foreman to sit down for coffee, asked what he was willing to pay to have the slave returned.

"Three thousand *akcheler*," replied the cannon-maker.

"I will inquire to see whether any of the thieves holds a complaint against you. If not, something perhaps can be done. Come back in two days."

The same night, I went to the bagno and told Ix-Xabaw that, should anyone ask, say that he was Lorenzo's slave who had been stolen by thieves and had ended up in the galleys.

"I do not understand this, Cikku," answered Pietru when I had given him these instructions.

"I do not myself. Pray tonight."

Two days hence, Lorenzo returned to the Sheik, who told him that the thieves who had stolen the slave demanded six thousand *akcheler* for his return.

"Six thousand!" cried Lorenzo in outrage. "For a Gozitan galley slave of no use to anyone! That is a robbery twice!"

"In addition they require an oarsman to replace him."

Lorenzo fumed angrily. "There is no shortage of slaves these days! How dare they!" The foreman came back to me and explained what had transpired. "No friend is worth that sort of money," he said, "unless he is a nobleman. Were I in your shoes I'd let him rot. And the demand for a replacement ... !"

"Fortunately," I said, "you are not in my shoes. These people are merely haggling. You know such matters better than I. Return to the thieves and say we will pay six thousand, but that they must hire an oarsman from this money. Let them take a convict. I'll not buy one slave by selling another."

Lorenzo appeared a third time before the Sheik and was told once more to return in two days. We waited with bated breath, but the offer was at last accepted. And so, in this strange land, in this strange manner, the deal was struck.

I cannot say with certainty whether it was God's pleasure or the Will of Allah, but after three years on the galleys and in the bagno, Pietru lumbered into the Foundry and said, "Good morning, Cikku. Thank you."

We would waste not a breath more. Immediately I set off to the taverns of Galata. Seeing the myriad vessels of all flags lining the docks of the Horn, it was all I could do to hold myself from jumping onto the nearest and disappearing with the wind. Yet the dangers in that road lay everywhere. Janissary patrols were everywhere about and, as I had now been in the city for three years, I was known to many of them. Nor was being caught by the janissaries the only peril I dreaded.

I entered one of the taverns. All about were sailors and merchants indulging in their taste for wine, coffee, whores and dancing girls. I listened closely in the din, hoping to find a captain—a Spaniard or a Venetian—who would undertake our passage. Every face that glanced in my direction carried a great risk. Having secured the fare, many of these jackals would sell a fleeing Christian slave back to an infidel corsair for the mere profit of it. I caught a whiff of Spanish from two men playing cards on a bench and asked to join them.

At first they ignored me, then the first looked up, staring hard. "Stand away from me, Mahometan dog," he said.

Tho' I spoke to him in my native tongue, he regarded my dress and took me for an infidel. "I'm a Spaniard, you fool," I said.

"You don't look like a Spaniard to me," he sneered with derision.

"What an idiot." I stormed out of the tavern.

All night I passed from one tavern to another, drinking in vain as I attempted to find someone in whom I might place a great trust. The next evening went by in like pursuits, and the next. After a week I overheard a conversation between two merchants, one of whom who wanted to bring tobacco from the Newfound World to Turkey through Sevilla, and import coffee to Spain.

"I lived in Sevilla, as a boy, for two years," I said, telling one of the tavern urchins to bring them more coffee.

The merchant, as the fellow a week earlier, stared at me, but neither did he dismiss me. "You speak Spanish as if your mother did."

"My mother did indeed, and that is because she was a Spaniard and may be still, if she yet lives." I crossed myself. "And I, Francisco Perez de Barai, am no less a Spaniard than she, having been born and raised in Granada."

"You seem shocked to hear the sound of your own name in your own tongue," the merchant said, regarding me with curiosity.

"I am, Señor, I am," I replied and wiped a tear from my eye.

Yet, it was the mention of Granada that caused this merchant's face to brighten, for by chance he too hailed from the beautiful city. We fell into easy conversation and from my descriptions of the Alhambra, the river, my home and all else of the city, he could not but believe that I spoke truthfully. I said not a word of our plans to escape, only ascertained that Galçeran Peguera, this merchant, would be sailing for Venice in two weeks' time. Having found a fellow countryman in this far kingdom, he invited me dine with him the following night.

Peguera was naturally curious to hear my story, and I readily enough told him about Djerbé and what happened after. "Oh, what a great infamy that was for Philip to abandon our soldiers who fought so nobly!" he cried. "We expect a descent each passing year and look at you! You have become a slave to the Turks—a Turk yourself, it seems."

"No, I have not," I protested, averring that my dress was common enough for laborers here. Nor did I beg him for passage and was myself surprised when Peguera himself invited me to sup with him the next night aboard his ship. "Might I bring a friend?" I asked, thinking it would not be unwise on several counts, and he agreed.

Neither Pietru nor I perceived what was about when we approached the docks at the agreed hour. The embankments swarmed with people. The harbormaster and customs officials were present, as always, as well as the janissaries who watched the ships. We could not risk boarding Peguera's vessel for fear of being seized. The hour passed and at last the merchant himself stepped down the gangway onto the embankment searching for us. Catching sight of him from behind one of the fish stalls, I waved and he approached. "We will be arrested if we attempt to board. It is too great a risk."

Peguera suggested we buy Christian garments in Pera and return the following evening. We did. Dressed as naught else than two Italian merchants we again approached the vessel. The janissaries followed us with suspicion in their eyes, verily boarding the ship behind us, but we feigned ignorance of Turkish and with enough remonstrances from Peguera, those ruffians let us be. Oh, that we would have sailed that very night! But Peguera's intent was otherwise. Rather, inviting us into his cabin for supper, he said that he had had a special dish prepared for us. His steward appeared and set down before us two plates of bacon.

Nothing loathe, Ix-Xabaw and I dug in.

"Ah!" Peguera exclaimed happily. "You are Christians!"

Trust was now firmly established between us, and we and this good Spaniard set about laying exact plans for our escape.

Sixty-Four

"*Che piacere rivederla*, Comte Contremaret," said Giovan Barelli, smiling, as he took Balthazar's hand before the same iconostasis where they had met three years ago. "I am surprised. Have you longed for coffee so much?"

"Assuredly, Signore," replied Balthazar as he gazed again on the enthroned Christ, "Constantinople is not called the Gate of Happiness for nothing. Let me not waste time with jests. I am returned for two matters of urgency." At hearing this, the curly-haired Greek ushered Balthazar out to the yet mild air and green streets of the city. "The Grand Master is grateful for your constancy. Based much on your reports, he is convinced a descent on Malta is now inevitable and has asked me to find out every particular you may know."

Barelli remained silent until they reached the old Hippodrome, where the Byzantine emperors had raced horses and staged spectacles of combat. With time, it stood empty and in ruins. "You may be disappointed, Comte," Barelli said in this crumbling arena far from curious bystanders. "I have emplaced eyes and ears in the most sensitive places—the *most* sensitive. This has required no little time and expense, but be assured, I am now receiving news of every decision taken by the Porte itself." The Greek, Balthazar perceived, had not lost a dram of his energy. With hardly a pause he went on: "Parisot is correct that an invasion is coming after the delays of which I have written. No decision, tho', has yet been taken as to the objective. I can tell you it will be Sicilia, La Goletta or—Malta."

As he listened to Barelli, Balthazar gazed with curiosity at the ancient bowls of marble about them and the great columns rising from this deserted place, whose single remaining wall of vaults reminded him of the Roman Colosseo. He ran his fingers lightly over the hieroglyphs of a needle fifty *braccia* in height, and over the three-headed serpent of the bronze pillar near it. "What do you believe, Signore?"

"Some Viziers," Barelli said, not responding directly, "argue for La Goletta, as it is the last Christian stronghold on Barbary. Once seized, all of North Africa will be under Turkish control. But it is heavily fortified by the Spanish. Others declare for Sicilia as a stepping-stone into Europe. Their opponents point out that Sicilia is large and would be difficult to hold. From the other side, Malta is a small island with no more than a handful of Knights to defend it. The commanders believe that with little difficulty they could take it in less than a week. Then Europe could be invaded from north and south simultaneously."

Simultaneously, Balthazar breathed to himself. Regarding a great, overturned bronze of Hercules, he wondered not so much what civilization these antiquities around him had come from, but which civilization would next lie in ruins.

"I must say, Comte," Barelli was going on, "that if Parisot desires to avoid a descent, he would do well to rein in this Romegas. In the Divan and the Seraglio there are constant complaints of his forays."

"Indeed," the Greek recounted, "only a few days ago there was quite a scene in the Divan. Soliman himself was present, as was the *Kapudan Agha*, who holds responsibility for Turkish shipping and sees his money lost with each of Romegas's outrages. You can imagine his fury when the report came in that Romegas had seized two *caramusali*, carrying hundreds of pilgrims to Mecca. The *Kapudan* had hardly begged His Majesty to put an end to the despicable knights, when a corsair named Cocia-Cocia told how Romegas had sunk two of his galleys and forced him to flee hither. Cocia reminded Soliman that the jackal Romegas of late also captured the *Sancak beyi* of Cairo, and that the Possessor of Men's Necks and Star of the Most Happy Constellation, who has conquered much of the known world, could easily destroy these impudent dogs and should do so without delay."

"I must say," mused Balthazar after hearing the report, "the Sultan's intelligence is impressive. I helped seize those two *caramusali* with Romegas en route hither, and to be sure we encountered Cocia before that. I can hardly believe the savage spoke so eloquently." He smiled at Barelli. "Will Soliman act?"

Barelli, smiling slightly himself, shook his head. "He sat, impassive as always, and listened. Believe me, the old man wants only peace and quiet, away from these bickering advisors and screaming harpies of the Seraglio.

It is too late for him to act this year. But I say to you, Fra Balthazar, Romegas is salting the dragon's tail. Beware."

From the spy's account, Balthazar would have guessed he had himself been present in the Divan.

At this juncture Barelli asked, "You had spoken of a second mission?"

Balthazar told him of how I, Francisco, had been captured at Djerbé and been a slave here since, working at the Foundry.

"O, those rogues!" exclaimed Barelli. "Had I known! But this is an immense city and Francisco probably does not know how to find me. May I be of assistance in this matter?"

"Nay," replied Balthazar, "I think not. It is now merely a matter of negotiating a ransom. A propos, a strongbox awaits you under guard at Galata. Let us fetch it."

They had agreed to meet at sundown. Earlier, upon arriving, they had installed themselves at an inn and paid their respects to the Bailo, whereupon Balthazar had vanished. This gave Isabella some hours alone. She, as Balthazar and his comrades had four years earlier, walked the streets of Galata, curiosity and fear warring within her. In one sense the town seemed strangely familiar; truly, after that long, horrible voyage, she had returned to Genoa. And had not. In one corner of the piazzetta she chanced upon a dervish. With his tall hat and a skirt that flared out like a woman's, he whirled to the keening of pipes, the beating of drums and the rhythmic clapping of bystanders. A Venetian who happened to be at her side remarked that by this spinning, which was fast enough to make any ordinary person sick, the dervishes claimed to come closer to God. For an instant, Isabella tried to imagine herself spinning in the same way, but was quickly overcome by revulsion at the heathen rite.

Stranger were the few infidel women who glided silently by, shrouded from head to toe. Isabella crossed herself at the sight of these barbarian wraiths, counting herself fortunate, and walked on, suddenly composing verses in her head. She paused on the wharf, taking in the smells of fish and coffee. Isabella had already experienced her first taste that morning and wondered whether she might import the elixir to Italy, but at that moment her eye was drawn across the Golden Horn to Constantinople itself, with its countless mosques and minarets. She decided to have a closer look and paid a ferryman to take her across the channel. Not long after, she was staring up at the great mosque built only a few years ago by Soliman. Just as Balthazar had on that day when he first beheld it, Isabella swallowed hard in awe and terror. By now the sun had fallen and the muezzins were calling the faithful to prayer. Isabella took a step beyond a beggar near the mosque, retreated and put a coin into his hand, then hurried back to Galata, where she met the Bailo's servant who was to escort her to Abdallah-al-Waryagli's home. Balthazar had not appeared and she decided to go alone.

Luckily the *chavush* was home and when his servant, with some surprise, presented Isabella, Abdallah-al-Waryagli immediately invited her to supper and ordered his wife Fatma to bring another plate to the table. Tho' Fatma, unveiled in the house, was no longer young, Isabella thought her rather pretty, if shy. She bowed often to the unexpected guest but could not speak any language Isabella knew, and so the two were reduced to exchanging curious glances and wary smiles.

"My wife says you are very beautiful," the Moor translated into Spanish. Fatma offered Isabella much food.

Isabella accepted the compliment and such food as she was able, but wasted little time in explaining her presence. "Señor," she said, "I have travelled to Constantinople to ransom Francisco de Barai, who is your slave."

As she pronounced these words, a shadow crossed the *chavush*'s countenance and, thought Isabella, a sensible sadness. "Señora," he said, drawing out his words delicately, "I fear you have made a long and dangerous journey to no purpose. I cannot accept a ransom for Francisco."

"Why is that?" Isabella asked with confusion and, suddenly, a sinking heart. "Are you not his padrone?"

"You see," the Moor went on with equal delicacy, "I have treated Francisco well, and he has become as a son to me. No less is he valued by the Porte itself, because he works as an esteemed caster of guns at the Imperial Foundry. What I am saying to you is that Francisco has seen the advantages of working for the Padishah—may peace and glory be upon him!—and has accepted the True Faith."

Isabella could hardly comprehend the words that assaulted her ears. "Do you mean, Señor, Francisco has become a renegado?"

"As you infidels say," Abdallah-al-Waryagli nodded, "he has turned Turk. He has become a free man."

Feeling faint, sick to her stomach, Isabella unsteadily rose from the floor as Fatma glanced at her husband. "My wife asks whether you are ill, Señora."

Isabella barely managed to find a reply. "No … I am sorry, this news is greatly unexpected," she said, casting about helplessly. "Please excuse me, I … I must go now. Accept my gratitude for your hospitality."

"Will you not remain for coffee?" the *chavush* asked politely, unable to conceal a certain satisfaction. By now Isabella could only shake her head as Fatma said something in Turkish with a concerned expression. "My wife asks whether she might have the honor of your company at the baths tomorrow."

The remark brought back the stories Isabella had heard of the unnatural depravities that took place in Turkish baths. Filled again with revulsion, she also realized it mattered little; after what she had just heard, she could hardly consider such an invitation and she begged her leave. Abdallah-al-Waryagli ordered a slave to escort her to her lodging.

Once we had agreed on our escape, Galçeran Peguera advised Ix-Xabaw and me to lay low until the day his ship was to set sail. Still, reconnaissance was necessary. For some days Pietru and I took turns watching the activity on the docks in order to ascertain the best way to elude the harbormaster and the janissaries who patrolled the wharfs at all hours. With Peguera we decided that he should set sail without us and we would hire a caique, as if making only across the Horn, and meet him in the middle of the channel.

It was a good design. A week before our intended departure, tho', a turbulent group of janissaries was carousing past me on the embankment. Among them was Yakhshi and the lot of them was drunk to their eyebrows. Catching sight of me, Yakhshi stumbled up and put his arm around my shoulder, asking with foul breath how things stood at the Foundry. As always, I told him. "But how is it that you have been drinking, my good Mahometan?"

Yakhshi regarded me with a quizzical expression, then turned to his comrades. "We must have this *kafir* to the *tekke*," he said, "and show him the real life in Constantinople."

"I cannot enter a *tekke*," I answered with some trepidation.

"Stupid *kafir*," Yakhshi replied, fairly grasping my beard with his hand and staring me in face with the wide eyes of a drunkard. "The Bektashi don't care whether you are Christian or Mohammedan. I will come for you at the Foundry in a week."

He named the day after our escape. I nodded to Yakhshi, having no intention of honoring this rendezvous, and went about my business as if nothing had occurred. Pietru and I met Peguera in a tavern a few days ahead of time to agree on the hour, which would be late in the evening, paid him half the money. We got our Christian clothes ready and waited.

After three years, the day arrived. To my everlasting regret, so did Yakhshi. In his drunkenness he had named the wrong day for the ceremony and showed up at the Foundry just before the evening gun. He would hear nothing of my protests and he and his comrades fairly dragged me off. I managed to take Pietru aside, told him to get my clothes and meet me at the Galata Tower at the appointed hour.

I stilled my pounding heart, assuring myself everything would go according to plan. Not long after, the janissaries led me to the Bektashi lodge in Pera. Had I been in a mind to enjoy the revel that followed, I would have. My distraction was such that I scarcely took in the debauch unfolding about me. This *tekke* was no mosque. Calling themselves "divine moths," the janissaries launched into song and a frenetic dancing that went on for hours. And drinking. Some, before downing their first cup, would let out a shout, warning their soul to stow itself in some odd corner of the body, or leave it altogether, lest it be defiled by the drink to come. Others intended to drink to oblivion, averring that as it was a sin, the penalty would be the same regardless of quantity.

The presence of freely flowing wine was only the beginning of this astonishing rite. My eyes simply could not credit that among these infidel revelers sat women, unveiled women. Some got to their feet and danced with the same abandon as the men. What sort of ceremony I was witnessing, I formed no conception, nor at this moment did I wish to. As Yakhshi plied me with drink, I thought only of the passing moments. At last I could wait no longer, and while the *Boluk-bashi* joined in the ecstatic dance, I stole out the front door.

Pietru was waiting. Despite the orgy in the lodge, I had gotten to the tower in time and all was proceeding in accord with our intentions. Ix-

Xabaw led me to a deserted spot behind a warehouse, and I quickly changed clothes. We made our way to the waterfront.

But the Bektashi ceremony had ended immediately after I had quit the lodge and the janissaries were now on the streets, carousing with the same sanguinary drunkenness they had a week ago. Pietru and I had gained the embankment. The moon was up, providing a bright evening and the taverns were closing for the night. Unexpectedly, a voice called out to me.

"Francisco!"

I turned to see a man and a woman, not ten paces away, she raising her hand as she hailed me. I could not believe my eyes. Isabella and Balthazar. Alive, and at long last they had come for us! For a confused moment I could not decide whether to abandon our plan and throw myself at their feet, or go on. I took a step toward them—halted. The decision was snatched from me. In that fatal moment of irresolution Yakhshi, alerted by Isabella's cry, spied me before the taverns, now dressed fully in Christian garb. Who knows what was going through is drunken mind, but he raised his hand, commanding us to halt our movements, and stepped briskly toward us.

Pietru and I glanced at each other and without a word dove into the Golden Horn, hauling with every strength out into the channel, peeling off our clothes as we did so. We did not make it to Peguera's ship. As we closed in, the cabin lights and lanterns swaying before our eyes, a caique cut us off. It wasn't filled with janissaries. We stopped, treading water, attempting to swim around it. One of the men aboard the boat fired an arquebus shot as a warning. We halted, heads above water. With weapons pointed at us, the corsairs laughingly hauled us aboard and took us to their galley. So it was that Pietru and I became slaves of Cocia-Cocia, the Executioner.

Sixty-Five

We did not spend a year as prisoners of Cocia-Cocia, but it might have been eternity. Dragging us onto his galley, his men threw us at once into the hold. Whether this was to hide us from the Turks, who would claim us, or to break us in, I can't say, but we sat in that darkness for over a month, fed only through the grate, while the corsair's galley sailed out of the Golden Horn and south.

When they finally let us out and, squinting in the sun I struggled to my feet, I first beheld the Executioner and he first beheld me. He was standing not far away on the *spalla* and his first words cast in my direction were, "I don't like Christian dogs looking at my tattoos." After the *gumi* flogged me with his stick, Cocia-Cocia laughed, adding his infamous boast, "I am the Devil incarnate, *it*, and if I am to spend an eternity in Hell, Christians'll get a taste of it here while I'm alive."

They were the only truthful words that ever issued from Cocia's disgusting lips. The savage standing before me was naught more than a beast on two legs. His swarthy, bald head—covered with tattoos almost as much as the rest of him—his huge dark moustaches, his bright pantaloons and the sash girding his waste … it was a demon from the dark world. There on the *corsia*, before they chained me, I managed to stand erect and gaze at him with burning eyes. Cocia ordered me beaten again.

"I think I'll kill this one slowly," he said to the *gumi*.

We wintered at Gallipoli, building new sheds and slipways at the arsenal there. The bagno was darker and filthier e'en than the one in Constantinople and the guards beat us for pleasure. One day Cocia appeared in the bagno and, catching sight of me, he ordered me to eat a live rat, or he would have his way with me. I ate the rat and called myself lucky. The Executioner often raped virgins and pregnant girls and then, in the way of these barbarians, took the men when it fancied him. They returned from his tent in tears, broken forever by his hideous, unspeakable acts.

"Forgive me," I said to Pietru on one of those days in the grey sequence of days whose beginning had quickly receded beyond recall, and whose end lay beyond imagination.

"No, Cikku, you did everything for me. A man cannot ask for more."

I do not remember us saying much of anything after that, for in the Gallipoli bagno and on Cocia's galley, I at last gave up hope. There was no longer any chance of a ransom, none of escape. I fell into a stupor, an unthinking, animal stupor. My eyes clouded over; I ceased to pray. The slaves built, rowed; Cocia beat us. God alone knows why I lived thro' the winter. Perhaps some dim image of Balthazar and Isabella flickered in the recesses of my mind, beckoning me, but if such was the case, I failed to discern it. We had been fully defeated.

In that state, in spring *anno* 1564, we sailed back to Constantinople to deliver cannon to the Arsenal. Rowing Cocia's galley was itself a greater torture than on any other I'd been chained to. The boat was built like an ancient trireme *alla sensile*. Each man held his own oar, instead of three men on one. They said this way was better, faster, easier to maneuver, but more was required of each slave and fewer western boats used it in recent years. It also allowed less room to sleep between the benches.

One day, exhausted, I let my oar slip and the *gumi* unleashed his stick on me. I turned, senselessly, grabbed it, then his arm, then struck him down. Cocia saw this and ordered me beaten. I turned to Pietru at the oar next to mine and said *à Dios*. They pinned me down on the *corsia* and the punishment began. Ten strokes, twenty, thirty, on the back, on the soles of my feet. They would have kept at it until I died, but when I was passing from my senses, Pietru shouted to beat him instead. The offer seems to have tickled Cocia's fancy; they unchained Pietru and began to beat him. I wasn't aware of what was happening. They'd thrown me down onto the *corsia*, where I passed out, but when I came to my senses, they were still beating Pietru and his back was a bleeding mass of skin and bones.

I lifted my hand and croaked, "No, me."

Nothing loathe, they changed us again.

There wasn't much left of either man by the time they stopped. We remained alive, barely, both wishing we had rather departed this earth.

Some of the Turkish convicts carried salves in their bags that they stowed under the benches, and as we rowed into the Bosporus, they smeared us with their ointments, but by then the scars were too deep.

Cocia-Cocia walked by me. "Your false God did not listen to your prayers," he scoffed.

I struggled to my feet and glared at him. "Kill me," I said.

"Oh, I am," Cocia replied. He had the *gumi* cut off my earlobe.

The Executioner put into Constantinople to deliver his goods, intending to provision the boats and go on to Italy for his yearly plunder. The plans changed suddenly when we were engaged to escort to Venice the galleon of the Chief Eunuch of the Seraglio, a ship laden with fabulous merchandise purchased not only by the eunuch, but by His Majesty's wives and concubines. About a dozen galleys surrounded the *sultana*, as the whole fleet slowly made its way toward the Morea. During that voyage a fierce argument erupted between one of the corsairs and Cocia. Why were they escorting this ship when they could be ravaging the Italian coast to greater profit? Cocia plunged a knife into his chest, tore out his heart with his bare hand. He had the carcass chopped up and thrown overboard and gave the heart to one of the animals aboard, which ate it for breakfast. The next day, for no reason anyone perceived, Cocia had a slave stood before the muzzle of a cannon and discharged it.

Praying for death as the only release from this hell, we rounded the Morea and continued onward between Zante and Cephallonia. It was precisely here, on that bright, hot summer morning, when an unexpected shudder of excitement ran thro' the *ciurma* and Pietru looked up.

"It's the Knights," he said.

Nothing is so graceful, or so dreaded, as a galley dashing into battle at top speed. I have already told His Majesty at the outset of this tale how Romegas ploughed straight into our vessel with a great crashing of wood and splintering of oars and how, calling to the long-sought Cocia with curses on his lips, he defeated the Devil's son in a single combat. Aye, we the slaves then tore flesh from him with our own teeth as had he been a fatted calf and we a pack of sharp-toothed jackals, and we cast what was left of Cocia into the sea. Pietru felt his newly straightened nose and knew a miracle had occurred. We were free at last. And so we stood on the ruins of this boat, bodies all about, and watched as the fleet of the Religion, having scared off or taken all the enemy galleys, attacked the *sultana* of the *Kapi Agha*.

When Captain General de Giou received the warning shot from the Turks, signaling that they proposed to fight, he, Romegas and the five other galley Captains agreed to make a continual circle, each firing on the approach to the target, such that there would be no cessation. At once they got underway and first Romegas, followed by the six other Captains, emptied their pieces against the heavily-armed galleon before reloading. This plan, tho' succeeding, did not last long. As if ordained, feuding quickly broke out. Romegas, Commander of de Valette's personal galleys, and de Giou, Captain General of the Fleet, each wanted the entire glory for himself and so they soon left off the formation and began to attack the galleon as each saw fit.

"Do they never learn?" Pietru said, feeling again with some disbelief his nose as we watched, both thinking that our freedom was being sold back before we had tasted it.

It seemed they did not learn. The battle lasted five hours, de Giou instantly hit by the full fury of the janissaries—cannon shot, arquebus, arrows, balls, stone and fireworks. A ball from the galleon blew Romegas's wale to pieces, killing over twenty men and forcing twenty more to leap into the sea. Seeing a great cannon levelled, preparing to take him betwixt wind and water, Romegas retired, as de Giou had. With its heavy armaments, the Turk held no thought of surrender even as the Order's other galleys relieved Romegas and de Giou, two to the enemy's port and three to starboard, pouring fire into her broadsides.

We learnt only afterwards that, so greedy had the Turks been to fill the ship, the heaviest guns were trapped amongst bales of merchandise and couldn't be moved. And so thus it fell out: The Knights finally boarded, overcoming the janissaries, and took prisoners. They had lost sixty men in the undertaking, and the infidels above eighty.

When a week later this fleet at last sailed into the Great Port of Malta, the Knights towed their great prize to the moat between Fort St. Angelo and Birgu, where it remained for one and all to see. Pietru and I staggered onto the embankment, and Ix-Xabaw dropped to his knees in thanksgiving. After four years, our nightmare of captivity had ended.

Others were not so fortunate. A Greek caulker named Baptiste had been circumcised and when the Knights saw this, they arrested him. Our deliverers could plainly see the rest of us had not been caponed and let us go.

I walked into town, asking at the Auberge de France for Balthazar. He had been living in Birgu since the Grand Master's *Citazione* a few years ago had raised the alarm for war, but had at last taken rooms of his own. I found him there. Upon seeing me, dirty, torn, scarred, bloody, he rose to his feet and I, more dead than alive, collapsed into his arms.

GREAT PORT–MALTA
1565
Gallows' Point
Fort St. Elmo
Castle St. Angelo
Marsamxett Harbor
Guiral's Post
Mt. Sciberras
Post of Sanoguera
Porto
Marsa
Fountain
Grand Master's Garden

N
Rinella
San Salvatore
Kalkara
Kalkara Creek
Sta Margherita
Heights
Borgo/Birgu
Galley Creek
Fort
St. Michel
Bormla
Wall
Senglea
Mandra
Heights of Corradino

Book IV

Barelli

At last the army crossed the Danube, where it was greeted by John-Sigismund of Transylvania, an ally who Soliman regarded as the rightful ruler of Hungary and who warred against Emperor Maximilian. John-Sigismund's Grand Marshal led a procession of one hundred janissaries carrying sumptuous gifts for the Sultan, including one ruby alone valued at fifty thousand ducats. In exchange, and for the kissing of his hand, His Majesty ceded to John-Sigismund all the lands between the river Tisza and Transylvania. They then discussed plans for defeating Maximilian.

During the negotiations, Soliman had little time for the likes of me, but at night continued to listen to my story before retiring. He remarked that I seemed to have provided some service to the Porte, even as I admitted to escaping, but he was confused on certain matters. I imagined he was, I answered. He especially could not understand how a man, having seen the splendors of Constantinople and of the Empire, could be reluctant to embrace the True Faith. I replied by repeating a story I had once heard from a wandering dervish near his palace. A mad king, having received some favors from an idol, vowed that everyone should worship it and commanded his soldiers to seize the first three people who passed by his castle and force them to bend to the image.

The first of these, a scholar, when ordered to do this, said to himself, "Force compels me to my knees, and thus I bear no responsibility for this sin." He bowed to the idol.

The second, a descendent of Mohammed, said, "Through my veins runs the blood of the Prophet and so my actions purify anything." He also bowed to the idol.

The third, a whore, said, "I am but a whore, and understand little of this world. I only know that I cannot worship this idol, whatever you do to me."

The king's madness thereupon left him; he ordered the first two decapitated but set the whore free.

Soliman gazed at me, stroking his beard thoughtfully, and said, "We shall see."

Sixty-Six

Balthazar now had some forty years to him. Grey hairs had begun to assert themselves on his temples and in his beard, and his skin was no longer the smooth hide of a youngling, but at first glance he seemed in higher spirits than during our dismal sojourns in Constantinople and on Djerbé. Aye, those keen, sparkling eyes belonged to the spry man I once knew, thirteen long years ago. Without delay he ordered his to servant wash me with seawater, bring fresh clothes and thereat led me to an inn for a decent meal.

I nearly retched.

"*Vertu de Dieu!*" he exclaimed, "have you become so unaccustomed to proper food?"

That was it exactly, I nodded, excusing my lack of appetite. It would take time to grow accustomed to living. Truly, I felt walled off from my surroundings, as if an unseen glass prevented me from touching anything, from feeling the breeze or the sun. Balthazar sensed my distance, acknowledged it and made no attempt to unlock my soul by force. Rather, he waited. Others nearby us in the tavern were pouring over the prophesies of Nostradamus, who of late had become famous throughout Europe. Listening to the babble, Balthazar leaned over conspiratorially with his cup in hand, elbow on the table, and addressed me in a voice loud enough for all to hear. "Who be this Nostradamus? When I met him in Catherine's court and had him standing on his eyebrows in drink, the charlatan admitted forthrightly that he wrote his quatrains about events which had already taken place. 'All the astrologers do it,' he said."

Without hesitation, Balthazar commanded the book of prophecies be given to him, licked his forefinger and read:

"'From great dangers the captive is escaped.
Little time, great fortune changed.
In the palace the people are caught.
By good augury the city is besieged.'

"I say, what is this but Francisco's escape from the Turks and the threat to Malta! Nay, Nostradamus confessed to me that this verse and none other refers to Attila's sack of Ravenna and Galla Placidia's flight to the Goths."

Tho' in no merry humor myself, I could hardly restrain a chuckle, and neither did many around us. When they returned to their study of the astrologer's prognostications, I said to Balthazar, "It is good to see you in such cheer."

"Why not?" he replied, "I am at my *acme*—so the Greeks say." Now the Knight leaned back, regarding me. "You, on the other hand, look like a starved rat … one with sinews of iron."

"Aye," I said quietly, "the Fates have made me hard to kill off, haven't they? Let me thank you for your voyage of deliverance to Constantinople last season. Had I but known, I would have waited for you to ransom me."

"Think naught of it. I had business there in any case." Hereon Balthazar abruptly changed the subject. "Tell me, how is your sword arm?"

I had not picked up a rapier in, oh, four years, tho' I held little doubt my skill could soon return.

"Good, we will begin practicing on the morrow. And your Turkish?"

This question struck me as odd, but I told him likely as good as a janissary's. The Abbé cocked his head, and so I explained that, as all janissaries were stolen from Christian families, their Turkish was far from perfect, much as my French.

"*Ouy*," he said, and we fell silent.

"What disturbs you, Balthazar?" I said at length. "These high spirits methinks are some disguise, and your questions hardly idle."

"This rich *sultana* Romegas has seized from the *Kapi Agha* … " Balthazar shook his head. "The Commander has salted the dragon's tail once too often, and we shall soon feel the fire singing our breeches, believe me. We must strengthen ourselves for everything and lay in vast quantities of good cheer, for surely that is what will be in shortest supply. Now," he said, handing me a purse, "you will want a room."

I accepted the money with as much gratitude as I was then able, telling him I would soon repay it, somehow.

"What of Isabella?" I asked at last.

"Why," Balthazar replied, "she may tell you herself, for she is not one hundred paces from here, caring for her mother, who has been unwell." The Knight's countenance dimmed. "I must be honest with you, Francisco—Isabella was crushed when your padrone told her you had turned Turk, and that he could not accept a ransom because you were a free man."

"Truly?" I said, not comprehending any of this or sensing its import. As the Knights had observed with their own eyes, I hadn't been caponed, tho' in truth, the Turks did not require that mutilation to take up their faith. I was about to offer an explanation when Balthazar raised his hand.

"I have seen men enow return from captivity. Save explanations for her. We shall meet in the morning, if your strength has returned." With that he slapped me on the shoulder. For some reason it came into my head to ask him about his studies of Niccolò. "I no longer read him," he answered.

"How so?" If I had been capable of expressing astonishment at anything on this the day of my return, my astonishment would have been complete.

"He is under suspicion by the Inquisition. What of it? There are newer authors to be read ... somewhere." Again he slapped me on the shoulder and said with the slightest hint of gravity, "Take care."

The sun stood yet high in the sky, and as I stepped into the heat of the day, I gazed on Birgu with the same sensation that everything within my sight lay beyond my fingertips. I was as a walking ghost haunting these former environs, nothing more. I did not at once set about to find lodging. Dimly I perceived that I must again begin life anew. How? What sense to remain here? My thoughts were not so much a jumble as absent altogether. I could barely string together enough words to utter a sentence, but in the next moment Dr. Jean de Vigo passed me on the street and forced me to.

"*Buenos dias*, Francisco," he said, glancing up briefly from some papers in his hand, "it is good to see you again." In his distraction he evinced no surprise at my presence, as had he seen me a week ago. Only after taking a step beyond did he halt and, removing his prized Venetian spectacles, gaze upon me from head to toe with a wrinkled brow.

"I ... I heard you had been ... *away*," he stuttered and rushed to embrace me. "It *is* good to see you again."

"As it is you," I replied. Then, not able to think of ought else, I pointed to his papers. "Into what have you buried your red beard now, doctor?"

"Ah," he replied with enthusiasm, "it is quite remarkable. Gabrielle Fallopius—you of course know the famous Italian physician—claims to prevent the spread of syphilis by covering the male member with a sheath of linen tied by a pink ribbon. He has this year tested the invention on over one thousand men—so he writes to me—with perfect results."

"Perfect results?" I mused dully. "I can imagine the perfection of that experience."

"Yes, hmm, I imagine there is some room for improvement ... Francisco," the physician suddenly peered at me with a serious mien, "how are you? You were taken on Gelves."

I nodded, revealing that for four years I had been a slave in Constantinople and on a galley.

"You are a lucky man to be alive," Vigo replied. Am I? I wondered. He turned my head with his hand to regard the missing part of my left ear, then peered at my teeth. "Umm, not so ... bad, I can tell you have grown accustomed to the *siwak*. We can fill the teeth ... " His expression at once became serious. "I do hope, Francisco, you have not escaped the kettle for the fire, for our friend Barelli in Stamboul has been sending messages. Work in the Arsenal and Gun Foundry there seems to be ... *increasing*." Aye, I imagined. "There will be a descent on Christendom in the coming year. The Turks have not decided the objective, but everyone is terrified." Well they should be, well they should be. "Francisco, I must return to the Hospital. We shall speak when you are ready. *Vade in pace*." With that the good doctor departed.

I walked about Birgu, gazing at the small but now bustling sea port in which I found myself. On the main square some inspectors were burning books in a small bonfire as dogs barked around them, and nearby I noticed that on the doors to churches and taverns nameless denunciations, *libelli famosi*, had been posted: one charging a Knight with secret Lutheran practices, a second *scriptum diffamatorium* accusing a brother of bawdiness, a third charging someone with owning a Bible in French.

Book burnings would not take place in Venice, I thought. I watched for a moment, kicked a dog from my path and moved on. While I wandered aimlessly, infused at each step with the same sensation—the absence of it—that I was here but a spectre, a familiar voice shouted my name and I turned to see Pietru with a white-mantled woman at his side.

"I have wanted to ask whether you will want to share a room," I said to him in Italian.

"No, Cikku, I have found my wife. She is Grezz."

I glanced again at the woman, who so far as I could judge thro' her mantilla seemed plain enough, shorter e'en than Pietru and no less sturdy. I could scarce believe the words I'd just heard. Grezz said she had been a slave all this time in Argier and had finally escaped on a Christian ship. After thirteen years the two were reunited. I wiped a small tear from my eye. "You never gave up hope, did you, Xabaw?"

He shook his head. "You helped me hope, Cikku."

I do not know how he received my attempt at a smile. "Where will you stay?"

"We will farm on the other side of the island," they said.

"I shall visit," I answered and we parted company.

With amazement at this small mercy blinding my steps, I found myself before the Guasconi door and before I knew what I was doing, I knocked. A servant admitted me to the big room where Isabella sat alone in the light of a window, embroidering. She glanced up. For a moment she gazed on me without expression. Then, as a thousand emotions crossed her face, she dropped her embroidery and rose slowly to her feet. We stood apart, she with her hands clasped before her.

"Francisco," she said.

"Isabella," I bowed stiffly.

A moment of silence and awkwardness passed, whereupon she offered me a chair. We sat facing each other, the silence continuing as the light played on my cross that she yet wore and the *imprese* with two extinguished candles. At last I said, "There is much to speak of, or perhaps nothing."

"I think much," she said, lowering her head, "or perhaps nothing." She glanced away, biting her lip as tears came to her eyes. She dried them with her handkerchief, then said, "Excuse me for this outburst. Your presence is ... unexpected ... Let us walk, Francisco. I need the air." Isabella threw on a *faldetta* and we walked out thro' the city gates, past the stables and ramshackle houses encroaching on the new bastions, past the small chapel and onto the hills where a decade ago we strolled among the flowers and buzzing of insects.

The companion beside me was no longer the girl I once knew, but a grown woman, whose *faldetta* could not disguise a certain sadness in her bearing. Her eyes seemed deeper, darker than of old, but her hair, tied back, was still dyed blond and she did retain some resemblance to the women of that painter Balthazar spoke about, Botticelli. "I am indebted to you," I finally said, searching for a place to begin, "for your attempt to deliver me last year. To journey to Constantinople was as futile as it was dangerous."

"Truly, it was more dangerous than I had foreseen," she acknowledged, "but I have since wanted to kill myself for causing your escape to miscarry."

"This was ordained. You were not the cause ... Isabella," I said, taking my place on a large rock, "Balthazar has told me ... You believe me to be a renegado."

She nodded silently, painfully, and remained standing.

"You saw me dressed as a Christian, at the moment of our flight."

"Renegados often escape from Barbary," she said, "dressed as Christians."

"Because they have not turned in their hearts. God knows that." I told her how my padrone Abdallah saw that I had become of value at the Foundry and how he made the conditions for my release ever more difficult. "I do not doubt he would say such an evil thing to keep me there. Turks often refuse to ransom doctors, for they prove too valuable."

Isabella turned full on me with the same pained expression on her face. "How am I to believe you, Francisco?"

"Can a man be a *felo-de-se?* Because lying scoundrels have claimed that Moorish blood flows through these veins, you believe it would be easy for me."

"Yes."

I had no words to convince her and sat silently in the bright sun as she stood before me. As if she somehow perceived the inadequacy of words, at length Isabella bade me, thro' her eyes only, to rise. I did so, understanding what she requested, and as I towered above her I stripped off my shirt, letting it fall to the ground. The infinite mass of stripes that covered my chest and back, many received in recent months, now confronted her and she recoiled, putting her hands to her mouth in horror. When she gathered the strength, with great tentativeness Isabella extended her hand and ran her fingers along those scars, my disfigured ear, and her tears flowed freely.

"I do not want your pity, Isabella; I have survived."

At that, Isabella fell to her knees, clasping my cross before her. "If you will not have my pity, Francisco, allow me to beg your forgiveness, I beseech you."

I had no understanding of this. "I have ne'er known a woman to beg forgiveness," I said, kneeling with her. "Of what do you speak?"

"Of that time o'er ten years past when in a senseless terror to save myself, I gave you up to the Inquisitor." I nodded. It was long ago, but I conceded I had never understood the necessity or circumstance. "I beg you even now," she said with a sudden edge, "not to ask. Let us forgive each other for the sins that lie buried in our hearts and try to find each other again."

"I can forgive you," I said, with a great hesitancy touching the sweet, wet face before me, "but we are no longer the children we once were. We are strangers."

"Yes. We are strangers who have each passed through trials of our own and no longer see the world as before, but strangers may meet and come to know one another. Let us try."

We prayed in that nearby chapel of Santa Margarita as chickens roamed about and we walked side by side across the hill covered by a warm breeze and dragonflies. We spoke little and about nothing of consequence. In this gentle way Isabella quietly undertook to bring me back to life. I asked her to relate to me the events in her own life and the first thing she said was that late this past year Michelangelo had died.

"His nephew brought his body to Firenze in a bale and buried him in Santa Croce. Much of the city came out, I among the crowds. He painted the portrait of me hanging in my house—such a difficult man. But with his passing, Francisco, an age has ended, I feel it. Of all men of our times, God's divine glory shone through him in its full splendor, and he will be remembered as the highest, do you not think so?"

I told her that the question was stupid, ignorant. What answer could she want from a man who had spent four years thinking of naught but food and flight? She apologized. After a silence I asked, What of herself?

At that she laughed quietly and said, "Is it not strange how we are destined to travel along the same invisible circles all our lives, like the planets. I had thought to escape this island and its malicious gossip to a better life, but here I am again. I think my greatest accomplishment in Firenze was to whisper in Duke Cosimo's ear to build new offices next to the Palazzo Vecchio." Isabella went on to boast lightly of suitors who knelt at her feet, tho' she pointedly exclaimed that she rejected them all. She could not herself express the reasons, but the distance she kept and her downward glances revealed a woman who had become accustomed to a solitude of spirit. "I have," she said, suddenly more playful, "published two books of verses and received much praise, all because of you, Francisco. But ... " her mien again grew more pensive, "it can be of no consequence."

What was she saying?

"Francisco," she turned to me, yet standing apart, "another age is ending. I am frightened." The Turks? "Yes. A great trial of strength is approaching. An invasion will come soon."

"Every year tongues say there will be an invasion," I scoffed. "The Order's intelligence is shit."

"Francisco, do not play the fool. You, I am certain, know better than others."

"Yes."

"What are we to do?" Her voice was filled with true urgency.

Return to Firenze, I told her. "Parisot is a soldier. He knows the business of war. When attacked by a foe, you fight as you have learnt. That is all. Go home."

The silence about us became entire. Not a toad sounded or a cricket chirped. Isabella bent to pick up a sprig of thyme, shaking her head as she smelled it. "No. My circle has brought me hither. Mother needs me. Parisot will need me. He will need all of us."

"I had thought to return to Spain," I said.

Isabella turned full on me with a hard glance that at once softened. She nodded. "If I asked you to remain?" I made no answer as her deep eyes gazed into mine. "Come, let us speak to Parisot," she said.

Outside the Grand Master's house a small crowd of Knights had gathered, celebrating the capture of the *Kapi Agha*'s galleon with its fabulous riches. Among this lively rabble stood Vergã, wearing the half-cross of the confrater on his mantle, surrounded by his bravi. As on that time at Crete, he failed to recognize me when I walked past. Catching sight of Isabella, tho', he bowed graciously to her and she curtsied in return. Only then did Vergã realize who stood at her side.

"By the Holy Vow I made when I was freed from the Galleys of the Infidels!" he exclaimed in the highest spirits and outright disbelief, "Esforzado is alive! Hah!"

"I do not grant you use of that oath," I answered, staring dully at him as he offered his hand.

"And you refuse to embrace me?" he said, and with a glance to his bravi added, "Four years ago we put aside our quarrels, did we not, Francisco?"

I had little choice and slowly our arms locked. All the while Isabella watched this reunion with curiosity and suspicion. "En route to Constantinople," she remarked as we left the crowd and stepped thro' the door, "he saved me from a certain death. I do owe him my life."

My surprise at hearing this was great, but we spoke no more of it, for inside de Valette and Romegas were raising their cups in a salute. Parisot, in a good humor after the Commander's success, invited us to join them, which we did, his lioness sitting amongst our feet. Shortly afterwards, Romegas departed, already planning to set sail again and we were alone in the Grand Master's presence.

"Parisot," Isabella said, "do you remember Francisco de Barai?"

"I do," he nodded, extending his ring. As I kissed it the old man asked where I had been these past years. de Valette was an old man now, of mayhap sixty-five years, with the frown of yore surrounded now by a fully white beard. His eyes, tho', shone with some inner fire that hadn't diminished over the seasons. I briefly answered his question. My tale did not strike him as unusual, as indeed he and so many others here had passed thro' suchlike histories. He nodded in a matter-of-fact way, taking in my stripes, the nick out of my ear, glancing at the shackles above the door. Then he said, "Good. Tell me, Señor, should God will a descent on this island, what advice would you give me?"

I did not think long. "Beware their weapons. I assure you they are terrible as I have cast many of them myself. Moreso, give all respect to the foe, Eminenza. The *yenicheriler* are trained soldiers, as are the Porte *spahiler* and the *silahdarlar*. They show more discipline by far than the unruly soldiers under your command and are willing to die for their Sultan and their faith. They are greater warriors than the Knights of St. John."

de Valette raised an eyebrow. "Indeed. Then the outcome shall be a matter of who holds the greater faith, shall it not?"

"There is another thing," I ventured. "Once I asked you to tell me about Rhodes. Perhaps now is the time."

Parisot nodded pensively, then, as forgetting me, turned to his ward. "You, Isabella, what advice would you give?"

She sucked in her breath, glanced at me. "Parisot," she replied after a long silence, "I am able to ride a horse, but of warfare I am ignorant, you know that."

"Go on, Isabella."

Nervously, Isabella found the lioness's ear with her hand and began to scratch it. "Parisot, the simple people on this island fear you greatly and many Knights do as well. Were I to presume to advise my own guardian, I would say it is not enough for your subjects to fear you. They must love you. You must inspire them, and they must be willing to die for you."

"Not for me," de Valette replied sternly, "for God."

Isabella curtsied. "For God, then, at your behest. O Parisot, our men have been defeated in battle time and time again because they are without loyalties. You must find that which commands their loyalty in here." With a momentary hesitation, then resolution, she pressed her hand firmly to his chest.

Startled by this, the Grand Master ushered us toward the door. "Thank you children for your advice," he said. "Now leave me to think on it. I have much pondering to do."

I bowed, Isabella curtsied again, and we took our leave. "You were right," I said on the street, "another age is ending. The last Crusade has begun." I stiffly bent to kiss Isabella's hand and we parted company for the day. We all had much pondering to do.

Sixty-Seven

Early next morning Balthazar and I made toward the hills to the west of the Borgo for our rite of swords. Just outside the gates our attention was diverted by some Greek fishermen, who with baskets of fish at their feet and their long rods resting against the walls, were selling the morning's catch. They joked that I looked in need of a proper meal. More than one, Balthazar agreed, ordering his servant to buy a few fish to cook up later, suggesting also that they might find more famished soldiers yonder, in Fort. St. Michel. Happily they set off in the direction Balthazar pointed. When they had gone I remarked that the fish did not appear to me entirely fresh.

The Chevalier replied, "Remember, boy, it is not fish you are buying but men's lives."

We climbed to the spot beyond the little chapel with its wandering chickens and took up our rapiers. As the fish mongers observed, tho', I had recovered neither strength nor sword arm and proved a worthless fencing partner. Before long I called a halt, fairly collapsed on a rock and gratefully accepted wine from the hand of Balthazar's man.

"Forgive me," I said in a stupor, as falcons perched on nearby rocks observed us. "I fear I am not who I was."

Balthazar sat down, wincing as a sharp pain from Gelves shot through his side, sighed and also took a cup of wine from his servant. "Nonsense, you are weary after your ordeal, but we both know that when your strength returns, it will be greater than before."

With this Balthazar, like Isabella, undertook his efforts to bring me back to life. I despaired that anything would come of it, our first lesson having just ended in disaster. He would not agree to leave off, tho', for reasons he kept to himself, and insisted we resume on the morrow. With my breath yet heavy, I regarded this Knight, sitting easily on a rock by me. After all these years, he remained something of a mystery.

"What do you search for, Balthazar?" I asked him.

He gazed far off to the horizon. "As a youth I thought I would accomplish epic deeds. As a Knight I battled the Infidel to an end that grows ever more distant. As I have grown older, the Religion has sent me on more missions that require delicacy over muscle. Now, with the great contest looming, I should like to find a place in which a man can live, but as Thomas More understood, utopias are nowhere to be found."

I had not heard of More or utopias, I said, yet puzzled.

"'Tis not to be regretted," Balthazar answered easily, "if his books have not already been reduced to ashes on the square, they soon will be." For a moment the Knight regarded the falcons feeding nearby, then we gathered up our weapons and walked down the hill.

The next morning Isabella was coming from market with one of her servants when she encountered Blaij Vergã. He himself was walking with a few bravi toward the house he had recently built in this quarter. For a moment Isabella felt a sharp resentment of the rabble who built houses for their mistresses within sight of her own, but she put it aside when Vergã bowed to her. As on each encounter with him, Isabella recognized the man's commanding demeanor, which showed clearly in the deference his friends granted him. Isabella extended her hand, sending the servant home.

"That is a splendid mirror you have purchased, Señora," Vergã said in a boisterous voice, meant as much for his audience as for her, "tho' the reflection any glass could give would be but a pale shadow of the face gazing into it."

Isabella blushed in spite of herself, but found a reply: "I must apologize for the sin of vanity, Señor," she said, regarding Blaij while likewise speaking to the others. "Were this a true convent and we true brothers and sisters, we would not permit such wicked contrivances into our cells."

"I am surprised Parisot has not outlawed them," Vergã remarked.

"An excellent thought," said Isabella. "I shall mention it to him and, meanwhile, burn my own." At that Blaij bowed jovially again for his comrades, whereas Isabella suddenly shuddered unnoticed, thinking she must have bought the mirror to divine the future, which hinted at witchcraft. She *would* burn it. Abruptly, she took a step back and nodded to them all. "Yesterday I saw you and Francisco shake hands. I trust, therefore, your ancient quarrel is truly and finally behind you."

"Señora," Blaij replied, "some years ago I put away my grievances. After all, despite the accident of our births, my prowess has made me rich and esteemed by my comrades, while Francisco's path has led to his ruin in the hands of the infidels."

"Ruin? He has survived his trial and, Señor, he has not been ruined by the infidels so much as others have by pride. Your grievances? As I recall, it was you who ten years ago on these docks nearly killed him, for no reason."

Vergã's bravi, seeing a different sort of duel unfolding, quickly found excuses to depart. When at last the two were alone, Vergã answered. "Señora, I remind you that it was he who stole a woman from me, one named Isabella, and it was he who first attempted to kill me. Of what do I stand accused?"

Isabella quickly saw that she was opening old wounds and yielded a step, but not two. "You count his birth against him, Blaij Vergã. Why is that?"

"Ah, Señora Guasconi, again you wrong me. I hold nothing against him. I confess to you and you alone, that in our youth it was difficult to see him receive every advantage merely because his father acknowledged him, while I was the worthier and of purer blood. But, I say again, I have risen far and our quarrels are over."

Despite his protests, Isabella found little sympathy for this arrogant confrater. "Señor," she answered, "I know something about not knowing one's father. Each of us has a cross to bear while traversing this defiled earth, and yours is neither so rare nor so heavy as to justify the grievous sins you wrought against another."

Blaij perceived he had been insulted, but as he was unable to draw arms against this opponent, he bowed again. "Milady, a year ago I had the honor of saving your life. If that is not enough to win your esteem, I beg your forgiveness."

While Isabella remained speechless, Blaij moved on.

A few hours afterwards, Vergã departed on another caravan with Romegas. At about the same time, without mentioning her encounter, Isabella invited me to lunch in Mdina, where her mother was this day. We rode out in a silence broken only by Isabella, who at odd moments would begin singing merrily, then halt with a start. The city had changed hardly at all since Strozzi had repaired the walls after the *razzia*. Catching sight of Matteo Falzon's mansion, I asked about the heretic, almost my first words since leaving Birgu. Isabella lowered her head and said that they had not associated during these long years since the Tribunal; the Falzon family had withdrawn entirely to Mdina, having almost no contact with anyone. We trotted past the house and I gazed at the shuttered windows, wondering less than I ought of what ghosts haunted the inside as I did the out.

Lady Emilia had aged greatly, and if ten years ago she had seemed disposed to worry, her frail and narrow frame now gave her the aspect of being more so inclined. At table I inquired after her health. She replied that she had of late been full of complaints, from her heart to her bones, but that the useless physicians could not describe her malady other than to say old age was nearing; fifty years, after all, did lurk around the corner. I heard her words without truly listening.

"Isabella says you have been in Venezia and Constantinople," she offered. "I do not like Veneziani much. Was it terrible among the Turks? Did you see the harem? I've heard so many stories about the harem." She went on to inquire about my plans.

From her questions I could in no way discern whether Emilia knew I had been a slave. I made no answer.

"I have asked Francisco to remain on Malta," Isabella replied for me, laying her hand briefly on mine.

She elicited from me only a rebuke. "I told you I must return to Spain," I said harshly. "Lo those many years ago, Vergã stole my life and now I intend to reclaim it."

Isabella gazed fixedly at the bowl of fruit before her. "What will you find in Spain, Francisco?" she asked at last. "I know you are bitter about the fate that befell you on Gelves—"

"What can you know about that, Signora? To be betrayed by your King and cast onto the galleys among the vermin as if you were no better than they? To eat them and be grateful to have food?"

Isabella stifled a sob and excused herself, seeing now that her presence could not in a day salve the wounds inflicted by years of servitude. But she refused to abandon this bitter man to his prison. She picked up her lute, which to my surprise she had learned to play in Firenze, and sang. Listening to her elicited from me the faintest of smiles, which pleased her. Before we returned to Birgu, she bade me kneel before the image of the Blessed Mother and pray with her. I knelt, but some time on Cocia-Cocia's galley the last prayer had escaped my lips. Isabella did not upbraid me for my failure to pray. She prayed for me.

"Isabella," I said on the ride back, "a part of me died on the Executioner's galley, and you must accept that what of me still lives is of a different color than before."

When Isabella suddenly perceived that I had been a slave on the galley of the same Cocia-Cocia who had very nearly raped and killed her, she shuddered with a greater understanding. Yet she refused to yield. "I have seen men return from captivity," she replied as we trotted past a few cows lowing behind stone walls, "and I vowed to Balthazar I would not allow what happens to them happen to you. I have kept your crucifix all these years, dear Francisco, and I know you shall find strength in what you have passed through."

"I cannot e'en say when I lost your kerchief," I retorted, "I think when Balthazar and I swam for our lives at Djerbé."

It was like that. Isabella and I met daily and somehow not. When the bells sounded Paternoster and Ave Maria she prayed next to me; a distance always separated us. We walked, we rode. On the hillside Isabella often broke into song. I asked wherefore these tunes and she answered anyone who did not sing in Firenze was a barbarian, but thereat she would halt, naming it sinful. We rode on.

Over the days, weeks, the sensation that I was cut off from the landscape about me diminished, but a full resurrection, I perceived, was never to be granted. Not long after my arrival, I spied a gaunt Ramon Caravajal one day in a tavern; what was left of him had of late also been freed from the Turks in a sea battle.

"I would kill every Turk alive," he declared with all vehemence to those gathered near, "and I mean to do it."

At the table sat a Provençal, Pierre de Massuez Vercoryran, the same Colonel Mas who had been taken prisoner on Djerbé and since ransomed by Busbecq. He replied gravely to Caravajal, "*Per Dominum Nostrum*, I am ready to sell my life in battle, but not before I take the heads of one hundred Turks."

At that moment both men caught sight of me, the usual pause of bewilderment crossed their faces; then, raising their cups, they growled with cold steel in their voices, "*Uscança dy guerra.*"

"*Uscança dy guerra*," I returned the toast. I saw much of me in them.

Isabella attempted without force to dissuade me from returning to Spain. She was correct; my parents were likely dead and the first Isabella was surely long married with a family of her own. I could not explain e'en to myself why I desired to return, other that to discover someone who once knew me and prove that some trace of Francisco de Barai was yet to be found on this earth, and that his blood was pure.

After a month on Malta, I passed a gun-maker's shop and with no warning to myself asked for work. The shop master agreed and I set about fashioning some arquebuses, including a fine wheel-lock for myself. I spent much time ornamenting the stock with brass and ivory and it pleased me greatly. Seeing that I was far the best gun-maker on the island, some of the soldiers ordered weapons from me and soon I was able to repay Balthazar's loan.

At the Knight's insistence, the two of us continued our daily practice on the hills with both rapiers and the *montantes* Balthazar preferred. I never did overcome my distaste of those great two-handers, and whenever he demanded we try them, my despair at ever recovering my skill redoubled. The Abbé astonished me. His youth was behind him and he often suffered pain from his wounds, yet he husbanded his strength and when we bouted he evinced hardly more concern than on that long-ago day in Africa when we'd first met and fought. Truly, he watched like a hawk, denying me any opening and, worst of all, when my attacks were as slipshod as a child's, he would distract himself by telling a story. "Let me tell you about the time in Italy ... " he'd offer, just before he caught my arm and pinned me to the ground.

But we persisted and he proved right; before too many weeks passed I had a sword arm again. Finally one morning we were bouting when suddenly I felt the rapier thro' from pommel to tip. My arms, legs and mind were acting together. In an instant I had disarmed the Knight and held a dagger at his throat.

"You see," Balthazar laughed, "the first day we met, lo those many years ago, I foretold you would someday best me. Now you have." He offered his hand.

The cannons on Fort St. Angelo were booming, and as soon as the townsfolk realized they'd heard naught but a salute, all Birgu rushed toward Galley Creek. Balthazar, who happened to be walking thro' the square, ran down with the rest. Triumphant fanfares of trumpets and drums greeted them, fanfares announcing that Commander Romegas had returned from his latest foray on the Grand Master's galleys.

The vessels docked. Moment by moment, as the crews disembarked and told their stories, the murmuring of the bystanders increased. One hundred Turkish prisoners were marched off, followed by two hundred *negri* and Moors, followed by Mahomet Bey, the new Governor of Cairo, followed by the Sanjak-bey of Alexandria, followed by four sailors carrying a woman old beyond old in a chair.

"Who is that?" Balthazar asked as she was taken past him.

One of the crewmen answered: "The nurse of the Sultan's daughter Mihrimah."

Balthazar lost not a breath. He crossed himself and left the docks to seek out the Grand Master, but the Council was in session. By the time he found de Valette later at his house, the Monsignore had been well informed of the caravan's success and was in high spirits, fairly rubbing his hands together in delight.

"We will ransom the Bey for twenty-five thousand gold *zecchini*," he said, and unable to restrain himself added, "At least that will to a degree make up for the Pope's failure to remember us at Trento."

Twenty-five thousand Venetian ducats! Balthazar thought—that is an enormous sum. "And the nurse?" he asked. "What will you do with her? She is too old—"

"One hundred and seven years!" de Valette cackled. "Can you believe it? The very nurse of the Sultan's daughter returning from Mecca! What a ransom she will fetch!"

"Eminenza," said Balthazar urgently, "you know exactly what ransom she will fetch. I implore you, set her free or with the speed of dark angels you will bring down the Grand Turk's full wrath upon this island."

de Valette regarded Balthazar with flaming eyes. "Fra Balthazar, have you forgotten our sworn duty to fight the Infidel? If war has been ordained, we cannot now prevent it." Thereat, the Monsignore began to pace. His lioness followed him with her own eyes, naught else. "A propos, I would like you to return to Constantinople, meet Barelli and hear from his lips the state—"

"Sir, you receive regular intelligence from Barelli, do you not?"

de Valette nodded. "His service has been unwavering, I thank you, Fra Balthazar. But letters traveling three hundred leagues go awry and at this moment above all we must have exact and trustworthy information. You have been in that city twice before, and your eyes will prove invaluable—"

"Eminenza—"

"Commander Romegas will ferry you as far as Crete. He will go on to attack Malvasia in an attempt to wrest it from Soliman."

Balthazar's innards froze from top to bottom. "Eminenza!" he exclaimed thoughtlessly, "this is mad! Soliman himself failed to take that crag by force. Malvasia is impregnable, I tell you! There can be no purpose to such an expedition!"

"Fra Balthazar, are you refusing to obey the Grand Master?"

"My vow has never faltered, Eminenza," replied the Knight, recovering a proper contrition.

"Then thank you for your advice. Leave me."

Soon thereafter, Balthazar found me at my room, appearing as gaunt and weary as if he had just returned from a campaign in Italia. "Come," he said, putting his arm around my shoulder, "let us eat."

We entered the shingleless tavern to find Blaij Vergã sitting in the cellar, dressed in clothes no poorer than a Spanish gentleman's, and surrounded by Knights and townsfolk eager to hear all about the great haul. He narrated the adventure, taking no notice of Balthazar and me as we took places nearby. One could almost believe Vergã as he recounted how they'd run across a great armed merchantman en route from Alexandria to Constantinople and accidentally put a hole in its hull.

"Too bad we sank it," he mused. "That boat carried one hundred thousand ducats of loot." Romegas allowed the women and children to escape to shore, and took only the men, the Governor of Cairo and the nurse. "The escort flew to the Devil, knowing the Commander was on them ... A few days later we sighted another ship bound for Constantinople. This one carried the Sanjak-bey of Alexandria ... "

As he finished, those by him applauded. "You'll be made a Serving Brother for sure," said one of his bravi. Aye, Vergã had not lost his foothold on the ladder.

"Even a Knight of Grace," proposed another with enthusiasm.

At this, Blaij glanced at me, smiling. "You see, Francisco, all spoils to the daring."

He raised his cup; I returned the salute, then with Balthazar's hand on mine, I turned away to see the Knight's eyes, which were more troubled at this moment than when we'd entered the tavern. "What ails you, Balthazar?" I asked, and quickly forgot Vergã.

Pondering the cup in his own hand, Balthazar recounted his conversation with the Grand Master. Of Malvasia I had only the vaguest knowledge. It was a tiny island, Balthazar said, off the southeastern coast of Greece, in the Morea. "The Venetians ceded it to Soliman as part of a peace, oh, twenty-five years ago. Before that Soliman had attempted to take the place by force without success. I tell you, it is impossible. The isle sits just off the mainland, connected by a bridge. It is a perfect crag, hardly different in aspect from Gibraltar itself, but with girth of only a league. There's a town but no beaches on which to camp, the cliffs rise straight up and a castle sits atop. Malvasia is a natural fortress. I do not understand what Parisot can be thinking unless ... "

I put the question with my eyes alone.

"He intends to provoke the Grand Signor, naught else. This is more than folly; it is madness." Balthazar abruptly halted himself, violently shaking his head. "Nay. Parisot is no madman. There is something unseen in this, I say ... " Without a pause the Abbé looked up. "Parisot has ordered me to return to Constantinople to meet Barelli—"

The gaze I leveled at him evinced not the slightest amusement.

Balthazar raised his hand. "Pâce. I must go. The question, which has arisen more than once during our association, is whether you will accompany me." Leaning back, the Chevalier smiled gravely. "Yes, your stripes have barely healed after four years of servitude—or perhaps they have not."

"If the plan is to gather intelligence—" my eyes had yet to leave his—"I am known at the Foundry and the Arsenal."

"The mission will be the most dangerous. You speak Turkish."

"Barelli speaks it perfectly."

"True. Parisot needs trusted couriers. I would advise you not to go for the sake of the Order—"

Hereon I stood, still not taking my eyes from him. "You well know I am unable to deny you, Balthazar."

Balthazar raised his head serenely. "I release you from any obligation you feel toward me. It is between you and the Turks, and that is all."

Between me and the Turks, and that is all. I sought out Isabella, only to find her in a small frenzy. When her servant admitted me, she led me by the arm to the sitting room, where I gazed on none other than the captured one-hundred-seven-year-old nurse. Her face resembled perfectly an ancient tree trunk, knotty and gnarled, and her beclouded eyes revealed she was near blind, but as she sat before us she gesticulated with wild frailty, unleashing from her two-toothed mouth a torrent of curses and oaths I would scarce expect to hear from the lips of a janissary, shrieking finally that Allah would wreak a horrible revenge upon the Knights and all unbelievers.

"What is she saying?" Isabella asked at hearing this jagged whirlwind of screeches.

She did not wish to know, I assured her, but she compares the Grand Master to a certain part of a dog.

Isabella scarcely blushed. "Please tell her that in the custom of the Hospitallers, she will be treated as an honored guest and be allowed to remain in this house. Her servant Feruc will, I believe, be permitted to return to Constantinople to negotiate her ransom."

After learning that the nurse's name was Giansevere Serchies, I translated what Isabella asked. This news pacified granny not in the slightest, and when a slave offered her a tray of fruit she knocked it from his hands with a surprising contempt, sitting before us with arms crossed in regal silence.

Isabella and I removed ourselves to the garden. "How is it that I find her in your house?" I asked.

"Parisot does not wish to put her in a dungeon."

"Truly," I said, "she and your mother should get along well."

Isabella all but laughed aloud, remarking that this was the first jest she'd heard from my lips since my arrival. But, she said, Emilia would certainly choose to remain at Mdina rather than live under the same roof with an infidel.

Hereat I turned the conversation to a more serious color, recounting what Balthazar had told me about Malvasia. "Methinks Parisot has not accepted anyone's advice," I said. Isabella shook her head in perplexity, answering as Balthazar had that Parisot was far from mad and something must surely lie behind this. I told her then that the Abbé had asked me to accompany him to Constantinople.

Isabella regarded me for a long time with her hands clasped at her waist, understanding all the conflicting desires in the man standing before her and in herself. "Francisco," she said at long last, "I ask you to consider one thing only: All Christendom hangs in the balance."

Sixty-Eight

The Grand Master's two galleys, a galiot seized from the corsair Yusuf Conciny, two brigantines, a *fregata* and an old Greek set sail for Malvasia at the beginning of September. So important did the Monsignore deem this undertaking that he had named his own nephew, Commander François de Valette, also called Parisot, chief of the *Philippe Corona*. He regretted speaking to Balthazar of the enterprise, and so secret became the exact preparations that he revealed to Romegas himself little more than the destination. Only when we were approaching the Morea did Romegas and Parisot open the sealed plans in the armory of the *S. Gabriele* and did the Greek explain to the Knights how those plans might be accomplished.

Afterwards, Balthazar found me below in one of the holds, trying with others to catch some sleep on a blanket among some grain sacks in these rough seas. "I believe I misunderstood Parisot," the Knight said gravely. "There is a strategy behind this mission." I sat up rubbing my eyes as he perched himself beside me on one of the bags. "So apprehensive is de Valette that a descent will fall on Malta that he has sent Romegas and Commander Parisot to seize Malvasia in the hope that the Grand Turk will instead divert an invasion to that place. In the meanwhile, he hopes to convince other Christian leaders to send forces thither to use as a base for the war against the Turks."

"It is an attempt to save Malta, then," I repeated as in a fog.

Balthazar nodded. "A desperate attempt."

I could not entirely grasp it. If the place was impregnable, how did Parisot think to succeed?

"The old Greek aboard, Antoine de Ravenne, hails from Malvasia. He says he can conduct us from the mainland across the bridge, which is entirely unguarded, to a cave large enough to shelter five hundred men. From there he says a secret footpath leads up to the fortress atop the crag. The castle's walls are low and can easily be scaled. From there it will be easy to skirt the sentinels. Inside the fort, he says, there are no more than one hundred soldiers, old and crippled."

I listened to Balthazar's relation of the plan with some concern. "You say 'us.' Is not our mission otherwise?"

"Malvasia is but a step to Crete. I say we lend a hand with this undertaking. Then it will be an easy matter to return to Candia and arrange passage to Constantinople."

"Balthazar, I replied, shaking my head, "this is unwise. Should I perish in an assault, so be it. Should you perish, the mission to Istanbul is foiled. We cannot risk it. You are disobeying orders."

He began to sing that song: "Talk to me not of the frowns of Fate or adverse Fortune; nor offend my ears with tales of slavery's suffering in Argier ... You are correct, Esforzado, I shall tell Romegas to drop us off at Candia."

Underhanded rogue. Balthazar knew his companion too well. Francisco Perez de Barai had slowly come to understand that he held no high principles or deep beliefs, and of late he found naught within him except a hatred of his captors and a stronger desire to build his life again. Yet the youthful smile he saw in Balthazar's eyes reminded him of days when, truly, he had been *esforzado*. He got to his feet.

We had reached the Morea only some leagues from Malvasia when, within the sands of a watch, a phalanx of black clouds swept over the clear evening sky. The wind suddenly whipped itself into a fury and raindrops began pelting us like rocks. Each man raised his eyes to the heavens, crossing himself, but before we knew what was happening God had leashed from his hands a tempest the likes of which few of us had seen.

St. Elmo's fire lit the masts and spars so brightly that we expected the ship to burn up right then. It nearly did; a lightning bolt stuck so close to the mast, accompanied by a deafening thunderclap at the same instant, that every heart aboard ceased to beat and each one's owner thought he had died.

Romegas steadied his hands. "*Arria vela!* Strike the sails!" he commanded at once, feeling that hard rain lashing his face.

At his signal the *comiti* were already shouting, "Row you dogs!" but the rain and thunder were drowning out their words. "Row for your lives! *Tira! Tira!*"

It was no use. The whips came down again and again on the backs of the slaves and they heaved for all they were worth, but they made no headway toward land, which lay within easy sight of us.

"We must make land!" shouted Romegas to his pilot.

Night was falling but the lightning that flashed all around lit the coast as were cannon firing. "Look at those rocks!" shouted the pilot as he lashed himself to the tiller. "We try to make land and we'll end up splinters!" He glanced into the darkening sky. "We're losing light. We ride it out."

With a nod from the Commander, the *comito* ordered the canvas raised. The crew and *ciurma* huddled underneath—to no avail. Driven by that unearthly wind, the waves crashed again and again over the wales. The deck was awash, the bow was under. Surely, we would founder in the next moments. "Toss the artillery overboard!" Romegas ordered and the *gente* went at it.

"Give me a damn knife!" I cried and sawed at the tackle holding the gun carriages in place. Balthazar and five others put their shoulders to those pieces as I cut the ropes and together we tipped them over the side. Such was the water's turbulence that they disappeared without a splash. Suddenly, the *S. Gabriele*'s bow came up and for a moment we were saved.

"Better guns than wine," remarked Balthazar. More men were struggling up from the holds with cannon balls in their hands or other weights and heaving them over. In this way, we managed to survive the night, but as the sky slowly changed from pitch black to dull grey, the rain never let up, nor did the waves decrease their fury. The only thing we could discern was that this canvas was in tatters and we threw what was left of it overboard.

"Where are the other boats?" Romegas shouted, peering through the slashing rain and the feeble dawn, not being able to see much farther than the end of his nose. The *Corona* lay off to our starboard, buffeted about with the same violence as we. The *comiti* tried signaling with lanterns. The galiot, farther out, was afloat but we descried no sign of the *fregata*; it had disappeared overnight. Another wave crashed into us. As the arquebusiers and Knights held on to the cables and wales for dear life, the same torrent drove one of the brigantines straight into the rocks and smashed it to pieces. Moments later we espied two or three of the men climbing onto the rocks, but the others had gone. Now the second brigantine foundered and disappeared.

Still the tempest showed no signs of abating.

"We must make land or we are lost," said Romegas to the pilot. He personally ordered the *ciurma* to row for shore. The pilot leaned on that tiller with all his might to steady the ship but it was no use. Another wave rose up and tossed us towards the rocks. Oars splintered as we grazed the deadly eminences. Cables frayed against them and snapped. A block loosed flew against the head of the soldier next to me and knocked him over.

Everyone thought we were gone. Somehow we had to get in between those rocks. Of a sudden one of the young boys appeared from the hold carrying a large net, which had a thin rope running through an end of it. "Let us throw it over one the rocks," he said to the *sotto-comito*, both steadying themselves against the mainmast. "We'll pass a bigger rope through it and pull ourselves in."

They tried. Once, no. Twice, no. Vergã joined them. Four times they cast the net until it caught one of the nearest rocks and stayed. They tied a larger rope to the end of the smaller one, passed it thro' the net, then tied a cable onto that and pulled that one thro'. Finally, when they had passed a larger cable thro' the net, everyone pulled, and somehow with the *ciurma* steadying the boat with their oars as well as they might, we managed to guide the *S. Gabriele* to shore.

The storm went on another day. When at last the skies cleared, all the small boats had been lost, the large ones damaged and any number of men drowned. The rest of us, half alive, dragged the supplies ashore. Some gave thanks to God for their deliverance. I muttered to Balthazar, "A step to Crete, eh?" but the Knight, peering into a wine cask he had just opened, said only, "In truth, God has delivered us."

With what strength remained we spent still another day repairing the galleys and fishing for the artillery, which we managed to recover from the crystal clear water. The old Greek Ravenne assured Romegas that we had landed only four leagues from Malvasia and so the Commander took the *S. Gabriel*e a short distance up the coast to a little port where we hired two barques from the local people. Then a small group, led by Ravenne, rowed further to the place where the bridge joined Malvasia to the mainland. It was as Balthazar had described.

Impregnable.

"Where is the cave?" asked Romegas, gazing at that rock which towered a hundred *brazas* above the water.

"Above that eminence," pointed the Greek, "halfway up."

All the Knights in this party glanced at one another. "That is a sheer cliff," Romegas said. "Are you certain, old man, we can get to the fortress?"

Ravenne nodded. "Oh yes. We'll climb to the cave. The path is above it."

Romegas's hands were beginning to tremble. He steadied himself, shot Ravenne a burning glance and we returned to camp, not a man among us thinking this could be done.

That night, we loaded all the hammers, ropes, spikes and other things needed for climbing, and about one hundred Knights and arquebusiers crowded onto the barques and some other small boats we had borrowed, and set off again. Half a league south of Malvasia we abandoned the boats and marched up the coast. The Greek had been right: no one guarded the bridge. Under cover of darkness we crossed from the mainland to the island in good order without encountering a soul. Ravenne led us across the shallow apron of land that surrounds the rock and within moments we had reached the wall. Each man craned his neck and gazed to the sky. We could see well enough under the *Via Lactia* and a half moon. Close up, what had seemed a precipice from afar appeared hardly less so, but among us were men as agile as cats. They fastened ropes and hammers about their waists, found hand and footholds and began the ascent.

An hour passed while those below awaited in silence with weapons at the ready. Now and again a small rock or pebble tumbled down from above but no one observed our presence. At length, the climbers signaled that they had gained the grotto and the rest of us, putting hand to rope, followed. Vergã was up immediately, I behind him on the same rope and Balthazar behind me. Halfway to the cave, the rock below my foot dislodged, hit Balthazar in the shoulder and suddenly I had lost my footing. There I was, hanging in mid-air by one hand, thirty or forty *brazas* above the ground. Without hesitation Vergã lowered himself to the ledge directly above me.

"Here," he said, giving me his hand. At once I took it and Blaij pulled me up to the ledge. But a moment later Balthazar slipped in the same spot and was hanging far above the rocks as I had, by a hand. He uttered no cry for fear of the enemy hearing. Not knowing what had happened, Vergã continued up. I knelt as I could on this narrow shelf, wrapping one arm around the rope and grabbing Balthazar's arm with the other. He found the ledge with his free hand. We both groaned and I pulled. Soon he was standing beside me.

"Once again I am in your debt," he said, brushing himself off.

"When the full count is tallied, I fear I shall never be able to repay mine."

He slapped me on the shoulder and we climbed.

Two more hours passed before all the men were safely in the cave. "Now where is this path?" said Romegas to Ravenne when most of them had gathered.

The old man replied that there was a crevice nearby, a chimney that would allow us to attain the summit. Immediately Romegas ordered his climbers to find it. After some time these mountain goats returned, not having seen anything in the dark.

"I'll go," Vergã said at once, but Balthazar and I were already out the grotto's mouth.

Truly, we could see almost nothing. Nearby was a narrow path, but after a few steps it ended at a sheer drop. We tried to climb above the mouth of the cave. "There's something here," I whispered, sensing a deeper shadow within the darkness. It was a fissure, a crack, something that ran upwards. I wedged myself into it and pushed, Balthazar close behind me. Vergã also wasted no time, scrambling up behind us. This time, tho', it was Blaij in his haste who slipped, just at the entrance to this chimney. He slid downward, losing his balance on a toehold beneath him, tottering backwards. Balthazar instantly let himself down. For a heartbeat I thought he hesitated; I must have imagined it: He grabbed Vergã by the shirt and we continued up the chimney. But it shortly ended, blocked, and here was no way forward. Carefully we climbed down again to the cave.

"Well?" Romegas asked.

"No," said Balthazar, shaking his head in the dim light. Someone had lit lanterns. "We could not find a way."

The Commander was ill-pleased. "It'll be daylight in a few hours. What do we do?"

"We might leave a few men in the cave to find the path during the day," Balthazar suggested, "then summon the rest of us tomorrow night."

Parisot did not approve of the idea. "If we climb during the daylight, we are certain to be found out," he said. "It's too dangerous."

Romegas agreed. Glaring at Ravenne with hands trembling, he said, "We do not even know that there is such a path." Forthwith, he ordered his men down the ropes. The retreat was carried out calmly and we made good our escape before sunup, but so enraged was Romegas at the faulty intelligence that at the entrance to the bridge he suddenly halted and spun about, pointing to the old man.

"Hang him," he said.

Not a soldier stepped forward to do the job, so much did everyone pity the poor fellow.

"Hang the traitor, I say," barked Romegas, but still no one moved. Descrying the first rays of sun, the Commander growled, "To the Devil with him then." With a disgusted wave of his hand, he abruptly spun around again and set off for the boats. We left the Greek behind.

A few days later at Candia, Balthazar sought out his go-betweens, found no letters waiting from Barelli and booked passage for the two of us to Constantinople.

Sixty-Nine

I will not tell how we made our way toward Constantinople near the end of that foul season, the storms we weathered, how we were all but shipwrecked on Chios where Balthazar, contacting Genoese agents there, yet found nothing from Barelli, or how later, stranded on Lemnos with no round ship in sight, the Knight in a final desperation hired a *fusta* to make the remainder of the journey, or how at last we neared our destination, waterlogged and exhausted, only at the beginning of December.

As the throne of the Infidel drew us league by league into the Bosporus, my apprehension grew. A year ago, scarcely more, I had been a slave in this city. The thought of being recognized did not sit well, but my mind had been set and I throttled any protests.

Balthazar saw thro' my silence. "I know there is a slight danger here for you," he said, gazing onto the wondrous sight of mosques and domes floating past a grey sky. "We will give a wide birth to your old haunts and find disguises at once."

So it was. We docked at Constantinople proper rather than at Galata and immediately sought out Barelli at the church of St. Theodosia. Shortly, the wiry Greek arrived carrying a rooster he intended to cook, and the three of us embraced. "I am glad to see you alive," he said in his perfect Italian, slapping me on the shoulder. "I had feared the worst."

"So had I," I replied without the slightest jest.

Barelli didn't need to be told of the urgency of our mission and immediately led us to the Hippodrome, filled with its mournful relics and vaulted conduits nearby.

"Parisot also fears the worst," said Balthazar, "and as we have had no letters from you in the past months, he ordered me to ascertain the exact state of affairs. When I was here last you affirmed a descent would fall but were uncertain of the date or objective. We must know both."

Barelli, standing before a colossal marble engraved with the history of the place, nodded gravely. "It is right you have come. Matters are quickly reaching a head. News of the attempt on Malvasia—"

"They know already?"

"They know."

It must have been the old Greek, Balthazar and I said to each other, or the peasants we encountered crossing the bridge on our retreat. Mayhap word had leaked from Malta before our departure.

Barelli walked to the Egyptian needle, crouching at the base of it. "The final decision will almost certainly be made in the coming days," he continued. "Meanwhile, I want to show you something at the Sarai."

"The *Sarai?*" I whispered with marked disbelief.

"Yes. Many say that the Ottomans have perfected their government, as none of the high officials apart from Soliman himself are Turks. As you know, everyone here is a slave." Barelli paused as a water carrier walked by us, offering us a drink. He waved him off. "One must concede that the policy works splendidly, but the loyalty of a few remains with the mothers they have been stolen from rather than with their abductors. Nor do all great pashas share the Grand Turk's love of austerity. I have become a trusted friend of one who will receive me in two days in the palace. You shall accompany me."

"How?" I asked, feeling my brow constricting.

Barelli regarded me, placing his fine dark hands around my face and asked me to speak with him in Turkish. "Good," he said after a moment. "We shall shave your beard down to the moustaches and dress you as a *yenicheri*. You will pass. As for you ... " With his hand on his chin he regarded Balthazar. "No. We shall find a safe house and you will wait."

At once we began the preparations. Barelli installed us in a room near the church. Balthazar crossed to Galata and again purchased the robes of a rich Venetian. As for me, the spy carried out his threat: he shaved me to my moustaches, dressed me in the kaftan and headdress of a common janissary and gave me a stick to carry. I protested that this would make me yet more visible to the *yenicheriler* themselves, in particular those who might know me. Barelli agreed and for the next day I walked the streets in the baggy pants, loose jacket and turban of an ordinary Turk. I remained on the Stambul side of the Horn and no one recognized me in the immense city.

At dawn of the second day, Barelli appeared. He stood before us, tho' adorned in the robes of a wealthy merchant, entirely himself. "You will go without disguise?" I asked.

"My face is well known in the Sarai," he replied. "As far as the Porte is concerned, I am merely a merchant engaged in opening new routes for coffee and ... rhubarb. Your face, on the other hand, is new and must fade into the background of the palace canvas." Barelli adjusted my hat. I shot a glance at Balthazar who merely nodded, quipping cheerfully as he picked up a cup of tea that we would see each other in a few hours.

Barelli and I walked to the Sarai. As always, passage thro' the Imperial Gate was open and the first courtyard miraculous in its silence. But as I regarded the hundreds of janissaries milling about the armory that had once been a church, sweat poured unbidden down my arms and with force I stilled the pounding of my heart.

Evincing no concern Barelli strode to the Gate of Salutation, where near the columns bearing the heads of the newly executed, he presented to the *bostanci* his letter of invitation. Janissaries accompanying ambassadors, officials and merchants are the most common sight in the city, and the guard said not a word to either of us. For the first time I entered the second courtyard of the Sarai. If possible, the silence was even more profound than in the outer yard and only the sounds of an ostrich trampling on the flowers and a stag scraping its antlers on a cypress broke it.

Barelli walked under the portico to our left, across from the cupolas of the royal kitchens, and thro' a door. Soon a vizier, wearing as one of his rank a rich kaftan and tall hat, received him in the friendliest manner. The two men exchanged pleasantries and spoke of the spell of warm weather. The Vizier then cast a hard, questioning glance at me, but Barelli assured him I was a friend. Only at this juncture did I fully realize how successful the spy had been in his long endeavors. This man standing before me was one of the half-dozen most powerful pashas in the realm. With money, skill and patience, Barelli had penetrated to the very heart of the Ottoman government.

Once assured, the Vizier said quickly that we had but a short amount of time and he waved us behind him through a long corridor, where he finally paused at another door. He ushered us into a not overly large chamber, richly ornamented in blue tile, which was at this moment empty but for a large table in its center. As the Pasha watched the door, I walked up to the table, my gaze transfixed. Before me sat an image of Malta. On it was carved the Great Port, perfect in every detail, Birgu and Fort St. Angelo, crafted with no less exactness, Fort St. Elmo, Fort St. Michel, Mdina, the harbors, the inlets, the chain across Galley Creek ...

As I stood examining the miniature, another official stepped into the room. Catching my breath, I turned to the door. With the utmost possession the Vizier introduced Barelli: "You have met the merchant Michael Ramberti. He considers whether to help finance the projected descent upon Malta."

"Ah," the other official replied and, with a respectful bow to the Vizier and a nod to Barelli, departed.

I turned my attention back to the table. "How?" I whispered.

"This summer past some engineers were sent to the island with tools to measure it. Is it a good likeness?"

"I ... it is perfect," I answered gravely.

"Come," the Vizier said, peering into the corridor and waving us out. Two more palace officials passed by, but threw at us hardly a glance.

"*Putant quod cupiunt*," remarked Barelli. "It is human nature to believe what one expects. We are here, therefore we should be here." Natheless the Greek politely declined an invitation to remain for coffee and we forthwith removed ourselves from the Sarai.

"Well?" Balthazar asked as we entered the room and I removed my hat.

My words fell slowly. "In the Sarai they have built a perfect image of Malta and its fortifications." Balthazar raised his eyebrow; this gesture was sufficient. "Engineers, we were told, were sent to the island with measuring rods to survey it this last summer—"

With my abrupt halt, Balthazar and I stared at each other for a moment. Then: "Those fishermen!"

"Indeed, we paid dearly for those fish," said the Knight. "You were correct that they seemed not entirely fresh." Now, stroking his beard, he took a deep breath and spoke resolutely: "Thus, it is decided."

Barelli and I nodded. An invasion of Malta was imminent.

"We must know when," Balthazar went on.

"Yes," agreed Barelli. "My confederate has told me the final decision to proceed will be made in the Divan next week. I intend to be there, if possible." He glanced at me. "So shall you."

If possible. It could not be so.

"I need to reflect more on this. Should we be discovered ... " The Greek had no need to finish his thought. "I go now to write dispatches to the agents on Chios. God granting, the messages will get there ahead of you. In the meanwhile, you must go to the Arsenal and the Foundry and make an account of the activity there. I can tell you it is great."

"The risk is also great," I replied. "I am known at those places."

"Francisco the slave is known at those places, Muruvvet the *yenicheri* is not. I shall speak to you tomorrow."

But the danger was too real for me to appear at the Foundry; Balthazar decided to go thither himself. I had spent far less time at the Arsenal and might pass without being recognized. Steeled by our success at the Sarai, I approached the gate at dawn. Some *yenicheriler* were crouched about a fire, warming their hands and eating their usual breakfast of garlic and vegetables. As I stepped toward them, carrying my stick, I kept an eagle's watch for Yakhshi, who was usually posted around here. I saw no trace of him. God is smiling on us, I thought, feeling the surge of excitement that accompanies perilous undertakings. I hailed the janissaries, intending to stride past. In my recklessness, tho', I had not counted on being invited to breakfast. To refuse would have been more reckless.

I crouched down among that circle, huddled about the fire in their winter kaftans. One of the fellows eyed me as if I were familiar. Indeed, I recalled his face from previous years and my breath slowed. But before that one could decide, one of his mates asked where I was from.

"From Gallipoli," I answered.

"*Evet?*" one of them said. "I am also from Gallipoli. I have not seen you."

"It is a big place," I answered.

"Do you know Ridvan the dungeon-man?" he asked.

"I do," I nodded, not having any idea of who Ridvan was. "I do not like him much."

The janissary laughed. "Neither do I. He stole a cow from me."

Barelli was correct: people believe what they wish to believe. "I have a message for the *Kapudan*," I said. "Is he here today?"

They all nodded with various degrees of certainty and waved me into the Arsenal.

I wandered about freely. The craftsmen were just arriving, but I could already see that far more carpenters, oarsmakers and caulkers were at work than last year. Every one of the hundred sheds contained a ship, either being built or repaired. I struck up a conversation with one of the novices tallowing a hull. "How long have you been here?" I asked.

"A month only."

"How many ships have you waxed?"

He shrugged. "Many many," he said. "More than I can count."

"How high can you count?" I asked, but he did not understand me and went back to his job. I talked to others. No word had come down on the plan for the ships or when they must be ready, but I left the Arsenal certain the fleet would be far larger than the one that had destroyed the Spanish armada at Djerbé.

I had advised Balthazar to pose as a Genoese merchant seeking arms at the Foundry. We had decided wisely that I should not go, for the first person he encountered at the sheds was Lorenzo himself, now chief foreman in charge of guns.

"You look like a Veneziano," Lorenzo said to the Knight, as he wiped his hands on a rag and regarded the stranger from top to bottom. Every forge was going; dozens of men ran to and from the casting sheds. Each chimney belched smoke into the sky.

"I was in a hurry to buy new garments after a long voyage," Balthazar replied.

The foreman continued to eye the visitor with his customary suspicion. "You don't sound Genoese to me," he said.

"I have spent many years in France," the merchant conceded. "Listen, I am a busy man and have no time to argue with the likes of you. Everyone knows Genoese arms are shit and so they buy from the Veneziani. If you can produce cheaper goods, people will buy them from you. What do you say?"

"Oh, the Veneziani have shown the Turks how to build guns, I can tell you that," replied Lorenzo, glancing at a pony that had wandered into the shed. "Our guns are as good as theirs, I'd wager. I admit they're heavier. The Turks like 'em big." He chuckled to himself. "But we have too many orders to fill from the Porte now. Come back in a year. Then we'll talk."

"You cannot fill any orders before then?"

"No, look around you, man. All these pieces are for the Porte."

Balthazar walked about the sheds, gazing on dozens of pieces of all sizes, from the smallest falcons thro' cannons and culverins to the most immense gun he had ever laid eyes on. Then he bade Lorenzo good-day.

"I believe I saw your basilisk today," Balthazar said when we met later in the room. "Truly you cast that behemoth?"

I nodded with pride.

"It is regrettable ... for us," the Knight sighed.

We agreed that the invasion would be large, frightfully large. How large we could not know. While we traded surmises, Barelli knocked on the door and stepped in. The Imperial Council, the Divan, would meet at dawn.

"Without doubt we will have a report," the Greek said. "But at such a crucial juncture I would prefer to be present myself. Francisco, I want you to accompany me, in case ... "

His voice trailed off. I knew only that whatever the Greek was planning was a supreme risk. Yet he betrayed no fear. I would not either.

In the morning, hours before first light, there was another knock. I opened the door, expecting Barelli, only to see a complete stranger—a Jewish physician. Quickly I slammed the door shut again, as Balthazar went for a knife.

"It is I," a familiar voice on the other side said. I opened the door once more and Barelli stepped in. "Today is entirely otherwise," he said and we set off for the Sarai, I again a janissary.

As we entered the first courtyard, Barelli whispered, "I once told you that to get into the third courtyard of the Sarai is impossible. Today I am going to attempt the impossible. I want you to stay in the second yard. When the Divan adjourns later, if I do not appear, you must find the same Vizier we spoke to and get his report. God willing, I shall have the report up here." He tapped his temple.

"How ... ?" I shook my head.

For the single time in our association I saw Barelli gulp. "As you must know," he said, "the Sultan often listens to the deliberations of the Divan secretly thro' a small window above it. But today, I am assured, he will be present himself for the meeting. That chamber will remain empty. Unfortunately, it must be gained from the third courtyard."

"It is impossible," I said, falling silent as Barelli presented his pass to the guard at the Gate of Salutation. Everyone knew the third court was guarded by twenty-five white eunuchs who allowed no one, *absolutely no one*, thro' the High Gate—beyond the Sultan's immediate household, pages and retainers. And an occasional doctor. We walked in the darkness to the High Gate, where one of those eunuchs—judging from his dress, someone of rank hardly lower than the *Kapi Agha* himself—ordered the guard to admit Barelli. The physician bent to the ground, kissed the threshold of the gate and without uttering a word more passed through the Sublime Porte.

Only Barelli and the members of the Divan ever knew exactly what was said at the meeting, but of all others who live and breathe, I was closest to those ears on that fateful morning, which would be remembered as the greatest victory of intelligence in the history of the Order, if not in Christendom altogether. Barelli gained the Sultan's room above the Divan, secreting himself with infinite silence behind that small, grilled window. How much he saw I know not, but Barelli had visited the Divan before and knew the chamber beneath him was of blinding opulence. The gilded dome illuminated all below with the daylight that had yet to come: blue, arabesqued tiles encrusted with gold and precious stones, the crystal fountain standing next to the silver mantlepiece; pillows, divans, carpets.

As dawn did break, the Council quickly assembled: Grand Vizier Ali Pasha; the Viziers and Chancellors; the Chief Equerry; the *Kapudan* Agha; the *Yenicheri* Agha. After they had gathered, the Sultan himself appeared, wearing his customary white turban, not a large one, with only three fingers of crimson atop it, and a golden rose bearing a ruby at its center. Pearls rather than buttons fastened his kaftan and a pearl the size of a hazel-nut hung from his ear. As he entered, every one of the Pashas kissed his ring and he seated himself on a sumptuous cushion. The others sat on the divans or on the floor.

Without further ceremony he ordered a page to read two letters he had received in the past days. Both were from captives on Malta. "We remind His Majesty, Lord of Lords and Possessor of Men's Necks," began the first, "how the galleys of the Knights of St. John have inflicted immense harm on the fleet of the Ottomans. His Majesty well knows the unsurpassed insolence of the pirate Romegas, offspring of the Devil and filled with the poison of vipers, who earlier this year seized the *Beylerbeyi* of Cairo and the galleon of His Majesty's Chief Eunuch of the Seraglio. Now the impudence of this fetid son of a snake carcass has exceeded all human bounds by his capture of the new *Beylerbeyi* of Cairo, the Sanjak of Alexandria and His Majesty's daughter's former nurse, Giansevere, all of whom—may Allah pity them!—are being held for great ransoms."

Tho' the counselors knew of these events, a strong murmur of anger ran through the Divan. At the Sultan's nod, the page read the second letter, which spoke of the nurse herself. "O Mighty Lord, do not forget the many slaves who are held on Malta and this high-ranked lady who was once the nurse of your own blood and was cruelly taken into slavery as she returned from the Holy City of Mecca in fulfillment of her sacred vows! Death is preferable to the treatment of your subjects at this place and to a life in captivity! How is it possible that you, the mightiest lord of the mightiest empire on earth, allow such a small, weak island to insult you with continued opposition to your power? We beg you on our knees to take pity on us and relieve us of our desperate plight!"

Servants entered the chamber with drinks for the Pashas, who were moved to tears by this letter. Truly, Vizier Daoud, rose to his feet in great agitation, reminding His Majesty that his deceased wife of blessed memory, Hurrem, never ceased urging him to destroy the Knights completely ,and that the *imamlar* had told him this was the only path to salve his conscience. Nor should he forget also that his beloved daughter Mihrimah was beyond herself with fury.

Yes, the Sultan nodded, Mihrimah had spoken to him since receiving the news, on more than one occasion.

Another Vizier, Hiferat, stood to remind those present about the assault on Malvasia, of which they had only just heard from the Bey there, which, tho' unsuccessful, was unsurpassed in brazen effrontery. To the astonishment of everyone present, at this remark the Sultan got to his feet and paced across the entire chamber, as furious as if the island had actually been taken. The Venetians had ceded him Malvasia. It was rightfully his, and while Allah was Lord in Heaven, he Soliman, would not let it fall into the hands of the impudent knights. Only after some moments did he calm himself enough to sit down crosslegged at his place.

Of all those assembled, tho', by far the most agitated was the *Kapudan* Agha, who continued to suffer the most from the Order's depredations. "Invincible and Mighty Lord," he said, bowing, wringing his hands, "if I thought it would be necessary to incite Your Majesty by my words, I should offer more profuse and eloquent arguments, but I have no doubt that nothing can convince you to revoke the order you in your wisdom have already given, that we should utterly destroy this insignificant island—which I am ashamed even to name. I only regret that it should be necessary to send your invincible fleet against such a trifling objective simply because no one else has bothered to destroy the accursed place. It seems we Turks are no longer the descendants of those who once served this great house of Othman, for they conquered the warlike Syrians, drove the Shah into his mountain fortress, conquered Trebizond and many other places.

"I will not weary His Majesty by speaking of his countless victories in our own time, against Hungary and other places, and say only that the people of that nameless island shall have reason to know the might of Your Majesty, especially after the capture of Rhodes, which was much stronger and better fortified than this nameless island. Majesty! I humbly beg you to pity your subjects and to mercilessly punish these knights, for they have shown no gratitude for the forgiveness which Your Majesty has treated them on so many occasions. Let your preparations assure you of victory and humiliate these monks, who yet remember with unjustified pride how they resisted for six months the powerful attack on Rhodes that Your Majesty led in person."

At the conclusion of the *Kapudan* Agha's speech, all the Pashas in the Divan rose to their feet, nodding assent. The Sultan immediately sent for *Kapudan* Piyale Pasha, who arrived not long after, and asked him whether he could take Malta without difficulty.

"Of course, Your Majesty," the dashing Admiral answered. "It should require but a week, then we can pass on to the Goletta."

The answer pleased the Sultan, who ordered Piyale to put all the ships in fighting order without delay and build twenty new ones.

"At once, Your Majesty," replied Piyale, bowing. "Indeed, preparations are underway."

Thereon Sultan got to his feet again, telling his advisors that he would send a *chavush* to Turgut, ordering him to gather all the corsairs under him and that he would recall Mustafa Pasha from Hungary. Piyale would command the navy, Mustafa the land forces. He addressed the Pashas.

"Excellent counselors," Soliman said with his habitual seriousness, "I give you my thoughts. I have no fear of any of the Christian powers, but as Piyale and Mustafa will be so near Sicily and Naples, two realms of the Spanish Bey, he might attempt to frustrate my plans while they are engaged in the siege. If we are successful in this enterprise, we shall try to accomplish what my father attempted—the conquest of Calabria. The capture of Malta would bring us great wealth, because we should then be able to send our fleet into the western seas, and in this way gain glory for ourselves and inflict great harm on our enemies. We should in time be able to take Sicily, the fertile granary of the Romans who once ruled in places where we now rule—all praise to Allah and his Prophet. We could then carry the war into Italy and Hungary until the great German Empire will have been gained for us, and then we should extend our empire to the ends of the known world, and the names of my generals would become immortal.

"We shall give out that Piyale and Mustafa are sailing not only against Malta but against all of Italy and in that way keep our enemies in a state of uncertainty and divide their forces. I command you, Piyale, under pain of my displeasure, to work with Mustafa in harmony in all things. If you do not, our labors shall be in vain."

His Majesty knows better than I how well his words were recorded, but with this speech the Divan ended its deliberations and its members dispersed. By this time I had stood in the second courtyard for many hours, not knowing Barelli's fate and at every moment concerned for my own. More than once a page or a servant passed by me under the portico and into the palace, and each time I expected to be questioned, but so many *yenicheriler* were about that no one concerned themselves with me, not e'en the *yenicheriler* themselves. At last my vigilance relaxed and I was hardly aware when Barelli appeared at my shoulder and whispered into my ear that it was high time to get out of here. Before I could collect my wits, we were well into the courtyard and, as a gazelle leapt past us, we sped through the Gate of Salutation.

"That was a pleasant few hours of solitude," he remarked as we rushed thro' the outer courtyard.

"You have nerves the likes of which I have never encountered," I told him.

He thanked me for the compliment, observing that mine were respectable as well. Unfortunately, at that moment our string of luck ran out. In our haste we collided with a group of the janissaries standing about the old Byzantine church. I stood face to face with Yakhshi. At first he did not recognize me, but when I tried to release myself from him, he demanded an apology and refused to let me pass. I mumbled a few words, which were enough to let him hear the voice of the slave he knew not long ago. In the instant of confusion, Barelli and I were off, running for our lives with a squad of janissaries behind us.

We bolted out thro' the Imperial Gate and into the city, hurtling toward the great bazaar with those praetorians at our heels. Into that immense warren of arcades and shops, tearing off our hats, shedding our robes; but even as we darted this and every way—overturning baskets, dislodging veils—we could not lose them. We emerged at the other side into a crowded part of the city where churches and mosques stood at almost every corner. Still the soldiers, coming from every part of the bazaar, were after us. "This way!" Barelli waved me and we ducked, exhausted and panting, into the nearest Greek church. The janissaries halted, forbidden to enter, yet their shouting outside told us that we had only succeeded in trapping ourselves.

"Come!" ordered the Greek, who I now perceived had not chosen this way by chance. He waved me down into what I took to be a crypt, then through a hole in a wall from which we emerged into a long, stone channel. "This city had the most extensive water supply in antiquity. It is riddled with aqueducts and conduits now dry, having fallen into disuse centuries ago or having been destroyed by tremors." We stumbled along in absolute darkness through spider webs, kicking vermin from our path, finally discerning a faint patch of light. Barelli made for it, and we emerged through the cellar of a shop not far from the Church of St. Theodosia. Balthazar was awaiting us patiently in the room; we grabbed him and ran to Barelli's rich home, which stood but a few streets away.

Upstairs, in a crowded study, without having lost a breath, the Greek sat down at his desk and narrated to our incredulity what he'd overheard in the Divan, even as he scribbled down the same onto a piece of paper with a quill dipped in lemon juice. "We have no time," he said. "The janissaries are searching, *con un po' di fortuna* for no more than an escaped slave. We shall hide you in a church and you shall depart tonight with this letter to the Grand Master. Memorize what I tell you. I'll also make several copies and send them with other couriers. God consenting, one will get through." Suddenly Barelli halted. "To the Devil! I've run out of lemon juice!" He abruptly downed a half-empty glass of wine and held the goblet out to me. "Francisco, a glass of your piss, if you don't mind." After this day I was ready; quickly I opened my trousers and fulfilled the request. Barelli kept on with his furious writing. "It works almost as well, believe me." When the spy had completed the letter and waved it dry, he wrote over it in ordinary ink a mundane business letter addressed to someone in Sevilla, then handed it to Balthazar. "Your doctor will know how to read it. Give him my regards. Now—we are gone."

Downstairs, Balthazar handed me the letter and went to scout for the janissaries. Soon he returned with word that soldiers were searching everywhere, heading this way. We ran what seemed like half a league to another Christian church, where Barelli hid us behind the iconostasis. Hours later, after it had grown completely dark, he returned with fresh clothes for us and we three carefully made our way, eluding one night patrol of janissaries after another, not to the Golden Horn, but to the far side of the peninsula, where we found a broken section of wall and passed through it. Shortly after, we came to a deserted spot where a *fusta* awaited. There Barelli bade us farewell.

Would he not accompany us? I asked. Surely his life was now in great peril.

"Nay," he answered, laying his hand on my shoulder, "the costume is off and the janissaries will have no recollection of my face. I am who I was. We have come clean away."

"Natheless," said Balthazar, "it is likely we shall never see each other again. Allow me to say with every honesty, Sir, I have been honored to know you and, be assured, you will be rewarded beyond your dreams for your services to the Religion—nay, to Christendom. For what you have done today may have saved the West."

"Let us not exaggerate, Comte," Barelli smiled, taking Balthazar's hand. "You will be hearing from me as I learn more. And I sincerely trust we have not seen the last of each other."

We all embraced and Balthazar and I climbed aboard the boat. "You once promised me," I said with all gravity as the oars dipped into the cold waters, "that you would not make a profession of such matters."

"Ah," he replied, smiling with equal seriousness, "you were rightly named, Esforzado, do not deny it."

We set off on our homeward journey then, carrying a warning whose immensity lay beyond our ability to grasp.

Seventy

As Balthazar and I made our way thro' the winter waters, from Lemnos to Chios to Crete, repeating Barelli's report to every trusted courier in the net of agents the Grand Master had established, Isabella dreamed. Better said, dreams visited her nightly, angels, demons. On occasion she found herself walking through fields of artichokes and woke up wet between her legs. Parisot often appeared, shielding her on all sides so that she remained invisible to other men. Last night she danced with those Botticellian nymphs with whom she had more than once been compared, not without justice, until they disappeared into the forest. She took this to mean that her life in Firenze was vanishing—that her wealth, the praise of her pen, the gaiety of her banquets, the pleasantries of the lute and dialogues extoling the virtues of the ancients would become things of dreams, and only of dreams.

Awake, she attempted to keep Giansevere alive. At first the haughty old witch's refusal to eat or drink exasperated Isabella, then alarmed her. She couldn't make out a word among the hideous sounds spewing from the shrew's rotted gums and relied on her slaves to translate what they could. She told Giansevere that her servant Feruc had been allowed to return to Constantinople to negotiate a ransom, but to Isabella's surprise, the news only increased granny's anger.

"He is not my servant, he is my son!" one of the slaves translated, cowering in fear from both women.

"Milady," replied Isabella with perplexity, "if he is truly your son, he will surely obtain your release."

The slave rendered her words, but Giansevere's answer was unexpected. "Hah!" she shouted e'en more sharply. "He is a worthless son! Why do you think he posed as a servant? If these pirates—may God have their carcasses fed to the birds and ravens pick out their eyeballs!—knew he was my son, they would put him in chains!" True, Isabella was forced to agree; the Knights would have ransomed him too. "He has abandoned his mother!"

Giansevere clammed up again. Nearing wit's end, Isabella had her slaves forcibly feed the nurse with juices and soup, but she spit up everything. At length one of the slaves suggested yoghoort and Isabella ordered him to make some. When they spooned it into the nurse's mouth and she tasted it, for the first time she calmed down; she asked for more. Afterwards, Isabella ordered her servants to cook anything the toothless witch wanted.

Giansevere's age astounded her. Isabella slowly comprehended that she had been born only four years after Constantinople had fallen to the Ottomans. She had been captured as a girl in a raid on Italy and because of her great beauty was brought to the Seraglio during the reign of Mehmed the Conqueror himself. Giansevere dimly recollected stories about how Mehmed defeated Vlad the Impaler and other barbaric people, but her whole life had been spent behind the doors of the Harem.

"You must tell me about that," Isabella said.

"Oh, the Seraglio is where everything happens, where everything is decided!" Giansevere said, her clouded eyes lighting up. "There is not another place like it in the world!"

"I have heard," said Isabella, thinking that one hundred years was a long time to be locked up in a cage, even the most opulent cage in all the world.

On a dreary day some weeks after, Isabella and a servant were walking to market to find proper food for Giansevere when she again encountered Blaij Vergã, now long returned from Malvasia, whistling on the street.

"You dare whistle in the Convent, Blaij Vergã!" exclaimed Isabella, e'en as she hummed the tune herself. "You'll bring the Devil upon us!"

At once Vergã broke off with a marked laugh, which annoyed her. "Pardon, Milady," he replied in a voice that revealed he took her less than seriously. That also annoyed her. "I had no intention of summoning spirits, merely to ward off this lifeless day." Natheless, he quickly glanced over his shoulder. "Tell me, Señora, how is your guest?"

"She is beyond old and frightened beyond fear," Isabella deigned to reply, but only after she too had glanced over her shoulder. "Giansevere will not live long. Are you proud to have taken her, Señor?"

Blaij merely shrugged jovially. "Granny is a prize, nothing more. She will bring much money to the Order to fight the Turks. I bear her no ill will."

"No, I suppose you do not." Isabella turned to depart, halted. "I see you are back from Malvasia, alive. I have heard it was ... difficult. Why did you not remain a further day and make the attempt again? Parisot was furious."

"I suggested as much," Vergã replied, suddenly serious, "but waterlogged spirits thought we'd be discovered in the daylight. So we returned."

"And of Francisco?" she asked. "What news?"

The feared confrater shrugged. "We got him and Fra Balthazar to Crete. That's all I know. On Malvasia I saved his life. He nearly fell to his death on the rocks, but I snatched him."

Isabella hadn't expected this and gathered up her mantle against the wet wind, which had picked up. "If that is true, Señor," she said finally, "I am glad to hear it, for it goes some way to repaying the harms you have done him. Further, the ancients also tell us, do they not, that true valor has no need to call attention to itself."

"My apologies, Señora," Vergã replied with an embarrassed bow. "I shall not forget the lesson. Now, if you'll excuse me, I have affairs to attend to."

Balthazar de Marans des Homes-Saint-Martin had resolved that neither pirates nor winter seas would deter him from gaining the Convent, and he spared no expense, throttled more than one thief and ran more than one oarsman to his death in getting there. I had never seen the Knight so grimly determined. With his indomitable will overcoming every wave and protest, we became the first of the couriers to reach Malta, if only by days, and he lost no time in seeking out de Valette. February was close upon us when we docked at Galley Creek and a moment had not passed after the gangplank hit the embankment before Balthazar was dashing off to Fort St. Angelo, me at his heels. We didn't bathe. The Council was in session and the guard outside the Magisterial Palace lowered his halberd. Balthazar, in no mood for argument, knocked him aside.

The Knights within, all black mantled, at once broke off their discourse at the unexpected intrusion. de Valette glanced up from his throne and raised his hand, about to call for the guards, when he recognized the disheveled and dirty figures before him for the men he had sent to the realm of Satan.

"Eminenza," Balthazar said, bowing deeply, "a descent on Malta is underway, a descent of such magnitude that this island, mayhap all Christendom, has ne'er seen."

The murmur that ran thro' the chamber was of equal parts disbelief, terror and defiance. The Grand Master, standing, raised his hand for silence and cast a glance at me. "Is this true?" he asked.

Catching my breath, I nodded. Balthazar handed de Valette Barelli's letter, which the Grand Master ordered immediately deciphered. Exhausted and resembling half-drowned rats, we told the Council all we had seen and heard.

That evening after vespers, Balthazar and I entered the Monsignore's home to sup with him. As we stepped into that grand but austere place, de Valette turned from his mantlepiece and emptied into Balthazar's hands a sack of priceless jewels. "Your service to the Religion, Fra Balthazar, shall ne'er be forgotten."

Balthazar bowed and replied, "It is Giovan Barelli in Constantinople who deserves every reward, Eminenza, and this one." He raised his hand to me. "I did but get him there."

Smiling, Parisot took the gold and ruby ring from his finger and placed it in my palm. "Thank you, Señor Barai, the knowledge you have brought this day has given us a chance."

By now the word we had brought to Malta had spread throughout Birgu, if not the island entire, and a throng of people holding lamps and tapers had gathered outside the Grand Master's door. He decided to address them. de Valette made no speeches. "Yes," he said without raising his voice, "God in his wisdom has willed that our Religion and Malta be tried this spring by a descent of the Infidel against us. We shall announce measures in the next days. You must prepare yourself for great sacrifice."

Lady Emilia and Isabella stood in the crowd and, as we turned back into the Grand Master's house, they stepped upon the threshold. Isabella, holding out her hand to me, was unable to restrain her tears, tho' what portion were of joy at seeing me alive and terror at the news we brought, I made no attempt to discern. de Valette was hardly insensible to her emotion and a frown crossed his face, but at this moment I stood in his favor and he invited the women to join us.

At least the Grand Master had told the people outside the truth, I thought as we all sat down before the candlesticks, which was more than d'Homedes would have done. Truly, that evening de Valette revealed himself of an altogether different cast than the Spaniard who had faced the earlier invasion. Before his servants had poured wine, Parisot was thinking ahead.

"Tomorrow we shall begin strengthening the unfinished parts of the fortifications. I will issue a *Citazione*. We shall at once send boats to Sicilia and Italia and summon all the Knights who are dispersed throughout Europe to return forthwith to the Convent. At this time of testing, every Knight of the Order and every arquebusier in Europe will be required. I shall also tomorrow write to His Holiness and King Philip, telling them what you have learned and asking them for money and troops." He paused then, regarding in turn his lioness asleep under the table, then the goblet of wine in his hand. "Thus, at last, the great contest between the forces of Evil and Christendom nears its culmination and the full might of the enemy will be brought to bear on this tiny island. Everything depends on us."

Thereat he glanced up, his tone becoming entirely practical, and asked, "Fra Balthazar, how many fighting men are on Malta at present?"

"You must know better than I, Eminenza," the Knight replied in like voice. "I would guess several hundred Knights and somewhat more common soldiers. Of the Maltese, mayhap one thousand or two are skilled in arms."

Such a quiet descended on the table that one could hear the sizzle of the candle wax, but de Valette himself soon broke it. Smiling with a cheer strange for him who so rarely smiled, he said, "In that case, we must redouble our prayers." He turned to Emilia and her daughter. "Prepare to leave the island. I shall send all women, children, prostitutes and other useless persons to Sicilia."

Emilia made no response, while Isabella lowered her head. At length she replied with a voice full of entreaty, "Parisot, it is difficult for me to remember those events ten years and more ago. I was only a girl then, but it seems to me that Monsignore d'Homedes attempted such a plan to little effect. Those who live here will do all to remain to defend their homes, and to die for them."

Isabella near batted her eyelashes and I well perceived she had mastered the art of speaking to potentates. Parisot did not anger. With some visible affection he said, "We shall see."

Afterwards, Isabella saw her mother home, then met me on the ramparts above Kalkara Creek, the place we had parted that earlier time, years ago. This night, in the driving winter wind, she approached me, all cloaked, and collapsed against my chest, again in tears.

"O My God, Francisco, you cannot know how I feared for your safety. But He has willed your return." She stood away from me and began sobbing outright. "Forgive me, I—"

"Isabella, we must get out of this wet place," I said and we descended to the base of the ramparts, where we hid ourselves from the rain in a guard's niche.

"And so, it finally comes," she said.

I nodded, grimly.

"Will you return to Spain now?"

"No," I said, shaking my head. "The decision, meseems, has been made. Balthazar will fight to save all that is good in Christendom. Vergã will fight because he relishes the fight. Ix-Xabaw will fight for this island his home. Parisot will fight for God. I shall fight—" I halted, then said with a sneer: "Such high things mean nothing, Isabella. When faced with the foe, a man fights, that is all."

"Truly you feel nothing more, Francisco?"

"Nay." I told her Balthazar had once more taken to calling me Esforzado, and I had belatedly come to acknowledge that the exhilaration of perilous undertakings had seduced me time and again. "I am not proud to say so, Isabella, for there comes a season in a man's life when he wishes to fight for some purpose other than adventure."

"You have not found it?"

I shook my head. "Vergã has been right all along. The only thing that will matter is powder and a blade." Isabella regarded me with sadness and, in return, I breathed deeply, gathering my courage. "Isabella, you have tried to restore me to life, but you have expected too much. My soul was lost on the galleys, and all that remains is that empty hardness." I glanced to the stones. "Forgive me; the song says we should not speak of the proud one from glory tumbled down. I am in no way different from half the men on this island. The Turks do not reckon the hatred that will face them."

Isabella, hesitant beyond measure, pressed her head against my chest. "I refuse to sing a lament for you, Francisco, for tho' you feel only ice, I sense the spark heating your breast." While we stood silently in that alcove she handed me a new kerchief, embroidered with her name. "Do not lose this one," she said with a certain admonishment.

The token forced recollection of the vow I had made as a youth to fight for her. "Have no fear, I shall wear it always. I will fight for you, for Balthazar and for Pietru. That is what remains to me."

Hearing these words, Isabella abruptly kissed me full and passionately on the mouth, declaring, "And as you will fight for me, so I shall fight for you." Then, flushed with shame, she drew most slowly away, held me at arm's length. "Francisco, did Blaij Vergã save your life on Malvasia?"

"As Balthazar saved his," I shrugged. "The way to the citadel was treacherous and each man aided the other. What of it?"

Isabella shook her head in a genuine confusion. "I don't know. He declares your quarrel to be over, yet ... oh, for all his worldly success, he cannot hide his envy of better men."

"Isabella," I said, mounting the ramparts again, "why fret over such trifles? Of what consequence can they be now?" I waved my hand across the shadow of Castle St. Angelo looming to the left and to Kalkara Creek ahead. "Everything must pale ... I cannot describe to you what I sensed in Constantinople, but such a terrible force is being unleashed against this island—" I halted as the rain lashed my face and Isabella ran headlong, embracing me. "Everything must pale ... "

Seventy-One

Yakhshi had been at the Arsenal since dawn, ordering the hundred men under his command to their various tasks. Since the Sultan's final blessing for the invasion had come down two months ago, the entire city had been alive with the preparations and nothing else. *Hiyer*, the entire Empire. He himself had ridden into the provinces with some *Subashilar* to inform the fief holders that the time had come to sacrifice. Under penalty of losing his *timar*, each *timarji* had to supply a horseman, a *spahi*. A few here and there failed this duty and lost their fiefs, maybe their heads, but most upheld the duty of a *kul*, and over the past weeks flocks of *spahiler* were arriving in Constantinople, where they practiced their archery daily in the nearby field and awaited orders. Probably ten thousand had come by now, but only the best would be taken.

With so much horseshit around, Constantinople had become noisy. Every day, Yakhshi saw arguments breaking out about who would get what *timar* should the owner fall in battle or fail in his obligations, but this was customary. He was more worried about his own, the *yenicheriler*. In former times, the *yenicheriler* had kept their pricks to themselves, being forbidden to take wives. Only officers and old ones unfit for duty were allowed to marry. But under Soliman many did so. This divided their loyalties, and sons fought for the same privileges as their fathers. Just today one of his men was sucking up to the *Ashibashi*, the chief cook, for a promotion over another because his father had been a standard-bearer. This habit of marriage was causing a lot of trouble; it weakened the vigor of the corps. Yakhshi shook his head in disgust and spat on the ground. The *yenicheriler* weren't what they once were, but they were still the best warriors in the world. Compared to them, even the fanatical Maltese Knights were untrained slugs of lords who hadn't ploughed a field in their entire lives and who ate all the time. He was looking forward to the contest, to ridding the world of those fat insects. It shouldn't be difficult with the size of this force. Yakhshi briefly gazed over the activity about him on this fine day. The army wouldn't be nearly as large as the one Soliman sent to Vienna those years ago, or perhaps even to Rhodes, but it would be the largest fleet he could remember. From the stories told around the cauldron, it would be the largest fleet since the beginning of the world. He didn't know yet how many *yenicheriler* would go. There were about twelve thousand in the city.

One of his men dropped a bale of wool into the dirt that had been churned into mud. "Donkey!" Yakhshi shouted as the fellow picked it up and carried it aboard the galley. They needed to take everything. Malta lay three hundred leagues to sunset and, from what all the returning slaves and spies said, the place was a miserable, barren piece of rock. They were loading vast quantities of woolen sacks, old sails, old ropes, hides, old tents to cover the movement of troops ... for on that miserable rock they would not find any of these things. They had already stowed countless shovels, pickaxes, iron bars and wood for the opening of trenches and the digging of mines, not to mention thousands of sheepskins for water. Every fool knew that water was going to be a big problem. Just to get this number of soldiers to Malta would take—Yakhshi didn't think he could count so high. The army had soft men skilled in this sort of thing, *logistikos*. Maybe one hundred barrels for each galley. They would have to stop at Greece for more supplies en route and be provisioned from Barbary once they had landed. He knew that the Sultan had already sent a *chavush* to Turgut in Trablus, ordering him to join the venture, as well as to *Beylerbeyi* Hasan in Cezayir-i Garb with the same instructions and ordering him to get all the corsairs of Barbary.

Food would be near as much of problem as water. Despite the *yenicheriler*'s reputation, fighting men needed to eat. The Sultan in his great wisdom was generous to his soldiers' stomachs, and the Ottoman army was envied throughout the world as being the best fed and supplied. Fifty *dihrem* of rice a day, the same of *peksimet* and bread, even more of mutton. What more could a man want? Of course they would live off the land and catch fish, but it mounted up. Yakhshi regarded the galleys docked along the Horn as far as the eye could see. Ten or twenty thousand barrels of rice and grain were going aboard, how many thousands of sheep? The *Boluk-bashi* laughed as one of his men dove for a fat one that had gotten away and ended up in the water. The baaing of the animals was filling the air with quite a racket and their droppings were all over the place, but his men were managing to herd the bleaters aboard. I'll wager my sword, Yakhshi thought, the number of livestock we're taking is enough to provision the ark of Noah. For a moment he wondered about the weight of all the coins that would be used to pay the troops each day.

"Over here!" someone cried then and Yakhshi turned toward the voice. There was some commotion at the Arsenal gates and he strode over.

"You goats!" he shouted when he saw what had happened. About a hundred men had been trying to drag the giant stone-thrower through the gates and the transport had collapsed. Now the fore-piece of the gun was stuck in the mud. Mustafa Pasha had ordered that one of the old stone-throwers used at Rhodes be brought up from Gallipoli. He'd also ordered all the artillery cleaned and bored again if necessary, and Yakhshi wasn't certain whether this basilisk was the one from Rhodes or the one Francisco had cast. For a moment he wondered what had happened to that slave he was certain he saw at the Porte two months ago. That was a strange thing. If Francisco was trying to escape again, dressing as a *yenicheri* wasn't a bad idea, but what was he doing at the Sarai? There were rumors of spies in Constantinople, but the *yenicheriler* never found a trace of him. It was all too bad; he rather liked the fellow and owned a fine wheel-lock because of him. Yakhshi shrugged. The Porte was right to have dropped the hunt. Final preparations for the expedition had begun the very next day and by now the Venetians, if not the entire Abode of War, would know what was going on.

"You stupid goats!" Yakhshi shouted again, beating the nearest men with his stick. "Why do you try to bring that gun in here? It would be easier to bring a barge out."

They spent two days struggling with the basilisk. They built a big frame with blocks to get the fore-piece out of the dirt, then spent a day dragging both parts aboard a big barge that had been specially allocated for it. A third day was spent getting the stone balls aboard. Each of them weighed over two hundred *okkalar* and the sight of four or five men trying to roll them up the gangplank had caused Yakhshi to burst out laughing. One man had his fingers crushed when his mates lost their grip and the ball rolled down over his hand. Of course slaves would cut most of the balls in the field, but Yakhshi was yet amazed that the barge didn't sink with the monster on it, and the thought that they would have to move the other one too didn't please him. He was glad all these chores would soon come to an end. By now they had loaded well over one hundred thousand iron balls on ten large boats named for this purpose, as well as fifteen thousand *kantar* of cannon powder. Apart from the two stone-throwers, there would be some other huge pieces, each weighing well over one hundred *kantar* and tossing balls of a *kantar* or more. Yakhshi wasn't certain how many guns had gone into the ships. They were taking two hundred cannoneers.

As the final ball was put aboard the barge, Yakhshi stood up and enjoyed the sunset that had lit the sky over Constantinople's mosques with a brilliant orange. All said, preparations for the invasion had proceeded in an orderly fashion, with the efficiency for which the Porte was renowned. There had been few delays and the spirit of the troops was high. As night fell, Yakhshi said his prayers and decided to go to the *tekke* for a last drink.

As he had every day for two months, on the twenty-sixth of Shaban, Yakhshi again stood in the Arsenal near the water's edge. Preparations were complete and yet not: The Horn was choked with ships even as more continued to arrive. Troops were boarding for departure while new soldiers joined the expedition. About five thousand *spahiler* and adventurers had lately shown up from Rouania. Some thousands more *azablar* dressed in every sort of costume imaginable had arrived, begging the Sultan to allow them to fight for the Faith, knowing that if they fell, they would enter Paradise. Yakhshi 'd bet his balls that many of these adventurers were in it just for the money, for Soliman had generously offered five gold *altunlar* to each man to equip himself. He wasn't certain that the great Joseph Nasi himself had helped pay for the venture, but many Jewish merchants had been arriving with their own ships, eager to revenge themselves against the Knights and to buy Christian slaves as the chance arose.

As he stood on the docks with his stick, ordering his men onto their assigned vessel, a loud cheering broke out not far away. Yakhshi turned to see Piyale Pasha and Mustafa Pasha walking together with Grand Vizier Ali himself as shouts went up all around them. The two *Pashalar* could not have been more different. Piyale had now about thirty-five years to him, Mustafa about seventy. Piyale had been born a Christian, Mustafa a Turk. Piyale was known for his daring, his success against Italy and, most of all of course, his triumph at Djerbé. Mustafa claimed lineage from Ben Walid, standard-bearer of the Prophet himself, and had fought long against the Persians and Hungarians. Christians would not get a drop of mercy from him.

"Remember," the jovial Ali was reminding them, "the Sultan commands you under pain of his displeasure to work together always in harmony."

Yakhshi thought he detected a slight twinkle in the Grand Vizier's voice, for everyone knew how Piyale and Mustafa disliked each other intensely. Foreseeing that this might cause some difficulties, the Sultan in his wisdom ordered them to defer to the advice of Turgut in all things.

"Remember, Piyale, to revere Mustafa like a father," said Ali, "and you, Mustafa, to look upon Piyale at a beloved son."

At that, the Grand Vizier ordered one of the sword-bearers to present to Mustafa the jewel-encrusted sword of command, which the Vizier accepted with a deep bow and handed to a retainer. Likewise he accepted from the standard-bearer the royal standard and everyone bowed before the big red banner, banging gently in the breeze against its pole, from which fluttered a horsetail and atop of which sat a golden ball. Watching this ceremony from some paces, Yakhshi thought he saw a scowl cross Piyale's face.

Having accepted sword and standard, Vizier Mustafa Pasha *Hazretleri* lost no time in climbing aboard his galley of twenty-eight benches, while Piyale, also bowing to Ali Pasha, walked onto his *barcha* of thirty-two benches. As he sent them off, Ali remarked to all within earshot, "Here are two men of good humor, always ready to savor coffee and *afione*, about to take a pleasure trip in the islands."

Yakhshi quickly ran to his galley and boarded himself, as did the other officers. He did not doubt yet more stragglers would arrive on the morrow and struggle to catch up, but the body of the fleet was now ready to sail. After all the little problems of departure were seen to, Piyale hoisted his pennants, the drumbeat began and the flotilla made its way in a stately procession across the Horn. Following custom, the galleys passed slowly before the Sarai, where they were greeted by cheering crowds, the blaring of trumpets and the salvos of guns. Yakhshi gazed at the garlands floating past the boats and felt the sea breeze on his face, thinking it was another fine day.

Seventy-Two

Overnight Malta changed completely. True to his word, the morning after our return de Valette wrote to the Pope and to King Philip. The same day he issued a *Citazione*, recalling every Knight of the Religion to the Convent, dispatching boats at once to the north and to the west. Senglea was de Valette's biggest problem. Tho' the previous Grand Master had put a wall around l'Isola on all sides but the one facing Birgu, the work was incomplete, especially on the farther side, that facing the fourth inlet coming off the Great Port. People now spoke of this creek as Poret de la Sengle or Porto di Senglea. The wall all along the Poret was very low; worse, it lacked traverses and parapets. His Eminence immediately put every available soldier, servant, slave and villager to work, raising it as well as strengthening Fort St. Michel itself. The engineers scoffed at its cavalier and ordered the ravelin to be repaired.

I went thither in the morning, shortly to be hailed by Pietru as he came to join the construction gang. "Xabaw!" I said as we embraced each other, "you were right—it seems our whole lives are to be spent hauling stones."

"This time I do it for me, *haqq it-torok*," he replied with a mixture of resolve and joy.

This ravelin, a big triangle-like platform standing across the ditch from the fort itself on the Poret side, had been built to protect St. Michel's curtain, but it was truly in poor condition. We'd have to rebuild it almost from the ground up.

As it happened, before I spent the morning on the ravelin, Balthazar came along to fetch me, saying, "Come, it is time to dust off your old accounting skills."

He and many other Knights had been assigned to ride to all the villages, count the people and muster all the fit men. This proved not so easy. We rode by those stone walls and rude huts to the south, sending men to Birgu, ordering the women and old people to ready themselves to leave for Sicilia. These suspicious souls sometimes greeted us but more often they fled, disappearing into fields and into the caves that pocked those seaside cliffs.

"Wide is the way and broad is the gate that leadeth to destruction," remarked Balthazar. He then sighed. "Mayhap better a friendly rock than a foreign pasture." Maugre our inconstant reception, before too many hours had lapsed, the first Maltese farmers began to trickle toward the Borgo from all parts of the island.

Late in the day our party entered Mdina to learn who was there. The Old City was quiet, only a few people on their way to market to be seen. As we passed Matteo Falzon's mansion, I dismounted, walked to the door and knocked. A servant opened and saw me in. Soon the Master Falzon himself appeared. I did not recognize him. More had passed than the dozen years since we had last set eyes on each other.

"Signore," I said, bowing, "you perhaps do not remember me. I am Francisco de Barai."

His eyes widened as his face assumed an aspect of pleasantry and despair. "Yes, I do remember. I never expected to see you again, Signore. But why do you speak Italian like a Venetian? Please, come."

The man who ushered me into the courtyard was old before his time. Falzon's hair had greyed, his eyes seemed duller than of yore. He walked slowly, and when he offered me a chair he winced at some hidden pain. I remained standing, while he seated himself.

"Sir, have you heard the news that has come yesterday?" I asked.

"No, Signore Barai," said Falzon shaking his head. "I have not. I rarely leave the house."

"We know now that a Turkish descent will fall on Malta within a few months. All able-bodied men will be required to bear arms."

Pouring two glasses of wine, Falzon offered me one. I took it with thanks, noticing then that the statue in the nymphaeum had grown only a little greener in all these years. "No," he said, "as you see, I am no longer able-bodied, but even if I were, I would not fight."

"How is that, Sir? Malta is your home."

"My home!" he scoffed with unexpected vehemence. "My family's home was stolen from us when the Knights arrived on this island and my life was almost stolen from me by their Inquisitor. It took years for my arms to heal after the torture, and even now they remember the pain. Do you recollect Giuseppe Callus, the doctor who on that fateful day interrupted our lunch there in the dining room—" he lifted his hand—"to tell us of Cubelles's Tribunal?"

Yes, I could picture the doctor walking in as were it yesterday. I did not recollect exchanging words with him.

"No matter," Falzon said, "five years ago he wrote a letter to King Philip protesting de Valette's appropriation of the *Università*'s revenues. The petition fell into de Valette's hands and His Eminence hanged him as a rebel. Strangely, only the Church stands up to that despot who has usurped every freedom. Under no circumstance will I fight for the Knights. Tell the Grand Master he can hang me; I would sooner be taken into slavery than lift a sword or a gun in his favor." As Falzon regarded me, I took a seat on the cloister wall. "How is it," he asked, "that you come here again to fight for these disgusting thieves and brigands?"

That story, I feared, was too long to recount at present. "Let it suffice to say, Signore, that I have been taken a slave by the Turks and have no desire that it happen again."

"Why then not leave?" He seemed genuinely curious. "Return to Spain."

"I am reckless by nature," I answered somberly. "Signore, we both have reasons to distrust these Knights, but as much as you may revile them, you must concede that it is the Turk who invades us now, not we the Turk, and therein lies a difference. I also say to you, I have of late been to Constantinople and have seen the forces being arrayed against us. Malta is merely a stepping-stone in the Grand Turk's designs. What happens here concerns Christendom entire."

"You speak eloquently, Signore Barai; I am surprised." As I am, I replied. "Natheless, I say they have sowed—let them reap. I refuse absolutely to aid the Knights, with arms or money." Falzon got to his feet. "Now, if you'll excuse me, I have some reading I should like to do."

He escorted me to the door. "Master Falzon," I said, "You once did me a great service, which I never repaid; nor am I able to repay it now—"

"One should not live in debt," Falzon smiled. "One should merely live."

I paused at the remark, robbed for a moment of speech. "I'll tell the others you are unable to bear arms. You would do well to keep this door locked."

"Thank you, Señor de Barai," he said. "You have my gratitude."

"*À Dios*."

That evening I betook myself to Flaminia's house in the Borgo for the first time since my departure to Djerbé, five years ago. After being freed from the galleys, I had avoided her, but I knew that she lived and now I wanted to tell her what lay in store. To no one's surprise I found her readying a customer in the sitting room under the candelabra. To my astonishment, the house was full of the most expensive chests, tables and chairs.

"You have prospered, Milady," I said, regarding my surroundings.

"O Madonna!" she exclaimed, extricating herself from the fellow's arms on the divan and running to embrace me. "You are alive."

"I am." Months after my release I found those words strange to utter.

Flaminia, now with the better part of thirty years to her, dressed finely, had not lost her figure and in her dark eyes candles yet sparkled. As a pet dog came up wagging its tail to greet me, she asked the merchant eagerly awaiting her services to tarry a while and told her daughter, now almost a woman herself, to bring drink. My long-ago mistress noticed my ear and inquired after my health. When I told Flaminia my story, she replied that her own husband had been captured at Djerbé five years ago and never came back. It was just as well. They never had much to do with each other and, if they had, it might've proved unhappy for him. Sometimes a stupid judge sent men to the galleys who knowingly allowed their wives to be *quiracas*. More than once Flaminia had paid a bribe, and of more than one sort. *In qualsiasi caso*, her trade prospered, and she confessed that she had indeed become one of the richest women in Birgu.

"We must set aside reminiscences, Flaminia," I said without softness. "You must have heard yesterday's news."

Her head bobbed nervously and she laid her hand on mine. "I have, *mio cuore*, what do you expect me to do?"

"You shall be sent to Sicilia," I said, pulling my hand away, "and I tell you to go with all speed; take your daughter. The Turks will be here soon enough and naught of this island will remain when they have finished with it."

"Again Sicilia! Jesus, Mary and Joseph! Who must I pay, Francisco, to let me be?"

"You know better than I," I answered soberly, natheless conceding that a healthy sum toward the defenses would be looked on with favor.

"Flaminia," I told her, "Remember how terrified you were during the *razzia*? I swear on the graves of my parents that next to the nightmare facing us, the *razzia* will have seemed a pleasant daydream. Leave; you can be of no use in what is to come."

Flaminia replied that if she had survived the Inquisition she could survive this. The merchant had been listening to the entire conversation with the keenest ears and would sooner follow my advice, but I had said what I'd come for and made to depart. Flaminia found a talisman in one of her chests and gave it to me, attempting to put it around my neck, but I saw it was of infidel origin and merely took it in hand.

The number of people on Malta changed by the hour. The Grand Master had rearmed the *Kapi Agha*'s galleon, and it escorted the constant stream of boats ferrying old people and young children to Sicilia. Romegas and Captain General de Giou led the convoys, which on their return journeys brought every needed supply to Malta—wheat, corn, wood, gunpowder, ammunition, arms. de Valette had sent other Knights to levy men in Sicilia and Italia. Colonel Mas of Auvergne went forth himself to raise a company and everyone prayed for his safe return. In the midst of this, the Order, following custom, went ahead and held a Chapter General. Romegas broke off his convoys to discuss promotions, clothing and wine at the auberges.

At the beginning of April, a few weeks after the Feast of the Annunciation brought *anno* 1565, Don Garcia de Toledo disembarked at Birgu with twenty-seven galleys behind him. Mounting the summit of Fort St. Angelo, Toledo, now nearly fifty, greeted the Grand Master with a bow and explained that King Philip had received the Monsignore's letter. In his great alarm, the King had immediately appointed him, Don Garcia, the new Vice Roy of Sicily. For the past weeks he had been racing with the wind to confer with His Holiness and the leaders of Firenze, Napoli and Genoa. Now—here he was.

"Eminenza," said the same man who fifteen years ago had seen the way to defeat Turgut at Africa, "His Holiness has asked me to convey his great love and esteem."

"Gracias, Eccellenza," de Valette replied with no hint of humor, "*de momento prefiero el dinero del avaro*."

"On this occasion," the Vice Roy replied, smiling, "I am finally able to say that the Pope has matched his piety with his purse." He ordered his men to open the chest containing ten thousand *scudi* that His Holiness had sent through the Order's Ambassador.

de Valette glanced into the box and nodded as an audible sigh escaped his lips. "Not the ransom of a Sanjak-bey, but far more than that of a Grand Master." Unable to restrain himself, he added for the Vice Roy's benefit: "We lack every necessity to face the enemy, and for several years the Turkish menace has put us to huge expense at rates of interest so onerous that I fear we shall never be able to redeem them. Natheless, have no doubt, Illustrissimo, that I shall write Pius in gratitude."

Toledo bowed slightly and the two men set off to inspect the fortifications. As they rode on horseback around the Great Port, de Valette remarked that the Vice Roy appeared uncomfortable.

"My health isn't entirely what it once was," the speckle-bearded Toledo returned. "The gout, you know." Atop Sciberras, the two paused to look upon Fort St. Elmo far below. "I have brought three thousand troops with me," the Vice Roy said to the Monsignore, pointing to his galleys placidly rocking on the harbor's blue water. "They are at your disposal, if you wish, tho' I'd not wish it upon any man to be caught in that fort should the Turks emplace batteries here."

de Valette nodded as the warm wind whistled thro' the tall grass around them, causing it to ripple in waves. "According to Barelli they will and there is nothing to be done about it. As for your troops, we do not know the exact size or whereabouts of our foe. I understand you must also protect la Goletta, which is the portal to Spain." True enough, the Vice Roy told him. "In that case, take them thither, if you can supply me with another company later."

"You may be certain, Illustrious Señor, that Philip views the defense of Malta as he does of Sicily itself. He has given me instructions to raise twenty thousand foot. Of course this will take time. Meanwhile, I promise you every possible succour from Sicily, perhaps a thousand arquebusiers. I have already ordered that those sent to Sicily be treated as Sicilians."

"That will do for the moment," said Valette and they proceeded down Sciberras to Fort St. Elmo, where soldiers were positioning cannon and carrying up powder barrels from boats docked below.

The Grand Master never explained his refusal of Don Garcia's offer of troops and it has always remained a mystery. Many, Your Majesty, aver it was simply a mistake. Others that he believed la Goletta must be protected at all costs, and that the knowledge of a relief of twenty thousand foot being prepared allayed his fears. Still others say de Valette held no fear, that his somber countenance reflected a certain fatality, or that the perils he saw to be inevitable inspired him with a resolution superior to all events. For me, I had seen Parisot angry, often enraged, a few times mirthful; once or twice in my sight he had ventured tenderness. I had never seen him afraid. Nor, I believe, had anyone else.

When they arrived at St. Elmo, the elderly Grand Master and the younger Vice Roy were saluted by the men. de Valette walked among them casually, but when they passed the old chapel now enclosed by the a south wall of the fort, he unsheathed his rapier and bade them pray with him. Everyone around gathered at his side and knelt. Afterwards, he and the Vice Roy mounted the ramparts.

"How many pieces do you have here?" Don Garcia asked, surveying the fort.

"Twenty-seven," de Valette answered.

The Vice Roy fell into silence, walking with some discomfort to the northwest side, facing Marsamxett. "That is not bad, but you see this wall is entirely exposed and cannot be protected by the guns from St. Angelo." He turned around, pointing toward the fortress that lay over six hundred paces across the harbor. "We must build a new ravelin outside this wall."

de Valette concurred and the Vice Roy promised to send an engineer from Sicily forthwith. True to his word, the moment they returned to Birgu, Don Garcia sent a *fregata* northward. The next day, promising once again before the entire Council that anything the Knights required would be at their disposal, the Vice Roy sailed on to la Goletta, leaving his son, Don Federico, who had just professed, as his deputy.

Seventy-Three

The Vice Roy's engineer arrived a few days later and work on a new ravelin for Fort St. Elmo began precipitously. Truly, as the splash of the Turkish oars and the beat of the galley drums grew louder, louder, toil on the fortifications proceeded with ever more fury, ceasing neither day nor night. The stream of boats between Malta and Sicilia likewise saw no interruption, carrying peasants on the outbound journey and, at last, soldiers on the return. Colonel Mas had succeeded in raising three hundred fifty of the bravest men in Italy, who were greeted with cheers as they disembarked at Galley Creek. Knights themselves began to arrive from Italy, e'en Germany and France, rushing hither to answer the Grand Master's call. Those too old or sick to make the journey instead sent huge sums of money to the Religion's aid, often the greater part of their estates.

One day tho' Balthazar remarked mournfully, "Villegaignon will not come. He is too old."

"He must be but fifty-five!" I retorted.

"Mayhap he is weary," Balthazar answered, without saying a word more.

de Valette, in truth, knew that little was to be expected from France. Wracked by religious strife, the country's coffers were empty. He would place his faith in Italians, Spaniards and Spain.

By April's end, I continued to make guns but spent more time at the powder mill under Commander Maimon, a Catalan, and Rafael Salvago, a Genoese. In the open air just outside the city walls we collected soil from around dung heaps and tombs, mixed it with water and filtered it to get saltpetre. We mixed the saltpetre with charcoal and sulphur in tubs to make the powder and finally corned the powder thro' sieves—coarse grains for cannons and finer grains for arquebuses. We gave new life to the old stock and churned out nine fresh quintals each day, atop of what was being brought from Sicilia.

A week after Easter celebrations de Valette strode out to inspect the progress of the work. I was amazed at how agile the old man had become once again, as had he regained his youth. "Eminenza," I said when he approached me. "I would the ingredients for fire weapons. Much is here—pitch, tar, tow, gunpowder. We also require the proper wood—cedar is best—and brass cauldrons for distilling the liquid resin and other parts."

He nodded. "At Rhodes," he said, "the most valuable man was Fra Gabriele Tadini da Martinengo, an engineer who saved us time and time again by his knowledge of mines and fire weapons. We have not forgotten. Fireworks are here. For liquid fire, the doctors may have the necessary alchemical apparatus. If not, tell Romegas or one of the others what supplies are required—or go to Sicilia yourself to fetch them."

Thereat I went to see Romegas at the special post he been assigned between St. Angelo and the slave bagno, and found his men busy emplacing several heavy pieces while aiming them across the harbor toward St. Elmo. They called this post "the Towers" because it was so well fortified by solid rock on each side. de Valette would require Romegas to be near him at every moment, but at this moment he was not to be found, being somewhere between Malta and Sicily. Vergã was there, tho', and I told him what I wanted.

He said he'd see to my request, then laughed, wiping his forehead. "By the Life of King Philip, you've brought a mountain of work with your news from Constantinople, eh?"

By now both of us well perceived how our lives depended on each other, but despite his joviality, after my conversation with Isabella I could not find it within myself to lay aside every suspicion.

I went to the Guasconi mansion nearby. Servants and slaves unloaded large jugs and urns of water from a cart, from which they filled the cistern in the cellar. Many houses in Birgu had such cisterns, themselves almost as large as a house. No one quite knew then to what extent our lives would depend on these reservoirs, but the Monsignore ordered them all filled from the island's biggest spring, which was a fountain at a place called the Marsa near the inner end of the Great Port. Once all the cisterns were filled, he would poison the spring.

I found Isabella inside, listening with despair to old Giansevere chattering about the Seraglio, about how the dream of every girl in the

Empire was to be taken there and to be noticed by the Sultan. Oh, how young girls threw themselves at raiding parties just for the chance to be numbered among the few hundreds of concubines in the Harem. If luck smiled on her and she caught the Sultan's eye, she could rise to the greatest heights of power. Did not Soliman's wife wield the same authority as the Queen of England?

I listened to this babble with equal impatience before taking Isabella aside. "What are you doing here? You must go to Sicily before it is too late!"

At my words, Isabella flew into a small panic, putting her hands to her ears. It was plain that she felt trapped on every side. "My mother in Mdina does not wish it. What am I to do with the nurse?"

"Go," I said sternly. "Go with Vergã if necessary. He will be sailing at any hour for provisions."

Isabella stared hard at me. "You would send me with that man?"

I did not hesitate. "Isabella I'd sooner renounce she who bore me than trust him, but we have sworn peace and—there is no choice." I departed.

By May the Port was in the throes of a constant, purposeful chaos. Everywhere thousands of dark, sweaty men, hair tied back with cloth or rope, most wearing nothing but breeches and many only loincloths, heaved and hoisted stone. Marsamxett and the Great Port were clogged with boats. The *sultana* of the *Kapi Agha* was secured again by Fort St. Angelo in Galley Creek. The Chevalier St. Aubin sailed to Barbary on the Order's *patrona* to discover what Turgut was up to. Men continued to run supplies and munitions up to Fort St. Elmo. Pietru, half naked like everyone else, helped build a gun platform at the side of Fort St. Michel to be manned by the Maltese. Crossing from Sicilia, Captain General de Giou met a Genoese galley laden with wheat. Her Captain at once proceeded to Malta with all his men. Commander Andrada in Napoli raised two hundred foot at his own expense, and the Order's galleys brought them to Malta. Adventurers followed by ten men here, twenty there, arriving each day from Genoa, Napoli, Tuscana, each one of them eager to fight.

With the Majorcan Knight Ramon Fortuyn, we tried out some combustibles of our invention. Having covered some barrel hoops with caulking tow, we steeped them in a cauldron of boiling tar. After the tar dried we covered the hoops again with tow, once more immersed them in tar. We repeated this process until they were as thick as a man's arm.

"What do you plan to do with these?" Balthazar asked when he caught me at this activity on the Salvatore hill above the powder factory.

"Watch."

We lit the hoops and rolled them down the hill, all afire and giving off great quantities of smoke.

"The Turks wear light robes," I said.

"The hoops are heavy," Balthazar said. "They are for rolling, not for hurling."

We made them lighter.

After services on the first Sunday in May, trumpets and drums sounded. Shopkeepers ran to their doors, arquebusiers grabbed their weapons, every heart in the Borgo ceased to beat. It was not the attack. The Grand Master had called for a review of all the Knights to determine their present number and to make certain they were properly armed. Each servant dressed his master in his armor and, once attired, each Knight took his place at the post that had been assigned his langue along Birgu's wall: the Post of Provence atop the St. John bastion, the west-most bastion on the landward side; the Post of Auvergne atop the St. James bastion to the east of it; the Post of France on the curtain running between the two ...

I tell you, Your Majesty, rarely had Malta seen such a spectacle. A good breeze was blowing on this fair day. The Knights, fully armed, stood in all their glory beneath the banners of their langues, and the common folk and soldiers followed the inspectors around as if they had been at a grand tournament of old. Each Knight wore armor according to his taste or wallet, and the spectators applauded or jeered as each one presented himself for inspection. The poorer Knights dressed in armor of plain steel plate, but some of the richer Germans had chosen the fashionable Maximilian style, with its fluted breastplates and helmets. The slashes in the steel strengthened it and caused arquebus balls to glance away, but so ornate were such suits that they seemed made for women rather than warriors; Balthazar named their decadence the end of civilization. Others of wealth chose what we in the Arsenale called *anime* breastplates. No single plate here, the cuirass was made of hinged narrow strips that moved with the wearer. Many of these rich suits were decorated with scenes from the Gospels or from the heroic times of antiquity.

Like a menagerie of exotic birds from the Newfound World, every imaginable sort was on display. Full suits, half-suits, open helmets; old-fashioned helmets with visors—the best protection, but they'd prove unbearably hot in the summer. Plumes of red, purple, orange; here and there helmets surmounted by lions, claws or falcons. A shield resting by every leg and a broadsword in almost every hand; in many those mighty two-handers.

Armor had been changing much, even in my memory. The increasing strength of the arquebus prompted many armorers to turn out thicker wares. Some of the full suits weighed far more than a quintal, but being expertly tailored for their wearers, the Knights moved in them with the slow ease of giants trampling down dwarfs. And more than one breastplate before us carried its maker's proof—the imprint of an arquebus ball. Some men, feeling that there was no escape from muskets, chose lighter armor—for its still certain protection against arrows—and many were convinced that soon enow the musket would spell the end of armor altogether.

Pietru and I came across Balthazar standing amongst his brethren under the banner of the Langue of France. Since Djerbé he had purchased a new Milanese suit, which blinded us as it deflected the rays of the sun. To be sure, engraved on Balthazar's cuirass an ancient sun god blazed forth. As he had in the past, Balthazar had chosen a half-suit for speed and lightness. Before him, its tip planted in the rampart, stood his beloved *montante*, with which he could cleave a suit of armor in half. Tho' he'd chosen an open *salade* for a helmet, he gazed off somewhere into the distance and failed to see us. As we passed, his servant draped over him the red and white tunic of the Order.

As we walked past these splendid ranks, the Grand Master himself came and everyone bowed. Too old for fighting, de Valette had natheless donned his cuirass for the ceremony. The breastplate was a simple one, resembling a doublet. It was decorated with St. John and the Lamb, and it bore the inscription, "*Ecce Agnus Dei.*"

When the review was complete, the inspectors announced that five hundred forty-eight Knights and Serving Brethren stood among us. A small number, aye, but these were the most dedicated and fervent of the Knights of St. John, and everyone left in raised spirits.

The tempo of preparations increased. The Council met night and day and, unlike that earlier time, decided that Gozo must be defended at all costs. Hardly a soul yet lived on the island, but if the worst should pass it might well prove to be the only road to Sicily. Pyres for signaling were put atop the rebuilt castle there and at Mdina and signals arranged. The Council ordered that all the fields on Malta be cleared and the crops brought into Birgu, along with the livestock. The number of Maltese could not have numbered much above twenty thousands and surely half had been carried to Sicilia by now. Natheless, a slow stream of carts filled with wheat or oats and with livestock tethered to their frames began to appear over the landward heights. The grain was stored in Birgu in immense underground cisterns, like the ones for water, which were sealed by great stone caps. The streets began to grow crowded until the Grand Master commanded the peasants to go back into the countryside.

It was a Monday, the day after the feast of St. John Porte Latine and thus the seventh of May. de Valette ordered the new chain to be fixed in place across Galley Creek. Some time ago the old one had rusted thro' and a new one had recently arrived from the Venetian Arsenale. When word of the order came down, everyone was certain the attack must be imminent and many of us rushed to the inlet to see what was happening. Men aboard a galley under Don Francisco de Sanoguera were trying to lower the chain with hooks and ropes, while other men maneuvered small boats and rafts under the chain as it came down. The thing was so heavy that the work was taking forever, so those of us watching went out on skiffs to lend a hand. I ended up on a raft with Vergã, who said, "We brought the provisions you wanted from Sicily."

I thanked him and asked whether the fleet had been sighted.

"No," he replied.

We worked for hours to get the chain in place. More than once it fell. When the monster finally lay across the creek, water streaming from the links, each more dear than the kiss of a Venetian whore, Sanoguera's men fixed the far end on the tip of Senglea with the immense anchor from the *carraca Santa Anna*, which they wedged amidst the living rocks. Soldiers and slaves winched the other end with the great capstan to raise it to the proper height. Galley Creek was sealed.

But the spur of Senglea was without a fighting platform or parapets. Only the old windmill vanes spun beyond too-low walls. Without pausing for breath Sanoguera's men set to work at what would become their post.

Still galleys came. Every hour the stream from Sicily increased but now ships usually docked in Marsamxett. The day after we put the chain up, a galley arrived there from Barbary bearing a Moor, his wife and son, who the Grand Master had sent thither as a spy. By nightfall the news they brought had spread throughout Malta: Tunis had seen a poor spring harvest and bread was scarce, but the King there had collected a great quantity of raisins, dates, honey, oil and other things to provision the Turkish fleet. Turgut had sent him many pieces of silk and some bronze artillery to win him over.

"Then Dragut has indeed received word of the descent?" the Grand Master wanted to know.

The Moor regarded de Valette with a disbelief. "Your Eminence," he said, "Turgut and the Bey Hasan of Algiers are gathering every corsair in Barbary to come and destroy you."

Two days later Don Juan de Cardona, Captain General of the galleys of Sicily, arrived with two vessels bearing a company of Spaniards under the famous Colonel Andres de Miranda. The moment Cardona docked at Marsamxett, he ran up to Fort St. Elmo and told everyone: The Turkish fleet had been sighted at Navarino off Modon, where they were replenishing their stores. Modon sat just on the other side of the Morea from Malvasia—the nearer side.

"It is but a week's voyage," I said to Pietru when we crossed paths before the armory below the St. James Bastion, whither he had come to collect arquebuses.

"*Iva*," he said, and ran off with an armful of guns.

Ix-Xabaw had been on the Santa Margarita heights teaching the Maltese irregulars how to shoot. Spring was in full blossom, the day warm. The hills were covered with the green of the wild grasses and the blue and purple of the flowers. The Maltese honey bees were buzzing everywhere. A few days ago Balthazar had told him to get the arquebuses out of the armory and ready the men. Row after row of farmers, merchants, lawyers, doctors, a few priests and a corrupt judge awaited their turns at the target.

Many of these goats hadn't fired an arquebus in their entire lives. He showed them the difference between the fine powder for the pan and the coarser powder for the charge, how to wear the twelve apostles, how to use the scouring rod, how to light the match, which end of the gun to aim with ...

"*Mur inharaq!*" he erupted when one of them burned his hand by accidentally igniting the powder.

To another who couldn't hit the target they had set up on the ridge, he barked, "If you can't do better than that—*ejja erdahhuli!* You might as well be a whore!"

Spirits, tho', were high. The men laughed. Pietru surveyed the companies practicing near him and the other trainers. Between the companies of Colonel Mas, Colonel Miranda, Captain de la Cerda and the Italians, he thought about one thousand soldiers had arrived. The galley soldiers, the Greeks and Sicilians living on the island, the oarsmen and the hundred men who garrisoned Fort St. Elmo, Pietru heard numbered another thousand. As for the Maltese—he shrugged. With all the people coming and going, no one had any idea. Pietru was convinced they had three thousand, maybe four. God alone knew how many were still roaming around the countryside. One thing Ix-Xabaw was certain of: Only half knew how to shoot. The Grand Master had decreed each man should get three balls for practice, an extra if he hit the target. Not many were hitting the targets. It didn't matter, Pietru decided, they would soon have practice enough.

In the midst of the unceasing activity, de Valette appeared a moving center. Never still, he now oversaw the placement of artillery, now took the first spade for the new ravelin at St. Elmo's, now appeared at Senglea as stones were hoisted by sunburnt men, now wrote dispatches to Sicily, now inspected the irregulars while they practiced. Yet, it was as if he never moved, as if he was encircled by a steely calm, no longer wearing the melancholy frown of yore but some more invincible armor. When Pietru saw him on the practice hill, he recalled the long-ago image at Zuara when, amidst that terrible rout, de Valette held his sword aloft and marched his company and slaves to the boat.

What above all impressed the common people about de Valette during those strangely elevated weeks was that each day after vespers he walked calmly to the Sacra Infermeria and fed the sick and poor with his own hands. Dr. Jean was himself in the midst of every preparation and often saw the Monsignore on his rounds.

"He has changed somehow," he observed when we met outside the Hospital one morning. "You see him and you know that ... he was born for this moment. His destiny is upon him."

"He is seizing the *kairos*," Balthazar remarked a few evenings later in a tavern, "the moment of grace and opportunity."

What is this *kairos*? I asked Balthazar, of which he spoke once or twice in former years.

"It is exactly that, the ancients understood, the moment of grace and opportunity, the moment when the heavens pause and the gods grant us the single chance to alter destiny. Parisot senses the *kairos* has arrived, and he has seized time by the forelock. He knows the moment will pass as soon as it has come."

Isabella sensed the moment was fleeting. All these days she had delayed her departure to Sicilia, not knowing what to do about Giansevere, who was too toothless to go anywhere, or her mother, who refused to move. Her dreams had not helped. Nightly she saw herself moving about in no more than leaps and bounds. Natheless, tho' with all else to occupy him, Parisot had set the matter aside, Isabella knew he would eventually force her removal, and at last she forced herself to a decision. She would say farewell.

Isabella found her Godfather at his home late in the afternoon. The anger that flashed across his face left no doubt he was surprised to see her on the island. He did not erupt and she seized the hesitation. "Parisot, you have weightier matters on your mind, but I could not creep away without a word."

"You are finally leaving?"

"I intend go to Mdina today to fetch Mother and we shall sail tomorrow. The servants will look after the nurse. She will die soon." Silence fell on them for a moment. "Parisot, I cannot bear the thought of any anything happening to you, and to never see you again."

Her guardian gazed on her with an expression reserved for his ward alone and took her into his arms. "I would have you with me during this testing, but if I am to fall, God has willed it, and I can think of no better cause."

"If you wish me at your side, allow me to stay," Isabella pleaded in tears. "You will need more than warriors."

"Only one thing would grieve me more than seeing you depart," he said with a sensible hesitation and a tear, "and that is seeing you harmed. I could never forgive myself. Go, my dear. Find an escort to take you to Notabile." Isabella ran from Parisot's house, yet crying. For a moment he stared after her; then, with his lioness purring at his side, he wrote dispatches to the Vice Roy.

As it happened, on the street Isabella encountered Blaij Vergã, who offered to accompany her to Mdina. They took a servant and an extra horse for Emilia. The sun was by now close to the horizon. Not long after they departed, Vergã abruptly began singing, "Lucia, Heaven above, ah you rascally girl ... Georgio sings to you as to a countess, to a highness, to a Madonna ... "

Isabella well knew the tune from Firenze and at once joined in. "*Giorgia sporcata pisci' a lo lieto!* O that pig Giorgio pisses in bed! Don't tell me it's just sweat. You stink like rotting fish, black face, scabby hound!" "Ah," Isabella said, breaking off, spirits for the moment soaring, "how is it that every Italian song is about Lucia? Who is she?"

"I don't know, but what a wench she must be to have so many songs sung to her charms! Surely, she takes after you, Milady. How is it so many men have thrown themselves at your feet, but that not a one has captured your heart?"

Isabella perceived that she had stumbled into Vergã's unexpected question of her own accord and at once assumed her previous demeanor. "Do not think on such unimportant matters, Blaij Vergã," she replied sternly. "From this day forward your heart and mind must be devoted to the Grand Master, to God and to the salvation of Christendom."

Despite her harsh admonition, Blaij persisted as they trotted along in the growing twilight. "I accept that Señora does not think this commoner worthy of her," he smiled. "She should know that he will soon profess. Romegas awaits a special dispensation from the Pope."

"Señor is to be congratulated," Isabella replied haughtily, at the same time unable to deny the accomplishment. "No one from the rabble, yet alone a bastard, has ever achieved such a feat. But lest Señor forget," she reminded him, her voice losing none of its high tenor, "if he professes he shall swear to a vow of chastity and shall put aside all thoughts of women."

Vergã laughed in a way that both conceded and dismissed the lady's observation. "Alas from the rabble many of us are, but allow me to tell Señora another thing I have never revealed to a soul. Francisco de Barai and I share the same father. It was, after all, not easy all those years watching my unworthy brother obtain every advantage, while I suffered the shame of being born a bastard. As I have said, tho', the table has been leveled and what is past is past."

The news, divulged so casually, stunned Isabella, but when she had recovered her senses, she perceived it explained much about Blaij Vergã. At length she answered, "Would you swear on the Holy Book to what you have just told me?"

Vergã nodded. Then and there Isabella took a Bible from her *boursetta* and he swore. The señora, tho', yet found little sympathy. "I have told you so before, each man has a cross to bear in this life. My father—"

"Yes?"

She momentarily faltered. "You have at least known who he was. Blaij Vergã, do not seek to win prizes by deeds of glory. Think only of your duty to the Order and to God. In the coming days you will have enough opportunity to display true prowess." Without thinking Isabella Guasconi crossed herself.

"I have said as much to Francisco," he replied softly.

Isabella never spoke of this conversation to me until much later. She acknowledged to herself a certain flattery in the popular brute's attention and, despite her words, his confession did extract a measure of sympathy from her. She natheless was tempted to dismiss him with the ill-formed contempt she had felt all her life for the rude people. He did sing. Isabella shivered.

At Mdina she found her mother delirious with fever and raving that the Almighty had unleashed the Apocalypse on Malta. Isabella at once sent for a doctor from nearby Santo Spirito Hospital. He soon arrived with a prescription of *doronicum* but said the matter was grave and that Emilia must not travel. That the matter was grave Isabella held not the slightest doubt. She sent Vergã on his way and remained the night in Mdina.

The next morning, bells rang atop the Conventual Church of San Lorenzo, calling all the Knights thither for a service the Grand Master had ordered. By now the streets were crowded with mercenaries and villagers, and the sight of armored men walking amidst yapping dogs had become commonplace. The summons brought many common soldiers as well, and after the pages and criers had collected everyone, de Valette mounted the steps of the church and addressed all who had assembled. I stood among that crowd and saw a man who had traveled far. Afterwards many swore that angels surrounded him. I say that the discomfort wherewith Parisot had addressed his men in the past was gone and that none gathered in that square ever forgot what he told them.

"What force Soliman prepares and what a great battle he brings against us," de Valette began with a voice that rang the stones, "you who have been with me of late well understand. The enemy is known, his insatiable ambition is known, his strength his known and his mortal hatred against us and the Christian faith is known. Wherefore, let us as one reconcile ourselves to God and prepare this day for war." Some townspeople walking by heard these words and stopped to listen. "To appease God's displeasure, we must cleanse ourselves with confession, and we must worship Him with such prayer that puts a steadfast trust in His help. By these two means alone our ancestors obtained many victories against the infidels of the East, and neither can it be doubted that if we shall in godliness join together, we shall frustrate all the force and fury of this proud tyrant. But God helps those who labor and take pains, rather than the negligent and slothful. We must therefore join unto worship and cleanliness that which our profession and the course of war requires. For victuals, armor, money, we shall so provide, such that no man will complain, sparing neither cost nor pains. I shall pour out all my store, neither shall I for desire of life refuse any danger.

"As for the other Christian princes, I cannot believe that they will lie still in the face of so great a danger, which threatens not only our estate, but their own. I will exhort every one of them by letters and by messengers, and I do not doubt but that we shall have aid enough from the Pope, the Emperor and the King of Spain, such is their Christian zeal, and I trust they will move the rest. As for you, the princes and light of this Sacred Order, I am well assured you shall fight for the most Holy Religion of Christ, for your lives and property, and for the glory of the

Latin name. You shall fight against a most cruel tyrant, the destroyer of true religion, of all civility and good learning, the plague of the world, enemy of God and man, and he shall feel the sharpened points of the Cross he so despises; he shall feel them across the sea, he shall feel them in the far city of Constantinople; yea, he shall feel them e'en in his houses of pleasure. But in order to make ourselves worthy of that honor, let us go, my brethren, to the altar, there to renew our vows and partake of the blessed sacraments, and let the blood of the Savior of Mankind inspire us with such a noble contempt of death, as can alone make us invincible."

After that, every Knight followed him into the church to give his confession and partake of the Eucharist. Some of the townspeople and soldiers followed as well.

The work didn't slow, but the same evening after dark many took an hour or two to gather in the crowded taverns. The mood had surely changed. I do not know how to name it. Ramon Caravajal and Colonel Mas were as always boasting of how many Turks they would kill, but this time more belief than bravado filled their voices. For myself, I felt no invincibility toward the approaching foe, and in Parisot's speech I perceived a glance toward the Venetian—arms over faith. For others, tho', the Grand Master's words had carried the touch of God, and no one could deny the profound strength infusing all his men.

Pietru had also rushed into the tavern to grab some bread and wine before returning to work on his gunnery platform. "Xabaw," I said, "I have been looking for you. Here." I presented him a wheel-lock I'd made, but he hesitated. "Take it and remember our vow. Stay alive."

Ix-Xabaw took the gun, kissing it, and departed.

Balthazar, sitting by me, remained in high cheer as he had promised and held in his hand a collection of stories just published in Italy by a Geraldi Cinthio, one an improbable tale about a jealous Venetian Moor who, convinced of the unfaithfulness of his beautiful wife, murders her.

"A tale for our time," joked Balthazar. "For is ours not an age afflicted by jealousy and vindictiveness?" Any concealed meaning in his words was well hidden, for without ado the Knight went on to show me some dialogues of a Venetian Knight of Malta, Aretino. What I say in the dim light caused my eyes to pop from my head. The doings of the nuns described therein were so licentious as to be unrepeatable by Christian lips.

"Believe me," Balthazar laughed merrily, "this is what the Knights are defending—until we burn it." At once he changed his tone. "And you, Francisco, your spirits?"

I related the story I had heard from a dervish about the whore who refused to pray before a graven image, tho' she could not explain why.

"The Knights of St. John could not wish for a better whore," he returned, slapping me on the shoulder. Thereat he presented me with a fine rapier by him, its blade of damascene, new and polished, a hilt chiseled of silver and inlaid with precious stones. Several curving fingers formed the guard; one side of the ricasso was engraved with the cross of the Knights, the other with a pair of galley oars. "I know swords are not your craft and you have lost at least one of these on my account. Please accept it. And I beg you, don't use it against me."

I took the proffered weapon into my hands, tears overcoming all resistance. Balthazar, tho', turned and called for more wine. He leaned back, comfortably, and smiled.

For all his mirth, I saw in it the last repose of a man who knew that repose would no longer be granted him. Balthazar said, "Francisco, all our questions of yore will be answered in the coming trial." Finally he spoke again of the *kairos*, and with the same noble fatality that had been on de Valette's visage in the morning, got to his feet. He saluted those about him and returned to his room to get what sleep he could.

His Majesty will forgive me from this moment onward for not mentioning every name worthy of remembrance, among our forces or his. They are beyond numbering, and I am but one man and saw only what one man can see.

End of Volume 2

For sales, editorial information, subsidiary rights information
or a catalog, please write or phone or e-mail
iBooks
Manhanset House
Shelter Island Hts., NY 11965, US
Sales: 1-800-68-BRICK
Tel: 212-427-7139
www.ibooksinc.com
bricktower@aol.com

For sales in the UK and Europe please contact our distributor,
Gazelle Book Services
Falcon House, Queens Square
Lancaster, LA1 1RN, UK
Tel: (01524) 68765 Fax: (01524) 63232
www.gazellebookservices.co.uk
email: melanie@gazellebooks.co.uk